Gothique Fantastique

Other Tall Tales

Gothique Fantastique

&

Other Tall Tales

Ron Clooney

Matador
5 Weir Road
Kibworth Beauchamp
Leicester LE8 0LQ, UK
Tel: (+44) 116 279 2299
Fax: 0116 279 2277
Email: books@troubador.co.uk
Web: www.troubador.co.uk/matador

ISBN 978 1848765 399

A Cataloguing-in-Publication (CIP) catalogue record for this book is
available from the British Library

Typeset in 11pt Stempel Garamond by Troubador Publishing Ltd, Leicester, UK
Printed in the UK by T J International Ltd, Padstow, Cornwall

Matador is an imprint of Troubador Publishing Ltd

For the one who said – "You can, so do."

Contents

Introduction

When I was at a book signing recently someone, who had read my first novel, asked me what I had done before I became a novelist. What she wanted to know was the $64,000 dollar question - where did my ideas come from? I told her it was what had happened in my life, experience transposed into print - which I believe it is. She wanted more detail. She was persistent and though I tried to dodge the unanswerable question, I gave the – Journalist and then a series of teaching jobs reply. I think that was what she expected to hear. But I had done many things before either of those.

I'd worked in construction, inside, under and on top of buildings. I'd served at tables and sold things, pumped gas, cleaned cars – anything basically to turn a buck or two in order to keep my head above water and the wolf from the door. In short, I'd experienced life with all of the horror and doubt left in.

During all of that time stories and experiences, I'd seen, or heard about, came into my head; some got written and published - some just remained crazy ideas locked inside my memory palace.

My very first thrill was to see a story in print in a magazine, or inside a collection of a "new authors," volume. It was the short story upon which I "cut my teeth," so to speak - it was here I learned my craft. In this volume I have interlinked all the stories in one way or another and there is a subtext of a narrative which runs throughout them. They can be read in any order and in any sequence and the sub-textual narrative remains, whilst each story stands alone and is a self contained experience.

The stories in this collection include some about my detective Giancarlo Pancardi, the principal character in Pancardi's Pride, and other characters that have appeared elsewhere in my work;

essentially the spider's web broadens and grows with every stroke of the pen, but there are other tales too; tales of things seen and known and tales of the unexplained and the inexplicable. The central tale which is never written weaves and winds and the reader must search their own imagination to fill in the missing parts.

I have tried not to let anyone pigeon hole me by saying, "Oh he just writes crime," or "he's a one trick pony." The trick is always in the tale and the pony is just part of the ride; the tail is on the pony and the pony is the tale.

I hope that you, the reader, will enjoy what this volume provides - a strange and eclectic mix of intertwined tales, the sum of parts; and that it makes you want to read more of my work.

On a personal note I would like to thank the artist Louise Amond (her work is available @www. louiseamond.com) for her cover design/s and the internal artwork for every story. Like all of my work, the picture does tell some of the story and her work has once again been superb in complementing them.

Ron Clooney
October 2010

gothique fantastique

*This story is dedicated to those
who keep the spirit of the Gothic in their hearts.*

Chapter One

"Minty!" the old man shouted, as he passed along the worn sea wall. "Minty!" he called again, his patience wearing thin. His voice was thin and rasped through the air like fingernails on a blackboard.

The dog appeared to take absolutely no notice.

That morning was cold; the crisp sharp air came in off the North Sea and stung his face. Salt spray hung in the wind as the slow winter dawn struggled against the moon which still hung full in the sky. Face reddened and blotchy with the dew eyed dawn he turned his back to the sea and looked up toward the ruin on the top of the cliff. Swirling mist enveloped the ancient stones which lay scattered like some ancient game of unfinished skittles. Stone steps pounded by the feet of pilgrims and tourists had, over the centuries, worn grooves and hollows which yearly tripped some unwary tourist and sent them headlong into the hospital. Wrists, ankles, shins and even whole arms and legs had been shattered in desperate attempts to avoid the long tumble into the old cobbled streets which lay below.

He loved this time of year when the winter swells sent waves crashing through the harbour entrance, bringing with them the deep sea fish so well loved by the estuary fishing boys. One year a whale had been thrown onto the beach and he had wondered how such a supposedly intelligent beast had failed to find a way back into open water. Some of the old fishermen had said it was a suicide. Whales, one old salt had claimed, once mate-less in the vast oceans, pine and then eventually cast themselves ashore in lonely desperation. He would have liked to believe that story, it was romantic and at heart he was a lonely romantic too.

It had been six years since Jean had died from the cancer which ate her to the bone and he missed her intensely. When she had died the whole of his world turned on a knife edge. Life became unbearable and his mind began to play tricks with his imagination and reason. Some mornings, even now, he still set the breakfast table for two; an automated response which often caught him in mid-preparation and brought a wail from his throat and a tear from his eye. Six years of nights when he saw her dead face and had to get up and make himself a nerve calming early morning tea; six years of grief and misery. At night he drew the pillows from her side of the bed down into a long mass which he could cuddle. A mock body made of down and feather which served to support his arm as Jean's waist and hips had done. Once he knew she had been there and had wriggled her backside into his lap like a young woman as they spooned; he could feel her body rising and falling as the breath entered and left it. A smooth rhythm that had been his for all the long years of their marriage bed. In the morning there had been the scent of her on the pillows, he could smell her in his nostrils, but she had gone. Now it was just Minty and him.

He had bought the dog as a runt puppy and taken the time to feed her well and train her and she, in turn, had rewarded him with absolute loyalty and love. Like all dogs she showed her affection by licking him. Licking his bare feet, his face, if it happened to get too close, and by trying to get next to him on the sofa. Those deep dark eyes stared into his soul and at times he could swear she understood so much more than anyone could imagine, and he loved her.

As a boy he had always craved a dog but it had not been until he met Jean that they had their first. A great lolloping hound with no real common sense but bags of energy. Some of his family said Lola had been a child substitute, but she had been more of a whirlwind substitute. Minty, his current dark-eyed beauty, had become his Jean, his walking companion, his muse and someone to talk to in the cottage which Jean had bought, with her pension lump sum. Jean hardly lived to use it and now the house in London belonged to someone else too and he lived like a recluse. Minty he swore understood him, just as his dead wife had done. At times Jean and Minty seemed to be similar, so similar that he toyed with the notion of reincarnation. For no logical reason he had noticed the gun dog kennels one afternoon and the advertisement the following week. The very next day he went and examined the six possible puppies from which he could chose - five bitches and one dog. As they ran over his feet he noticed the smallest female, she hung back behind the others, timid and shy she waited her turn. Eventually as the others tired and continued with their play she came to him and he knew – knew in that instant that she was the one. Dark eyes sparkled at him and she licked his palm as he held her aloft; it was a union made in heaven for the salvation of both – he called her Minty after Jean's favourite after dinner sweet treat.

He sometimes wondered what might have been different if they had been parents; would he have become the grandfather babysitter or the lone parent visited out of duty, rather than choice? The fertility problem had been him and not Jean and yet she had stayed when she could have made a different life for herself. Deep down he knew how important it was for Jean to have a child – that had been her sacrifice. He had been grateful for that and their love deepened as a consequence.

It was November the first and the sky was open as the dawn continued to break over the ruins of the abbey. Minty was fast and free and he wondered how long it might be before that turned into shortened walks and long sits at the fire, the two of them bemoaning their arthritis together.

His dog was down on the sands now - barking. The air was filled with the sound of her imploring some thing to get up and get on. The old man knew his animal well and guessed that the dog was barking at someone. It was not an aggressive bark but one which had within it a slight tinge of anxiety.

"Minty!" the man called again. "Bloody woman dog," he said under his breath, as he began to walk toward where the dog now sat, barking at what looked like an old sheet partly submerged at the waters edge. He thought it might be a seal or a small dolphin washed in on the tide.

"What is it girl?" asked the man of the dog, as he approached, as if the animal might reply. Her tail was wagging, as he came up behind her, making arcs in the sand as it pulsed from side to side.

There in the water was a body – a body in a wedding gown. The woman was small, slim, and her hair, which was moving in time with the tide, was a bedraggled jet black. The face, which was turned toward him, was young, pretty and innocent, the eyes open and opaque like a fish on a fishmonger's slab. Her skin was white - too white he thought. He thought of 17th century powdered lead and imagined this girl applying the deadly compound for the sake of fashion. Her fingernails were jet black, long and well kept - she was so obviously a town or city girl. The velvet wrap on her shoulders had lost its sheen and was a sodden mass of drifting colour which strikingly contrasted with the stark white of the wedding gown.

Using the telephone at the bottom of the Abbey steps he dialled 999 and spoke breathlessly, "That's right," he repeated, "Tate Hill Sands. A body, young woman at the water edge. Was my dog that found her. Looks like she may have been washed ashore."

A female voice at the other end of the line spoke calmly, "Please wait at the scene sir," she said. "One of our officers will be with you shortly and they might need to ask you some questions. Can you wait sir?" she concluded, coaxing, "I just need to take some details – your name and address?"

"Yes, I'll wait," he replied, "how long?"

"A matter of minutes, there is a squad car on call right now. Did you say the girl was dead?"

"Yes, she looks dead to me?"

"Have you checked?"

He felt foolish, "Err no, but she looks like she's been in the water for a time."

"You see it's Goth weekend," the woman continued, "and they do play some pranks on people from time to time."

Now he felt ridiculous, "Well I don't think this is a prank she looks very wet," he said in his defence. It was all he could think to say.

He hung up and began to walk back down to where the corpse now lay flopping, face down on the tides edge. Why hadn't he checked, he considered as he approached, then he thought of pulling the body ashore but his judgement took hold as he thought of the forensic evidence. Soon it would be stranded like the whale had been and the sand ballast barge before that; the one which Sutcliffe had photographed on the single glass negative. The tide was already retreating down her body, undermining the fine particles of sand around the soft edges of her face and insects had started to gather. One cheek anchored in the sand, a fly crawled into a nostril and he knew that his was no prank. Her rhythmical movement gave the impression of a person attempting to crawl ashore. Of course she was dead, he had stared death in the face too many times not to know it when he saw it. He studied the face - it had no emotion, no ecstasy, just heavy mascara, black eyeliner, and dark red lips. She was a Goth, part of the ensemble that gathered in Whitby twice yearly to celebrate Halloween and Walpurgis Nacht. So she hadn't fallen overboard from some wedding cruise which he initially thought a possibility. He wondered what her name was and where she came from, she wasn't local that much he knew; her colouring was all wrong, she might even be foreign - German, or Finnish. Her lifeless eye stared at him and the wedding dress billowed in the lapping tide. He could see that she wore suspenders and stockings and what looked like a Basque. He noticed that she wore no underwear or at least nothing that covered her backside; he looked more closely, a thong perhaps but nothing else and it had to be a small one at that. He studied the pert backside and wondered. She looked too young but the saturated translucent dress revealed a tattoo in the small of her back which had the words, fuck me, intertwined with what looked like some ancient Celtic symbol. He studied it hard as if watching a great beauty showering behind obscured glass. He could make out the narrowness of her waist and the broadening of her hips and the tautness of her skin. She couldn't be more than fifteen he thought, but he knew she must be older.

"What a waste," he said to Minty.

He wondered how many young men had seen and read those encouraging words but now she was no more than crab food, a piece of human flotsam and jetsam cast onto a remote North Yorkshire beach.

Many Goth girls came to Whitby and he had admired them. They were often dark, mysterious and very beautiful. The clothes they wore spoke of sex and confidence and he had imagined the things which they got up to in the quiet hotel rooms or the boarding houses which overlooked the Spa pavilion. There had never been any trouble and the youngsters brought money into the town. October was the end of the season and yet all the hotels were full.

The local vicar had complained about - goings on - in St. Mary's churchyard late at night when the Goths were in town. Councillor Bessy Golling had openly said they were Satanists who held black masses, but what did she know the interfering old busy body. She hated any youngsters that came to the town. He however, he didn't mind what they did. They might be copulating like rabbits for all he cared – they never caused trouble or got into fights and they didn't roll around in the mud like pigs. They were polite, spent well, ate well, and drank too much, but it was always with the spirit of fun. In fact he liked their stylish clothes, they made the onset of drab winter a little brighter. The moaners - they'd have a field day now, he thought. He could see the headlines in the Whitby Gazette. Girl dies in bizarre satanic ritual that goes wrong.

He looked at the corpse again and wondered what her father might say when he found out she had died, most probably from binge drinking or a silly accident. Would he cry? Would he have to identify the body? The Bessie Gollings of this world would have their say and not even care a jot for the real tragedy. That was why he liked the mornings - nobody about and he could walk his dog in peace. Peace had become his main aim now, he was not sociable anymore and the death of Jean had made it worse. He wished he could just be on an island somewhere, far away from the chattering masses. His needs were simple, something to read, plain food to eat and a warm fire; he had come to realise, far too late in life, that work was just that - work. Smiling, he thought of the old saying that people never wished they had spent more time at work. He missed Jean too - at least she would have understood what he was thinking.

Minty lay on the sand looking at the corpse; she too was bemused by the human woman that had gone into the water. Mostly they didn't do that - they simply threw sticks for her to jump after. Sometimes they petted her and some; some had treats for dogs in their pockets. The dog wondered what the girl was doing and why she was not moving; wondered why they were not moving just standing? She wanted to go home now and have some warm milk like she did most mornings and chew on perhaps a pig's ear. She placed her square Labrador head onto her black outstretched paws and closed her eyes – waiting.

Chapter Two

Sergeant George Warlonger was an unfit man whose stroll across the soft sand of Tate Hill made him sweat profusely. He had the complexion of a man who oozed continually which gave an illusion of stickiness and this in turn attracted dirt which filled his pores and gave him the air of a grubby unwashed slob; but his mind was sharp and his conscience clear and he knew his craft. His hand out stretched he advanced. Minty rose from her doze and sniffed at the man's feet. His palm was dry and his grip firm and that alone was enough to instil confidence in the older man.

"Warlonger, Detective Sergeant," he said warmly. "Are you the gentleman that found the body?"

His accent was broad, his voice loud and his smile infectious. He took a pencil from his pocket and using a sealed sharpener he began to address the issue of honing.

"I hate those new fangled palm pilot - electric things," he said, "give me the good old fashioned pencil, perfectly serviceable and less than half the cost."

The older man wondered if the policeman had been briefed to expect an older person and his opening gambit had been tailored to suit his audience, to put him at ease. He noticed that the shaving receptacle was full and then thought that the man was probably a dinosaur like himself and he liked that – he smirked.

"So," Warlonger said, as he licked the tip of the newly sharpened pencil, like a carpenter, and produced a note book. "You sir, found the body?"

"Yes," the old man replied, "I was walking Minty here," he motioned to the Labrador and she wagged her tail at the mention of her name, "when she went down to the waters edge and started barking."

"Strange time to be out," said the policeman interrogatively, but still smiling. "There are not many people about at dawn on a November Saturday morning. Quite windy too – sharp, a chill in the air?" He shuddered slightly as he spoke to accentuate the remark and then blew on his fingers to warm them.

"Not for me it's not," the man replied, "I'm always up at dawn or thereabouts and I like the cold, it keeps people away from the beach and me," he checked himself, realising what he had said, "and anyway Minty loves the sand," he qualified.

"So you were walking your dog?" Warlonger scribbled, "Were there any other dog owners on the beach, fishermen?"

"No, nobody just the two of us."

"Well at least there won't be any Vampires," the policeman chuckled at his own banal joke. "They'll all be away to their coffins to nurse hangovers. Let's take a look shall we?"

Warlonger looked up toward the Abbey and saw that the church yard was empty. He was glad, at least he wouldn't have to trudge up the 99 steps to interview witnesses – he could get one of the younger officers to check that out when they arrived.

"You were saying your dog discovered the body?" he asked, as they approached the corpse. "Was the body just like this, face down in the sand?"

"Yes but the tide was higher and she was almost totally submerged then."

"I see, so the body looked like it might have been washed ashore?"

"I don't know," replied the old man, "but she was nearly submerged then and the tide goes out so quickly."

"So you were walking the dog," Warlonger stroked the animal's head, "and she started barking?"

Warlonger noted that the man referred to the body as she rather than an inanimate object body – sensitive, he scribbled in his pocket book as an evaluation.

"Yes, we were on our way back to the cottage, there." He turned and pointed up the hill which rose steeply behind him. "See the one with the gable window facing the sea."

Warlonger nodded, "So you haven't touched the body?" he asked.

"No."

"Not even to check for a pulse?"

"No I could see she was dead."

He was making notes quickly now.

"I like the peace and quiet, I'm a kind of recluse," he said, having no idea as to why he had qualified his lifestyle.

"Yes you said that already," Warlonger remarked. "Nice aroma up there though?"

"Well I'd rather smell the smoke houses of kippers than the smog of London. That is enough to make me choke."

"On holiday?" asked the policeman, "you and the wife?"

"No and no," the man replied, "that place is mine and ……

"Your name sir?" he interrupted sharply, the nice face turning nasty. Force of habit made him shift his style to unbalance any potential quarry during interview.

"Squirrel."

The policeman looked up from his note book and wanted to make a comment but thought better of it. All he could think of was Nutkin. His mind raced through all the weird and wonderful names he had dealt with in his long career but to date this had been his first Squirrel.

"That's Squirrel with an i," he began to spell, "S, q, u, i, double r, i," he paused accentuating the final i before ending with, "L."

"And the Christian name sir, unless that was it?" He smiled broadly at the man who in turn smiled back with a forced grimace.

The old man was used to the sarcasm, it had been part of his life since early childhood and stock ammunition for the school yard bully. It had made him stronger and more self reliant.

"Yes I know it's unusual," Squirril quipped, "but I am not related to Nutkin if that's what you're getting at. Martin, Martin Squirril."

Warlonger continued to write and his tone became serious, business like. Realising he had overstepped the mark he tried to regain the momentum.

"You are a local sir - address?" he demanded.

"Look, I am local and I don't appreciate the sarcasm, or the prying. I was out walking my dog. A walk I do everyday. I was on the beach and she started barking, that's it. I don't," Squirril paused, "I'm not some form of nut. I like to walk alone. In fact I like to be left alone. My wife is dead. I worked in London and now I'm retired. What else do you want to know?"

The tone of the police officer softened, "I was just trying to ascertain."

"Ascertain what? Whether I am some from of nut?"

"No," Warlonger was firm. "I just need to make sure that everything you say is correctly recorded."

"I'll give you all the details that I can, but..."

"Understood sir, point taken." Warlonger became apologetic, "You see I've spent too many years in this game and well," he paused, "I've met a few in my time."

"A few?"

"Nuts and fruitcakes."

"Well I'm not one of those," Squirril replied, "I just like to be left alone. That as far as I know is not a crime."

"Point taken sir," was Warlonger's terse reply.

Martin Squirril was a recluse but he had the air of authority which men who have been accustomed to giving orders and having them obeyed possess. It was not so much what he said, but the way in which he said it that made the significant difference. His irritation levels were rising again and he could hear Jean's voice in the back of his sub-conscious whispering - blood pressure. That was enough to make him draw in his horns and attempt to get the interview over with as quickly as possible. Soon the local gossips would be abroad and he wanted to be back at home to avoid their wagging tongues and inquisitive eyes. Whitby was a lovely place to retire but he hated the ever present net curtain twitchers – the women who had nothing better in their lives that to pry upon others. He saw them in the shops, heard them in the town and knew how lucky he had been with Jean. She had been too busy living her own life, rather than watching someone else, or a soap-opera substitute.

After a few minutes of tedious questioning Martin Squirril and Minty walked slowly up the beach and vanished into the cobbled alleyways. He had been told that further questions to aid with the enquiry might be needed once the doctors had established cause of death. Warlonger was precise and took the time to explain that often witnesses had seen things even they did not recall as important at the time, because they were mundane or seemingly unrelated. If he did think of anything perhaps he could telephone the station and ask for George in CID.

"Whitby's such a quiet little place usually," Warlonger had offered, "not often we get a dead girl washed up on the beach."

"I know," Squirril replied, "I've been coming here for years."

Warlonger was onto the possible mistake in a flash, "But you said you lived here sir?" he questioned quizzically.

"Yes I do now. But for years the wife and I had been coming on holiday. We had a little flat, well more like some rooms really round the back of the White Lion. When we decided to retire my wife got ill."

"Got ill?"

"Cancer."

Warlonger was quick to see he had opened a raw nerve and his retreat was as swift as his attack, "Thank you sir," he said.

"Good luck," was the older man's retort though he wondered why he had said it.

The beach quickly became a crime scene surrounded with red and white tape and sealed shut by uniformed officers who were now ushering early risers from the area. Children on their way to school were standing on the swing bridge as the reporters arrived and the forensic crime scene tent was erected. The S.O.C.O. was young, not much older than the victim and like the dead girl dark haired. She was full-breasted and Squirril wondered if she were pregnant – he had seen that body shape before. Martin Squirril turned and walked away and then some yards later turned again and studied the activity which had moved into high gear. Minty turned too, and then silently they slipped back into the obscurity of the cobbles and wind swept walkways.

Minty walked without a lead her head full of warm milk and the excitement of the corpse on the beach fading from her memory.

At the Ellsinore Pub later that morning, and at the Spa later that night, the word was spreading among the Goths. Girl, a Goth, found dead on the beach, who was she became the question of the day? The Goths were checking out the people in their parties, people who hadn't come back from the revelry of the previous night. Those who had slept in strange beds received calls on their mobiles from anxious friends.

A dark haired girl in a wedding dress tended not to narrow down the possibilities as it might have done in other places - many girls wore them. A tribute to the bride of Frankenstein idea or the formal madness of Miss Havisham, either way such a dress attracted attention - made people look. And that night at the Spa, when the Damned played and brought the house down Sensible and Vanian tried to get the crowd to give up an identity. She was, "One of their own," they had said, "every one needs to co-operate with the police however alternative they might feel."

The Goth crowd remained at the event but the Abbey above the town had few visitors on that night, and almost none of them female.

"And if you do go off somewhere?" Dave Vanian announced, "Don't go alone. There's some monsters out there. And, and if any of you girls are in need of some company well, we in the band," he hugged himself and lowered his voice to a sexual drawl, "well we are ready , willing and able."

The crowd burst into life as the sound of sharp guitar bounced from wall to wall.

Chapter Three

"Whitby, what in Yorkshire?" Inspector Michael Stokes wasn't happy. "Jesus," he was snorting through his nostrils, "they don't even have roads up there do they?"

"That's right," came the terse reply.

"Bloody hell chief," he exclaimed. "Why me sir, Whitby's bloody miles away from our manor?" Stokes was irritated. "It's all cow shit and funny accents up there. Half of the buggers can't read and the other half – well they do funny things to the sheep don't they?"

"Now, now, you can't say things like that, you'll upset the locals, or is that what you want me to think, you crafty bugger? You're going, and that my old son, is that."

"Why me? Why can't old Johnny Witt do it? He likes walking about in the country, poncing about in the wind and the rain. I bet he's even got some walking boots."

"I'm sending you Stokes," the voice became official, "because you were on the Kelsall Green murder, with that berk Slevin. You remember that one don't you? What a bloody mess," the tone was sarcastic now.

"How can I forget it?" Stokes replied.

"Well it seems that we have another, only this time in Whitby," he paused, "and I don't want that back wheel skid involved this time, he's a first class berk." He waited for a reaction - there was none. "So get up there and sort this bloody mess out. We have some sort of looney on the loose and I want you to feel his collar by Christmas. So no press calls, no bollocks, just find the little shit. This is becoming a bit of an embarrassment. Fix it pronto."

Stokes nodded.

"Forensics are up there now." A file was tossed across the desk at Stokes. "Background reading, for the journey," he said, "some of it's in there. Read it and get the locals to do the business, they know you're coming and they will co-operate fully."

Stokes knew that Slevin had Yiddish ancestry and that Keene was a pure racist, but even he had to admit the cemetery murder had been a public relations disaster. Slevin was too eager for success; he wanted quick promotion, but the police talking about a real vampire prowling London made them a laughing stock and Keene had blamed Slevin for what he saw as a fiasco. For the police who could not explain a murder, let alone catch the culprit; it was a public relations disaster. A junior officer banging on about the possible existence of vampires had turned the whole investigation into a farce. The Daily Mail had a field day with headlines like, "Spectacular Dracula," and offering special vouchers on garlic from Tesco. Vampire experts came out of the woodwork, with some even going on the hunt in London's cemeteries complete with Gladstone bags packed with wooden stakes and crosses ready to execute the undead.

Jack Keene was a Chief with singular views. He never wore a suit and dressed in Harris Tweed jackets with black trousers. Usually he wore a green tie and a checked shirt which made him look like a rural squire rather than a Chief Superintendent. The illusion was added to by his ruddy and well scrubbed face with a large bulbous nose, which glowed slightly like an established country farmer who had imbibed once too often. Stokes looked at the shoes Keene wore and marvelled at the hard leather which glowed from the military style polishing and the clash of their deep burgundy against the green of his tie. He looked every inch the country gent. Unfortunately he also exhibited most of the worst traits imaginable on race, colour and creed, alongside a profound intelligence for the solving of crime. A strange dichotomy of a man he was intensely likeable at times and at others he was disliked as a bigot. However, he was fair, scrupulously fair, honest and open; and for that single reason his political incorrectness was tolerated by those above him.

"Young girl," Keene said, "drained like the girl in Kelsall.

Halal style. I put my money on some mad Muslim, weirdo sect. Some strange group out to get even I suspect. They do women don't they? Cowardly bastards."

Stokes looked up. His face showed no emotion - he had learned not to question Keene but even after all these years the extreme racial remarks grated on his nerves. He would have liked to laugh out loud but ironically, on this one, Keene might be right.

"We have a serial on our hands, Mike." Keene waited, "Same MO, same marks on the throat and same bloodless corpse. This time it's one of those Gothic types up at the Whitby Goth weekend. That's the irony though, spend all their lives looking for vampires or pretending to be them and now they've got one," he laughed heartily, " I bet they're shitting themselves. I bet there are some arseholes clenching up there tonight." He snorted. "Find the little shits that are doing this. Get some collar felt. I don't care how you do it," he paused, "but don't do it in the bloody media spotlight. And keep that berk out of it."

"Same marks you say?" Stokes became professional.

Keene nodded, "Puncture wounds to the jugular and the blood gone. Only this time she was washed up on the beach. Some local guy found her. The forensic people are up there now, so you had better piss off up there toot sweet."

Stokes looked intensely at his superior officer, "Why just me though?" he asked.

"It won't be just you. There's some hot shot Italian on his way over from Rome."

Stokes looked puzzled.

"Apparently," Keene continued, "the I- ties had a problem too. Four years ago. Same MO. A girl in the English cemetery in Rome and three more in Florence, then nothing, it stopped as suddenly as it started. Like bloody Jack the Ripper Mike. Do you know Florence?"

"Been there once," Stokes replied, "the wife wanted to see the art galleries. Left me a bit cold. I thought it was a bit dirty – smelt of piss. Not enough toilets, but we marched around the place chasing the sights. "

"Well," continued Keene, "the daygoes aren't that clean are they? They piss and shit everywhere," he smiled, "but they are sending their best man on this case. He sounds ok but a little eccentric. Their press called it, il Mostro de Firenze; translated it means, the monster of Florence. This Italian chased this one down, spent two years on the cases and as he got closer the killer made like an oozoolum bird and disappeared up his own arse. Just like he starts - he stops. We have the Kelsall murder and now this Whitby one - same MO. So when there's a problem who do they send for, not the bloody Ghostbusters, but us. I think it's more than one person. Could be a cell of Muslims designed to get panic moving among the Christians. Play on their dark fears of legends, get some mistrust going. Christ when I think about it, it makes my blood boil."

"That's all I need, some Italian with a monster case to solve, is he young?"

Keene shrugged, "Don't know, looks it," he said, tossing a poorly reproduced ID card across the desk. "He's bloody Italian though, bet he stinks of garlic."

"Do I have to chief? I don't need some millstone hanging around my neck."

"Whether you need it or not you've got him. So read that file on the plane," he paused, "and you had best work with him, he's supposed to be mustard."

"Why me though sir?"

"Why you? Because you my old son are going to solve this. If there is some nutter who thinks he's a Vampire out there, you are going to feel his collar and Broadmoor the bastard. If it's Muslims then we do the lot in one hit. I don't want some smart arse Italian piggy - backing our investigation. Get up among those Goths before the weekend is over."

"They're not going to want to talk to us are they?" Stokes blurted.

"Listen there's a lot of old nonsense spoken about people. You know that. This is one of them. They aren't going to like what's happened. What if the council shuts them down? Then what happens, where are they going to hold their do?" He was looking Stokes in the eye, "Anyhow it's female dominated," he continued, "like the fetish scene. Those girls up there aren't going to like this are they? It kind of screws up the profits and buggers up the locals."

Chapter Four

When the small plane took off from London city airport Inspector Michael Stokes knew he had just one hour to digest the information within the file. He pored over the papers which had clear photographs of the Italian victims. The first girl had almost lost the whole of her neck. Her right ear was touching her collar bone and the throat had been torn away as if by a frenzied animal. Police at first thought it might have been a ferocious dog of some sort. However, the body had been almost totally drained and virtually no blood had been found near the crime scene.

The second victim had been partially dismembered and once again the blood had simply vanished like someone or something had simply sucked the juice from every body part like a dog sucks marrow from a bone.

The third victim had been hung by her ankles in some woodland like an animal, the jugular opened and she was bled into some form of receptacle; the blood had never been found nor had the receptacle. The body had simply been left and the theory had been disturbance, that had driven the killer away before he had an opportunity to clear up. Stokes noticed the girl's saturated hair which hung like a wet dish cloth and from the spread of blood he deduced she had been conscious of the bleeding taking place-she had struggled. Her killer would have been sprayed with blood, if he had been close enough to watch the gruesome spectacle. That, if they could ever find clothing, would supply them the forensic evidence they needed to convict.

The last girl had been dispatched in a much more subtle manner. Two puncture wounds to the jugular, the blood had been drained again but this time the frenzied mess had been replaced by clinical precision. Then as suddenly as the attacks started they had stopped only to start again in England.

Stokes looked at the picture of the Italian detective assigned to the case. Giancarlo Pancardi was a man in his early forties, dark hair, striking eyes - he looked sharp, intelligent, and intense. Stokes looked at the eyes and wondered if he was a career cop or a real cop. His hair was tufted and gave him the distinct image of Tin Tin the cartoon character. Stokes imagined the man in plus fours with long socks and golfing shoes, his face cracked into a smile and he rested his head against the seat back and closed his eyes. His mind drifted and he saw himself chasing a man along the beach at Whitby, the man was dressed like Bela Lugosi and Tin Tin and Snowy were just ahead. He was running hard now and the running man ahead began to lift into the air and swoop to the left and he was looking in awe as the little dog barked at the giant bat which the man had now become.

The plane banked hard to the left and Stokes woke to see a glimpse of fields approaching. The pilot was barking about landing on open grass but Stokes could not make out the precise wording of his complaint over the dull drone of the engines. He studied his watch - they were ten minutes early.

It was a bleak and isolated place on the edge of the North Yorkshire moors set high on the heather a short drive from Whitby. A grey and skulking place, a place where bitter winds sucked the marrow from the bones of beleaguered sheep, a desolate place. Stokes began to feel sick as the small plane bumped toward a pair of corrugated hangers which clung to the edge of the airstrip like two lone limpets on a weather beaten rock.

He noticed the biting east wind and drew his overcoat about him as he disembarked and walked toward the waiting car. The engine was running. He could taste the salt on his lips, and smelt the richness of aviation fuel mixed with the poor carburetion of the car and sensed the day had hardly broken.

Looking around he saw the pilot shiver as he exited the plane, quickly pulling a sheepskin coat which had seen better days, around his shoulders. Stokes checked the sky – it was overcast, packed with dull grey clouds which rushed in over the water.

"I've been sent to collect you," said a young man, as he appeared from the shadows of the building to greet him.

The man was dark haired and pale and his skin seemed to have bluish tinge. He was tall and elegant with movements that seemed light of foot, like those of a dancer. He smiled a toothy grin which showed teeth which seemed too full for the thin-lipped mouth which surrounded them. Stokes grunted a short reply and followed the younger man toward the waiting car.

In the rear of the black Bentley he sat next to the Chief Constable of Yorkshire, who had not thought Stokes important enough to brave the elements for. Stokes resented that from the outset and within seconds had the mark of the man; political bureaucrat full of public relations and posturing and not a clue about real police work. Stokes glanced at the driver's mirror once or twice during the short conversation and realised that the young driver was of the same opinion. He said nothing but his reflected eyes showed a clear understanding of his force leader.

"I need a driver," said Stokes suddenly, "or at least a car while I'm here."

The Chief Constable acted without hesitation, "Take young Vincent here. He's off to Leeds Bradford airport after he has dropped me back at the office after that he's all yours. I'm sure we can find you a car too, what do you say Vincent?"

The driver studied the visitor in the mirror, "Yes sir," he said calmly.

"You're not staying Chief Constable?" asked Stokes.

"We have some of our best men on the investigation, and," he replied, "now you and this Italian expert Campari are on the case I am sure that you won't need me. It's not everyday that we get so much interest in one of our local events."

* * *

The television cameras were rolling near the beach and interviews were being conducted on passers by and the Chief Constable's concentration upon them had already marred his recollection of any names other than his own. He talked like a man absorbed by a television screen, much as a moth flutters toward a light in the corner of a darkened room. He seemed unable to concentrate and in consequence his speech seemed disjointed. As he strode confidently toward the press gathering to preen his feathers publicly, he became totally oblivious of the east wind driving up the estuary.

Stokes' irritation grew as he watched the man stride out of ear shot, "Gobshite," he hissed almost inaudibly. Vincent smiled and Stokes wondered if he had heard.

"What time do you go for Pancardi?" he asked, stepping into to the open air.

"He's on the three o'clock, sir," Vincent replied, closing the door behind him.

"Right, I want him back here as fast as possible got that. Get rid of bloody Prince Charming there," he nodded toward the Chief Constable. "And you get our man back here sirens blazing. Get rid of that bloody Bentley and get us a proper car – nothing flash. We don't have time to mess about showboating. I don't want to be driving around this town in some great big motor. Might as well have a ten foot flag flying from my nut which says plod in thumping great letters."

The young constable nodded and grinned, "I'll get a small inconspicuous car?"

"Too bloody right! What's your name son?" Stokes continued, nodding.

"Vin......"

"Not that one, your full name," he interrupted.

"Vincent Drago, sir."

"Right Drago cut out the sir crap. It's Stokes right? DI Stokes right?"

"Yes sir."

"Come on son you don't want to turn into one of those do you?" He nodded toward the Chief Constable again who was now explaining to the whole world how wonderfully important he was. "He'll be a real sir one day," he slurred the, real, in a broad American twang, "sure as eggs are eggs."

"Yes DI."

"Better Drago. Now piss off and get Cinderella there," he nodded once again toward the Chief Constable, "back to the ball before midnight and get me my expert Italian."

With that Stokes leapt cat-like over the edge of the path wall and dropped the five feet into the sand below. Two constables rushed up to eject him but he flashed his warrant card and he was led toward the white plastic forensic tent.

At the entrance he drew the two plastic covers provided over his shoes and disappeared behind the overlapped entrance into the mass of shadows at the waters edge.

Vincent Drago noticed the tide was on the turn and he could smell the salt which stung his nostrils. There was no way he was going to cross that piece of flowing water tonight. He thought of food and then looked up toward Whitby Abbey; the winter light was murky and the emptiness in his stomach needed to be slaked - but it would have to wait until later when he had run all of his errands. He glanced at the Chief Constable and then back toward the tent, listening to the distant conversations within; the explanations and the excuses of those trying to solve the unsolvable.

Back inside the car he glanced at his watch and wondered just how fast he could get the Italian back to Whitby once he had dumped the Bentley and it's charge. He had a need which wanted servicing and this weekend was one of the best chances.

* * *

"The body? It's at local undertakers at the present time," replied one of the officers.

"So anything found on the beach here?" Stokes continued with his questions. "Have you anything at all you can offer Doc?"

"Just this Inspector," came the reply, "in about ten minutes this tent and the whole area is going to be under about six feet of water. I have a couple of metres of sand left to sift so time is rather pressing. I'll conduct the autopsy later today but here, so far, there is nothing."

Stokes knew that there would be nothing found but he needed to know if this had been the site of the killing.

"So this is not the crime scene?" Stokes continued.

"Most unlikely. The body seems to genuinely have washed up. Perhaps the killer just dumped the body at sea and the tide brought it in. In Whitby that happens quite a lot, whales, ships, all sorts of things land here."

"Are you certain?"

"Totally."

"So where was it dumped from?"

"Could be from the cliffs, a boat or virtually anywhere," the doctor replied, "I'll know a lot more when I've completed the autopsy."

"But it's Goth weekend, and she's a Goth. She doesn't seem dressed for another sort of outing. You don't need to be a rocket scientist to work that one out."

"That may well be so," the doctor seemed bemused by the urgency of the Inspector who was irritated by the incoming tide which lapped at his shoes.

"Any of you local boys fishermen?" Stokes raised his voice to the gathered police ensemble - two hands were raised. "I want to know about the currents and where the best places to see them are," he continued. "I need a guided tour, now, before the light fades."

"It's only lunchtime sir," one of the younger officers replied.

"Well it looks bloody dark to me."

"We could walk along the sea wall and up to the Kirk sir, that'll give you a vantage point for all of the rips and the locals will be fishing there now on the turn of tide."

Chapter Five

Stokes could see the circus below him packing up ready to leave town. There was scurrying and rushing to lift equipment beyond the incoming tide. The wind was biting his face and he had turned to view the town spread out below him and to catch his breath after he had toiled up the Abbey steps. The Doctor was issuing orders below and the constables were moving to and fro like an army of dark blue ants ferrying the spoils of an unguarded picnic hamper away from the tide as fast as they could.

"It's a bit of a walk sir," said one of the local Bobbies.

"That's an understatement," Stokes replied, "it's lung splitting."

At the entrance to the Church yard the officers made for a narrow path which led around the cliff head and Stokes followed as dutifully as a puppy.

"The path goes right round and you can see everything from it." One constable pointed, "See," he pointed again, "there's DS Warlonger, looks like he's interviewing the fishermen in the boats at the dock. Perhaps he's got the same idea sir?"

"Perhaps."

"If you look sir you can see the water moving in dark vein channels across the mouth of the estuary. Anything that gets thrown off this cliff ends up on the sands. Anything thrown further out at sea well somewhere in Northern France might be reasonable."

"So if that girl was thrown from along here, you're saying that she would naturally end up on the sands."

"Yes sir, every local knows that one. The local kids have tossed allsorts of stuff from here. Used to be message in a bottle when I was a boy. Pirate codes and all that."

Stokes was examining the cliff edge.

"Careful sir," said the second constable, "there's more than one or two ended up on Tate Hill sands that left from here when they didn't intend to."

Stokes could see foot prints but no real signs of a scuffle.

"Loads of foot prints," he said, "do lots of people come up here then?"

"Not that many this time of year, but every night during the Goth weekend it's heaving with them. Once they had candles burning and even fireworks. The whole cliff was lit up like a Christmas tree. One idiot even climbed to the top of the ruins in the dark to have his photograph taken, with his cape billowing in the wind."

"There's been better than that sir," piped the second officer. "One year there was a duel fought at dawn."

Stokes laughed, "You can't be serious," he said.

"As true as me standing here. Two of them in shirt sleeves one had a deep cut to his arm when we arrived. Something to do with a woman and they had seconds and swords – the whole works. But they claimed it was a first blood of honour duel and if they had been left alone the whole matter would have been settled. Never seen anything like it, nor had the magistrate. They came to court all dressed up in cloaks and boots. Like a period drama from the telly it was. Made the Sunday papers too, but that was some years back now. Mind you they are a weird lot. One guy came to the Old White Lion and he wouldn't come in, not until Bert Cumming came to the door isself and invites him. Now old Bert is no fool and seeing as the fellow had a dinner for 40 people booked he humoured him. Funny though the bloke didn't eat a thing according to Bert. Just sat there and watched the others guzzling red wine by the bucket and eating," he paused, recalling the gossip, "now what was it they had?"

"Paprika chicken, Hungarian style," piped the other officer.

"Yeah that's it."

"Mary, the cook, she was sent a recipe especially for it."

"By the weirdo who wouldn't come in?" Stokes asked.

"She didn't say, but it was a funny thing to do."

"I wonder where the recipe came from?" Stokes asked.

"Probably some book or legend, you have no idea how weird

these Goths are. But this is the first time we've had anything like this, a girl's body."

Stokes raised his eyebrows, "Were they local?" he asked.

"Who sir?"

"The men having the duel?"

"No these were city boys. Having a laugh for the papers and the others here. They're a weird lot you know. Just look at the things they wear. They spend a fortune on clothes and meals and jewellery. The antique dealers love them, because some of them spend like Sheiks in Harrods."

Stokes laughed inwardly at the country-boy vision of London and Harrods and wondered if either of these constables had even been inside the place. He wondered how their wives might react to London sights and then observed that neither of them wore wedding bands.

"So the killer's not local," he suddenly said.

"Not if you ask me," the first man replied. "If he dumped the body from here somewhere, he perhaps thought it would not be found. No local boy would have dumped from here."

Stokes reflected on their ease of acceptance. The girl could have fallen, it could have been an accident but the two local men had accepted murder and a male as the protagonist. He wondered if the Sergeant below was as easily swayed by the locals he was interviewing.

They walked the whole length of the cliff and the sea wall, there were no signs of blood anywhere. Stokes and his two companions had covered a complete circle of the harbour before returning down to a café which opened onto the main colonnaded market square. It reminded him in a small way of Florence - the market of the boar, a covered square and cobbles. He wondered if that was the reason the killer had chosen Whitby, familiarity.

"Three teas please," Stokes requested as the party sat at a table.

"There's a shop over there," the younger constable pointed across the square, "that makes Dracula coffins."

Stokes raised an eyebrow.

"Not real ones," the younger man laughed, "chocolate ones, full of praline."

Stokes nodded.

"For the tourists and weekenders. A lot of them come to see the Goths as they wander around the town. They've become an attraction in themselves. Everybody loves the vampires with their long teeth and funny gestures."

Stokes was watching the younger men who clearly relished the appearance of Goths in the town. These were local village Bobbies out of their depth and trying to make light of a plague which was about to hit their sleepy town. He looked at their fresh faces and wondered what the Italian would make of them. He could retire to a place like this he thought. Grow prize roses and leave the world to get on with its own destruction.

He played the scenarios of the crime scenes in Italy in his head and then overlaid the Kelsall Green murder in his mind. If they knew what he knew, would these young men be quite so eager to laugh off the cares of the world.

"Hey Sally," one of them called to the waitress, "have you got any of that lovely carrot cake – the homemade stuff?"

"Why William Turpin," she replied in a mocking flirtatious tone, "you'll be as big as a house one of these days. I won't be able to take you to meet my mother if you gets as big as old George."

"And why should I, Sally me girl, wish to meet with your mother?"

"Why to ask her proper."

"I only want your carrot cake."

"Mmm well as long as that's all you wants Billy Turpin," her tone became serious, "that's all you'll get." She held out her hand, "That's five pound twenty."

"What for a bit of cake Sally?"

"Three bits," the girl replied.

"Don't we get a special rate?" Turpin teased.

"Just cos' you're a Bobby don't mean you'll get anything special from me Billy Turpin. And you'd best be at my house by seven iffen you want me to go the pictures."

The young girl turned and walked out toward the kitchen her nose held high.

"I don't know why Sally even likes you Bill," said the second constable. "One day she'll catch you out, all those birds you bash about with and then you'll be sorry."

Stokes watched the reaction in Turpin's face.

"What the eye don't see the heart don't grieve," he replied.

The door of the café flew open as the waitress returned with the cakes.

"Constable Turpin!" Warlonger exclaimed as he entered.

Turpin and the other officer were on their feet.

"Sit down lads," his voice had a jovial ring. "Have they been looking after you? Tea Sally please," he said, without expecting a reply from Stokes. He stretched out his hand in greeting, "Warlonger," he said, his face opening into a grin. Stokes noticed he was missing some teeth in his lower jaw and that his chin was deeply scarred. "You must be Inspector Stokes from London?"

"Yes," Stokes replied, gripping the hand outstretched to him.

"Well," said Warlonger as he drew out a chair to join them, "we have been given orders to hand over the investigation to you. I've interviewed some of the fishermen and they saw nothing. I spoke to the man who discovered the body, strange name but he seems Kosher to me."

Stokes was bemused by the scene. He was taking afternoon tea with the investigating officers of a suspicious death possibly a murder and they were chatting about it freely in a semi-deserted tea-room, with a waitress who could hear everything. It struck him as surreal, like an out-of-body experience, the script from a bizarre and obscure artsy foreign film, all it needed now was a pouting clown carrying flowers and mime artist and the whole thing could be a dream. Stokes studied his watch, and wondered when the Italian super sleuth would arrive.

"I need to find the Crescent Hotel," he said breaking the cosy quaint atmosphere.

"It's on the West Cliff sir," the officers piped in unison.

"Which is?" Stokes questioned.

"We'll walk you up there sir. It's just over the swing bridge and then up through some alleys to the kop and then on from the whale bones. Not far, but it's not exactly the Ritz. But you'll get a good breakfast."

Stokes looked at the men and knew that they had reached the high point of their careers. William Turpin was more keen on finding out what lay underneath the waitress' skirt and Warlonger was edging closer to retirement by the day. He suddenly realised that he did not even know the name of the other younger officer.

Chapter Six

Julianne Doppodomani studied the scars on her neck in the vanity mirror above the sink. She touched the wrinkled skin which felt soapy and smooth and almost like plastic against her fingertips; a single silent tear rolled down her cheek to drop into the basin below. Mornings always reminded her of him. The coward who had run, once that bitch had done her worst. He could have stayed but he ran, ran to his hideaway and found himself another model to play house with. If she could see him now she'd only speak a curse or two. Now, like then, the pain would always be there; but this pain was the worst sort - the constant emotional reminder. For that she could never forgive him.

She had been a beautiful young woman once, though her youth was fading now and she should and could have been one of the most beautiful women. Dark hair which shone a raven blue - black in the light, dark soft eyes which could invite any man to bed. But she had chosen the wrong man; the one with a crazy wife, crazy jealous, crazy enough to end up in jail for attempted murder. He had screwed them both in more ways than one.

She examined her reflection, the cheek bones were high and the lips full and luscious. It was a mouth men had wanted to kiss, though other models had a hastier take on its use – they had been jealous of her natural lips. She had deserved the accolades of her youth and once she could have commanded armies to sack the towers of Troy. That had been stolen from her by the jealousy of others and now she had to watch as these lesser women stepped into her spotlight. Cocaine snorting bitches, half doped or half sodden with booze, their fame aided by sexual favours. It was hard to watch as these young girls screwed their way up the greasy pole of fashion success- she loathed them, hated them, despised them.

She patted and studied her firm stomach below the navel as she spoke, "For this you have been destroyed. To have him here was your fate, and look what it cost in return." She turned to the mirror again to examine old scars, "What a price to pay for love?" She stroked the scarred skin around her neck.

She drew a high necked blouse from a chair and as she turned the wrinkled skin stretched across her back and right shoulder. The burn scar was deep and had to be treated almost daily now to keep it supple. Luckily she was small breasted and could get away without a bra, that too was blessing, not to have the chafing of hard lace irritate her. The treatment and surgery was working and it wouldn't be long before the scar would be better and then she could step back into the limelight- regain the momentum of her career and get back to the top alongside some of the other models that had since surpassed her. Admittedly, she reasoned, I'd have to do the more mature market, at least that was what she kept telling herself; repeating it like a mantra. It was the last bastion of hope left in a life which had been destroyed.

She stroked her hips as she smoothed her dress – her figure was still good and if Twiggy Lawson could do Marks and Spencer, she thought, "So can I."

The shoes were Gucci, high strapped, elegant. She stood tall and proud with long legs and fine hips. Her ankles were slender and her feet were perfectly proportioned. For several years now she had made a sideline of pants. The catalogue market had been kind and they didn't care if she had a hunched back and warts on her nose as long as the waist down shots worked.

At times she dreamt about him and that fateful afternoon. He had said the coast was clear and she had wanted to be in his London flat – she loved him. Taken a flight from Paris to be with him and in return the boiling water had stolen virtually all of her life and her self esteem. And he was a typical chicken, a mercenary, who ran as fast as his cowardly legs could take him.

She glanced at the clock - she was late.

She could still remember the room now. The fine paintings on the wall and the statues. Spoilt bastard, son of an art dealer or something, he had inherited things from his parents and he had it all. Smooth as the Devil himself he was.

Her mobile phone rang – she answered, "Hello Franco," she said, her voice slightly husky. It was a voice which other women envied, and men listened to.

"Good morning Principessa," he chortled in a cheery mood. "And how is Julianne today? Not busy are we?" The word busy was accentuated to infer the innuendo of illicit sexual activity.

Even after the terrible scars this man still spoke to her as if she were the most beautiful creation on the planet, and she loved him for that alone.

"Fine," she replied, "and for the record there is no one else here."

"And you expect me to believe that, after gorgeous George was all over you last night? Not fair you get all the best ones."

"He was drunk and wine has a way of making even the ugly beautiful," she replied.

"Dearie me who didn't get much sleep last night then?" he snorted.

"Me I'm fine and dandy, just fine and dandy," she was fixing an earring now and had flipped the handset to loudspeaker mode as she squatted on the toilet seat. "It's all organized though; I don't know why you settled for the name." She was speaking loudly now.

"Gothique Fantastique? Don't you like it then?" he asked.

"You know I don't." She waited, "It's so 1980's."

"Well Gothic is back. It's the new look and Jean-Michel wants you to handle all the lose ends. So it's Whitby first and then Paris to add the new to the old." He laughed, "It's time to make pure, raw sex, a focal point of fashion. We want to cause a little ripple, shake a few old plums off the tree. Vampires and Werewolves whatever next? I hope you enjoy it. I know it's not New York, Florence or Rome but the weirdoes up there should embrace you. You never know there might a Count available," he paused, "if there is bring a brother back for me there's a good girl. This man belongs to me and all that. Get me a Count Dracula and I'll drink from him."

"I'm sure you will; Franco you are a complete tart, haven't you got any shame?" she laughed in reply.

"Listen dearie, a hard man is good to find."

"Shameless."

"I know," Franco replied, "but the early bird gets the worm."

"Shameless."

She had dreaded the idea of a long weekend in Whitby. The only saving grace was that it would be Goth weekend and the place would be loaded with eccentrics and snappy dressers and she could blend in among them. The burn might even look like some special make-up. It would add to the illusion of horror.

"Make sure our girls behave themselves," he chided, "you're in charge now. All those aristocratic vampires. We don't want any funny business now do we? No bellies full of arms and legs when they get back."

"And don't I know it?" she replied.

"The reason I called was that Madeleine thought you could do some of…"

"No, I'm not accepting charity Franco. I'm not doing all the lace knickers while she gets the ball gowns. I could do some of those gowns, the scars on my neck are nearly gone. Anyway the treatment is working it won't be long before I'm back on the catwalk full-time."

"Sweetie," his voice soothed, "it may be a little while yet."

"You think it won't work don't you?" she snapped. "Well screw you and thanks for the encouragement. Do you have any idea how dangerous my treatment is?" She didn't wait for a reply. "No you don't. Do you care? No you don't. Sometimes I wonder why I try so hard for you. That bitch got what she deserved for what she did to me. She should have tried harder to keep him if she wanted him so much, instead of taking it out on me. Now look at them back together I bet and me, I'm fucked up."

His voice was placatory now, "You know that's not what I said. I just think you shouldn't get your hopes up too high. And anyway there's not a model alive has better legs and arse than you."

"Yeah," she replied, "but shame about the disfiguring scars eh?"

"Listen Princess you know you are my best, don't go all weird on me, this is your Frankie here and he loves you." He blew a kiss down the phone.

"I'm not doing all the bums and panties though," she snapped, "one of the others can do some too. And if you think I'm doing knickers in a churchyard you've got another thing coming."

"That's my girl," replied Franco, "feisty bitch oooo ar."

"Off the phone then you little monster, and let me get ready."

"Better whip your knickers back on then dearie and give gorgeous George the boot. No time for toast and marmalade now, and no going back to bed for seconds the car's on its way." He cupped the receiver in his hand in an attempt to muffle it, "OO hoo Lawson dear," she heard him call.

Julianne heard a voice in the distance and knew that Franco's butch lover would arrive for her within fifteen minutes.

"Go and get her ladyship for me there's a love," he had said, albeit as quietly as possible. There was a distant grunted reply.

"Julianne sweetie tums you still there, get your knickers on sweetie Lawson's on his way, about twenty minutes. So have your glad bags and hands rags on."

"Lawson's on his way is he?" she asked. "Did you let him out of bed then?"

" OOO you," he laughed at her chastisement.

* * *

Lawson Bell was a large man. That was precisely why Franco liked him. He stood six foot three in bare feet and wore a forty six inch jacket. Everything about him was large and had he not been gay Julianne could well have found him attractive. Franco had often remarked that he was the large silent type and emphasized the large, alluding to the fact that in his book size did matter. When he arrived at Julianne's apartment he rang the door bell and waited for the buzzer to sound him up.

"Miss Dopdo.." he had trouble with her surname.

"Come in Lawson," she said at the door, "my case is over there."

Julianne noted his prodigious strength and knew he could probably snap her neck like a twig if he chose to do so. Though not bright, he was incredibly loyal and Franco, in his usual fashion thought the world of him. The two had met at a shoot in London and over the past twelve years had become firm friends, lovers and bedfellows. She had found her reaction to the situation one of pure jealousy; and, as a result often wondered at her own inability to make the "one" stick. Once the scars had healed she was certain she could find him, a man to love her for what she was.

As the car moved through the traffic her mind began to drift back to the horrific events of the attack. She remembered every second and image as they replayed in her waking dream, for what seemed to be the millionth time.

The room was heady with the scent of jasmine and sex. She could feel the man between her thighs as he pushed and drove himself in deep. They were really together that afternoon. She had flown in from Paris and he had met her at the airport. The passion had been intense and they had torn the clothes from each other in their joy to be reunited. The two of them had rolled around the bed, him on top of her and then him standing and her kneeling before him. He had grasped her hips and pulled her to him and he nipped the nape of her neck when he leant over her. He had cupped her breasts and tugged on her nipples as his pelvis thrust forward. It had been passionate loud and intense, her orgasm had been powerful and shudderingly awesome and then they had slept. They had spooned and he had slid into her once again in the half waking world of a daydream.

Neither of them had heard the woman enter and neither of them expected what happened. In the throws of their third round of love making she had sat astride him her hips gyrating to his upward thrusts and then there was pain, intense screaming pain as she had never felt before. She had half turned as the flaxen haired woman screamed her name and flung the pan of boiling water over them both. She heard the words, "Fucking bitch, you fucking cock sucking bitch." She could see Ellen's eyes; in her nightmares they were flame red and she was spitting words which followed in the wake of the boiling water. He had burns on his chest and slight ones to his face, but hers were on her neck, shoulders and back - large painful burns.

In the hospital she lay for days covered in a plastic skin as fowl smelling fluid oozed into dressings. All the most modern techniques, and even frequent blood transfusions and high antibiotic doses could not save the skin. The blood transfusions seemed to help best of all and the skin did heal a little. At first it bubbled and blistered, then it cracked, then came the weeping and the flowers from friends and finally came the realisation that she would be scarred for life.

"Is it terminal three?" asked Lawson.

She snapped out of the daydream and noticed that her palms were wet with perspiration, "Yep that's it," she replied.

She knew that blood was a palliative, but she didn't care it had helped to avoid infection and it had made her skin less taut. Ellen Baxter was sentenced to seven years for the crime. Seven years for a crime of passion, the judge called it, and she Julianne, she had been vilified as the scarlet harlot in the press, as if it had all been her fault.

Ellen had sat down stairs while they made love and casually boiled a large pan of water; she must have heard him coming and then, as casually as you like, she walked upstairs and doused them both. Julianne's mind imagined Ellen doused in petrol as she herself nonchalantly flicked a cigarette butt at her. She saw Ellen writhing, twisting and clawing at the ground like a rabid dog until the silence came and her skin blistered and peeled like an orange. Some Daily Mail journalist, with a sanctimonious defender of the moral faith attitude, had written a story about her, said she got what was coming and that she shouldn't have been fucking somebody else's husband. Later she discovered that the journalist's husband had run off with a model, and that the venom in the story stemmed from that sack of poisonous bile in her own emotional turmoil. By then it was too late and the press had turned her into a monster-yet she was the one with the injury and the ruined career.

"We'll be there in a few minutes," Lawson replied. "Going somewhere nice Miss Dopopo...?"

Back in reality her mind flipped to the here and now. She wondered if he were a little simple. He seemed unable to grasp her name.

"That's fine," she said, "I'm sure it was terminal three."

"I hope it's warm," he said trying to make conversation. "I like the warm and the sea."

Now she was convinced that Franco liked him for his looks rather than his brain. "Whitby," she replied. "A god forsaken wind swept corner of England where we can get the Gothic feel."

"That's nice," he replied automatically.

"Nice? No, it won't be nice Lawson. It won't be warm, in fact it will be bloody freezing .They'll have us in our knickers in a churchyard. It will be cold and ..." she lost the will to continue and allowed her voice to trail off into the distance.

Chapter Seven

When the knock came at the bedroom door Stokes woke instantly. The room was dark and he reached for the light switch as he lay on the bed. His suit jacket lay crumpled beside him where it had been discarded. Cursing his own stupidity he opened the door to be greeted by Constable Drago and a slim man dressed in a long dark coat, knee high boots and a fur hat, he looked Russian.

"Sorry to be so long DI," Drago said, "but what with the chief wanting to finish off the interviews and then the traffic, I didn't get to the airport until after four."

A hand reached past the young constable toward Stokes, "Giancarlo Pancardi," the man on the end of it said.

"Oh right," said Stokes, not expecting what he saw.

"I have come for the Gothic Festival no, and," he turned a pirouette, "so Pancardi he dresses for it."

Stokes stood as if pole-axed as Pancardi pushed into the room.

"Do you need me anymore sir, I mean DI, tonight?" asked Drago.

"Nope," Stokes replied.

"Then I can go off duty and get something to eat?"

Pancardi was in the room now looking at the case file which Keene had passed over in London. He saw the picture of himself among the pictures of the corpses and grasped it immediately.

"So Inspector you have researched me no?" Pancardi asked.

Stokes spoke to Drago, "Absolutely, you have my permission to feast away but be back for seven a.m. We need to get to York for the autopsy report. Which I believe is being carried out as we speak. What room is Inspector Pancardi in?" He spoke as if Pancardi were not there.

"I am here next to you," Pancardi pointed across the hall,

"but first we must feast too no? Pancardi, he has been travelling and he needs to eat before he can do much more. I want to try some of this legend of the fish and chips and mooshy peas."

"Mushy peas sir," Drago corrected.

"Those too. Pancardi he must try this for the once he is here in Yorkshire."

"Well I am not eating bloody fish and chips out of a piece of old newspaper." Stokes was smiling, "Stuff that I want some proper grub. Something Italian I thought."

"I see you are making of the fun with me," Pancardi smiled. "This is good we shall have some laughing as we work no?" His voice lowered; he threw the file back onto the bed, "This is an ugly business and we are chasing a monster." His tone became serious, "I nearly had …"

As Drago turned the corner before the flight of stairs he heard the words Mostro and Firenze and knew that information was being exchanged. The door of Stokes' room closed and he knew the conversation would become extreme and intense, and he was not in the mood today. He was hungry, tired and in need of some serious recreation.

Once outside he left the unmarked Ford Mondeo parked in a bay opposite an unoccupied holiday home and slipped quietly off toward the gathering Goths making their way toward the Spa. He was going to do some of his own undercover work, once he had changed. He needed to look the part and get out of his work clothes but first he needed to make a visit.

* * *

The White Lion was warm and the dining room felt cosy. A large log fire burned in an open hearth. The brick walls had absorbed history and the low ceilings gave it the ambiance of a sea-faring inn. The Admiral Benbow would have been a good name for the place Stokes thought. He could see a drunken old sea-salt telling tall tales in a snug corner, offending the clients and throwing money all over the floor. Maybe even Cook himself had drunk an ale or two in the place before the Endeavour set off.

Horse brasses adorned the niches and beams alongside copper kettles and hunting horns. Candlelight struck the bare stone and glanced into the shadows where lovers sat and Goths brooded, under the crossed cutlasses which seemed to hang everywhere.

"I was close," said Pancardi, as he cut a chunk from his steak. "Much closer than anyone could imagine and then, how you say, poof he vanish. Like a true vampire, which he is not, he vanish."

"How's the steak?" Stokes asked.

"She is how you say stout?"

"Tough?" Stokes corrected.

"This is so," Pancardi continued, "he is a little hard to chew."

"Perhaps we should have had fish then?"

"That we must do," Pancardi smiled. "There is the batter made of the beer? This Pancardi he must try before he returns to Roma."

"Tomorrow?" Stokes offered.

"Mmm," Pancardi replied chewing heavily.

Stokes watched the Italian as he ate. He cut his food with precision and had exceptionally fine table manners. This was a man who moved in finer circles than his own. Yet there was something about him which oozed deep sadness. A quietness borne of solitude and a reserve, developed and honed to hide his innermost thoughts. As he ate he gave nothing away of his life and when asked turned back to investigations he had undertaken. He's intensely personal thought Stokes, a thinker, a man of reason and a lover of poetry. Now that did strike a chord with Stokes who loved Yeats. He made a mental to note to introduce this man to Yeats' poetry, a place where they were on common ground.

"This one, he is a monster," said Pancardi as he reached to take a deep draught of wine. "Il Mostro my peoples called him, how do you say, they nickname?"

"Yes nickname," Stokes replied nonchalantly.

"Monster is a good name no? You have seen what he did to the girls?"

Stokes nodded.

"Each one she is someone's daughter no? This one here she is a little girl who strayed too far from her father no? And she is dead no?"

Stokes noted the statements which ended in questions and understood how this affable detective got results. His eyes were bright, sharp and crisply penetrating, he was a watcher, an observer too.

As Stokes made observations of Pancardi - Pancardi did of Stokes. He noticed the large meaty hands, the hands of a labourer, and the hands of a man whose family had been used to toil - but the nails were clipped and not filed and they were scrupulously clean. His shirt, though creased now, had been perfectly ironed and either he had a wife who was proud of her man or he had military training in his past. He ate with precision but his manners were awkward - the result of late learning, confirming his origins from the lower orders. His eye was sharp and his mind clear as a running stream. He had no airs and graces and he clearly wanted to do his job well, rather than in a blaze of glory. That Pancardi liked, and for good measure the man liked poetry and Pancardi vowed to introduce him to Dante's sonnets.

To any bystander the meal would have looked like two scorpions circling their rival before stabbing to kill. Stokes studied the shirt - checked and ironed under a waistcoat of striking colour. The long boots gave the trousers the impression of jodhpurs and the hand tied bow at the neck finished the whole ensemble. Eccentric thought Stokes, off the wall with a touch of class.

"I nearly had him," Pancardi said again, "but nearly is not good enough and he slip through my net like water."

"So do we have anything on the man, a picture perhaps?" asked Stokes through a mouthful of food.

"He is handsome," Pancardi continued, "and totally insane," he paused, "I found his lair, a house alone in the back-streets of Florence. Rented under the name of Lord George Ruthven, funny no? George Ruthven, a lord, an aristocrat no less. He is after all a very clever man."

"So how come you lost him then?" Stokes asked.

"Well we stake the place out- he enters and when we come to

break in," he paused and his voice lowered, "poof he is gone?"

"How gone?"

"This we do not know, maybe up the fireplace or in the cellar, through the door which took us under the street. This we do not know for certain. My officers they have everything covered but he slip through and he is gone. He vanishes like mist. He must have his way out."

"Perhaps he never even...."

"Existed? Or he simply flew away disguised as a bat or a rat?" Pancardi interrupted.

"No...went into the trap?" Stokes questioned.

"He went in, this even Pancardi saw," he referred to himself in the third person again, "and Pancardi is no fool. To fool him is not so easy."

Stokes was warming to the Italian. He was clinical, sharp and critical of his own errors, he had humility and strength of character and that he could work with; he was so glad that the man was not some form of social climber with political aspirations. The man was self evaluative and not self obsessed, that alone was worth its weight in gold in present times.

"So you found his lair?" Stokes quizzed.

"Yes, a bare rented house. Just a few sticks of furniture a TV and a coffin."

Stokes spluttered, "A coffin?"

"Yes and a fine one too. Full of silk and lace and padded."

"Strange?"

"And even more strange than that there was earth in the box. Under the lining, a thin layer. Now Pancardi he have this analysed."

"Analysed?" asked Stokes incredulously.

"Yes the earth it comes from Romania, from the Carpathian mountains, to be precise, near the Borgo pass. So this man has been there - to vampire territory. He actually believe he is a true vampire and this makes him like Byron mad, bad and dangerous to know. He is totally crazy no?"

"What about blood, or murder weapons?"

"Nothing, the place is bare and after we break down the door he is vanish. Then the murders they stop and now he is here across the water. In Whitby? Does he think he is Dracula?"

"Well he started in London," Stokes said, "killed a girl in Kelsall Green cemetery. Two puncture wounds to the neck and the blood drained. Not in the cemetery, he must have killed her somewhere else and dumped the body for us to find."

"Clever no?" asked Pancardi, as the dessert arrived, "but he started in Italy. Why Italy? Is he one of my countrymen?" He gulped a spoonful of custard, "He comes to here and…"

"Bugger me," said Stokes suddenly, "it's got nuts on it. I specifically asked for no nuts. I hate almonds and anything to do with them."

"Marzipan?"

"Tastes like soap to me."

"What is this boo-gar?" Pancardi asked.

Stokes was angry, he called the waitress over, explained the colloquial meaning to Pancardi and moments later a nut-less dessert apologetically arrived.

"This we have in Italy too," Pancardi laughed, "but the Pope he does not know it happens. Maybe our monster he is of this kind too, and he has to take revenge on women for being women, no?"

"Nope," Stokes was emphatic. "Our man is heterosexual, he might be metro, but I think he has something far worse about him. He is a pure psychopath. Something is buried deep inside his subconscious and he enjoys killing – the act of taking a life."

"Why so?" Pancardi was licking the back of his spoon.

"The third girl. He stood and watched her die. He bled her to death like an animal, like he had done it before. She would have struggled," Stokes paused, "and he simply slaughtered her like a pig without getting any blood on his shoes."

"Perhaps then we have the records of a boy with the cruelty to animals?"

"It might be worth a trawl."

"Pancardi he too thought of this," the Italian chirped in triumph. "We have checked all the records we have worked and worked and interviewed many. Nothing. We spend many hours on these kind of children and men and not one thing she come out of it."

"Perhaps he's not one of yours?" Stokes offered.

"This it is true, but then we can never find him. Then why so many in Firenze?"

"Perhaps he likes it there and went on holiday?"

Pancardi laughed. "This it is of the joke no? You wish to make Pancardi seem the fool?"

"No I'm being totally serious." Stokes spoke calmly, "We had a couple who went on holiday and their idea of fun was killing other tourists. They went to a different location every year and every year the killings happened. No records, no data, until they made one silly mistake. Everybody likes to do the things they like when on holiday - they liked to kill." Pancardi raised an eyebrow, "I know it sounds crazy but it was, is, true."

"Which was of the mistake?" Pancardi asked.

"The trophy, the memento. A small silver ring which they brought back with them and which was identified purely by chance via a TV call in programme."

Pancardi was nodding, "This is the chance no?" he said. "In Italy we have no of the chances. There are no trophy. The trophy for this one it is the blood. So Pancardi ask what does he do with the blood?"

"Drink it?"

"Then he is a vampire no? Only he is real no?"

"Real chuffin' crazy more like?"

Pancardi pulled a face and then asked, "Chuffin'? What does this word mean?"

Stokes' face went slightly red. "It refers to a lady's private bits - their chuff?" He pointed to his crotch.

Pancardi laughed out loud. "Today I learn so much of the English and I give you no words of Italian in return. This I must do. But first coffee. Pancardi must have his coffee if he is to think."

When the two men left the White Lion to begin their slow meander back to the hotel, Goths had appeared on the streets. Some were making their way to the Abbey, despite the police warnings, while others were carrying crucifixes to ward off vampires. One man passed clanking in full cavalry uniform complete with sabre. Stokes knew that would be confiscated by the local plod at the cemetery so said nothing.

At the swing bridge the two detectives watched as a series of young Goths began to climb the steps up to the graveyard. They noticed the young women among them, before turning into the alleys leading to spion kop and heading back to their hotel.

Chapter Eight

At 7 am sharp Vincent Drago arrived at the Crescent Hotel to collect both Stokes and Pancardi - their destination was York. His smile was broad as he remembered how the resistance of the girl had broken down and he had screwed another victim for his pleasure. When it was over she was as still as a boned fish – limp, and he had slept for an hour replete and satisfied.

"So this monster of Florence that we're after is he a real vampire?" asked Drago mockingly as he swung the car through the traffic with all sirens blazing.

"Of course not," replied Pancardi, "Vampires do not exist but he thinks he is one. That is precisely why he is mad and dangerous. He must not be allowed to get away again."

Drago smiled and knew that blood sucking, life draining, leeches were everywhere and Whitby was no exception. It fact it was prime hunting territory for a sexual predator like himself, especially at Goth weekend.

"So you now think he is here in Whitby?" asked Drago.

"Absolutely." Pancardi was self assured, "If he thinks he is a vampire then he will try to…"

"Kill again?"

Vincent Drago looked into the rear view mirror to observe Pancardi's face. It was thoughtful.

"He believes he is a vampire and needs blood to survive, he must kill again it is his nature," Pancardi said coldly in reply.

"So when will the next one be?"

"Soon," said Pancardi, "very soon. But this is not like werewolves, every month when the moon is full, silver bullets and molten crucifixes. This is serious. This man, for a man it is, is a monster - a leech that engorges himself on the lives of the living. He is one who enjoys the conquest; he kills for the pleasure of the hunt. He is wicked as the devil and as dangerous as any wild and out of control animal. We must destroy him. "

Stokes felt like a novice as he listened and the feeling
intensified as the Italian unveiled some detail of his investigations.
Pancardi began to recite as if he were telling a story, as if he were
narrating a fairytale at some ancient fireside.

"It all began," he said, "with the body."

* * *

"My God this season is it so hot," said Roberto Calvetti, as
he wiped his hands into a handkerchief. "The flesh it is dried and
it begins to stink. It smells like a butchers shop. I hate the sweet
smell of ripe flesh in the sun, it is putrid in the warm, sickly."

"Always moaning Roberto that young wife of yours she will
soon turn her eyes to another man if you are not careful. It is old
men that moan. A fashion model no less, what does she see in
you?" Pancardi was looking at the corpse near the grave of John
Keats in the English cemetery in Rome. "Pietro you have a
strong stomach and no sense of smell you take a look at the
wound," he continued.

"A thing of beauty is joy forever," Calvetti replied. "Besides
she is a good Catholic girl and she sees a father of her children in
me. She is beautiful, kind, wise and an amazing..." Pancardi
grimaced, which made Calvetti change course, "And me I am the
steadfast man with morals and her mother likes me."

"Why me?" piped Pietro Grillva, as he produced a pair of
latex gloves from his pocket.

"Because I tell you to," Pancardi replied.

"I have seen the mother," said Grillva as he set to work.
"Very beautiful and the bust this is well - wonderful. Long legs
and for a woman of her age she is a beauty, but," he paused
thoughtfully as he knelt down, "she often comes to the office
with a white stick."

There was resounding laughter at the implication from all of
the officers at the crime scene. He snapped the gloves into place
and began to examine the wound on the corpse.

"Wild frenzy," he said as he worked. "Good grief, it is as if the body was torn apart at the neck." He used a ballpoint pen to lift flaps of lose flesh that were already turning green in the heat of the afternoon. "Could a human have done this?" he continued under his breath.

"Perhaps it is the mother who you should set your eyes upon then," Pancardi chortled.

"If your mother-in-law looks so good when she is fifty then you have something to look forward to," Calvetti replied.

"This is true," said Pancardi, "and your wife she does take after the mother."

The laughter was quick, as the team began to study the surrounding area. The detectives were looking closely at the ground around the body.

Grillva stood up from the examination of the neck wound. His face was slightly drawn and his eyes resembled those of a stalking Chameleon.

"It is easy for you Roberto," he said, "to see the girl but how easy will it be for your girl to see you in years to come? Blindness is hereditary you know."

There was more resounding laughter. Laughter was the manner in which these men dealt with the extremes of policing.

"It looks to me as if the neck was torn away," Grillva said. "I would say a wolf or a very large dog," he paused, as if buried in thought, "something with fangs, big fangs."

Pancardi studied the corpse with its head virtually severed from the body. He wondered who the girl was. She had been pretty and her skin looked wonderfully clear on her face. Her complexion was white, as white as a ghost and then it suddenly dawned upon him.

"Where's the blood?" he asked

Calvetti turned and saw his colleague examining the ground around the corpse.

"With that sort of wound," Pancardi continued, "there should be blood everywhere, the whole place should be sprayed with it." He waved his arms in a seed casting motion to indicate a spraying action.

"Perhaps the animal drank it?" Pietro Grillva proffered.

"Then where are the paw prints?" asked Pancardi. He dug his heel into the soft earth of the cemetery to prove his point. "Look the ground she is soft. So soft that any animal here would leave a print and there are none. The woman she would have struggled to fight with death. That is the natural instinct, to fight, to run." The other detectives knew when not to contradict Pancardi. "Besides that, where are there any foot prints...No foot prints?" He continued to reason, "So how did the body get here?"

Angelo Massimo had been studying the sky line around the cemetery and it was then it dawned upon him. He tapped Pancardi on the shoulder and pointed to a large crane which was carrying building materials from one building to another.

Pancardi simply nodded.

"There is no way I am going up that," said Pietro Grillva.

It was now Roberto Calvetti's turn to mock, "So you have no head for heights Pietro? You must stick to women with short legs then. Nice dumpy, frumpy types, you wouldn't want to fall off now would you?"

* * *

"And what did Roberto find?" asked Pancardi.

"Nothing?" replied Stokes.

"Correct. Not one drop of blood. Nothing on the crane."

"So how did the body get there?" Stokes queried.

"You tell me," replied Pancardi. "Maybe she was dropped from a plane?"

"The body would be mangled," Stokes reasoned.

"Yes - we could not see how this was done. So I study the vampire and try to understand the myth," replied Pancardi.

"This is ridiculous," laughed Stokes.

"Then you must help me work out the puzzle? No footprints, no crane, no plane. How did the body get there?" Pancardi smiled.

"You've got an answer," Stokes laughed, "you just want me to be a fool."

Pancardi gave detail on the history of vampires; the whole thing was so far fetched that Stokes felt he had stepped back into the pages of some nineteenth century penny dreadful. Pancardi's interest in the legendary night at Villa Diodati had been delivered with such excitement that Stokes found himself being drawn into the nightmare visions of Byron and Shelley. He had watched vampires like Christopher Lee and the old Hammer movies; Pancardi however, had researched the matter to a far greater depth, to him the case had almost become a possibility. Stokes' mind turned to Slevin and Kelsall Green, surely this Italian was not going to make the same mistake?

The car whisked through the traffic and the two detectives shared their thoughts on the matters in hand. Pancardi impressed Stokes with his methodical approach. The more he learned of the Italian – the more he liked him.

"He likes to kill," said Pancardi thoughtfully. "It gives him power and presence. He watches his victims die and he enjoys their torture, this much I know - he is weak."

Vincent Drago looked up into the rear view mirror once again to study the Italian. He looked for signs of compassion and saw none. Instead he felt the cold hard stare of reality coming back at him through the eyes reflected in the glass.

"In reality he is a small man," Pancardi continued, "with little or no personality. The kind of boy who is bullied at school and then becomes a loner who lives with his mother. A very sad and very strange hateful individual. A man who now has to feed on others, a very dangerous man, a monster."

"But what the hell is his motivation?" asked Stokes.

"I think it is control."

"Control of what though," Stokes continued. "He drinks blood? If he does that it doesn't sound like control to me it sounds like dependency, addiction?"

"Ah then Pancardi he is wrong?"

"He's crazy," Stokes replied, "that gives us the edge if that's what we need."

"So his motive?" asked Pancardi. "It is not control, it is pleasure?"

"No it's need," Stokes contested. "He needs to feed, the issue is where was this crazy notion put into his head, when did he get the crazy."

"If this we can find out then we can catch him no?"

Vincent Drago parked the car as close as he could to the coroner's office and watched as the two detectives walked through the double glass doors at the front of the building. He had listened intently to their conversation, but he was glad they had now left him to his own devices. For a moment he sat motionless and then surprisingly Pancardi reappeared at the entrance beckoning him to join them.

He left the car and began to walk. The sun was up and the warmth of the morning was beginning to irritate. He was only too glad to join them in the cool of the darkened building.

"You should be with us on this Vincent. It is Vincent no?" asked Pancardi.

Drago nodded.

"An unusual name for a Yorkshire boy."

"My father was Italian," Drago replied casually.

"Do you speak?" Pancardi asked as they joined Stokes, who was at the far end of the corridor.

"Afraid not - too lazy to learn and my father always made us speak English at home."

"Was he a prisoner of war?"

"Yes, how did you guess?"

"Ah well most, no some Italians who were here had nothing to go back to and there were many local girls who liked the dark eyed, dark skinned Mediterranean men. But you must have the colour of your mother no? She was blonde?"

"Right again Inspector. You seem very perceptive."

"Your skin it is fair but your hair she is dark no?" He turned to Stokes, "Vincent here he is Italian," he said.

"Half," Drago added.

"Half? This is better than none. Italy she is God's home land. We Italians often say that when he created the world he started with Italy and then worked his way out. You see that is why everything that is best is Italian. The best wine, the best food, art, culture, sculpture, and of course football. We invented football that is why we win no?" Pancardi laughed as he spoke and ushered the others before him.

"Tottenham?" was all Stokes said in reply. "Jimmy Greaves? Invented football my arse."

Pancardi laughed at his own joke, "London always London with the English," he said, "Fiorentina."

"Good morning gentlemen," said the Doctor, offering his hand as the three men entered, "don't worry I've scrubbed up," he chuckled. "What can I tell you?" He pulled open a drawer and a sliding table appeared to roll forward, "Female, approximately 18-22. Not a virgin. No sign of sexual assault, no semen deposits, no skin under the nails. She's been in the water for 12-24 hours."

"Cause of death?" asked Stokes.

"Heart failure."

"What? Heart attack?"

"No, no, Inspector, Heart failure."

Pancardi knew what was coming, it had been explained to him in Italy.

"Heart failure," the doctor continued, "due..."

"To the blood being drained out, no?" Pancardi interrupted.

"Precisely," affirmed the Doctor. "Bled to death."

"Jesus!" Stokes exclaimed. "Where did all the blood go?"

"I'm afraid Jesus couldn't help this girl," the Doctor continued, "she's had virtually all of the blood drained out of her. She must have had a strong heart for it to keep pumping for so long before it failed. As to where the blood went I was rather hoping you might enlighten me." He looked at Pancardi. "Usually we have three pints or so left in the body because once the heart stops the flow stops. In this case the cadaver is virtually blood free. Either she was drained mechanically or..."

"Or something sucked the blood out of her?" Drago interjected.

"What like a vampire I suppose?" The doctor laughed, "Absurd."

"But is there a machine that can do this then, drain the body of blood?" Pancardi asked.

"There is," replied the doctor, "but access to such machinery is limited and the skill needed operate it is high. Your killer would have to be medically trained and have access to heart monitoring equipment and be able to have privacy to use it. I hardly think that is possible."

"So it's a vampire then?" Stokes mocked.

"No of course not. The girl's heart could have been exceptionally strong, rare but not impossible."

"So where did the blood go Doctor?" asked Pancardi.

"The wounds at the neck are consistent with the bleeding. Loss from the jugular can be very quick."

Stokes looked at Pancardi for reassurance that the Doctor might be near to the truth, he received none.

"This too they said in Firenze," chirped the Italian, "but our man he is clever no? He is an expert in death and he is getting better. These machine they could come from Italy or Europe?"

The Doctor nodded.

"Right," ordered Stokes, "Vincent get on the blower to Warlonger. I want every import of hospital machinery into England or Scotland in the two months. No wait."

He turned to Pancardi, "When did the last killing take place in Florence?"

"May 18th," the Italian replied.

"Since the 19th May last," Stokes concluded.

"That's a tall order sir," Drago commented.

"Quite frankly son," said Stokes, "I don't care if the whole of Yorkshire police have sparks coming out of their arseholes, I want the job done. I'll get the flying squad involved on the tracking too in London. I don't want to find another body somewhere and be a bleedin' laughin' stock. This bloke is a screaming fruitcake."

Pancardi liked his style. Stokes didn't seem to care who he upset as long as he got the job done.

"We need a vampire expert," Stokes suddenly said. "Someone who knows all the myths and legends, Knows them better than you Carlo." He used the Christian name to put the Italian at ease.

"I see," said Pancardi, "if he thinks he is a real vampire then he'll behave like one?"

"Precisely. If it acts like a vampire, talks like a vampire and smells like a vampire it probably is a vampire. Sleep all day and party all the night." Stokes made dancing moves as he spoke. "They turn to dust at day break don't they?"

"Well it is said," Drago interrupted, "that vampires can walk abroad during the hours of daylight but their powers are weak."

"What like they need glasses, or what, are you kidding me?" Stokes laughed.

"To the Goths we must go then," chimed Pancardi, "in there must be many who can deal in the legends of the vampire."

"Right, so back to Whitby, Vincent," Stokes ordered.

"Right Gov. I'll get the car"

"However, this is absurd. In fact it's the most stupid case I've ever worked on. We aren't after a vampire otherwise we would have to stop for holy water, stakes and what else silver bullets?" Stokes was directing his questions at Pancardi.

Pancardi was talking to the doctor now, asking about the cost of the specialist machinery and where such might be located in the U.K. Stokes was irritated, but that was soon replaced by the sparkling idea which Pancardi suggested on a whim.

Chapter Nine

The siren wailed as the car sped through and zigzagged past the stationary York traffic. As they sped across the moor Drago began to seem calmer and as the daylight began to fade he finally removed the sunglasses he had worn throughout the drive. He turned the siren off.

Stokes was looking at the note which Pancardi had hastily scribbled and passed to him - he read it for the third time. It was simple and straight to the point - *Let us go to the Gothik ball,* was all it said. Stokes noticed the error but then realised how utterly ridiculous the whole idea would be. They had no clothes, and it was late in the afternoon.

"We'll be in Whitby in fifteen minutes," said Drago.

"Good," Pancardi laughed. "You can leave us at the Ellsinore pub, and we won't need you until the late morning we're going to interview some of the Goths."

"Would you like me to come along?" Drago asked.

"No need," Pancardi replied, "we're just after the background no?"

Stokes nodded in agreement - he was still in shock at the absurd notion of Pancardi's ridiculous plan.

* * *

As Drago drove away with the evening free he felt elated. The two detectives could spend the night investigating and chatting to boring Vampire experts while he could get to grips with something young and sweet. Goth girls were, in his opinion, sumptuous, voluptuous, extremely sexual, and mostly dressed for sex and the thrill-he loved it. At the vampire's ball tonight he would find himself a fine specimen. Something vibrant, leggy, with a willing mouth and a passion for experimentation; intimate body piercings would not go amiss and by the end of the evening he would be totally replete.

Pancardi watched the Mondeo disappear around the corner, and then he placed his hand on Stokes' forearm to hold him.

"Wait," he said, "there is time to go to the pub later. First you and Pancardi we shall buy some clothes to merge in."

"You have got to be kidding," said Stokes in reply.

"Pancardi he does not, how did you say? Kid. And he was not making of the joke in the note. Tonight my friend we go... undercover."

"But the blokes wear make-up," Stokes protested, as Pancardi led him to the door of a shop which was virtually ready to close.

"See the Goths, none, the street she is empty, they are getting ready and now we can shop unnoticed," Pancardi snorted.

Above the door Stokes read the words *Pandemonium – Goth emporia.*

"Come on," said Pancardi and tugged at the stoic's arm.

"We're just about to close," the girl said, as they entered.

"It says six on the door," Pancardi replied.

"Yeah usually, but tonight it's the ball and I need to get ready."

"But you already look so wonderful, and we are not tourists. We too are going to the ball, but our suitcase they have been lost at the plane and we need total outfits."

The girl did not believe them but tilted her green and pink hair coquettishly to the side. She had owned the shop for several years now and this weekend had not been as good as past years. She looked at the clock it read 5.34; she looked at the men and knew she could get them kitted by six and still be ready by eight.

"I don't hire," she said.

"Oh no?" Pancardi smiled, "then we shall buy," he replied.

"It's expensive?" she rejoined.

"This we know," said Pancardi. "But to look beautiful is always expensive no?"

The girl smiled and asked, "Where you from then?"

Stokes was dumb struck, his mouth open. He could not believe what he was about to do. His superiors in London would think he was mad. But he had to agree with Pancardi, the most likely place for the murderer to be was the ball. If the killer liked Goths and genuinely believed he was a vampire then he'd be there. He'd be the Count Dracula look-a-like. Stokes then reversed his decision as the girl began to produce outlandish clothes for him to wear.

"I'm guessing classic Goth?" she said.

Pancardi nodded, and the girl knew that neither of them were true Goths and the next half an hour would make her trading weekend.

"So, one frock coat, one cloak, two shirts - you had the silk ones. Two yards of silk, for the bow-ties. Breaches, white luminous nail varnish." She continued to add up the items, "Boots, one pair of ankle heels, belts, braces, boot straps."

"My boots they are at the hotel," Pancardi had confirmed, "so only one pair."

"Oh the dress jewellery," she continued, "two wigs and two hats. One Tri-corn and one Top in Victorian silk. Canes two - silver topped - antique."

She checked the list a second time, "I think that's all," she concluded.

"Gloves," said Stokes.

"Oh yes gloves, nearly did myself out of some.....That's One thousand seven hundred and thirty nine pounds and eighty two pence. We can call it One thousand seven hundred even and I'll throw in these crucifixes, just in case you meet a real vampire. They're rolled gold so they won't go green straight away. You can wear them over your shirts and everyone will assume that you are dressed as vampire killers. Oh, I have a leather Gladstone bag with some stakes and a mallet. It's not for sale though," she hesitated, "you can borrow it and come back with it." She hesitated even longer, "That is of course unless you come across a real vampire, in which case you're going to need it more than I do."

Pancardi nodded.

"You're not Goths are you?" she asked. "You're the cops

who are after that girl killer. Well I hope you get the fucker. Let me give you a tip, just mingle and don't ask too many questions or if he's a true Goth he'll spot you right off."

Stokes took the credit card receipt, this was going to be hard to explain on expenses, he thought.

"There's some right creeps in there," she continued, "you want to know about modern day vampires. Speak to someone in vein, Mick is your best bet."

"How will we find him?" asked Stokes.

"You won't need to," the girl replied, "he'll find you."

"How?"

"Because I'll tell him to," she said, glancing at the clock. It read 6.04. Not bad she thought. "I'll give Jo Hampshire a ring too and let her know who you are. She's the organiser and that way you won't need to show your warrant cards at the door. I suppose that's what you were going to do?"

Pancardi nodded.

"Well you are ready for now. So can you please fuck off and let me get closed and dressed for the ball too."

Outside on the street Stokes held his bag of Goth gear like a life raft, "This is utter madness," he said, to a grinning Pancardi.

"But fun no?" laughed Pancardi. "You can blame this on me when it is all over. Say I was a mad Italian who forced you into it, but if we get this monster it will be the making of us both."

"I'm not interested in that," replied Stokes

"No? But we can get that, not by, how do you say - licking of the arse, but by genuine solving of the crime. Stokes and Pancardi capture il Mostro de Firenze."

"Listen my little friend," Stokes replied, "this is England not bloody Florence and we had better get a feel of his collar or we are both going to be a laughing stock. You in Florence and me in London – bugger me the boys will have a field day."

Pancardi turned downhill and then crossed the street to avoid being seen before turning a corner and blending into the back streets.

* * *

Vincent Drago parked the squad car for the night. He had made his way through the back alleys and vanished into the cellar room of a large disused building. The air smelt musty, stale, and yet sweet and he lit a scented candle to cover the pungent aroma. The room was dark and dank but his clothes were inside a suit hanger and bone dry. They were all that was left now, the rest had already been loaded.

He sat on the blanket which covered a long box as he pulled his boots on. He thought it would be pleasant to move again, to rest, but that could wait. Tonight he was off to the ball to try and find a fresh young girl to delight him.

As he left the building he locked the door and clicked a padlock into place.

He walked to a Dark Blue Ford transit, which was parked down the street from the squad car, opened the door and placed some keys in the passenger foot well.

The white writing on the van side said, **Demon Antiques and Speciality Artefacts.** He closed and locked the door quietly and taking the time to check for movement in the darkness bent down as if to tie a shoe lace, at the same time he slipped a key inside the wheel arch before straightening himself to a full standing position.

Vincent Drago was now prepared. He checked his ticket for the night and began to blend into the Goths who were on their way to the event inside the Spa.

* * *

Giancarlo Pancardi was chuckling at Stokes who was standing in front of a full length mirror attempting to tie a bow tie from a yard of silk.

"A couple of counts, my foot," he said, "more like a couple of cun..."

Pancardi was almost in tears now, "My friend," he said breathlessly, "tonight we shall be Abraham Van Helsing and

Quincey P. Morris, he who carried a big Bowie knife and killed vampires. I shall be Van Helsing and you will be Morris."

"I can't get this tie to work and the wig - well that just looks weird, and we are not in some sort of talent contest. Well I'm not, but you might be," Stokes replied.

"But we shall be the vampire hunters no? And you do look very dapper and every inch the Victorian Gentleman."

He tossed a cane at Stokes, which he in turn caught with his left hand and then touched the rim of his top hat with his right like Fred Astaire.

"Now you must vogue," Pancardi laughed, "like in the Madonna song."

"What?" said Stokes, "Vogue?"

"Well you must strike a pose, like this."

Pancardi stood like a male model from a catalogue and then moved to strike another pose, and then another.

Stokes laughed, "No way I'm doing that, I feel like a tit already," he said.

"But trust me my friend," replied Pancardi encouragingly, "you look like a real Goth now, so you must act like them no?"

"Well this stupid wig itches," replied Stokes. "But," he looked at their joint reflection in the mirror, "at least we look the part I suppose."

Pancardi clapped him on the shoulder laughing as he did so; he was clearly enjoying the whole escapade far too much for Stokes' liking. Pancardi relished the idea of being the centre of attention and this sort of charade was just what he craved. The silver topped walking cane he was leaning on was to become one of his most favoured possessions in the years to come; and often his mind would be drawn back to this moment when it stood in the hall stand at his home in Rome.

Chapter Ten

"I can't hear a damn thing," Stokes shouted at Pancardi. "This music is terrible, let's go to the bar."

Pancardi nodded.

"What a din," said Stokes, as he returned with drinks.

As he sat down a tall thin man with an aquiline face approached them. He was all in black except for an antique globe which he carried like a lantern. He smiled and his teeth were white and sharpened to points. Stokes wondered if they were his own.

"Good evening," he said, "welcome to my home," and he gave a courtly sweep of his arm. "I am Michael, Prince Michael von Hessen of Sacre, how do you do?"

Pancardi looked at the man and tried to place his age; his touch was clammy and there was hair in his palm; his finger nails were sharpened to fine points. All in all the make-up was excellent and Stokes wondered what the man might look like the morning after.

"A friend tells me you wish to know something of our kind?" he enquired.

Stokes considered the accent, Russian he thought at first and then it dawned, of course - Romanian. The man was feigning a courtly Romanian accent, although the name of Mike destroyed the illusion.

They were ushered into a small corridor to the side of the bar and then into a small dressing room.

"What would you like to know?" the Prince asked.

Stokes was the first to fire, "Vampires do they exist?" he asked.

"No one really knows," the Prince replied, "some say yes, some say no. The man you seek exists, of that I am certain, whether he is a true vampire only you will know when you confront him."

"What we need to know," said Stokes "is what rules he and thus we, will follow."

The Prince tilted his head to one side and then the other as if reflecting before he spoke, "What you want to know is how to catch him?" he said.

"Yes absolutely," Pancardi interrupted.

"There are many myths about these creatures which go all the way back through ancient cultures," he said, as if reading from a text inside his head. "Vampires can move in daylight, they are weaker and the light hurts their eyes but they can walk and talk just like you and me. They won't vaporise like they do in the movies. They hate to cross running water, rivers especially. They must sleep on the sacred earth of home; some keep turf in their coffin."

"They sleep in coffins?" exclaimed Stokes.

"Yes, and they often have taste. They dress well, are neat, tidy and organised."

"No," Stokes interrupted, "I think you missed the point. What we want, no need to know is...... are they real?"

"Oh, they are real, more real than you will ever imagine."

"No," Stokes, was getting frustrated now, "are they immortal, undead?"

"We are all the undead," the Prince retaliated, he too was beginning to show irritation.

It was Pancardi who smoothed the way and gradually over some minutes the detail required by the detectives was forthcoming. Both men began to realise that the adversary they were chasing was a highly intelligent man. Someone who was fit, lithe, fleet of foot and yet highly disturbed.

"So they like to kill?" asked Pancardi.

"It often starts as a necessity, but ends up as a pleasure. Listening to the heart stop is the pleasure – the ultimate sexual climax. The last throws of life ejaculated into death- la petit morte."

Stokes was wondering if the idiot before him needed a mental health assessment. The Prince was, in his eyes, clearly disturbed and the question for any jury would be whether it was eccentric nonsense performed for the stroking of the ego, or whether he really was a stock-broker whose life was so tedious that he had to dress up at weekends. Stokes began to wonder if he drank blood or if he himself had killed. He wondered if the fantasy had taken over his reality, and then it dawned, that in the man they sought, that was precisely what had happened - the balance had gone. Prince Michael of Hessen at the weekend and Michael Biggins in the week. A quiet man who lived with his mother and played video games for amusement. A withdrawn man; a man without friends, other than Goths, and certainly a man without a girlfriend; though deep down inside it was the one thing he really craved. Stokes began to feel sorry for him and saw a small pathetic creature locked inside a false reality. He tapped Pancardi on the arm and they made their excuses to leave.

"Enter freely of your own will," the Prince said, as they re-entered the whirl and rush of humanity in the auditorium.

Stokes wanted to say, "Oh please you pathetic twerp," but held his tongue and council for Pancardi.

"Wheeze," he said, once the Prince had passed out of earshot, "he's a real loony tune." He twirled his finger at his temple, "Basket case I'd say - just a short hop into the big yellow taxi. If they are all like that then the reality and fantasy must get blurred and if he has a deep seated mental illness – bingo."

Pancardi smiled, "I think I need another drink after that, come," he said and he pushed through the crowds to get to the bar.

As he did so, Stokes, who had been following close behind, noticed a couple who were talking intimately in a corner. He tugged at Pancardi's sleeve.

"Look," he said, "over in the corner there, behind that column. It's Vincent Drago or someone who looks like him."

Both men stood watching as Drago leaned in to make physical contact with the girl who sat opposite him; he was touching her hair and looking into her eyes.

"Hypnosis," said Stokes, "that's handy for when you go on the pull."

"On the pull?" Pancardi asked, as he took a long swig from the beer before him.

Stokes noticed that Drago had no drink and that they were in the direct line of sight to the bar, but Drago appeared to be making no effort to obtain a drink or even look in the direction of the bar.

"He's on the prowl," said Stokes. "Look he wants to keep a clear head he's not even drinking."

"Prowl? As a lion prowls?" asked Pancardi.

"More like a poon hound actually," Stokes chuckled.

"What is this poon hound? Pancardi has never heard of this animal."

"They're easy to spot," replied Stokes, "they're usually young, energetic, eager and all prick and toe nails. Just like Mr. Drago there, they like to hunt out girls like bloodhounds, and play hide the salami."

"Now this I know," said the Italian. "It is a game we play in Italy."

"I think," said Stokes, "it's played all over the world."

Pancardi laughed, "And our driver is here tonight, to play?"

"Perhaps he just likes Goth girls. There are some real beauties here."

"But why did he not tell us?" Pancardi was beginning to become suspicious, "He comes here surely he would know that….."

"What that we would be here?" Stokes interrupted, "still waters do run deep." Stokes was sarcastic now, "Us two dirty stop outs - men about town, on the trail of some poon? I think it unlikely."

"But the police would know him."

"How? He's from York. He's as much a stranger as we are."

Pancardi thought a little more, he hated the metaphors and riddles of the English; much better to have the gesticulations and inflections of the Italians.

"We need to talk to him," he said and suddenly stood up.

Stokes grabbed his arm, "Sit," he said, "have a little patience and tomorrow we can rib the boy a little. It will give us the chance to have some fun. Don't be so harsh, let the boy sow some oats."

The metaphors were lost on Pancardi. He knew it was similar to being, in the same boat, but when there was no boat it did not make literal sense. Sowing oats and other riddle-me-ree wasted his time.

As the night lengthened the detectives realised that the idea of a vampire pretending to be a Goth, pretending to be a vampire, whilst plausible at first, was in fact absurd. They needed to take stock. They circulated around the building and found an assortment of drunks, some cocaine snorters and a couple who were smoking a joint. Some of the Vampire Society members were off up to the Abbey and the crowd had thinned out. It was almost one a.m.

Vincent Drago was kissing the girl when they returned, she was blonde, unusual for a Goth; her mouth was locked to his and her features were slim, and sharp. She had small pert breasts which Stokes estimated as a B cup. When she stood up to leave she swayed and Drago placed an arm around her waist which was narrow and fine, delicate even, but it fanned out into an ample set of hips and Stokes knew that Drago had got very lucky. The girl was dressed in PVC which clung to her like a cat suit. Her legs were encased in thigh high boots which accentuated their length. She was striking - her body alone made her memorable.

A friend came over to the girl, a darker counterpoint dressed in platform boots and a torn tee-shirt; she seemed satisfied and left the new lovers to it.

Stokes looked hard at the swaying blonde, she was clearly under the influence of something, she stumbled, and then fell toward Drago who caught her with a laugh.

"You lucky young bastard," he thought, "you'll be up that tonight and probably in the morning too." He was envious of youth. "Giancarlo," he said.

"Yes Michael," came the sarcastic reply.

"I think it's time to fuck off, dear heart."

"I agree," Pancardi affirmed in an affected English accent.

* * *

Vincent Drago was at the hotel as instructed in the morning. He wore dark glasses and his neck was covered. Stokes deduced that he had been nesting all night and that the cover up was to hide the bites of passion the young blonde had inflicted during their torrid love making. Stokes had a momentary vision of the girl bucking on Drago like a cowgirl riding a horse. He imagined her forcing him ever deeper into her. A thought flashed of his own wife, dull, homely, boring, but safe. Not a trophy like the blonde but someone who could make a man happy and in his case fat. His wife was a jam maker as the blonde was a prick teaser.

"What did you get up to last night?" he asked Drago.

"I should say ten inches shouldn't I?" Drago laughed.

"Only if you want to," Pancardi interjected from behind a mouthful of bacon. He loved the English fry up and had one at every opportunity.

"Well if you must know," said Drago, "I had an early night."

"So that's what they call it these days - it's a wonder you can walk at all," said Stokes.

"Ah to be young and thrusting," Pancardi chuckled, at his own word play.

Both Stokes and Pancardi burst into united laughter. Drago instantly rose to the bait, ready to make a hasty embarrassed exit.

"Sit down boy," said Stokes, as he kicked out a chair. "Have some coffee, relax. The old Itie here drinks it strong like tar. So strong you could surface a road with it."

Realising the language he had used, he looked around but no other tables nearby had heard his jocular remark - he was relieved.

"So what's the news?" Stokes changed the subject. "We need to get into the bizarre bazaar and talk to the Goths. So we want you there too. Three officers working the room and all that. But have some of this coffee first it'll blow your head off."

"No thank you," said Drago, "I want to keep a clear head. And I never drink coffee."

"Suit yourself," replied Stokes, "but I'm having one to keep me awake after the ball last night."

"Me too," said Pancardi, fully aware of what Stokes was doing.

It seemed to work, Drago froze, "You were there?" he asked.

"You bet ya," Stokes laughed. "We had to go and get some expert advice from one of those vampires. We met a right tosser, called himself a Prince no less, but he did seem to know what he was talking about

"All night?"

"Yep," Pancardi said, and winked.

"So we saw you with that blonde, you lucky boy," Stokes laughed.

Chapter Eleven

At the top of the Abbey steps the photographers were busily arranging girls in a variety of poses, first with Goths then without Goths. Mannequins of the fashion world; Victor Drago studied them, the slaves to fashion and wondered what they really thought. The girls were beautiful and showed no signs of embarrassment as they changed ball gown after ball gown behind make shift screens and tented walkways which led into the foyer of the church. He could see quite plainly the flashes of naked thigh or the odd breast as clothes were place and replaced on hanging rails.

"Beautiful aren't they?" Julianne Doppodomani said, as she approached behind him. She had walked around the cliff top to clear her head - he sat on a benched tomb.

"Stunning," he replied.

"I meant the dresses," she chided.

"So did I," he grinned, "but I suppose you don't believe me?" he laughed and to her ears it was reminiscent of water babbling - a small country brook. It was hypnotic and enveloping.

"Well Mr. Officer man," she flirted, without knowing why she did, "as long as that was all you were looking at."

"So what's this all about then?" Drago asked.

"It's called a fashion shoot. We take our clothes off and then they take pictures of us. Sometimes with other clothes on and then they sell those pictures. And people come to buy the big new line of clothes called Gothique Fantastique. Somebody makes lots of money and I get paid too."

His voice was slow and rhythmical, deep like the hollow echo of a well, it soothed and delighted as he spoke. Angels danced as he asked and she answered questions, and it seemed to her comfortable, like speaking to a grandfather who was full of admiration. It felt natural like the ticking of a clock in some ancient hallway of a mansion. His voice soothed, explored and yet reassured all at the same time.

Drago noted the woman's lustrous hair as he spoke and the scars at her neck. She noted the movement of his eyes, the pulsing of his pupils.

"Dreadful isn't it?" she asked.

"I'm sorry," he said.

"Oh please don't be sorry, every fucker is sorry, but nobody is more sorry than me."

"I'm lost," he said politely, his voice soothing more deeply. It poured like molasses from a jar and stayed in her ear like the ring of Christmas bells. His voice excited, delighted and invited in each breathy, heady expulsion of syllables which rhythmically exploded inside her animal subconscious.

She wanted to sit down, wanted to put one leg either side of his and sit on his lap; she wanted to kiss his mouth and reach down between them both to guide his manhood into her; wanted to force herself onto him to give him more pleasure than he had ever known, yet she could not understand why. With one hand he reached forward and touched the scars at her neck. She felt no fear, no shame, just the shuddering control of his fingers tips.

"Please don't," she returned softly, as if answering an unspoken question from deep inside her. "I have these and," she exposed her neck fully to him, "they will revolt and disgust you, just like they do me."

"But you have the best arse in the business," he said.

"How did you know that?" she laughed.

"You just told me," he cooed.

"Oh did I," she soothed, "I didn't remember, sorry. I'm here doing the pants shots, you know bums and legs."

Drago looked at the woman now, she was striking. Her natural beauty shone from beneath the scars and her face sparkled; when she smiled her whole being lit up as if it were an antique globe glowing in the darkness. He knew then that he wanted her.

"Accident was it?" he asked.

"That's forward of you," she replied. She wanted to say nothing more but he seemed disarmingly easy to talk to and as he was in police uniform, he was safe. But the fantasies built, and his voice comforted and she began to tell her tale. "Actually," she continued, "it was deliberate. This," she exposed the scars once again, "I'm afraid is the result of an act of jealousy. One which cost me my career; but I'll be back, the treatment is working well."

"Surgery and skin grafts?"

"That's a bit personal," she replied.

"What then?" he soothed.

"I have to have special blood transfusions and hormone injections, if you must know. I even have to drink blood at times. There, sickening isn't it?" she replied, unable to close her mind to the gentle probing.

"How does that work then?"

She could not believe what she was doing. For some unknown reason she was giving out personal details on herself as if she had known this stranger all her life. She had lost the will to refuse his questioning.

"When do you finish?" he asked almost casually.

She looked into his fierce eyes and felt the last vestiges of her will evaporate, "Couple of hours?" she offered.

"How about I get out of this uniform and we go and get some dinner or something?"

"Mmm, it's the or something bit I need," she replied, unable to control herself.

"Well how about dinner first?" he confirmed, "then the something later?"

"Fine," she answered willingly.

His eyes were locked on hers now and she could not help but look into his. She felt herself drowning in intrigue and sexual expectancy. She wanted to kiss him, take him.

At the cameras a young photograph in leather trousers started shouting, "Pants, pants, suspenders and pants everyone." He was clapping his hands, wildly ushering the girls through the screens and into the church. "Where's Julianne?" he yelled, "Julianne? Julianne?"

Her mind snapped back into reality, as if from a trance, "Just coming," she shouted in reply.

"Well don't make a mess dear," the photographer quipped.

"I'd better go," Julianne said.

"The name's Drago," Vincent said, "Vincent Drago," and he kissed her hand.

She was some distance away now, "Julianne Doppodomani," she called.

He watched her move, it was languid, sexual and carried a promise which he had never seen in a woman before and he had known many throughout his lifetime. In that respect he had been lucky. The injury was nothing - in fact it could work in his favour.

She was entering the church now and he realised that he did not have a number or a hotel. He was on his feet and flying the thirty steps into the walkway.

"Oi, no fuckin' way son," said one of the burly security guards as he approached, "there's ladies in there."

"Police," Drago replied. Grabbing the guard by the wrist.

The guard stood aside instantly.

"Shut your eyes ladies," Drago called, as he entered, "I'm coming through."

And true to form the models all shut their eyes as commanded or covered their faces as he passed, even though many were naked.

"Julianne," he said, as he reached his quarry. "Do you believe in love at first sight? Give me you and I will give you every one of your dreams and much much more in return."

* * *

The body was found in a builder's skip. Goth weekend had come and gone and it wasn't until the Monday morning when the plasterers arrived that the gruesome discovery was made.

The labourer had been told to take the wood out of the bin and burn it and that was when they found her - a pretty blonde. Her eyes were open and yet glassy and opaque. The pathologist estimated death two days previous - only because the rigidity of death was being replaced with the flexibility of decomposition.

The neck showed two small puncture wounds and the PVC clothing had been torn from her body to give access to her throat and vagina. There were bite marks on both. This attack had been prolonged, frenzied and sexual. Around the wrists were ligature marks - the girl had been bound while the man or men had taken their pleasure of her. There was semen on her pubic hair and her scalp line also showed some residual fluid encrustation. Her face had a bluish tinge so the first estimation of cause of death was strangulation but by the afternoon this had been revised to blood loss - death had come from prolonged bleeding. The body was as dry as a husk.

Chapter Twelve

When Stokes and Pancardi arrived, the skip murder had once again been converted into a media spectacle. Vincent Drago had been recalled to York to continue his longer term driving assignment with the Chief Constable and Stokes was now driving. The Chief Constable no longer wanted to be associated with a failing serial killer hunt and was busy distancing himself; what he wanted was results and if those were a long time in coming he wanted to be sure the media were useful. Stokes hated it, the political posturing and constant courting of vanity but he had to except it, they had no alternative.

Stokes had his team in London trawling the international files. He wanted similar cases of unsolved murders with the same MO. He was surprised just how many there were. He had expected a few, but in fact there were dozens; the Interpol computer was working overtime sifting both past and present information like a thing possessed. But worse still this style of murders - they seemed to mysteriously start and then just as quickly stop again and he had fears of this turning into a long and drawn out investigation.

Stokes had a great deal of respect for the computer "geeks" as he called them. Usually fanatics who knew everything there was to know about systems, data and the latest bits of silicone. He preferred silicone inside a girl, but he admired the dedication and persistence of these police, for police they were. It was they who crunched away at the slow tedium of police work until they gave him something to work with. The press, however, he despised as real leeches, bloated leeches that fed off the misfortune of others - in this case a murdered girl. It was they who were the real vampires. They had little regard for family, mothers and fathers who would now be crying over the loss of their daughter and wondering why it had been their child that had to die. The vultures would gather to pick over the carcass and when the bones were clean they would be left to bleach in the sun, to petrify - forgotten. And the story? Yesterday's news for wrapping chips.

"Get rid of those vultures," Stokes ordered to a junior uniformed officer.

And Pancardi had been just as terse when a Daily Mail reporter had accosted him with the story of the Vampire of Whitby. The tabloids had been running articles all week but this had pushed it to the limit. Pancardi was in no mood for frivolity, or the press and he shouldered his way through the forensic cordon.

"We know who the real blood sucking Vampires are here then," he said to Stokes.

"They are just as bad as the paparazzi in Italy. No probably worse," he paused. "It is the curse of money plain and simple. Well plain at least."

Both detectives were in the skip now.

"Let's take a look at the ......" said Stokes, lifting a sheet which lay casually draped over the body.

Both men recognised the girl instantly. Stokes was the first out and on the radio.

"The Chief Constable now, put me through immediately," he screeched.

"Car get the car," he continued to Pancardi.

A female voice answered him persuasively, "I am the Chief Constable's PA can I help?"

"DI Stokes love," he barked, "is he there?"

She hated the patronising word love and immediately froze into bitch mode, "He is in a meeting and cannot be disturbed I'm afraid Detective Inspector."

"Well I think he'd like to be disturbed for this, we have a suspect to the Whitby killings, and I think he would like to know who."

"Can you hang on I'll go in and see if he can be disturbed."

There was click and she was gone.

A young constable pulled up in a squad car next to Stokes

who was hanging on the end of the radio handset. The officer, who looked like he was twelve and had just left school, handed a file to Stokes. Simultaneously the radio connection spluttered and Pancardi bunny hopped the Mondeo to a standstill.

"Inspector Stokes this file just came in via the Whitby Police courier," the young constable was proffering a file.

"Stokes?" The Chief Constable's voice spluttered from the radio.

"Sir."

"This better be bloody good."

"We saw your driver at the vampire's ball with a blonde girl." Stokes was emphatic, "Her body was discovered in a builder's skip in Whitby less than an hour ago. We need to have Drago arrested and held."

"He's not here!" the reply cut into Stokes like a knife.

Pancardi was now standing next to his colleague, muttering apologies about the car.

"Not there?"

"No, he called in sick yesterday. I think he is at home... In fact," he paused, "Ruth get me Drago's home address. I do believe it's in Whitby."

Stokes handed the file to Pancardi, and switched the radio to receive only, "Take a butchers at this?" he said, "I have to deal with Freddy Fuckwit here."

Pancardi did not understand but gathered from the gesticulations that the file had vital information. It was marked Metropolitan Police and listed a set of killings which seemed to fit in with the MO of the current killer. He could hear Stokes getting angry on the radio and knew the tension was mounting.

"47 Royal Crescent, a basement room," Stokes said to Pancardi. He turned to a local policeman, "Where the hell is Royal Crescent?"

"Just up the road turn left and there opposite the sea, sir," the man indicated in reply.

"Carlo, we've got the bugger," he was smiling as he spoke. Stokes turned to the local police, his orders were low and yet forceful, "Royal Crescent," he said, "I want it sealed off, no one in or out. Number 47 under immediate surveillance. And do it quietly, no media, no cars or sirens and I want armed officers too and no chance for anyone to escape in the confusion. We are going to pay a little visit to Constable Vincent Drago - one I don't think he'll ever forget."

"My God," said Pancardi, "amazing, it goes back years."

"What does?" asked Stokes, looking over his shoulder.

"The killings, look, 1917 Vienna in the turmoil - the same type of killing."

He turned the page, "Then 1920, Germany: Munster and then Detmold; 1922 France, on the Dordogne. Then back to Germany 1932/3, Berlin, Leipzig and Munich, only this time it was undercover agents undermining morale, well that was the report. The Weimar republic falls and then nothing. It stops suddenly."

"Well perhaps the war got in the way and…."

"And what, there was no need for explanations anymore?" asked Pancardi. "1917 to now it doesn't make any sense. In fact it's nonsense, our killer would have to be well over one hundred and twenty."

"Perhaps these people inflicted others with a disease," said Stokes, attempting to mitigate, "and it is passed through generations, they need blood as a flower needs rain. Remember what that Prince geezer said, "the *thirst*," he called it. Maybe there is some weird truth in the whole bizarre thing."

Pancardi was sharp, "What that Vampires do exist…rubbish, total rubbish and you know this to be true and so does Pancardi."

Stokes nodded, he had seen incredible things in his time and this would be just one more scene in the weird and inexplicable path of humanity toward oblivion. It was true what they said though, that truth is often stranger than fiction.

"Right," he said, snapping back to reality. "Let's go nick this weirdo and stop mucking about. He may be weird and believe he is some form of Vampire. He might even be diagnosed with some funny illness – they do it to all the school kids these days.

We used to call them clumsy and thick, now they're dysphasic, dyslexic or dyspraxic, but this guy is just fucked-ups-ic and he needs to be locked up."

* * *

Pancardi had a revolver in his left hand and he stood with his back against the wall as he knocked with his right. If Vincent was armed he might fire through the door. There was no answer.

He knocked again.

"Vincent?" he said, "it's me Pancardi."

"Ah my little Italian friend, looking for il Mostro de Firenze," a calm voice replied.

"Come in do. Have you brought your imbecilic monkey with you?"

Stokes face reddened and he cocked the hammer on a standard issue 9mm Browning.

"He's rather stupid, don't you think?" Vincent's voice continued. "So stupid in fact that one wonders if he could find his own arse with both hands."

"That's fucking it," yelled Stokes, as he burst into the room.

There was a sudden flash of blue light and Stokes yelped in pain as he fell to the ground.

"Phosphorous dear heart, burns a bit don't it ?" Drago laughed.

Pancardi had not moved and the voice of Vincent Drago poured from the darkness like molasses from a barrel.

"You had better help your colleague," Vincent's voice said calmly. "There are some wet towels over in the corner. That should stifle the oxygen long enough for Inspector stupid here to reach hospital."

"You won't be able to get away," said Pancardi, "the whole street is sealed and there are armed police everywhere.

"Oh really?" said the voice, with a tinge of sarcasm, "I'll have to be a little scared then won't I?"

Pancardi thought he heard a low chuckle, turned and stood in the doorway. He expected a shot to hit him; a thud like the thump of a mallet as the impact hit the protective vest and knocked the wind from his lungs - none came. Instead he saw Stokes laying on the ground wrapping towels around his calves and his fingers glowing as the phosphorous bit into his flesh.

"Nasty stuff," said Vincent, "rather like Napalm and it has a distinctive odour when combined with burning human flesh. Rather like the sweet smell of a whore's cunt after she has copulated, don't you think?" He smiled and a fine line of white, sharp teeth showed. "Sorry," he said, noticing the direction of Pancardi's eyes, and closed his lips. "They do that after I have…"

"Shoot the bastard," squealed Stokes from the floor, "fucking shoot him!"

"That gun," said Drago calmly, "will do you no good here. You might as well be throwing cream cheese at a President in an assassination attempt."

Pancardi wondered if he too was wearing protective body armour, or if madness had engulfed all of them. "I could shoot you in the head," he said, "where you have no armour."

"Of course you could, but then you'll never find the two girls I took this morning, and then they'll just starve to death."

He looked at Pancardi who had replaced the hammer on the gun and was lowering it to his side.

"Intelligent choice," he said. "Constables, would you like to come and collect your Inspector here, before he has to lose that leg, it looks very, very, nasty."

"No you fucking don't you monster," said Stokes, "I'll see you in hell first."

"But you appear to have lost your weapon," Drago laughed. "What a good job I set the charge at calf and not testicle height or heaven knows what might now be burning. And I am not a monster, I am *the* monster. At least the Florentines have a healthy respect for the Prince of Darkness."

"Prince of Darkness," Stokes mocked through his teeth, "more like the pig of shit, you wallow in it for now but you're nicked and there is no way out. And then they'll put you in a six by six room to rot, you fuck."

Two uniformed officers were lifting Stokes under the armpits from the floor. His face was white and the pain was obvious. While Drago sat stock still in an armchair on the other side of the room.

Drago smiled at Pancardi, "Would you like to tell him what a Drago is inspector, in Italian?"

"Dragon," came the terse reply. "Where are the girls?"

"Not so fast inspector, I can call you inspector can't I?" he paused, "after all we're all friends here now aren't we?"

"You fucking piece of slime," Stokes spat out from behind clenched teeth. "I'll kill you with my bare hands."

"OOOh , see me quiver, see me shake," Drago mocked. "What a nasty little thing you are. Rather like an annoying bug that needs to be stamped upon."

"I'll track you to hell and back," Stokes threatened.

Drago's voice became calm almost bored. "In Germany they called me Drache, but I have had many names over the years and it has been many years. I'd like to travel to the Americas one day, but the water, so flowing so deep," he paused, "you came so close," he continued, "in Florence, but you don't believe and that is your failing." He caught Pancardi's eye, "I shall sleep for a few decades now and when I return you will be long gone, you see time is on my side and not yours. Vampires do exist, all you have to do is believe that they do and then, well you know what to do, don't you? Michael told you, he made it very clear. When you are old perhaps I will come to watch you die and see you gibber as you piss yourself with fear. When will you realise how ridiculous you both were."

"The girls?" repeated Pancardi.

"So gentlemen our time together is almost at an end."

Pancardi's hand tightened on the grip of the pistol, he was marking his spot. He thought he might have a split second and be lucky with one shot to the head. The Man was clearly insane and as soon as he could be certain that there were girls, and if there were, they were safe, he would fire.

"Two girls?" Pancardi repeated again.

"Oh yes two," said Drago, "fine rich blooded, young bitches. One was even a virgin, but that is a thing of the past now. To be penetrated and bled simultaneously must have been such exquisite delight."

Pancardi was cold, dispassionate even, "Where are they?" he asked again.

Drago raised his hand in a courtly sweep, "Just through that door," he said, pointing to his left.

A constable moved forward.

"Careful," Pancardi warned.

"Oh that is not booby trapped, I can assure you," Drago said. "I give you my word as a gentleman of wealth and taste."

The constable moved forward and as he opened the door the room was flooded with light. There was a ghastly sight of two naked girls suspended by their ankles from a beam. The floor was soaked in blood as if someone had taken a shower in their blood and then simply walked away.

"They are not dead," Drago affirmed. "Just a little empty."

Pancardi raised the gun and as he did so the light failed and the room was plunged into darkness. Pancardi fired, once at where Drago's face had been, twice at his body, a third time to the left and then he lowered his hand.

"Get some fucking light in here," Stokes screamed, as he felt a slight wisp of something pass over his head, it was fine like a spider's silk trail; he reached up, but it was gone.

Chapter Thirteen

A van sporting a Demon Antiques logo left its quiet parking place in Whitby and without hindrance drove toward Scarborough. Vincent Drago sat at the wheel, dark glasses obscuring his eyes - he was feeling very tired. Julianne Doppodomani sat next to him, her eyes were full of life and her skin was radiant, and perfect. All traces of burns and scars had gone; she was as she had once been, perfect. Like the driver she too wore dark glasses to shade her eyes. She had never felt better, never felt more free, alive; the bargain had been struck and the perfect companion found. She would be the greatest of all the supermodels. After the investigation died down it would be assumed that her disappearance was all part of the killing spree and she would soon be forgotten.

The beauty which once made her the toast of the town was back and would never fade, never become old and sordid. In the years to come she would once again be the best.

"You see drink from me and live," Drago laughed. "The people we shall kill are worthless, naked worms crawling. You are the most beautiful woman and we shall live forever."

The woman's smile was radiant, dazzling. Her lips were red and her teeth sharp with a slight protrusion over her lower lip. Her hair was lustrous and her complexion cream and white like alabaster. Her eyes glowed and she was beautiful.

"I know a place where we can sleep. Where time will forget us." He paused thinking, "And when time has passed, and the world is renewed we shall rise and feast. I shall be the Prince and you will be my Princess."

* * *

On the edge of the North Yorkshire moors there is an old

village, a village of grey stone and slate roofs and in it there is a cemetery. Outside the cemetery walls lie the graves of those who took their own lives. Among the briars and bracken, hidden in un-consecrated ground stands a mausoleum for an atheist family long past, long forgotten. People seldom go there for it is, Victorian, old, windswept, and overgrown. Even the trees struggle to avoid the wind and bend their backs to the sleet and rain which winter throws at them.

Young children say it is haunted and dangerous...it is an almost perfect place.

the hutschenreuther legacy

L.amond.2010.

For the those that made me,
What I was,
What I am,
And this brief candle that I light.

The Hutschenreuther Legacy

That year it had been particularly cold and timber was in short supply despite the proximity of the vast and eerie Teutoburger Wald. A dense forest of impenetrable pines which ran all the way from Detmold to Bielefeld. Tall firs hung heavy with the pregnancy of snow; icicles growing from daggers into swords in the alternating warmth and frost - waiting like the swords of Damocles to punch into the deep virgin drifts below. Picture post card, picturesque, tinged with the possibility of imminent death, it was a beautiful sight; an aphrodisiac of danger. Days had bright sun, almost warming, though human breath crackled as it fell to earth; but nights held the bitter and unforgiving cold.

The cross country route to Bielefeld was about thirty kilometres through solid forest and the kind of place where, once discovered alone, the wild pigs would attack - if hungry enough; and this year they were that hungry. Several had made their way into the towns to steal what they could from the refuse bins rather than rummaging under the trees for meagre pickings. It was as bitter a winter as any could remember.

There was a civil ban on cutting down trees. No one really knew why the ban had been placed by the Colonel-in-Chief, but the effect had been dreadful and demoralising; miserable cold, crying children and numbness which bit into the fingers and faces of the local defeated community. Food was scarce too and to be cold made the whole winter of 1954 that much worse. As temperatures plummeted, the water on the moat around, "The Schloss," froze and the local children began to skate; skate with all the manic fervour of the young. They had, in the near ten years past, already forgotten the loss of fathers and uncles and started to live a new life under new imposed rules. The war for them had ended and different men now gave them bars of chocolate through the gates of the barracks; and the once proud eagle which stood in the "Markt Platz" had been painted red, white and blue. Older sisters cast their eyes upon the young and vibrant men who had been stationed in the old barracks of the town. To the young children it did not matter, to the old men it stung like a summer wasp. Some vowed to get even, but these were just the hollow words of the vanquished, tinged with the bitterness of old age.

Detmold was and remains a traditional small Saxon town. There was and is nothing of significance there, except the huge Hermann's Denkmal. The great bronze statue, perhaps 50 metres high, which stands alone in the woods; a symbol of German unity, with his sword raised, not toward Rome but west toward Gaul – the old Celtic enemy.

The town is like many other towns, a combination of shops and small businesses which continue to thrive, despite the devastation of war. That winter was like many others before and like many since.

Children laughed and played away their hunger - that was until one fell through the thin ice and the girl was rescued by an unknown soldier. A big barrel-chested, Lance Corporal, a Welsh man. A man used to mountain snow, and ice and cold; a man of the hills and lakes. A man used to plunging into deep snow to pull out a distressed ewe. A man of the earth, like those of the Saxon farming community he and his comrades occupied. He plunged, without hesitation, boots and all, into the murk and mud to drag the spluttering infant out. Holding the young girl upside down he emptied her lungs and gave her crying, back to her horrified mother.

The local women applauded him and the old men, for the younger men had not returned from the war, gave him tots of Schnapps and wrapped him in blankets so his uniform could be dried. His blonde hair stood up in the frosty air as they loaded a brazier with logs cut from the banned forest. Somehow there was an absurd irony in the whole episode which made little sense to any observer. There were many profuse thanks which he could not understand, beyond the basic German which he had gleaned, but the smiling faces and the clasping of hands had told him that he was approved of. When combined with some of his colleagues handing out sweets and cans of food, the ice was truly broken. And by these small acts of kindness the occupying army gradually began to seem part of the future.

The main obstacle became the Berlin wall, which had not really been a wall at all, more like an elongated tract of minefield which snaked across a land smashed and broken by the opposing forces of capitalism and communism. On the western side a few white stones marked the border point, on the east the fences were high and armed guards patrolled the gaps between the look out towers. Binoculars flashed in the reflected sunlight and long barrelled rifles protruded from freezing vantage points. The irony was that both the watchers and the watched were Germans.

The premise had always been that if the free world should be attacked by the massed armies of Russia and the communist non free world, the meagre forces of British troops stationed along the border would hold them back. Rather like a wall made of cheese can hold back the ocean. That had always been the oxymoron, the art of the ridiculous made into public propaganda; worse than that – it was a plan devised by an idiot and executed by fools. The Russians, should they have chosen to invade, would have been in Cherbourg within a day, such was the massed strength of the Red Army. Bearing in mind that the allied ammunition would have run out in perhaps six hours, because that was all they were supplied for, for the rest of the time they could throw stones at the T54's as they rolled past. These were some of the truths that were never explained, things that the public never knew in the cold war; such was the fear of communism. I learned the truths my father told me, once I was old enough to understand what he knew, and how to hold my tongue in public.

And now? I am old enough to try to understand what he and she went through and how I came to be. Now I remember, in detail, a story. A story like no other, because to me it was me, the core of my existence, the reason for my being. I debated long and hard whether I should write it down. Whether it ever happened at all. What I am about to tell you is what I remember of the telling.

The 3rd Royal Tank Regiment had been on manoeuvres for the past week and now Sergeant Roland Connelly had the opportunity to do a spot of Christmas shopping; though for whom he could not really say. He loved the German Christmas with the candles on the tree and the cinnamon and ginger scents filling the air; though he knew the population were not up to their usual high spirits. He could only imagine what it must have been like prior to the war when the new prosperity had been so evident. His military experiences that winter had not been too good either, both in the small market town and on manoeuvres. He had been in charge of supplies for the mobile cook house, which were in a tent next to the encampment of tanks. Only this year, like never before, the pigs decided that they were intending to make a raid. And Pigs can be the most aggressive of animals once they have their mass mind set upon something. The result was one man having his calf muscle torn away as he levelled a well aimed kick at a brutish boar and another shooting two sows: It had been a mess.

The Colonel had told him to, "Sort the bloody mess out," which had been code for, "you fool Connelly – fix it pronto."

Connelly's home had not been a happy place his mother was a very dour woman, tough and yet unusual. Childhood came and went in the blink of an eye. His father an Irish ex-service man worked for the borough council of a city which he could so easily not be in. Liverpool or elsewhere had been the choice? And his father had chosen elsewhere, rather than the standard Irish drop off - Liverpool. The result? Roland and some sisters had been born on the south coast of England, the sons and daughters of a Cornish and Irish immigrant mix.

Connelly's father often joked how he had come out of the Irish bogs, hopping from clod to barefoot clod, a sack of potatoes on his back. Some of the family had gone to America, others came to England, while one or two went to Australia. He omitted the detail of leg-irons and brandings and convict servitude, but Connelly had sense and intelligence enough to understand the inference. He was also determined to make his mark in the world.

He had joined the army, as soon as he had been able, and been posted abroad to avoid the drunken rows and sheer sense of doom within his childhood home. Once in the services he had risen quickly by taking on challenges. The Berlin air lift, 1948; Singapore 1950-51; The Gulf 1953 and 1954 Germany.

Today he was interested in a particular piece which he thought might impress a local widow, who though ten years older than himself had taken a shine to him.

In his twenties and making a mark in the army he had risen from the two up and two down slums of the pre-war to a period of relative prosperity. A respected young Sergeant with a natural aptitude for organisation; already a veteran of the cold war and Berlin's check point Charlie, he had come to like this country and the people. In particular this widow. As time had gone on he saw that the German people were more like him than he had at first imagined and as a result his attraction to the experienced widow had grown.

Their first meeting had been a strange one as he queued for service at the food counter of the Sergeant's mess. She was working there as a cook, and part of the kitchen staff. The widow had been serving food and he had smiled at her, while she giggled in German with her colleagues. There had been lots of eye contact and much blushing, by both of them. However, somehow he seemed to have been given twice the portions of the other men - and he liked his food.

In his spare time he was learning German, as fast as he possibly could, and within a few weeks he had managed to hold the most basic of conversations with the widow. And she had tried, but had not been as successful, in learning some English.

They had begun seeing each other and at some point the flirtation tipped over into a relationship. As unlikely a relationship as anyone could have imagined. A relationship, which his mother and her father, disapproved of.

* * *

In the window of Reichman's porcelain and fine art shop the

statue stood in pure white, her arms outstretched to the sun and her whole being balanced on one leg, set upon a golden orb. Connelly's eye had been taken by it from the very first instant. He had to possess her. The perfect form, the beauty of it, the balance and ecstasy on her face, it was perfection and executed with all of Karl Tutter's precision and skill.

Porcelain, like the silver he had admired in the window of Flemings antiques as a boy, spoke of class and culture and he was a cultured man. This piece epitomised everything he desired in both a woman and fine art. It was the sort of item he had seen in the old houses of the wealthy as he rode his bicycle around the length and breadth of the Meon Valley. The glimpsed vision of things behind the leaded glass windows and part of the opulence of the nineteenth century which he so loved. Now it was for sale; for sale in a conquered country which had once been the centre of European artistic excellence.

"How much is that figure?" he asked casually, after he had browsed in the shop for about twenty minutes.

"I do not think that is for sale," the assistant replied in broken English.

"But it's in the window?" Connelly continued.

"Sometimes Herr Reichman puts things from his personal collection in the window. To get people into the shop. He hardly ever sells them."

"So it's not for sale?"

The woman shrugged her shoulders, "Who am I to say," she paused, "maybe, maybe not."

"That's a strange attitude, either it is for sale or it isn't."

" This I do not know," the woman replied, "but when he returns from the Selb factory tomorrow then I shall be able to, how do you say?" she paused, "as-cer-tain?"

Connelly's eyes swept over her. She was dressed in dark colours, bleak colours which gave her countenance a severity. Hair pulled back from her face she looked cruel with grey eyes and thin lips.

"What time will he be here?" Connelly asked.

"About eleven, I think he said," she replied.

"If it was for sale, how much do you think it would be?" Connelly asked, smiling broadly. An inviting smile which had an underlying expectant promise.

"That I cannot say."

"How about a guess then?" He winked. "You must have some idea? A shrewd guess?"

"I really have no idea." The assistant did not smile back. "But I do not think it will be cheap."

"Go on just for me – have a little stab at it?" Connelly was persuasive. He was also flirting and the woman knew that too. Knew that he had a way about him. He had the gift of the gab. A touch of the Blarney stone, as he was to say in later life.

"Why?" she snapped, trying to bring herself out of his persuasion.

"Because, I am a good customer?"

"Sergeant, just because you buy things from us does not mean you have special treatment by me. I cannot tell you if the porcelain is for sale or what price it is."

"I know, but I thought I'd try. You know me."

The assistant succumbed and wrote a figure down in Deutsche Marks and Connelly made a calculation of currency conversion. Nine pounds or thereabouts, his mental arithmetic concluded: Four weeks pay.

"What is it called?" he asked.

"Die Sonnenmadel."

"What does that mean? I'm learning but not that fast."

"Loosely translated, it means young sun girl. But others might say, young sun virgin." She smiled, her English better than his German.

True to form the following morning Sergeant Roland Connelly was at Reichman's: Eleven thirty precisely. He had calculated that he would allow the proprietor precisely half an hour to get himself set up for business and then he would pounce.

Perhaps he could haggle his way to a reduction.

The morning had been uneventful and with Christmas approaching Roland Connelly needed something impressive, a gift to charm the widow. The word of the dramatic rescue had buzzed around the town in less than twenty four hours and the uniformed men, who might be spending Christmas in Detmold, were being offered all sorts of Christmas cheer.

A small overhead bell rang as Connelly pushed open the plate glass door. The shop seemed empty, with Reichman nowhere to be seen. The female assistant had now been replaced by an old woman, Connelly wondered if it might be Frau Reichman. She had her back to him as he approached and had been crouching near a display case at ground level.

She stood up abruptly.

"Good morning?" she asked. Her English was poor.

"I've come about the Sonnenmadel?" he asked.

"Ah yes," she paused, "my daughter Erica told us all about it. I've spoken to my husband and I'm afraid he does not want to sell it."

"Perhaps if I spoke with your husband Frau Reichman?"

"There is no need. You cannot change his mind."

"I am prepared to pay a very good price and I could do certain things to help you out with ration cards?" As soon as he had said it, he regretted it, and didn't even know why he had.

"The piece doesn't belong to us, it belongs to someone else and he doesn't want to sell."

"Perhaps if I spoke with your husband?"

"Why? Do you not believe what I say? Why would I lie to you?" Her tone became sharp, caustic even.

"I'm not saying that you are; please forgive me if you thought that I was implying that…I just thought that I could negotiate?"

The woman opened a concealed door which seemed to be built into the display cabinet behind the counter, and there some distance away sat Reichman. He sat behind a large oak desk and he was speaking to a small fat man with heavy rimmed spectacles.

"Karl," she called, and both men looked up simultaneously. "This Englishmen wants to talk to you about Sonnenmadel. I told him it wasn't for sale," she paused, "but he won't listen."

Karl Reichman rose from his seat and turned to face the young Sergeant. Then stepping forward he smiled and asked, "Why would you want to buy my best piece? You must know that is a wonderful piece. Modelled by my friend. There is nothing like it anywhere else. He is the best modeller in the whole of Germany. Better than that, the best modeller, alive today. "

"That is precisely why I would like to buy it. It is absolutely wonderful I have never seen anything like it anywhere."

"You have good taste, young man," said the small man who sat in the distance. "Invite him in Karl so I can see him better."

Karl Reichman did as he was told and when all three were in the anti-room, the concealed entrance closed behind them and Frau Reichman resumed her vigil behind the sales counter once again.

"So you want to buy one of my Sonnenmadel?" the small man asked.

Connelly nodded.

"Before we discuss anything," Karl Reichman started, "we must have introductions." He paused and pointing at the small bespectacled man on the other side of the desk, said, "This is Karl Tutter, from the Selb factory in Bavaria. The man who created the Sonnenmadel."

Roland Connolly looked at the small man with the heavy spectacles who sat behind the oak desk. He looked average but his smile looked grotesque. It gave him the appearance of some strange gargoyle with a bag of broken teeth protruding from his mouth. An uglier runt of a man you could not find and yet there was intensity within his eyes. A pool of great knowing.

"I see from your uniform you are a Sergeant in the British Army. I expect you'd really like to be an officer one day?" Tutter spluttered.

"If I'm lucky I might make it to RSM," Connolly replied.

"RSM?" Reichman asked.

"Regimental Sergeant Major," Connolly coughed.

"So that is as far as the glass ceiling allows?" Tutter was cutting. "The highest point on the ladder through which you can see, but which you cannot pass." He was fumbling in a box next to the desk as he spoke. "Once it was the same for me. I could make plates and design but only now can I sculpt. That was what I really wanted to do." He changed the subject as he produced something wrapped in Hessian sacking which he placed upon the table. "You liked my Sonnenmadel, well this is my finest creation yet. It has all of my skill and all of my soul poured into it. It makes the madel look tame. It is without doubt the best I can do. And I have given my soul to be able to make the best for the sitter."

Roland Connelly knew Tutter's work, knew he was in the presence of a genius, or so he felt. "I admired your small cupid very much," he said, "and the woman I wish to buy this present for would love the Sonnenmadel."

"And so she should," Tutter continued.

Reichman who had sat listening suddenly interjected, "What if an object can be created just once. Like a child with a unique personality it cannot be repeated, it is born but the once. Once in the life of any artist a truly great piece is created; a David; a Mona Lisa; a Guernica; a vase of sunflowers; or a screaming Pope; this is," he paused to catch his breath in his own excitement "Karl's piece - his triumph." He reached over and started to unwrap the Hessian covering which had protected a figurine. "Are you familiar with Goethe's Faust?" he asked casually, as the strips of fabric were removed delicately, like the layers of an onion.

"Well I know that the story is based on Christopher Marlowe's Faustus," replied Connelly.

Reichman continued, "Well Karl has managed to encapsulate the whole spirit of Mephistopheles in this one piece. I had a joke with him that he must have sold his soul to the Devil to achieve such artistic mastery." He turned to Tutter, "Is that not so Karl? Like Faust you agreed to some hellish bargain in order to make your masterpiece. And I have no doubt Colonel Connelly, you can get what you desire too. You are persuasive and obviously know your own mind. "

Connelly did not know whether the reference to Colonel was a poor joke or something darker, but he chose to say nothing.

The pieces of Hessian removed, a beautifully sculpted figurine stood before them all. It was fifteen inches high and was a figure of a man beckoning. His left hand outstretched he cloaked his body with the other. Red and black were the predominant colours and the whole had a presence of evil which made it both fearful and seductively attractive.

"Henry Irving," Connelly squealed. "It's Henry Irving."

"And just who is this Henry Irving?" Reichman asked.

Karl Tutter picked up the thread, "Henry Irving? Why he is Count Dracula, or the man that Bram Stoker used for inspiration and he played the Devil in Faustus. Is that not so Sergeant?" He did not wait for a reply, "Henry Irving was a powerful actor, the Olivier of his day. Stoker arranged for a public reading of his novel to ensure it had copyright and Irving said it was," he paused to accentuate the word, "dreadful."

Roland Connelly was nodding.

"I see you are a literary man," Tutter continued, "and Irving was the man of his day, but," he paused thoughtfully, "he had his twenty five years of fame and fortune but it is Stoker's book that lives on. Do you know? Of course you do, that Dracula is the most published novel in the world, behind The Bible?"

"Mein Herr," Reichman interjected, "The Bible is not a work of fiction."

Tutter burst into loud and almost uncontrollable laughter, but said nothing in reply.

Connelly changed the subject, sensing that one of the taboo subjects was about to be broached. "I left school when I was fourteen," he said solemnly, "and went to work in a bicycle shop, repairing them: Burnett's! I expect they are long gone now, but that was where I learned to read. Not at school. The owner was an avid reader and he gave me books to read. Books for me were my great escape."

"And read you do?" Reichman asked. "To read much is to be self-taught? Is that not so, for what else do students at any university do? They read a subject."

"Five or six books a week," Connelly replied. "I read a variety of things and for me reading is a pure pleasure. Dickens was my favourite and Williamson now is."

"Ah this is good," Tutter exclaimed, returning to his subject. "So you know the story and you know that Henry Irving was the man that Bram Stoker was the actor manager for. Some say that the vampire Dracula is based on him and him alone. You must then know of Polly Dolly."

Roland Connelly was nodding as he spoke. "John Polidori, doctor to Lord Byron, uncle to the Rossetti family. The writer of the first vampire story in English; he created Lord Ruthven, Lord of the Isles? Some scholars say that Ruthven is in fact Byron. But they all stole the idea from you lot."

Tutter was becoming excited, "So you will understand this piece, yes?"

Roland Connelly looked at the face of the figure; it was cruel and hard with a goatee beard and a black cap perched upon the head. He had seen the style of cap before but could not place it. He thought Victorian bed-cap, but the colour was wrong. Curling above that was a fine royal blue feather. It gave the whole thing an imperious air, and balanced the whole look of the piece. The face was a sneering leer and the hand behind the back, which was shrouded in a black cloak, had two long fingers protruding. The effect was one of a shudder, but the execution and artistry was superb. But above all else the most striking feature was the eyes. Dark eyes which seemed to follow a person and move from one to another as they spoke: The effect amazed Connelly.

"So you see," said Tutter, "this is even better than my Sonnenmadel."

"Karl here," Reichman continued, "wants me to help him produce these, in a limited quantity."

"You see into this one piece," Tutter continued, "I have poured all of my skill, all of my knowledge and it is guaranteed to make me famous. Perhaps I will be known as the greatest modeller of them all. Better than Meisen, Wedgwood, Spode, this is my triumph."

Roland Connelly had to agree. It was without doubt the finest piece of porcelain sculpture he had ever seen. Many times as a boy he had passed the antique emporium of Fleming's in Southsea, with it's old clock tower; and just as many times he had vowed that one day he would have the silver tea service and cutlery; the works of art.

Though he had come from humble beginnings he had made a start at climbing the ladder.

His mind flashed to the widow and he wondered what she would make of such a piece. This much he knew, that she understood art, understood opera, and that there was more to life than being a slave to the system. He knew that she understood Goethe's poetry. In fact she loved poetry in general so she would surely know Faust.

Heinrich Heine and particularly Herman Lons were ones she talked about and he, as a result, was trying desperately to learn the language to keep her interested. Though older, he found that many of their aspirations were held in common and that seduced him most of all. His family would have thought him a snob, but he really didn't care. His life path was going in a different direction. In that instant he knew he had to have Mephistopheles; have her; have success. All he really needed now was the figurine. Everything depended upon it. Life itself depended upon it.

"How much is it?" Connelly asked casually, attempting to disguise his lust.

"Ah this?" Tutter paused, "this, this is not for sale, it is the prototype. The first and only one to be made, but there will be others. Those you can buy, but this one…"

He began to stroke the item as if it were a small pet, and for a brief split second Connelly thought he heard a sigh from the figure; and then dismissed it as a figment of his ridiculous imagination. He knew he was over tired now, his stint of duty had been too long. Also the gloom of the room hurt his eyes and he was finding the atmosphere oppressive, as if it was restricting his free thought. He wanted the figure but he also wanted to be outside.

"So you came for the Sonnenmadel and you now wish Mephistopheles?" Reichman smiled as he spoke. "You would be the first non German to own one. Even the great and the good would not have one of these. Because," he paused chuckling, "we are only to make twenty five. Just twenty five."

"Why so few?" Connelly asked, as he imagined the price slipping well beyond his meagre means. "If you only make twenty five the price of each will be astronomical. You could price yourself out of the market. These things go out of fashion." He could sense himself clutching at straws in his attempt to obtain one.

"One for each year?" Tutter laughed. "That is all I have been allowed."

"Each year?" Connelly asked, completely bemused.

Reichman was nodding now. Nodding like a dog, he spoke softly as if he didn't want to be overheard. "Our bargain, Sergeant Connelly, we will make only twenty five."

"And," Tutter continued, "for you we have number thirteen. The first twelve have already been accounted for, or ordered as you English say. How does that suit? You are not superstitious are you?"

As Connelly continued to study the piece he thought he spied a slight movement in the corner of the room, as if another person might be present, but realised that his eyes were playing tricks upon him again. He heard the chime of a huge clock in the darkness and realised that he would have to be on duty in one hour. It was now or never. Suddenly Tutter began to wrap the sculpture in the protective Hessian once again, and then slipped it below the table top: It was gone.

Having tantalised his customer, Tutter was now ready to close the deal.

"What would it cost me?" Connelly asked.

Reichman began to talk about the rarity, and the beauty and how this was the chance of a lifetime but was suddenly interrupted by Tutter.

"Exactly the same as the Sonnenmadel. Not a penny more. Do we have a bargain?" Tutter asked.

The reaction was instant. "Done," Connelly said, almost whooping internally with excitement.

Once again he thought he saw a movement in the dark behind the sculptor, but once again attributed it to the changing perception of his tired eyes.

"It will bring you all you desire; it will be lucky for you." Karl Tutter was positive, and smiling. "Thirteen is your lucky number. From now on you must remember that, thirteen will be a special number for you."

"When can I have it though?" Connelly suddenly asked.

"Right now," Tutter said, as he lifted a box from behind and below the wooden desk.

"But, I thought you said," Connelly began, but then stopped himself.

"Thought I said what?" Reichman asked.

Karl Tutter placed a box on the table.

Connelly opened the box and there within lay an exact copy of the prototype which both men had refused to sell. Once again it was wrapped in Hessian and packed for transit. He seemed to recall that they said no others had yet been made. But there it was, a copy with the number thirteen clearly inscribed in the base, alongside Tutter's signature.

When he left the shop that afternoon he knew that he could now get everything he possibly wanted. The figurine was in the box he carried, and though the widow was older and had two children, she could possibly give him a child. A girl, a daddy's girl perhaps, with golden ringlets that hung down over her ears as she threw her little arms around his neck to plant a kiss upon his cheek. Or a boy maybe?

Then there was the talk of promotion. Staff Sergeant perhaps and then RSM. On that afternoon everything seemed possible and everything seemed achievable. It was as if he could conquer the world.

* * *

Roland Connelly seemed to get everything his heart desired in the coming years. Promotions came thick and fast, at times so quickly that he thought he had a guardian angel on his shoulder. The widow succumbed to his advances and the two were married - living in 13 Langstone Crescent, a small suburb in Poole, Dorset. Life was good, and every time things happened he could not believe his luck.

In the regiment a combination of luck and good judgement gave him what he needed. Those above him conveniently fell by the wayside until there were no obstacles in his path to advancement. The RSM had died on the 13th April, and he , though only a young Staff Sergeant had been given the post, apparently he had been the thirteenth applicant, and a wild card to boot. No one had expected him to be chosen, and Connelly later said it was because of his lucky thirteen. Then with the same speed a commission appeared and suddenly he had become an officer. That had been on the 12th June 1966, and he had laughed at the proximity to the thirteenth. Occasionally he thought of Tutter and his rambling prophecy that thirteen was his lucky number.

The widow had produced their child, a boy, but to tell the truth Roland Connelly had little interest in the infant. At the birth, Roland had told the widow that he felt nothing and asked if that was usual in such circumstances. She had cried.

As time progressed Roland concentrated on his career and left his wife at home rather than travel with her using married quarters. In truth he had come to tire of her; she was older now and as his fortunes waxed so his love for her waned. He found her age an embarrassment to him, so he avoided public appearances with her at his side. His lack of love he communicated to her via his touch and kiss. Familiarity breeds contempt, but embarrassment kills love – it is instant death. The lines on her face became a little too deep and the grey in her hair a little too pronounced. In consequence, as he achieved what he thirsted for she became less and less important to him. And the boy? The boy became an irritation.

The strangest irony was the extraction of the widow from Germany, where she had friends and family and where he had found a real homeland, only to isolate her in a foreign land virtually alone. Her children, from the first marriage, moved on and married themselves and the small boy became the central stay of her existence. That was until her husband came home on leave; then the house would come alive, alive with music, entertaining, cooking, baking and laughter. It was a strange existence, for both the woman and the child. Most of the time the boy learned to amuse himself; he learned that books gave him an avenue of escape. Learned that music and being proficient at it won him friends. People wanted to make music with him, some even tried to persuade him to make a future career out of it. Like many teenagers he wanted the adulation and respect of his peers; his came from being able to play the guitar. So he practised and practised until a combination of fear and self doubt made him opt for the traditionally safe academic route.

He always loved to learn something new, whether it was history, art, music, science.

As the child grew Connelly's interest in him decreased, there was no real bond between them beyond that of dutiful father and respectful son. That was something the boy failed to understand as the years progressed, but he was sheltered and content within the cocoon of safety. It was his launching pad.

By 1967 the relationship between the widow and Connelly had run out of steam, and neither of them really knew why. Perhaps boredom had set in with the younger man; perhaps the love once claimed had never really existed. Connelly claimed, to himself, it was her age and the fact that she had, "let herself go." She had said, and accepted, it was because he was embarrassed by her, both were true and yet both were untrue. The embarrassment factor was the one which hit Connelly's wife the hardest; the one that hurt the most, especially when in reality he was no better than her. His issue, if it was one, was that he believed he was. The slum boy, made good by hard work, and the young girl who had married well prior to the war, only to have her world destroyed by world events. In reality they should have been a perfect match, but something went wrong. Something almost beyond their control. Connelly acted out of character at times, and the widow reacted in kind, reacted with fits of anger. Their fights became bitter and sometimes loud and recriminatory. She admonished him for bringing her to his country, while he told her that she had only married him to escape the penury of post-war Germany. The seven year itch had turned thirteen, and a severe downward spiral began.

* * *

As the boy lay sleeping he was not sure whether he was dreaming or waking in a nightmare – the image was so vivid.

He was alone in the house when the door bell rang. He had no idea why he was alone, but he was. It was dark and only being thirteen he was not sure whether to answer. Having no idea where his mother was he tried to make out the shape of the person standing on the red tiled porch floor. He could see a rather tall and thin shape which looked at him as it peered through the letterbox.

"Aren't you going to let me in?" a thin and rasping voice asked.

The boy shuddered.

"I know you're on your own in the house," the voice continued, "so come on you're number thirteen, and today is the thirteenth. It's time for me to collect."

"Collect what?" the boy asked.

"Don't you know? Didn't he tell you?"

" Didn't who tell me? My mother didn't say anything about any collection – besides she hasn't left me any money. You'll have to come back later when she's in."

"But it's not money little boy. I don't need money I've come to collect something far more valuable to me."

"So what have you come to collect?" the boy asked.

The figure let out a blood curdling laugh. "Why I've come to collect you. You and anyone else in the house. You're my lucky thirteen, and next year it will be fourteen. But this year it's you," he paused, "number thirteen."

The boy turned to run.

"Let me in number thirteen," the voice continued, laughing, "come in number thirteen your time is up."

It was seductive, laconic and yet as sharp as fingers being drawn down a blackboard. The boy's spine tingled with fear.

As the boy looked, the face bent down to the letter box and a foul and offensive breath passed through the small gap between them. He thought he could smell burning, burning flesh. Then he saw them, the flame eyes which glistened in the half light. The teeth, which were sharp, pointed and protruding over the lips. There was a cruelty like he had never seen before, a menace which was trying to bend his will to open the door. His hand began to reach for the deadlock, just an inch or two more and the catch would open and the…

He was awake now and his mother was giving him a drink, cold coke, gone flat. The man with the cruel persuasive voice had gone. He was coughing loudly. She was taking his temperature, and telling him to drink as it was full of sugar, and his chest felt heavy, like it was full and ready to explode. He coughed, a deep rasping cough which brought phlegm to his throat. His pyjamas were wet and clammy and he wanted to get them off, throw them to the floor. Pull on something dry, anything; anything at all to be comfortable. The air in his room crackled, crackled because there was no central heating, no fire in fact. He lay deeply shrouded under a traditional feather duvet, with his back to mobile radiator which was plugged in at a switch timer. The warmth eased his chest, as he lay with his back to the warm metal, but the air hurt his lungs and ice, made up of condensation, was forming on the inside of the bedroom window panes.

A sallow face passed outside the window, which lay to the front of the small two bedroom bungalow. A cruel face he had seen before. A face lit by moonlight and reflected beams from the snow, which had fallen like an iced glaze. A face with a cap and a blue feather; a face which winked and smiled a cruel smile. He jumped up and made sure the window was closed, checked the catches. Then he shuttered the Venetian blind in an attempt to blot out the image, but the face and the eyes, he could still see them clearly through the gaps.

"What's the matter Rolant?" his mother asked, in German, from the doorway. As always she sounded the "d" as a "t" in his name and her accent, despite living in Britain for thirteen years, was very pronounced. She wore a full length white night gown and the effect startled him: He jumped.

"The face," he said, breathing heavily now. "There was a face at the window like the figure in the front room. He said he wanted to come in. Wanted me to let him in."

"You're dreaming," she said, in broad German. "You have a strong fever."

He understood everything she said and was fully able to

switch from one language to another with consummate ease. Even as a small child he had learned two words for everything. Nothing was ever quite what it seemed, and nothing was simple, but unlike other children he had become bilingual. He had learned to be different, in fact he relished it. Being an outsider had advantages, it meant that people left you alone and you did not have to fit in with them. Even his school teachers did that; some because of his German ancestry and others because of linguistic dexterity: In either case he did not mind.

" You're dreaming," she reassured again. She took the thermometer from under his arm pit and switched on the light. "You're very hot, too hot. I'll get you a flannel."

The boy was cold now as the wet piece of cloth hit his forehead. The heat had gone and the damp of the bed was getting cold. Cold as the grave. He knew that if the figure came again he would be unable to resist that persuasive voice. So he intended to stay awake – wide awake, just to make sure nothing else could happen and that he could distinguish fact from dream.

"You must try to sleep," his mother soothed, "then by the morning your fever may have broken. Everything else is a dream, just think about nice things – sunshine and swimming."

The light suddenly went out.

He was jumping into a pond, no a river. It was deep and it was cool and he was feeling soothed from the scorching sun. They had walked down to the bridge by the ancient Abbey; and even though the farmer had placed a placard on a tree, which screamed, " private," he and his mother had climbed the wall to dip their toes in the cool water.

That was as far as they ever went. His mother hated to travel because she became violently sick on any form of transport. She had the worst case of motion sickness imaginable, but this was not imagination. She could projectile vomit after only a few brief minutes on a train, ship, or car, and that too had annoyed his father. He could have chosen more wisely and then perhaps a holiday or two might have been possible. As his father liked to travel she was forced to stay put. As his father liked to spend she became ever more frugal. They walked everywhere and were trapped in the provincial parochial little town – he knew he would break free whenever he could.

Then came the tapping once again. This time it was more insistent, more demanding and he was wide awake . A small thin voice was calling on the chill night air; a chilling, wailing sound which hurt the boy's ears .This time there was a thin hand gently tapping against the leaded lights of the single glazed windows. Suddenly he was cold, colder than he had ever been and the moonlight made a silhouette of the face. A smiling leering face, which began to salivate before his very eyes. Salivate like a rabid frothing dog, beckoning. He threw the covers over his head and lay motionless as imagined fingers ran over the duvet cover and his mind began to unravel. He coughed again.

He couldn't remember what happened next, whether he had slept or simply passed into a nightmare. But he lay in the dark terrified of the shadows on the wall and the hand that kept knocking. Knocking at the glass until he knew he had to do it. There was nothing else he could do - it was the only answer.

* * *

In the front room he could see the figurine in the firelight. It was standing one hand behind the back, the other beckoning him forward. The hand was moving, beckoning; the fingers were curling like claws, the figurine was moving; its eyes were glinting, flame red orbs in the darkness. Flames in the darkness. With sudden staccato movements the boy advanced and grasped the figure like a mongoose with a cobra. Then with a single swift and terrifying movement he dashed it against the hearth and threw it into the open fire. The object exploded into a thousand pieces which whizzed around the room like shooting embers. A hollow wail emanated from the shards and suddenly, as if a great weight had been lifted, the boy rushed back to his room. Back into darkness.

* * *

When the boy woke, the house was in total silence, but lights were dancing along the walls: He coughed. It was hard to breathe.

He could hear his mother's heavy breathing as she slept in the room opposite the bathroom: He coughed and called her name.

He wasn't sure if his chest had cleared slightly but he was finding it hard to move and he felt sick. He called to his mother again: He coughed.

Recalling the events of the night before, or was it seconds before? He had lost his equilibrium and the smell of burning plastic was invading his nostrils. He wondered what excuse he could provide for the destruction of his mother's prized figurine: He coughed again this time he was feeling light headed, as well as sick. He vomited.

He coughed and vomited again.

Without moving he opened the Venetian Blind and the crisp winter sun streamed in to hit his face. Snow lay on the ground, but there were no footprints under his window. Without moving he leapt to the front door and opening it noticed no single mark on the virgin blanket covering: He coughed; once twice three times. It was hard to breathe and he couldn't move. The stench was overpowering.

Inside his head he could hear wailing, long screams and screeches and the sound of car horns in the distance. The room was a magical blue colour: He coughed once, twice and then closed his eyes.

* * *

In Detmold Roland Connelly decided to pay an impromptu visit to Reichman's shop. It had been nearly thirteen years since he had been there last. It had been 1954, just before he had left Germany for a variety of postings, and married the widow. Connelly was hoping that perhaps he could find a present for the new woman who had just walked into his life.

At the corner of Krumme Strasse, he turned left and walked past The Schloss, which was now a municipal museum, and then on toward Reichman's shop. When he reached the site of the shop it had gone. Instead there was an ironmongery emporium.

He strode in and asked one of the girls behind the counter, "When did Reichman's close down?"

"This is Reichman's," she replied.

It was only then that he fully noticed the sign above the counter. Reichman's was emblazoned there clear as day.

"Oh, it's probably my German," he apologised.

The girl was very quick off the mark, "Your German it is very good," she said, smiling.

"What I was looking for was Reichman's porcelain shop. I bought something here," he paused, " back in '54; thirteen years ago, it doesn't seem that long, and well I was rather hoping to get something special once again."

"That is impossible," a voice sounded from a room behind the counter. "Ilsa can you sort out these bolts for me while I tend to the gentleman?"

A man emerged from the back room. He was painfully slim with a sharp and angular face. Roland Connelly thought he had either met him or seen him before but he couldn't place where.

" You said you bought some porcelain here?"

Roland Connelly nodded, "I was stationed here after the war and Reichman's always had the best."

"I agree," replied the man. His face was lined and his lips rather cruel, almost in a sneer, were stretched over particularly fine and sharp white teeth. His tongue flashed along them nervously.

"Well I came here in '54 and I met Herr Reichman and his wife," Connelly paused. " I also met his friend Karl Tutter, the modeller and I bought Mephistopheles. It was one of twenty five - I had number thirteen. The greatest piece I have ever seen. I was just hoping that Tutter had done a new piece."

"And this year is 1967," was stated in a matter of fact reply.

Connelly was looking at the man now, concentrating on his features. It was then that the singular thought struck him, this man could be a living image of the figurine he had bought all those years ago. If he had been wearing a cap with a feather, then perhaps, just perhaps, it could have been said that the man had been the artist's subject, transposed.

"What a shame the shop is different. Are you the new owner?" Connelly asked.

"I am, but I am not new. I am their youngest son. My other brothers were killed in the war and I grew up with an uncle abroad until I was twenty and then I came back to rebuild the shop."

"I expect the Reichmans, your parents, have retired?" Connelly was fishing.

"They are dead I'm afraid," the man said.

"I'm sorry, I didn't know." Connelly knew that his mouth had opened on too many issues. "Please accept my condolences, I had no idea." He paused and then blurted, "Connelly, Colonel Roland Connelly," proffering his hand as he did so. "Well soon to be , next month in fact. As soon as the paperwork is completed I take charge of the regiment.

The grip that met his was like a vice, but as cold as ice. Far too strong for a man of his stature Connelly thought. Immediately he loosened his grip and hoped that the man had not noticed his shudder of disgust.

"Gustav Reichman," he replied, " at your service." He then clicked his heels together in the most formal military fashion and bowed very slightly.

The effect totally unnerved Connelly, "When did they die?" he asked, though he wished from that moment onward he had not.

"And here is the strangest thing," Gustav Reichman replied. "We were a prosperous family, well respected in this community. Then in one night the work of three generations went up with a fire bomb which dropped into the attic."

"I am so sorry," Connelly said.

The reply he received both amazed and stunned him, like a sudden punch to the mid-riff. "Sorry? Why be so sorry, you work for the other side, and from what you say you are good at your job Colonel."

Connelly was silent in response.

"On that night we had to watch the people we cared about the most. The people we loved be turned to charcoal. My older brother died in the Afrika Corp in 1940, and Wilhelm in early 1942, in Russia. Do you know that I don't even know where they are buried? I am the last of my kind. I have no children but if I had, would you kill them too?" He was voicing all of his venom, all of his malice, all of his hatred, "This shop, the porcelain shop was destroyed in 1941. Both my mother and my father died in that raid, your raid." He paused, then continued with a really cruel edge to his voice, "The modeller you spoke of, Karl Tutter, was my uncle; he was here on that night too. They all died and everything was destroyed," he paused then repeated, "everything." He paused again before his final blow, " And you know the irony?"

Connelly was shaking his head.

"My family," Reichman said, "my family weren't even Nazi. In fact my father didn't support the man at all. He thought him a loud mouth." He paused once again, "But my family were slaughtered like pigs nonetheless. And you Colonel you wish to advance in such a profession?"

Connelly squealed, "I was here in 1954. I was stationed here. I didn't kill anyone. I liked the people."

Gustav Reichman said nothing.

"I was in this shop in 1954 and I bought a piece." Connelly said, "I have it at home right now: I can prove it."

dario's palazzo

This story is dedicated to my brother, who, like me loves Venice.

I

It had been a very warm summer that year and I, like the rest of the English tourists, had stumbled from ice-cream seller to ice cream seller, looking for the gelato which most resembled sorbet, and at last I had found one. Crisp smooth lemon, which bit into the tongue and lingered in the throat like a medicinal pill, was combined with the refreshing sting of pure ice – made from the water of deep earthy springs. Bottled in Milan, in a most fetching pink plastic and wrapped in a gold label it was shipped in to make the final ingredient of my personal heaven. Never had I believed that water would have tasted so marvellous, for I was of the clean tap generation who found the bottling of water rather absurd. I mean water drawn from underground springs, naturally filtered and then bottled in plastic? Absurd was the only word which came to mind.

I had also taken to carrying a large white pocket handkerchief, to ward off both the flies and sweat as I walked through the crowded alleyways. Dabbing my forehead and temples the white cotton, embossed with a rich royal blue R, had turned grey with use; while the fresh feel of ironed laundry had transmogrified into a rather pulpy mass of damp cotton, which clawed at my skin making it raw with every wipe.

All around the city it seemed to smell of decay and the lower levels of buildings seemed abandoned, the residents accepting that there was no way to stop the encroaching water. The Adriatic was slowly claiming back those parts of the land mass which made up these low islands. It was a potentially tragic loss, on a scale similar to the passing of the polar bear, or the engulfing of the Maldives. The residents here did not have the resilience and tenacity of the Dutch nor their engineering prowess. The Dutch would have long since surrounded the area with dykes and waterways which would have drained out the sodden mass. The

Italians were different, more accepting and less willing to fight the elements. It was a concrete exemplification of the difference between a Northern European stoicism and a Southern European, Latin, romanticism. The Italians would eventually do as they had always done – move on and seek out another new frontier.

My mind often questioned the differences between Europeans; why some should take the line of least resistance and others would stay and do battle? The answer which I thought would be simple never came.

The stoic British with their reserved and withdrawn nature; the Germans with their ability to organise; the French with their love of food and wine and the Italians with their ability to concentrate upon only those things which seemed important. I had tried in the past to understand nationalism but always floundered, much as I did with religion, when asked to take a leap of faith. I was riddled with the racist stereotyping which was, and is, of course utter nonsense, but it percolated through my views like the coffee of Brazilians. And there it was again this racial stereotyping which had been injected into me through the media and television. Television rules the world, and if you don't believe me just say you don't own one and watch the reaction from any square box voyeur. You'll get the, "I don't watch much television either," reaction as if to confirm the joint bestowing of deification.

There the test is passed, we have something in common.

Then there are those who ask incredulously, "What no television, you don't watch any?" To those I give a simple reply, "No, not only don't I watch one, I don't own one." The reaction to that would be virtually the same as public exposure of my genitals. A series of gawps and ahs as if I either need to be pitied or was and am totally, "strange."

Every humble living room across the land faces the grey screen of oblivion. The world sets a clock by the news and the entertainment ensures that all are the same; the thirst for thunderous mediocrity once begun can never be reversed. The moving finger writes and having writ moves on and I was a dinosaur. An old fashioned dinosaur, who, despite having had his hopes and dreams repeatedly dashed against the rocks, continues to believe in love and the power of humanity. Not in humans but in the broader sense of the word – as a life force locked into a planet which is spinning in a black void and going nowhere. A third stone from the sun which is a rock in itself and disintegrating slowly every day. Or maybe all the hocus – pocus of existence really is no more than a huge Monty Python sketch show, loosely held in place by a profound notion; the notion of chaos. That in fact, everything is chaos, nothing has a purpose, God is dog spelt backwards and that man created him in his own image. Or as some now say, after the birth of 1970's feminism, God is a woman?

I add this here because the tale I am about to relay is one relayed by a stoic, a non believer, unless of course you count lemon ice-cream sorbet as one of your own small faiths.

An ice-cream maker whose limone was so tangy and sharp that the tongue cleaved to the roof of your mouth with every spoonful. It was fantastically refreshing. One small spoonful and the zest and zing lifted the senses like an angel lifting the soul. Rather poetic for a man who believed in neither Angels nor Demons. It was a sudden and absolute delight, an explosion of fruit on a jaded palate. In fact, the lemon made we sweat all the more.

"Hey Mr Rickhard, a good one no?" my guide Giovanni laughed.

I nodded, and smiled at the way he simply could not get his mouth and tongue around the ch in Richard. He sounded Italian but either he had a very strong dialect, which was unknown to me, or he had some Spanish influence within his pronunciation. Either way his voice had an unusual sound even for a Venetian.

He smiled and his peg-like teeth stood like old individual tie-posts in some long forgotten gondola graveyard. Some were yellow, others chipped and cracked, while the majority were weather worn and tired.

"Theez is the best gelato maker in the 'ole of Italeee," he wheezed.

"Really?" I replied, noting once again the careful way in

which he pronounced words. He was a convivial fellow who smiled a lot and had arranged for a gondola ride for a "single" gentleman and he had served my pocket well. I had expected some form of ridicule from the gondoliers, because of my single status, but to his credit, and theirs, they had not questioned me in any detail and I, in turn, did not have to volunteer the history of my failed love-life.

I had been married but that had been a disaster. I had married in haste and then taken fifteen years to discover the self delusion within which I had lived. Like many men before me I believed that my wife had loved me, until she vanished across the horizon with some other stout fellow. There then followed a series of, relationships, which consisted of sex, and power struggle exchanges, until finally I had been cast aside for one last time.

I'm not saying I was perfect. I too had made some ridiculous errors of judgement and treated my previous girlfriend abominably. How? By cheating on her with another woman; it was not an action I was either proud of, nor able to reconcile with my own treatment at the hands of the opposite sex. But like all good fools I had been able to transpose some of the blame and thereby save my own sanity.

The experience had made me cynical and less than sympathetic to the plight of female kind. Some might have said I was verging on the misogynistic, others that I was a misanthrope, whereas I preferred to see myself in more romantic terminology. An old tree twisted by a bleak wind. I had often joked with the girls at the office that I had not been born this way but that years of systematic abuse by women had created me. Like Mary Shelly's God turned monster I was striving to re-find my soul. Like some dark Count Dracula I was still looking for my soul-mate, my Cathy, forever scraping at the window which faced onto the endless moor. In truth I would have given anything to have the kind of relationship I had seen others achieve. A relationship like the one between Rochester and Jane, one which transcended time and space and the conventions of polite society.

True there were those who thought themselves happy, but I had witnessed the nagging wife and the bitterly expectant children and seen the frustration in many a man. Once or twice I had seen true love, quiet acceptance one of the other, the peace, the harmony and the sheer joy that some couples experienced in the company of the other. They were the couples who spoke when they ate out, rather than those who had spent one too many days together and had in consequence nothing more to say.

Was I happy? That would be hard to evaluate truly; I was still persevering, though on one or two occasions I had thought about ending it. Thought about sliding into a warm bath and opening a vein or two and then just letting go. Why not? I had thought. The answer was that perhaps at this stage in my life I was not ready. Deep in the back of my mind the romantic spirit clung to me and I wondered if, by accident, one day she might appear; but I had not yet found my Jane Eyre.

"That's because," a friend had once kindly pointed out, "she doesn't exist. She's fictional. There are no Jane Eyres and you are not Edward Rochester."

At that point I had to agree. But I also told him that his single status was probably, like mine, brought about by a single common denominator. He had looked at me quizzically when I pointed that out to him.

"After all," I had said, "you've been out with young girls."

He nodded.

"Beautiful women, not so beautiful women, ball breakers, and those who were so professional they forgot to have a life."

"There are plenty of blokes like that too," he had cheerily defended himself with.

"And they're single too," I had pounced. "The single common denominator," I had cruelly pointed out, was him.

To his credit he had taken it well, and laughed at my cruelty. Taken a blow to the heart which most boxers would have winced at; and after saying it, I had wished I had not. However, the truth remained, we were both single. Whatever we might chose to believe, the truth was we were un-picked, old, second hand and dusty goods stuck in some bric-a-brac shop corner called life.

"And you're too fat, and too old. What young girl is going to look at you?" He had finally counterpunched with, but the impact had gone and the numbness was already setting in between us.

I had to agree. There was more chance of a jet engine falling on my head than me meeting my Jane Eyre. So I filled the void with travel, before slipping into some slow decaying old age. I could see myself, alone, old and broken in a nursing home. The only saving grace being the young nurses who wore wonder bras under their uniforms; the ever present reminder of what might have been. The bouncing prancing globes of youth which would be topped by the provocative pink peaks of desire, hard firm and enticing as they brushed against my face.

That was not the way I intended to go. Dribbling, smelling of stale urine, unshaven and lecherously ridiculous; being forced to listen to sub-standard entertainment provided by some church group or other. That would be utter torture. I was going out dancing; dancing on the ceiling, telling crude jokes, kissing the girls and still firm enough to get my hands up and under their skirts. My fingers were not going to be making models out of matchsticks on a Sunday afternoon; mine would be tracing figure of eight patterns or writing crude words in the small of some woman's back.

I had wanted to see the unusual sights of Venice before the place vanished into the Adriatic; and after receiving my redundancy payment, had finally taken the plunge.

At fifty four years of age I had suddenly discovered precisely how expendable I was. Despite ploughing years of goodwill into what I thought was a "career," at Christmas, in line with the spirit of goodwill toward all men, I received my marching orders. There were new chimps diving from greasy branch to greasy branch, and the old silver-backs had to go, even if they were better and faster than the younger men hired to brighten the image of the magazine. Age and experience count for little when opposed by sycophancy and cost – younger men are cheap.

I'd give you the name of the publication but they would probably deal out a libel suit and to be frank now, after nine months, I just can't be bothered with it all. The young bucks can do as they please and me? I intended to do the odd piece of freelance and write a novel. Call me weak, call me cynical, but I am going to take the line of least resistance before I finally belly flop into my shallow grave.

So that was what made me decide on Venice. I'd already done Rome, when I was younger and romance had been in the air; I'd done Florence too and now I wanted to, "do" Venice.

Being done in Venice however, had been more like it. The prices of everything had been astronomical and everywhere the tourist stalls and cafes jacked up their charges. Piratti della Laguna it said on some of the tee – shirts for sale. Tee shirts printed by five year olds somewhere in Thailand and shipped in and sold at four times their value. I thought the sentiment admirable - Pirates of the Lagoon. Venice was over-flowing with them: Pirates. Prices were jacked sky high and the alleys were filled with rogues. Not like when I had been in Pisa and some greasy fingered lout had taken my wallet with a swift bump and grab - this theft was more subtle.

My guide had come from the Albergo Barbaro-Bertellini and true to their boast he did a have a good knowledge of Britain. He even had the temerity to ask if I was related to Keith Richard of the Rolling Stones, and then broke into a few bars of Jumping Jack Flash, followed by an almost unrecognisably version of Brown Sugar. His voice was like two cats confined in a bag being beaten into submission by a cane of bamboo; in truth the noise was awful. But I had also been flattered, having a name which was famous by association gave life a little twist – added spice.

"Today," he chuckled, watching me wince at his dulcet tones, "we are going to the most amazing house in all of Venice," he said. "It is full of memories and some of the locals say it is alive with them. It is magical, beautiful, mysterious and like a good woman seductive and sensual. It is also dangerous."

I was instantly intrigued by his opening for the day. Only the day before he had taken me on a trip to Torcello, the romantic and desolate island which, prior to the silting of channels, had been the centre of Venetian population. In 638 a Cathedral had been founded there by the Bishop of Altinum. Santa Maria Assunta with its columns and arches now stood alone on the ghost island, which had been decimated by plague 500 years before. I found the place delightful with the literary links to Hemingway and Pinter and my guide had revelled in my enjoyment. Today, he said, he was intending to titillate my senses to reach even greater heights – already I was hooked.

Venice, as a city, has always been a haven for the rich and famous, the waterways draw them in. The glass of Murano reflects the mirror images that everyone wants to see of themselves. Everyone wants a slice of Hollywood even if it is no more than a fleeting glimpse. Film stars and multi-millionaires rub shoulders with street traders, prostitutes and the other assorted flotsam and jetsam of humanity. Everywhere there is the hustle and bustle of life and luck. Yet somehow the whole vibrancy of the place reminded me of New York in the way a cosmopolitan aura clung to the buildings like a fog. New York had no soul, no centre, it seemed to have grown like a giant carbuncle. Slow, reaching up into the sky until eventually the sun light is blocked out and all that remains is the water – Venice felt like that too, only it was older, more entrenched like a corn.

Venetian travellers to China had returned with recipes and spices, silks and slaves. This was a place of crossroads. Not the crossroads of humanity and exploration, but the Devil's crossroad of Robert Johnson. A place where every sin and vice could once be found and where those with wit and dexterity could achieve greatness. New York gave me the same kind of uneasy feeling, despite the bright lights of Time Square and the huge greedy sky-scraper fingers which reached grasping into the sky. It felt like both places had been built upon the heaped accumulation of human misery. It might as well have been down in the depths of Mississippi, down at the crossroads where everyone had a hell-hound on their tail: A stranger place I have never known.

II

When the water taxi left the jetty I had with me my customary Nikon and several spare films. I intended to have documentary evidence of where I had been, so that as I languished in a nursing home or hospice in my dotage, I could dull into submission visitors and nurses alike, with the enormity of my travels. On my head sat the battered Panama hat which had travelled with me to a variety of places around the world. The sweat band inside was decaying with the salt which seemed to be exploding from my forehead, and the skin on my face had never been so clear. The pores of my face had constantly emptied a steady flow of fluid into that handkerchief which I now wiped around the back of my neck to cool down. In my shirt pocket sat a small notebook which contained a collection of eclectic notes. I was wondering if I could formulate a story or two for a magazine - get some freelance work. Be like I was when I first left University, carefree and wild, able to punch well beyond my weight. Perhaps, I thought, I'll explore some travel magazine or other which didn't focus on muscular surfers and beach babes playing in the sun. Perhaps I'd try the middle-aged market; the market which was awash with disposable income – people like me. People who had seen life and yet still had a thirst for more, something cerebral. I'd done my fill of plastic boobs and vacuous blondes inside the Heffner mansion; from now on I was going to think about me.

"We are going to Palazzo Dario," my guide Giovanni said, as if I had some indication of what this might mean. "The," he paused to accentuate the word, "Palazzo Dario?" he repeated.

Again I said nothing because my ignorance was as it had been when I first heard those words. Had I known then what I know now my reaction would have been totally different.

The Grand Canal of Venice is without doubt a beautiful

place, a place of plenty, a place of refinement and a place where common folk had no right to the property which ran along the banks. These properties were reserved for the well heeled or the famous. The owners here, could play at being patrons of the arts, could live here happily eccentric among other strange incarnations. Strange Countesses whose servants served guests in the nude. Opera singers who took the sea air and tycoons who had made nonsensical volumes of money out of gadgets. The places were opulent, secluded and inaccessible, and we were cruising past all of them. Me a normal average Joe Smoe, with maybe my one chance to see the place before they threw sods on my box. I loved it - the way small canals drifted through the buildings and the bridges passed overhead; in parts the eerie silence unnerved me, but the structures delighted and enticed me too. Like a lover with a seductive smile who suddenly holds a knife to your throat to heighten the excitement in mid act. Venice had been everything I had expected and more.

"There," Giovanni pointed.

I could see nothing but a modest marble fronted building next door but one to the home of Peggy Guggenheim, which now housed her collection of modern art. A small building by Venetian standards, almost fragile like a house of cards. I was struggling with my memory, the Roladex of images flashing past and then repeating themselves, but I couldn't place it. I had seen this place before, there was an image that I could not quite recall. Like one of those lost memories, it would probably pop into my consciousness when least expected.

"Palazzo Dario," Giovanni announced, "an evil place."

Immediately my ears pricked up, "Evil?" I asked, "how so? It's just a house and a rather beautiful one at that."

The taxi driver had slowed the motor boat to drift speed and waited for Giovanni's instructions. My Italian was not good but there seemed to be some sort or exchange and argument which culminated in me having to give the driver an extra hundred Euro. I was for entering at the water level through the main arch but the driver was adamant that he would never do that. It had to be the end of the jetty or nothing. So the end of the jetty it was.

As the boat tore away into the heart of the canal, Giovanni looked at me and spoke almost with a whisper.

"This place the locals say is haunted, bewitched, bedevilled, possessed. I hope you do not believe in such idiocy?" he asked.

"Well thank you for asking ," I sarcastically replied. "Perhaps you should have asked me, before we got here, especially as the boat has now gone."

Giovanni nodded a muttering reply, suitably chastised.

I laughed loudly. "I am not superstitious, neither do I believe in the Devil, witches, or God for that matter and as for ghosts well that is almost absurd."

"I see then we are of the like mind," Giovanni laughed, but I could sense his unease at my remarks.

"So what is the story behind this place?" I asked almost nonchalantly.

In the bright sunlight with his back to the building he began his prepared history, to which I listened in detail.

"The house," he began, as my camera captured shot after shot, "was built in 1487 or 1488 by Pietro Lombardi. It was commissioned by Giovanni Dario." I smiled at the name. "Dario was a chancery secretary on the diplomatic missions to the Ottoman Empire. Venice traded a great deal with the Turks and many normal people made vast sums of money. Dario sank all of his into this place."

He turned to face the ornate marble which looked delicate like the frosted icing on a cake. It reminded me in part of the Duomo in Florence, the almost perfect marble carved and smoothed into a...

"It looks so fragile," he continued, "but the people say that Dario was a monster. A man who made his money out of deceit and slavery. There can be little doubt that his hands were soaked in blood. All the blood money he made he poured into this house.

There were some who said that he kept slave girls here, in this house, to wait upon him and serve his needs, and that was against the laws of the city. The Doge did nothing because Dario knew more than any man about their corruption and what he

133

could not use he could sell. Consequently, he was not liked, and some even feared him, but his house was constructed alongside the homes of the patricians and the nobility nonetheless. His presence was tolerated and yet they knew that their time would come to steal what was his."

"Claude Monet!" I suddenly exclaimed. "I knew I'd seen it somewhere."

My guide looked bemused.

"Monet painted this place sometime after 1900."

"That you should know this is amazing," my guide said. "Many people have come here and none knew of this before. Monet was a marvellous painter and you are right that he painted this house."

"But why, if the place is so evil?" I asked

"He loved this place. He could see it for what it is. It is a beautiful painting full of light and expression, he captured it just as it was. Though the balcony on the second piano nobile spoils the look and that was not there in the beginning. They put that up and spoilt the line."

"You know the painting?" I asked.

Giovanni nodded gleefully, "I know all about this house."

"Well are we going to get a look inside?" I asked.

"Are you sure you want to?" my guide replied with some trepidation. "I must warn you that this is not a place for the feint hearted. Only those with the strongest will can be trusted here."

"Absolutely," I replied, "now I'm here I want to see it all. I want to know all about the place. Want to hear every detail about it."

Giovanni nodded, "By the time we have finished," he said, " you will know as much about this house as I do. That much I can guarantee. Whether you will love as I do is another matter."

I have to admit at that stage I was intrigued by the obvious attempt of my guide to scare me. I had seen this before in both Egypt and Africa. An attempt to get the tourist enthralled to such an extent that they became engaged by their own mental hyperbole.

We began to walk under the large Doric doorway which had

a Gothic feel to it. I felt a sudden drop in temperature as the whole place seemed to darken. Giovanni's spirits seemed to lift and I noted that there would have been plenty of room for a water taxi to enter. That way we could have been in the heart of the building from the outset, but of course Giovanni would not have been able to extend and excite the narrative before we entered. I smiled a knowing smile. As a guide he was good at what he did; he had done something similar on Torcello and he must have noticed my response. Here again he was employing the same technique.

Two sets of staircases led from the central entrance moorings bay directly to the second floor, one to the left and one to the right. The ceiling was vast and cavernous a lacework pattern of marble and plaster, painted in hues of deep blue with golden stars. The expensive blue of lapis-lazuli shone above me; ground blue rock painstaking crushed in a mortar and pestle and then mixed with egg yoke and olive oil; finally applied in a blanket of translucent layers and interspersed with gold leaf – it was stunning. Dark, imposing and supremely beautiful. The camera flashed in the darkness and as it did so the whole area was lit with a brief radiant beauty. The opulence of the gold stung my eyes and I saw in the instant that the design was familiar and mesmerising.

"This is stunning," I said, "like in Florence, there is a chamber just like this there."

"I know," Giovanni mocked in reply. "And where do you think those damned Medici got their inspiration from? Money lenders and traders and thieves to boot." He was almost spitting now and his jaw clenched as if set against some imminent attack. His eyes widened and flashed in the darkness.

"The Palazzo Vecchio, the chamber of the sun? Or is it the council chamber? I can't remember the name."

"You have been to Florence?" he casually asked, his composure returning.

"Three times," I offered. "It is a beautiful city."

"I agree," he nodded, "but we must not compare this place with there."

"Why not?" I innocently enquired.

"Why?" he was becoming laconic, "because a diamond cannot be compared to a pearl, either in wealth or beauty," came his rather cryptic reply.

"But which is which?" I asked mockingly.

His voice raised and his jaw clenched, "How can one compare the money lender to the entrepreneur?"

"But surely both are needed to achieve the dizzy heights of ultimate success?"

"Bah," was all he said in reply, and even that was expelled as if he sighed the word under his breath.

The columns beside each set of stairs were laced in green and red, set with gargoyle faces painted in a dark relief trompe l'oeil which made them seem alive. Leering faces with eyes which seemed to follow those that entered wherever they went. At one point I was almost certain that one of the figures moved but then laughed at the ridiculousness of my own imagination. The air was still and a chill breeze entered the building despite the heat of the Venetian day which was now driving others to seek shelter from the raging sun. Seagulls bobbed on the water and seemed oblivious to the rumours which surrounded this house, and I too was thankful for the cooling wind.

Each stairway was shaped and rounded like a dark cave or cavern with a light fitting at its centre. The walls were decorated with fine murals which contained faces and ferocious figures of torment. The overall effect was one of entering a place unbidden and I could feel my breathing change in pace. The monsters looked on as I followed my guide into the darkness.

The lights hung like ornaments pierced into an epiglottis within a throat, only exposed now by a gigantic yawn. I was immediately reminded of a tongue upon which I, the unwary visitor had stepped. The terracotta tile steps stretched out before me and enveloped and enticed me toward the throat. I had a distinct feeling of unease, as if I might be a morsel of food wriggling for life before being plunged into the peristaltic darkness of the entry way. I was aware of a sudden sound of movement behind me and as I turned the water of the canal lapped a foot or two higher in the mooring area; and I would swear that it was the house salivating, or at least drowning in a guttural watery laugh.

"Come we shall go to the first piano," Giovanni coerced. "The most beautiful of rooms is there and I can tell you much more of the history of this building." And with that he jumped one or two stairs at a time to lead the way while I came a little less eagerly after him.

III

The first room we entered was magnificent, opulent gold and reds greeted my eyes and the colours flickered from the many candles which adorned the room. It felt like I was inside Christmas, with a warm glow of light all about me. Everything seemed to reflect as if a thousand glass blown baubles hung around the room; mirrors reflected back my own image which seemed to me to be less care worn. Even my hair had turned back toward the dark mousy brown, which it had been in my thirties, and the lines around my eyes seemed less pronounced. The room had a magical almost mythical quality. A fairy tale – I was inside a fairy tale.

"Amazing," I blurted, "absolutely amazing."

"It is," my guide smiled.

"It is? Is that all you can say? It's stunning I don't think I have seen anything like this anywhere." I wanted to add, except in Florence, but thought better of it considering my guide's reaction the last time I mentioned the Medici.

"You forget," he laughed, "I have seen this room so many times over the years. To me it is as familiar as if it were my home."

"What a place!" I exclaimed.

Giovanni let out a huge laugh and lifted his arms in acclamation and then turned three hundred and sixty degrees, at least three times. His face was lifted to the ceiling and his head tilted back with his eyes closed, as if he were in ecstasy.

"Welcome to Venice," he said, "and having now seen the beauty of home, never leave." He lowered his face and caught my eye, which unnerved me a little, "Venice is the kind of place that one can stay in forever," he paused, "if circumstance allows."

The ceilings were like something I had seen before and yet they were different; I was trying to place them but the location simply would not come. The room was bedecked in silks and the furniture was exquisite. On the walls hung carpets from Asia, highly decorative and yet somehow ancient and new simultaneously, as if they had been there for centuries, or placed yesterday. The room seemed dusty, but newly cleaned and the air clung like the fog of a damp winter morning, but light bounced in every direction. Ridiculous as it might seem, the room was cold, and yet it was intensely inviting, with a roaring log fire blazing in the central hearth. Everything seemed to be in diametric opposites, one huge oxymoronic work of enriching enchantment and fearful foreboding. It felt like my senses and my mind were struggling to assimilate the difference between the actual and the fictional. Things did not make sense. From the outside, the building looked abandoned, disembowelled, but now inside I was a child back in the world of childish fairytales.

Giovanni sat in a chair and threw one leg over the arm as if he were about to settle to watch an evening of TV in carpet slippers. I wondered at his disregard for the property of the owners and was about to ask more, when he launched into his prepared piece on the history of the building.

"The ceilings," he began, "are by Marco Cozzi and that," he pointed to a large painting which could be seen in a further room in the distance, "is by Vivarini."

"Who owns all of this?" I asked.

"Owns it?"

"Well I suppose I do," he replied.

"You do? Then why are you a tour guide?"

"That is to say we all do. All Venetians…"

"So it's a public asset then. A museum?" I interrupted him.

"You could say that."

"But we didn't pay to get in?"

"In Venice," he smirked, "one has to pay to leave, not to enter."

I took him at his word but had seen no other living being in the place, though I thought I heard voices from time to time. Voices of people who seemed to be looking for an exit or an attendant and were arguing as they did so. I presumed that some museum attendant would eventually usher them to the exit where upon the tax, or exit fee would be hefty. Venetians seemed to have learned long ago that enticing a person into a museum was the key and therefore often did not publicly display entry prices. A clever ploy to get the bodies across the threshold, but it did leave a bad aftertaste when the experience was over.

"This place is amazing, who designed it?" I asked.

Giovanni continued without answering my direct question. "Giovanni Dario was an unusual man," he began, "in that he was not a patrician but merely a humble citizen of the Republic. He made a small fortune in the missions to the Ottoman Empire. There were some who said he was a monster, trading women and young boys as sexual slaves to the wealthy, but that was always a rumour and never proven. There were many patricians who indulged in all sorts of practices which we today might find immoral, but you have to remember that times were different then and no man can be judged beyond the standards of his day. Slavery was not illegal and many women, girls, and boys for that matter, were sold for pleasure at that time."

I sat in a high backed chair and stared silently at the sheer beauty of the ceiling as my guide continued.

"The house did not stay in the Dario family for long, and many have said that was because he was not a patrician and Venice has the soul of a wealthy man. So the Barbaro family bought the property and for centuries it remained in their hands until death duties and the twenty first century came and the property had to be sold again."

I had heard the name Barbaro before, but was struggling to place it among so many which I had learned since coming to Venice. Then the penny dropped and I realised, The Albergo, my hotel, was called the Albergo Barbaro-Bertellini.

"So my hotel is owned by the Barbaro family?" I asked.

He nodded.

"So they owned this place?"

He nodded again.

"Ah, I understand, they sold it on, but they can do tours around it?"

Giovanni continued without replying, "That was when the history of this house was sealed. Henry James the writer described the place as a house of playing-cards, which might fall at any touch and he lived with the owners for a while, whilst in Italy on his grand tour. And, as you said, Claude Monet painted it in 1908, but the real claim to fame has been the string of unfortunate incidents which have occurred to the owners of the property since the Barbaro family were forced to sell it. They had invested centuries of work in the place and it is steeped in their history."

"Are you a Barbaro?" I asked, "Giovanni, are you related?"

My guide gave a broad smile, "Would that I were," he replied, "then there would be no need for me to be your guide. I would be able to invite you here as my guest. This house is now owned by an American family." He concluded, answering my original question, with a further broad smile. "The house has been full of suicides, murders and ac-ci-dents," he stretched the word so as to accentuate it. "But since the American in 2006 no strange things have happened," he paused, "yet."

It was clear from his delivery that I was the sap who now had to ask for the story to continue. I wondered if he might be expecting me to pay him extra to complete it, but once I issued my unpaid request he happily began once again.

"The room over there," he pointed, "Count Filippo Giordano delle Lanze, had his skull smashed in by his lover. The lover claimed that he had not been responsible, but no other person had been near the house and he had been the only other occupant. You might know of your playwright Joe Orton and the lovers spat which cost him his life? This was similar, so similar in fact that it was almost identical. In that room," he pointed again, "the sister of Fabrizio Ferrari was murdered. Her throat was cut from ear to ear and the floorboards so soaked in blood that the stains are there to this day. In that room the Englishman Rawdon Lubbock Brown committed suicide. Over there is the room in which the manager of the pop group The Who slept shortly before his fatal fall after leaving the Palazzo. In the fifth room there," he pointed once again, "a local prostitute was found bound and gagged and kept in a cage when the owners had left for a tour of Africa. When the family returned the putrid corpse was already maggot ridden and stinking and the resultant scandal made that owner sell up and leave Venice. He claimed he knew nothing about it. That the prostitute and the cage were somehow imported into the property whilst he was away. Nobody believed him of course, and some said he had a predilection for bondage games with young girls. That type of Chinese whispering has always attached itself to the owners of this house; some have even said it is alive. This house has a history like no other – it has a soul."

As I watched him tell the tale his body shifted excitedly in the chair and he seemed to be almost enjoying the sensational stories of those who died and those who experienced exiling scandal.

"So everyone who ever came to live in this place met with a sticky end?"

He gave me a quizzical look, "Sticky end?"

"It means unfortunate accident," I tried to explain; "like the stickiness of blood I suppose is what that refers to."

"Blood is very sticky that is so," he agreed standing and admiring the room again.

It was then that I noticed the odd arrangement of the rooms. A central cavernous room from which five small rooms led. I was trying to place the shape in my mind.

"So nothing happened in this room?" I asked.

"There are always more stories to tell," he replied.

"More stories?" I quizzed.

"Your Mrs. Browning, the wife of General Browning she came here. And she gained inspiration, though this is not Manderley."

My mind was racing, jumping from clue to clue. Browning gave me nothing except, a bridge too far and operation market garden. Manderley gave me Rebecca and that brought me to DuMaurier.

"Nicolas Roeg came here too."

Now I was lost. What did a film director have to do with this Palazzo?

"Walkabout?" I blurted, "I thought that was Australia." All the while my mind was trying to erase the thought of a teenage Jenny Agutter swimming naked in a blue lagoon.

"Don't Look Now," he almost squealed in triumph. "A film made by Roeg and based upon the short story by Daphne DuMaurier. The action takes place in the alleys of Venice. The dark alleys of ancient history. Those eerie alleys which hold all the old secrets."

"But that was a horror story," I replied.

"More of a psychological toying with the mind? I thought."

"Precisely," he smiled and hissed in reply.

"So how does that fit in with the history of this place?"

He smiled again and simply answered, "Shall we go to the second piano?"

IV

On the second floor I was guided through a further six rooms which I found hard to assimilate with the square exterior of the square marble façade, which faced out on to the Grand Canal. I felt as if I were inside an Escher painting; running up descending stairs; looking at flat rooms in three dimensions; while the perspective bounced me from wall to wall. I can honestly say that I have never experienced anything like it either before or since. It seemed to me that the place inside was not at all in the shape of the building outside, and that the five rooms and one central chamber, one floor below, felt totally at odds with the design above. What made it worse was the series of interlocking doors and passageways which could mislead and confuse. From the outside the building appeared to me to be small, compact and neat, from the inside totally the opposite, large, substantial and disjointed.

The light of the day was beginning to fade and I had lost all track of time. My guide seemed completely disinterested and the more the building darkened and became oppressive to me, the more light and airy his manner became. We were now seated again and I could see quite plainly the traffic on the canal below and the balcony which lay directly in front of me.

"Ugly isn't it?" Giovanni asked.

"No it's beautiful. The canal and the hustle and bustle of river traffic," I replied.

"Not the sea, the balcony?" he snapped.

"I suppose it is a little. It doesn't fit in."

"Precisely," he muttered, "it doesn't fit in. Doesn't fit in with the design at all. My design was perfect, is perfect."

We were sitting on two large oak chairs and the manner of his reply startled me somewhat, if not un-nerved me.

"Your design?" I asked casually.

"That's what you have been looking at all day," he replied. "And I believe you called it beautiful did you not?" His voiced hissed at me as if he were a serpent.

It was not the word, design, nor the word beautiful, which made me start. It was the simple possessive, "my," which stood out from all of his talk. It rang in my ears like a peel of bells. How could the house be his?

"This is meant to be my house," he said. "My house," and as he spoke his eyes grew red in the darkness. "There needs to be rumour here, rumour of death and haunting or they will rip it to pieces. They will remove the heart and replace it with a box which ticks money. Patricians are all the same – greedy. Why should I not keep that which is rightfully mine?"

I began to wonder if I were in the presence of a lunatic.

"You see the chair you are sitting in?" he questioned, "that was the chair in which the fat Barbaro sat and laughed after he had acquired this house from my weak-willed son. I would have been better to have kept the boy child of my slave, and made him my rightful heir, rather than drown them both in the Canal. Then at least some of my seed would have been carried forward. What did he do, that vacuous fop of a boy, my boy? Lost it all in less than a generation. Gambled away his inheritance and ruined himself in the process."

"This house is yours?" I asked lamely. My lips felt like lead in the growing darkness.

"The fat and indolent slug Barbaro. I spit on his name and I curse his family forever. A cheat, a slug, which should have been left in the sunlight to shrivel and die. He above all the others could not stand a common man like me to own a riverside property. What was he? Nothing! A man born from the slut of a mother, a whore; a whore who had been the pleasure hole of many." Giovanni's temper was rising and with it his whole stature seemed to grow and the air became close about him. "And his wine soaked swine of a father? A few generations back they were clearing the shit pipes which ran into the canals. Their main companions were the plague rats; carrion they should be carrion. The Barbaro were scum, pure robbing scum. Whores and thieves the lot of them, I curse them all. I cut his throat with this."

From behind his back he produced what looked like a small carving knife. He lifted it to his throat and imitated the action of cutting across the Adam's apple.

"He bled like a pig," my guide continued, "fell to the floor like a lead weight and his eyes begged me to let him live. Laying there in his own urine, he gargled and choked in his own froth as I kicked the life out of him."

Giovanni stamped his foot three times like Rumplestiltskin and then rose, "And now you," he said. "You have to be the silly tourist who mysteriously loses his life in the evil Palazzo Dario. No one must live here. For centuries I have guarded this place, and for centuries I will continue."

"But I am no Patrician," I answered as swiftly as I could think. "I am just like you a common man who has had his way barred on several occasions. Are we not one and the same type of person?"

"This house belongs to me; it can never belong to any other. Your death will simply be useful just like the others. It feeds the legend."

"But, I don't deserve to die." I could hear myself pleading.

"Deserve has nothing to do with it. Did I deserve to die? To catch the plague from the rats? There were many who survived that deserved death, and many who deserved life that died. My daughter was one such and had she lived then the Palazzo might have lived with her. She was the true re-creation of my being." He reflected as if recollecting a pleasant memory from long ago, "We are all pawns in the human race, but we do not know what we are racing against. All I know is that this house is part of me, it has my soul – it belongs to the rightful owner, me; and like me you must die."

With that he lunged toward me with a sudden and violent impulse.

At this stage of my tale I do not mind admitting how scared I was. My face had lost all of the natural colour, the ruddiness which was so part of my general characteristics. I was without doubt in the presence of a complete lunatic and one who believed he was the original Giovanni Dario. For the first time in a long time I could feel my heart race as it pounded against the inside of my rib-cage. In my clumsy attempt to escape the lunatic's blade, the chair in which I was sitting fell backward with a resounding thump.

"My house," he hissed at me as his ice-cold fingers grabbed my throat and the knife plunged into the oak chair no more than two inches from my right eye. I could feel his weight upon me as he prepared for a second and possibly the fatal strike.

That was enough for me and I spun first left and then right, to loose myself from his grip, which was both steadfast and merciless. In the quick wriggling struggle I became like a Dervish possessed, in the process both my camera and notebook fell to the floor. I was on my feet now but there seemed to be no direction in which to run. Time seemed to remain still, I was disorientated, confused, but like any mammal fighting for life, energy reserves became sudden and immense. The room seemed to be spinning and the doors changing their places. Again the knife plunged into the chair, this time close to my leg. Giovanni's face had turned into the face of some kind of maniacal demon; his eyes were aflame and his mouth frothing. I was convinced that this was the room in which I was going to die, and this lunatic was to be my final undoing. Then I saw the one spot which seemed to be a constant in the whirling maelstrom of my life versus death struggle – the balcony. It stood still, while the rest of the building seemed to swirl about it like snow blown in a storm around the base of a steadfast, mighty oak. I could see the rail in black cold metal but the features of the walls were moving, closing in upon me like some folding carton which was going to envelop my being. I had the feeling which I thought prey must feel as it is swallowed whole. I was the mouse which the snake was about to devour, the poor petrified mouse and Giovanni was the lunatic snake with a knife.

I leapt to my feet and threw myself forward using every once of will-power I possessed. Giovanni gave one last reactive stab at my ankle as he lay on the floor and cut a deep gash across both my trouser leg and soft canvas shoe. The pain was instant and terrifyingly real and that snapped me back into reality and spurred me on. One, two, three, four, five strides and then the cold metal met my hand and I grasped life once more.

As I leapt over the rail and plunged toward the Canal below the warmth of the day instantly hit me once again. Light punished my eyes – the hot afternoon sun, white clear, blinding. I was in the water now thrashing as I rose to the surface – gasping, breathing heavily. Behind me I would swear that I heard a howl like that of a lone wolf bemoaning escaped prey and then just as swiftly sudden silence. For a brief second the world stood still as if time and motion had ceased and then, like the flick of a switch, normality resumed. I was swimming now, kicking off my shoes as I went, aiming for the opposite bank as fast as I could possibly manage. My breath was short and my arms heavy in the salt of the Adriatic and although a good swimmer, by most standards, I felt that I would not make the far bank.

Fortunately for me that was when the motor boat arrived. The blue and grey of the police launch, and the wailing siren was an instant comfort to me. It was as I had always said, the unbidden arrival of the police in an emergency is always well met, but unbidden in interference less sought after.

"Get that idiot out," a proud and commanding voice ordered. "He's probably a drunk - a tourist. Get a line under his arms before the current sweeps him away."

I felt my body being lifted and as I left the canal a spray of blood leapt into the air from the deep gash to my lower leg.

"He's injured Sergeant," one of the officers yelled. "Bleeding everywhere."

I could feel my heart slowing and the shock of the wound pull me toward unconsciousness. I was fighting to stay lucid.

"There's a lunatic in the Palazzo Dario. He's got a knife," I squealed, as they bound a cord around my leg, just above the knee. "He's mad, tried to kill me. Tried to stab me."

I saw the Sergeant wave a second launch toward the Palazzo and then my resolve vanished.

V

When I came around I was in a hospital bed. A bed made up of crisp white sheets and hygienic smells. I was in a surgical gown and my arm punctured by a drip which fed fluid into my dehydration. Realisation dawned upon me as I reasoned that I must have passed out once aboard the motor launch. The combination of adrenalin, shock and intense pain must have driven my body into shut-down mode. I wondered how much blood I had lost from the wound to my foot. I tried to calculate my time in the water, and as I thought, I could not even place the approximate length of time inside the building, let alone in the water.

"That was a lucky escape," said a bland voice. "Nasty wound, that, very deep, twelve stitches, but it could have been worse. There are large boats which go up and down the canal. Not a good place to go for a swim. You could have been chopped into fish food. Tourists don't swim and certainly not in the Grand Canal. What precisely were you attempting to do in all of your clothes? Cool off?"

I could see the man in front of me now as my eyes re-focused and tried to read the name label above his shirt pocket. I thought it read Barbaro, but I was not totally sure if I was awake or dreaming. He was dark haired and his facial features looked somehow familiar. A squat nose and fat features made him look dispassionate, but his eyes were deep brown and warm.

"I wasn't swimming," I replied, "I fell."

The man did not seem to believe me.

"Honest I was in the Palazzo Dario and I jumped from the balcony into the water."

"Just a moment or two ago you said you fell. Now you say you jumped. Which is it?" he asked quizzically.

I knew that his interrogation of me would be close when he

picked up on the differences in my choice of words. His English was superb and he knew precisely what to look for in the nuances of word choice. Immediately my mind began to increase in speed and my recollection sharpen. I was wondering if I was being investigated, interrogated, or merely tolerated as a tourist simpleton.

"There was a lunatic after me with a knife. That's how I got the wound. There's a lunatic on the loose in your city. He works as a tour guide for the Barbaro-Bertellini Hotel. Giovanni, he told me he was Giovanni Dario. He said he owned the Palazzo."

The police officer said nothing.

"My name is Richard; I have rooms at the Barbaro-Bertellini Hotel. I have been in Venice for a few days. They will know me there," I added in desperation. "It is not me who is crazy. Shouldn't you be over there right now? Look," I continued, "my camera must still be there. I lost it in the struggle. It will be behind one of the oak chairs."

"At the present time sir, your clothes are being examined and we shall take you first to your hotel, to verify who you are and to collect dry ones and then on to Palazzo Dario to retrieve your camera. But you must know that the building is empty at the moment and is being renovated. There will be no furniture in the place."

"Rubbish," I replied, "I was there just a few hours ago. It is decorated exquisitely, tapestries all over the walls and the place looks amazing. There must be furniture there. How long have I been here?"

"We fished you out on Monday and today is Wednesday."

"Two days?" I squealed, "two days? What the hell happened?"

The police officer nodded but I had the distinct impression that he knew something I did not and that he was waiting for me to make a further error of some kind. I began to wonder why my clothes were being, "examined," and I felt rather than knew there was something else.

When finally I did get taken back to my Hotel, the guide Giovanni was not known to anyone on the staff. I tried to reason with them, that he had been sent to my room to guide me around the city for a few days-compliments of the hotel. No one however, seemed to have heard of him. Though the staff did say that they had seen me with an old man on a couple of occasions. A man with grey hair and a very odd old fashioned Venetian accent.

I tried, via lengthy explanations, to describe the man with whom I had visited Palazzo Dario and Torcello and Murano, but my remonstrations fell on deaf ears. The person I described was not known and on the islands we had visited, had gone unnoticed.

The situation at the Palazzo was even more astounding. The place was totally empty. Cement mixers stood where the terracotta tiled stairs once were and a lift shaft rose into the heart of the building. There was not a stick of furniture, no wall hangings and no trace of the rooms I had seen. The whole building was set squarely into the shape of the outside. The ceilings were light and plain. The whole building was bare and the gargoyles had gone too.

"This is ridiculous," I remonstrated, "absurd, totally absurd. When I was here, there were wall hangings and the ceiling was blue and gold and there were chairs and things and the rooms were a different shape. They were in the shape of a," I paused searching for the right descriptive word. Suddenly the word, which had eluded me in Giovanni's presence, popped into my consciousness, "A pentangle. Five rooms all running off a central chamber."

There, like some flash of inspiration I had recalled the shape - a pentangle. At that point I realised just how ridiculous I must seem to a man who dealt with facts and fine detail. A pentangle, the shape of the Devil and ancient witchcraft - I shuddered. The policeman made notes, but I could tell that he thought me unbalanced, strange, perhaps even a lunatic myself, a man who was given to bouts of exaggeration. I wondered how many other strange visitors this ancient city accumulated in the space of one season.

"Are you sure it was this building?" the policeman asked, stressing the this, as if I might be mistaken.

I nodded, "I'm absolutely certain. We came by taxi and if we could find that driver then he could verify we arrived together." As the hollow words left my lips I knew that the task would be impossible. It would be easier to find a needle in a …

"So you arrived and the rooms were a different shape and then a man with a knife attacked you?" The policeman was writing now.

I could tell that the whole incident was beginning to look more and more like some fantasy. The more I said the less likely it seemed.

"Why would I make this up?" I asked.

"Attention?" was the curt reply I received. "A short burst of glory?"

"Look I'm not some crazy neurotic," I blurted in surprised anger. "Some bloody idiot with a knife came at me and I have the wound to prove it."

"But are you sure it was here?" the police officer asked again. "There are so many buildings and on a hot day perhaps one looked just like another. The place you described is more like a museum than a home."

"You may think I am mad," I snapped back at him, "but I am as sane as the next man."

"Little do we know who the next man is," he replied, without a tinge of emotion in his voice.

"Well I know what I saw," I spat out in reply, "and you might think I am crazy but I know I'm not. And this is the place. I was here and I jumped from that balcony on the second floor."

"Then there should be blood?" The officer stated. "On the floor and on the rail? Shall we go and see?"

"You've already checked, haven't you?" I asked.

He nodded.

"And there isn't any blood is there?"

He shook his head.

"And you think that I'm confused, disorientated, or worse?"

The officer shrugged, "We are here and there is no evidence that this incident you spoke of occurred."

"Then what do you call this?" I pointed at the bandages

around my ankle from which a small crimson stain had seeped. "Scotch sodding mist?"

"Sir," the policeman became formal, "that kind of language will serve no purpose and you must agree that your whole story seems a little implausible."

"I know what I saw."

"And yet there is no physical evidence. No camera, no notebook? Might I suggest we take you back to your hotel and then you can rest before having that wound redressed in the morning?"

Reluctantly I nodded in agreement, and lamented the loss of both my camera and note book. I expected that my camera had already been sold by someone - perhaps even one of the police.

VI

After the police launch had delivered me back to my hotel, I took to my room.

Wrapping a large plastic dry-cleaning bag around my leg I stood in the shower as the warm water coursed over me. The ankle was a constant reminder of my sanity, even if the police now believed I was – delusional.

I towelled myself down and shaved in the warm sunlight before drifting into sleep in the clean bed which shrouded my nakedness. I was certain this had not been a hallucination.

I woke with a ravenous hunger and a pain in my ankle the like of which I had never experienced before. On closer examination my mobility had been considerably impaired by swelling and the bandage turned from white to a darker dull brown.

Reaching for a bottle of water, which sat by the side of the bed, I studied my watch trying to work out which side of midnight I was on. I sat up and propped myself against the headboard. It was then that I noticed my small notebook which lay on the seat of the armchair facing me and my camera which sat on the arm, like a single lid-less eye. A sudden chill ran through me and I jumped to the door which had been fastened as I slept - it was still locked.

I picked up the phone and spoke with the receptionist. She confirmed that the items had been delivered to the hotel earlier in the day – whilst I had been with the police. They had been delivered to the concierge who had then placed them in my room. Why I had not noticed them she had no idea.

"Who delivered them?" I asked. "At what time?"

The receptionist asked me to hold. When the concierge answered his words made me almost apoplectic with fear.

"The older gentleman," he said, "the one I saw you with

earlier in the week, he delivered them here. He said you had left them behind."

"Did he come into this room?" I asked.

"No sir, that is against the hotel policy."

"So who put them in my room?"

"The maid sir, I believe."

I picked up the camera and was rewinding the film as fast as I could, while I jammed the receiver between by shoulder and ear. "Do you know anywhere I can get a film developed now?" I asked.

"We do know of a facility," he replied.

"I can't walk, can anyone get it over there and back for me?" I requested with a slight tinge of the pathetic in my voice.

Ten minutes later the bell-boy appeared, and I told him that if he could both deliver and collect for me then there would be a € 50 tip in it for him. No sooner had I said it, he was gone with the speed of a bullet. I, in the meantime, examined the wound on my leg - out of curiosity. I unwound the bandages and removed the lint which covered the neat stitches. They formed the definite shape of a capital script letter D. It was like some crude gothic stamp carved into my flesh and I shuddered at the thought of what I recalled. Had I not been looking at the evidence and feeling the pain with my own nerve endings I too might have thought it some delirious dream.

When the bell-boy returned with my prize of 15 photographs, true to my word I rewarded the young man with € 50 as promised. As I closed the door I began to tremble at the thought of examining the prints which I now held.

I laid them face down on the bed and then poured myself a large double Scotch from the mini-bar. Part of me wanted not to view them, the other, more inquisitive part, wanted to go to it straight away. For some totally unrelated reason I thought of how the American Indians had refused to have their photographs taken in case it captured their souls. I was reminded of chief Crazy Horse, the victor at the Little Big Horn, and whose picture does not exist. Perhaps he had feared for his soul; perhaps, I thought irrationally, these pictures might take mine. Absurd I know, but my reason and sanity were becoming clouded. I poured another Scotch and turned over the first image.

It showed the outside of the Palazzo – I was there. I now had evidence that this was no hallucination, no dream. I took another gulp and turned over the second – blank. The third – blank. The fourth also blank. Then with complete abandon and renewed confidence, bolstered up by the liquor, I turned over the next few. The blue ceiling appeared, the rich silks and wall hangings and finally the long view with the Vivarini painting. There were now only two images remaining and I knew, no, that would be the wrong word, I feared, what the content would be.

The first would be of the central room on the second floor, resplendent in all its glory. As I turned the penultimate photograph the image which met my eyes was clear, bright and instantly recognisable. It was that room, the one in which I had been attacked. There were no tools, no cement mixers, here was the room precisely as I had seen it, and remembered it, and reported it to the police. Now I had it recorded on my very own film.

The final image was the one which I most dreaded, the face of my assailant Giovanni seated in one of the ornate oak chairs. As I turned it fully my hand began to tremble.

The image was not clear but it was instantly recognisable to me. There seated like some ancient potentate sat the figure of Giovanni Dario. The image was blurred and not well framed but I could see the man as clear as day. Here was my evidence which I would take to the Questura the following day. This would prove that I was sane and that, strange as it might seem, I was in that Palazzo. The photographs now proved it.

At dinner I sat and ate heartily. I wanted to laugh out loud and prove that I was still totally sane. A mixture of meats drowned in oil, served with oiled artichokes and Ciabbata bread, crisp and airy as only the Italians can produce. This was followed by pasta – linguini with scallops and squid, washed down with Valpolicella, sparkling water and one or two further whiskies. Dalwhinnie, a fifteen year old malt which tasted of the highlands and heather and although I am not a Scot it gave me the feeling of being home. I have always been a man of simple tastes, and the thought of some heavy pudding filled me with dread, while the heady aromatic whisky numbed the pain in my ankle and relaxed my very soul.

I talked with the other English tourists in the restaurant of the hotel and had almost forgotten my trials and tribulations of the last few days as we conversed. I spoke of the beauty of Torcello and how that island, along with the glass blowers of Murano were a must. They listened as I talked of the must sees, but as the evening drew to a close I thought it best that I retire, sleep well and clear my head before taking my, "evidence," to the Questura the following morning. I was imagining the look on the Sergeant's face as I produced it. The slight look of shock intermingled with horror. He would then have to accept that there was a lunatic on the loose.

I stumbled into the elevator, the first time since being at the hotel. I am, as I have already stated, a little corpulent for my age and one of the minor life-style changes I had instigated was to use stairs whenever possible. My meagre attempt at burning off the unwanted calorie or two. However, tonight, due to the leg, I was in the lift.

On the third floor the door opened and the lift attendant helped me clear. It was then that I saw him - Giovanni Dario, as clear as if he had been standing right before me. The shock made me step back and I almost fell.

There to the right of the lift hung his portrait encased in a gold frame.

"Can I get you a chair?" the attendant asked.

I shook my head. "That painting?" I asked as I pointed.

"Yes, it is rather scary isn't it?" the attendant smiled. "Eyes that follow you everywhere, creepy, but it's just a copy I'm afraid. The real works of art for the city are in the Gallerie dell'Accademia. The original of this is there. I think it was painted in 1500 or so. Giovanni Dario, the man who had the Palazzo, just over the way built." The man lowered his voice, "Apparently there was some sort of feud between the two families and well... The Barbaro family bought the place and all the artworks in it. There was a huge painting by Vivarini that's at the Academy now too."

The face I could see was the same face that had stared at me from the photograph which now lay in my room. My reaction was instant - flight. I removed myself to my room as far away as possible from the leering eyes of the portrait which followed me. They drilled into my back until I turned and hobbled Byron-like to the shelter of my room. I wondered who the painter might be? Thought of Velazquez and the portrait of Pope Innocent the tenth; the portrait which hangs in the Doria Pamphili Palazzo in Rome. Those eyes, dark and sensuous, eyes which follow you - it was a forbidding image. That image was rapidly replaced by Francis Bacon's screaming Popes and my inability to think lucidly.

At the Questura offices the following morning I triumphantly produced the photographs and negatives for the investigating Sergeant, who, to his credit did see me, after a thirty minute wait.

"I think you'll be surprised," I snorted. "My camera turned up yesterday, returned to my hotel anonymously. And before you ask, I don't know who or how or why it turned up, but it did."

He waited before he spoke.

"I had the film developed and there are images of the Palazzo and the man I saw and there is a portrait of him at the Academy and you can compare the two. It will prove that I am not a liar. And that I'm not barking mad."

I passed the unopened packet to the man in triumph and casually he flipped from one image to another and then finally lifted the negatives to the light.

"Are you taking the piss out of me?" he asked, scowling. "Is this some kind of sick joke?"

"What do you mean?" I replied in horror. "Those pictures show it all. The blue ceiling and the furniture - just like I described it. The oak chairs? The reds and golds and all the candles, it's all there. Now do you believe me? Giovanni Dario is the same man."

"Really?" he quizzed. "Then how come there are no images of him here?"

"What? That's impossible!" I exclaimed, snatching the photographs from his hand and examining the fifteen glossies – each was blank.

* * *

That was the last morning I spent in Venice and I have no desire to return, either in the long or short term. Of all the places on this earth never have I been so certain of my sanity. Nothing on God's earth, nor all the tea in China would lure me back to that spot on Dorsoduro. There is something evil which resides there; something best left well alone.

I packed in less than an hour and the Nikon camera, which I once prized so highly, is now at the bottom of the Grand Canal.

I was at Palazzo Dario; Giovanni Dario did attack me and I have the D shaped scar to prove it. The Questura were glad to see the back of what they thought was a crazy English tourist. The Hotel is still there and so is his portrait.

I have no witnesses, no evidence, no photographs - but I was there. So was the man who designed and built his Palazzo on the banks of the Grand Canal, over 500 years ago. I met him, talked with him and saw the result of his life's work. It was beautiful and dreadful with an attraction like some hypnotic predator. I did not hallucinate, or dream it as some people have tried to establish. And I didn't cut my foot and pass out and fall into the water. I jumped and I'd jump again. Giovanni Dario nearly killed me – I escaped.

And I am a sane man.

a perpetual harvest

l.amond 2010

Some there are that hide,
they hide among us and we pass them by.

A Perpetual Harvest

Father Peter Denker was a priest - a Catholic priest, but his real expertise lay in the production of rhubarb. Rhubarb which was firm, glossy and red stalked, topped by dark green leaf which hung like palms over the patch of land he used: His allotment.

On Sundays he carried the gold cross at the top of a tall, thin pole as he led his congregation to mass. The congregation had increased five fold since his arrival six years earlier. Everyone attributed church growth to his charisma. The Diocese had offered him a larger church, more salary, but he had been adamant: He wanted to stay there.

His masses were earthy, filled with incense, joy and inspiration. He ran the Sunday school classes with devotion and provided tea, coffee and biscuits for all the helpers. Sometimes he did bacon sandwiches and winter hot chocolate for the pupils. His milk bills were huge and he gave back more than he took from the congregation. At Christmas he made mince pies and mulled wine, which he and the parishioners drank before midnight mass. The teenagers, who supervised the younger children during the adult service, he paid, out of his own meagre pocket; the younger children all got a chocolate bar at the end of Sunday school. Everybody loved his manner and the way he genuinely cared for all people around him. In consequence, he was given a free Turkey at Christmas, which he then gave to a poor family of seven whose father had died in the war. Cheeses he kept and any home made wine too. That was his only weakness. He also liked a beer and on some hot sunny summer afternoons he could be seen in the allotment with his sleeves rolled up and his forehead sweating; that was when he liked a beer. A cold bottle of beer, preferably German and slightly sweet on the palate.

During the week he visited the sick, the lame, the dying and the elderly. He was tireless as he cycled from house to house or in bad weather used his van. He arranged for hospital visits, meals on wheels, free school meals and a myriad of other services for his flock. His white van, his gardening van he called it, was often seen out and about and nobody took any notice now. In fact he was out and about so much that he could not be missed. He added myth and legend to the whole process; saying his van was full of the secrets which had given him the best rhubarb prize at the county fair every year for the past five years.

His rhubarb was the envy of all.

The small seaside village of Crofton had once been a rural community, comprised of a few farms adjacent to Titchfield village. It had been an important place six hundred years ago, but now the surrounding towns of Gosport and Fareham had encroached and it had become a dormitory. Once there had been a mill, driven by water power and an iron foundry, the first iron foundry at the start of the industrial revolution, now it had returned to slumber.

The Church of the Immaculate Conception had occupied the same site since before the reformation, tucked away along a side road. Catholic or not it had managed to go untouched and essentially unharmed, due to the patronage of the Earl of Southampton during the reign of Elizabeth I.

Paul Denker had inherited that tradition when he moved to the manse, the tied house which came with the position of parish priest. He had the allotment at the back of the house. Allotment is not nearly the correct description. It was a strip of secluded land solely for the use of the manse occupier to grow vegetables and keep livestock. Chickens, he liked chickens and he kept them for eggs. Being a vegetarian he never slaughtered the old birds even though the villagers had tried to persuade him to wring necks when their laying days were done.

"Just because something is old," he would say, "does not mean it is useless."

"Waste of good grain on an animal that can't lay," the delivery man had said, as he humped sacks into the feed shed.

"God makes wonders and miracles," Denker had replied. "Every one of us has a purpose and every one has the right to life. From the smallest mouse to the largest elephant."

The delivery man was used to the eccentric priest. Even if he did let rats and mice get to the grain bags in the store. He'd have put a savage ratter in there, like Arnie Stolpinski's Jack Russell terrier; now that would sort out everything, rats, mice, cats and children. A small brown and white bundle of teeth and aggression that stopped at nothing except perhaps a bitch on heat.

"Why don't you get Arnie's dog down here Paul? He'd sort this shed out once and for all." He always said the same thing. Every three months on every delivery.

Paul Denker signed the delivery note. "Why would I do that? These animals have a right to life too. Everyone has a right to life," he had said.

It had now become almost a ritual which both men played out as if on camera.

"See you in three months then father?" the delivery man shouted over the roar of the diesel engine, before pulling away toward the main road.

Denker heard the radio go on in the cab. Then turning he walked down to the grain shed and scattered some of the fresh supply into the chicken pen before turning to his prize rhubarb patch. There he halted and looked a little forlorn.

"I think you lot," he was talking to the plants now, "you all need an extra feed. I hope to be able to provide that very soon."

* * *

Paul Denker had come to England at the end of the Second World War. No one, including the church hierarchy, knew much about him. He had come from Poland, a place with an almost unpronounceable name and had, with no more than a few shillings, managed to secure a job labouring. He worked hard and had one of those tans which only those who understood physical toil could call, "all over."

Then in 1947 he had started to study and graduated in two

years; he qualified for the priesthood a year later. After that he took on the most difficult of jobs in the worst areas of London before finally moving south to Crofton. He worked hard but always kept a low profile. Avoiding publicity he just worked his magic modestly – most people found that endearing, Christian and honourable. No one knew his birthday and when pressed he always avoided giving an answer. In consequence, he never received cards or gifts, except at Christmas and these he usually passed on to others. He was almost a recluse, but also not a recluse – an intensely private man he enjoyed working the land. His physique was muscular, wiry, athletic, without being muscle bound. He had a strength which was more prodigious than his frame would suggest and his blonde hair shone in the sunshine.

Paul Denker liked the summer sun, and often whistled as he worked. His eyes were an intense blue, piercing, perceptive and showed clear intelligence. It was obvious to many that he had seen some military service, especially when he was seen without a shirt. In the arm-pit of his left arm there was a tattoo a simple letter and a figure A +. Below that was a scar; a scar which had been created by either a knife or a burn. It was as if a chunk of flesh had been cut away and then the wound cauterised. Whenever anyone approached he always made sure his arms were down to conceal the marks. One of the local women once asked what had caused it and he, in response, replied.

"A long time ago," he said, "this was done to me and we must not talk of it anymore." Then he had lifted his index finger to his lips to sssh her.

She had told her friends and they had said that perhaps he had been in a concentration camp - because he was a Catholic. It seemed a reasonable assumption to make and the subject was dropped.

* * *

In the winter of 1953 the whole of southern England became more alert than it had been during the war. A boy aged 12 had disappeared in Bournemouth and the police suspected foul play:

It was headline news. In 1954 two more children vanished, one in Portsmouth the other in Southampton. By 1955 a frenzy of distrust had developed as three more children vanished. First in March, a girl of 9; then in May a boy of 10 and finally September another boy of 12.

The police investigations stumbled and then faltered. The last boy had been a choir boy at the Church of the Immaculate Conception and Paul Denker had been devastated. It had been hard for him to accept the fact that the boy was probably dead. He had consoled the parents and tried desperately to aid the police investigations. His van had been seen several times and now it was out and about almost daily as he conducted his own investigation. The boy had been seen at the manse on several occasions and had taken an active part in helping the priest with a variety of odd jobs; mostly gardening and tending to the chickens. Then one day he had vanished; vanished like all the others before him, into thin air. The priest held a mass to honour the boy and a special stone tablet was fixed to the inside of the knave to commemorate his life. Denker had paid for that out of his own pocket, but despite this the police had apologetically undertaken a search of the manse and the surrounding undergrowth, nothing had been found.

Then with the same suddenness the killing stopped and between 1955 and 1960 no more children vanished and the crime of abduction began to slowly drift back into memory.

In 1961 seven children vanished, almost at the rate of one per month. This time they were younger 7, 8 and 9 year olds; all from local parks and all in broad daylight. Each time there had been no witnesses except for the last. The last child, a little dark-haired boy had been taken as he walked home from his friend's house down a side alley at the back of a park. It was a secluded spot with easy access to the road.

Taken swiftly and silently, with a plastic bag placed over his head and held fast by the killer, his struggling had stopped quickly. The boy had then been lifted like a limp sack and tossed into the vehicle; tossed as if he were a bag of potatoes.

On this one occasion the killer had made a single mistake.

Like all crimes the unexpected happened and Lance Corporal Ernie Blinker had seen him and recognised him. Ernie Blinker had been in the wrong place at the right time.

Ernest Blinker was a chancer, a wide boy and a worker of scams. He also undertook a little light burglary to enhance his pay if he could see a quick opportunity. Today had been his lucky day. First the window of the bungalow had been open and he had slipped inside with the stealth of a cat. He had found old widow Meredith had left her jewellery nicely stashed in an ornate box on her dressing table. That went straight into his pocket, once back up in Caterick he'd flog the lot and make a tidy little profit. In the top drawer he found her passport and cheque book: He took neither.

There was a savings jar that she kept her pension in and that he emptied. That would give him a few good nights out. That was the beauty of the wealthy people in Crofton they thought they were immune to criminals. Ernie was never greedy and that's why he never got caught. He was careful and quick, in and out in less than a minute, never doing damage and never wasting time. There was absolutely no point in taking larger items and anyway he had nowhere to store them.

As he slipped back out of the same window, through which he had entered, he saw the young boy ambling down the path and cursed his bad luck. He knew the child and the child knew him, so he would have to wait. To avoid being seen he slid into a clump of pampas grass and watched the youngster continue his amble. Opportunities come around and only the swift and the skilled take them, Ernie Blinker never missed them, that was his special gift. He could always find the angle, the profit and today he'd been lucky. Then from the opposite direction he saw the man approaching; he crouched lower as the two met and began to talk. The boy knew the man and was laughing; the man gave the child something, it was purple and blue and Blinker guessed chocolate. As the boy turned to walk on the man moved with sudden quickness and a plastic bag was thrown over the boy's head. The man was lifting him now and the boy's feet were kicking and his arms thrashing. A hand was over the child's mouth and the man was looking up and down the path, checking he was not being noticed. Blinker knew he was the only watcher, tucked as he was out of site in the widow's garden. He knew he had seen the man before; he recognised him instantly.

* * *

Lance Corporal Ernest Blinker walked up the gravel path to the manse with a cock-sure manner. The stones cracked and crunched under his feet as he lazily scuffed his heels. He had never spoken to the priest before, had no appointment and was doing what he did best - taking a chance.

At the front door he rang the bell and immediately the electronic signal was relayed to the outside back-garden bell - which rang loudly. Paul Denker had been digging in his allotment and the sound disturbed his quiet afternoon. He knew he didn't have any appointments and unexpected visitors really got on his nerves these days, this was his time. The county show was only eight weeks away and the fertilizer would give the growth an extra push. Then the stalks would be extra firm and juicy. That would give him first place once again. Blood and bone meal worked well, but that was processed in a factory and his unique formula worked even better. It had worked well in Poland when he had been stationed there; rhubarb had always been on the menu.

Quickly he raked the last of the ground into place and threw some soiled clothes into the burning brazier which was converting extra bits and pieces into ash. That would be scattered on the surface and washed in with the rain over the next few days.

The bell sounded for the third time as the priest began to move toward the side gate of the manse. He was pulling his shirt over his shoulders as Blinker strolled through the gate.

"Hello," he said, as he cheerily approached.

"Can I help you, Lance Corporal?" father Denker asked.

"I just came to see you about something very personal," Blinker replied.

Denker had pulled the shirt into place and Blinker noticed

the scar in his arm pit and what looked like a knife wound to his abdomen: It was not an operation. The priest was muscular and toned and Blinker found that surprising in a man of the cloth.

He leaned his spade against the side of the house, as he fumbled with the small buttons.

"I don't do appointments today," the priest said.

"But this is an emergency," Blinker added, "and I'm certain you won't want to discuss this outside."

"Oh?" Denker sighed, "it must be very personal, if you don't want your business overheard?"

"Not for me," Blinker replied, "but for you." He looked into Denker's eyes. "That's a nasty wound scar you have there. Shrapnel?"

"That's very perceptive of you," the priest replied. "Very perceptive."

"Well some things can't be covered up and military people know when they see a combat wound" Blinker answered.

"And what else do you perceive?" Denker asked, as he picked up the spade and pushed open the back door.

"I saw you in the alleyway," Blinker blurted. "I saw exactly what you did."

They were inside the kitchen now and Denker closed the door behind them both.

"So you saw me did you?" Denker asked.

"Yep!" Blinker smiled at the priest, "I saw you put the polythene bag over that kid's head and watched you choke the life out of him. Saw his little legs kicking as he fought for breath. I don't blame you the little bastard deserved it. He was a right little shit."

"So why are you here?" Denker asked coldly in reply. "Should you not have gone to the police?"

"Now what good would that do? The little turd is dead. Best thing for him really." Blinker was laughing, "And what good would that do me?"

Denker was looking at the Lance Corporal, with his gleaming buttons and regimental insignia, "What regiment is that?" he pointed.

"Oh this?" Blinker was smirking, "Royal Armoured Corp.

Tanks and support vehicles. I'm a gunner." He paused, and then suddenly asked, "What regiment were you in? Panzers?"

"You are mistaken Lance Corporal."

"I don't think so."

"How so?"

"The scar under your arm pit. That's a blood group not a holocaust number. People are so stupid. You're a Catholic not a Jew."

Denker was smiling now and getting cups out of the over head cupboard. He placed the teapot next to them. "I have never been in the services," Denker was saying as he turned to the kitchen kettle and switched it on. A large cumbersome kettle with a loose lid and large spout. "I suppose we should have some biscuits?"

"You're so civilised," Blinker remarked. "I saw you kill a boy and you want us to have tea and biscuits together."

"Well it is obvious that you wish something from me, is that right?"

Blinker nodded.

"I would think you are SS Germania division? Weren't they, or should I say you, in Russia and Poland?"

Denker did not react.

"You start to retreat from Russia, and you end up in Poland. What happened? Were you wounded badly and left? What did you do pretend to be Polish? Then after the war you needed to get out so you burnt the unit name off from under your arm. What did you use?"

"All this since yesterday?" Denker asked. "My, you have been busy."

"Nope," Blinker replied. "All in the last few minutes. A blinding flash of inspiration."

"You are obviously destined for promotion. You'll be a Sergeant before you know it. So, here alone with your theories?"

"Look let's talk turkey, as the Yanks say." Blinker's eyes met Denker's. "I don't care about the kid and I don't care what the hell you got up to in the war. Do what you like I just want cash."

"Very noble," Denker replied, "and how much precisely?"

"How much would the SS pay not to have you caught?"

"You are assuming that you're right."

"Aren't I then?" Blinker asked quizzically.

The kettle was boiling now. Denker flicked the switch at the wall. Then he put three spoonfuls of tea into the pot and lifted the kettle from the stand.

"Do you take sugar?" he asked the younger man.

"Oh you're SS alright, and if you want to stay alive you are going to arrange to pay me a nice little bit of cash."

Then with a sudden and deft movement Denker removed the kettle lid and threw boiling water straight into the eyes of his accuser. Blinker attempted to let out a yell and as he did so a carving knife, pulled from the block, punctured his gullet and windpipe. Blind, bleeding and unable to speak he stumbled forward as a shovel blow shattered his knee; then he knelt as if in penitent devotion as the shovel edge split his skull like a cabbage.

Immediately, to soak up the blood, Denker threw a towel over the twitching corpse which now lay on his kitchen floor. Then he calmly filled the teapot with the remaining water and waited for the tea to brew. Thought and careful preparation had always seen him in good stead, and now he needed to remain calm. Calm and clear headed.

He was angry, angry for allowing himself to be seen this time. That had been a stupid mistake, and one he would never be allowed to repeat. The internal organs he would remove, as he had been previously instructed, but the eyes in this one would be absolutely no use. He would do as he always done and pack the harvested items in ice and despatch them to the same address. Only this time he had not been fully prepared and the packaging would have to be improvised.

Paul Denker started to strip, first himself and then the body. Usually he would perform the organ removals in the bath and then simply wash away the blood. He always worked in the nude, because blood was easy to wash off bare skin and impossible to remove from clothes. Today he would improvise and perform the dissection on the kitchen floor and then wash everything down. Towels and polythene were the key here; the whole lot could be folded away and then the brazier could do the work.

The body he could use, though it was bigger than a child's and the clothes he could burn, but he knew he would have to search the ashes for the buttons and insignia to make sure he didn't miss any. That would be his first task in the morning. If anyone came looking for Blinker he didn't want to leave even the slightest clue.

He dunked his biscuit in his tea and the chocolate began to dissolve. Blinker was an opportunist and a fool and the best use he could be put to would be medical research. The organs could go into the freezer overnight and first thing he would take them to the local post office and send them away. Each time he had done so in the past, the clerk, Mrs Jenkins, a fat frumpy widow with bad skin had told her neighbour that father Denker had been sending food parcels to Romania again. That he was, "A lovely man, a real Christian with morals," and like he always did there was no return address on the parcel. "Humble, he was a humble man," she had told her friend, "a man who obviously didn't want any credit for his good works." He was good looking too and if he hadn't been a priest then she might have, "Made a play for him," herself.

Denker worked quickly; he striped the body and removed the vital organs. Then he packed them into plastic bags and threw them into the freezer.

Usually he had a hole prepared but today he was not ready. That too would have to wait until the morning; if he started working now it might arouse suspicion. It was a gamble but Blinker would have to remain on the kitchen floor in pieces.

Denker showered and set out his plan. Tonight he would burn the clothes and the towels and every single cloth or rag in which the body had been wrapped or the floor and walls washed down with. The body was bagged in pieces and ready for burial. In the morning he would get up early, dig the hole, and then as soon as the post office was open get the package sent. He would be back by 10 o'clock and start his rounds as if nothing had happened. Standing on the slate floor he towelled himself down, and recalled the number of buttons Blinker's uniform had. Eleven, there were eleven in all and two insignia.

In his dressing gown he walked out to the brazier, which had already done the majority of its work. Throwing in his damp shower towel he returned to the house and flicked the television news on. A boy was missing; perhaps he should visit the parents, but then thought better of it. To appear too early could alert an over observant detective. Anyway he had had a tiring afternoon and he had an early start. That was the trouble with parents they'd probably be on the phone to him in an hour and he have to show concern over their little runts. He took the phone out of the cradle; he could always say there was an intermittent fault.

In bed he fell asleep quickly and rested with a clear conscience. He knew that what he was doing would complete the work his unit had started on the Jews. He drifted into wondering who was giving the orders for the organ salvage to continue, before his breathing began the slow and rhythmical purr of a sleeping predator.

* * *

Charlie Diamond was well ticked off. Because Eddie Hallam had called in sick he was going to have to do a double shift. And as Eddie wasn't likely to be back for a week or so, because of a bad back, he would have to take on the extra work.

This was just the second day and he had the drop sheets in front of him. Gosport, Fareham and Crofton they were all close enough for jazz, so he decided that he would take the chicken today and leave the hay bales in Petersfield until tomorrow and that way he could cut the mileage down.

Paul Denker had been up since dawn, he had cleared the brazier, retrieved all the tell-tale buttons and insignia. Re-lit it with logs and it had blazing merrily while he got several small holes ready. He thought about lifting the rhubarb crowns and placing the body in one place, but in the end had settled for several smaller holes. They were not as deep as he would normally have liked but they would do the job just as well. At the beach he had thrown the buttons and insignia into the sea and stopped at the surfer's beach café to get a coffee and a pastry. A little treat to reward himself for the exertion of the morning; he deserved it.

As he sat, one or two early morning dog walkers bade him good day and one even stopped to pass the time with him. Everything had gone smoothly and the disappearance of the boy coupled with the sudden absence of Lance Corporal Blinker might be tied together. No adults had been taken before, Blinker was the first and perhaps the police might make the quantum leap of thinking him a paedophile. Maybe he'd been luckier than he thought. Either way, despite orders, he would have to stop; stop providing specimens. At 9.00am, when the post office opened he had taken the package in and it had gone almost immediately.

* * *

Charlie Diamond came down the manse drive at break-neck speed. He was out of the cab and knocking on the door within seconds and his constant companion a sprightly Jack Russell, called Ted, was close behind. It was a pup he had bought from the old Polish guy with the funny name, but the dog was great. He was far more scary than any big dog and he made a good cab mate on long journeys.

Though a day early he was hoping the priest would be in – he wasn't. He checked the order, 4 bags of wheat grain and 2 of barley.

Ted was off down to the chicken pen, and as Charlie unloaded the 6 bags he surveyed the area. First the pup scared a chicken or two, then he was admonished and returned to hunt rats in the shed. By the time Charlie had unloaded the last bag, Ted had dug a decent sized hole in the rhubarb patch and retrieved a bone of some sort.

Charlie Diamond gave a whistle and the pup jumped up to answer the call. His legs rushed him back toward his master and within a few seconds the pair were back into the lorry as it reversed out toward the main road.

* * *

Paul Denker continued with his appointment to see Mrs. Sloan. An elderly woman who needed constant assistance. She reminded

Denker of his mother in her last years of life; though there was nobody watching the house and waiting for him, like there had been with her. His time at Buchenwald had been productive, around Goethe's favourite oak tree he had constructed benching and the rhubarb garden was highly effective. Blood and bone had always been the best fertiliser.

For following orders they hounded him. Hounded him until he had taken on the identity of the Polish peasant he had strangled so easily in that park in Warsaw. If that man hadn't been a homosexual he would still be alive today. Queer and stupid, very stupid; his sexual urges and soliciting had cost him his life.

SS Colonel Ernst Grossner vanished into the mists of history, by becoming Paul Denker. Paul Denker, in turn, floated in the sewer with all the other faeces until his bloated and corrupt flesh became the food of rats and worms and the bones fell silently to the bottom of the urine channels.

* * *

Charlie Diamond let the dog take the bone into his cab, where he lay and chewed on it as they drove to the next drop. Ted would be unlikely to give up the prize anyway without some sort of fight. He could be possessive of any real prize, despite being a mere pup. It wasn't until they stopped to comply with the taco-graph regulations that Charlie noticed something unusual about Ted's bone. Every so often there was a gold flash between the dog's teeth. Something yellow and shining was being turned in the dog's mouth.

When finally he did get the bone away from a snarling set of white teeth; it wasn't a bone at all, but a human hand with two missing fingers and a signet ring with several chewed teeth marks upon it.

Charlie Diamond only hesitated long enough to vomit before calling the police.

where's my golf ball?

For
Lulu - belle
Who was my inspiration,

Where's my golf ball?

"Fore!" Reginald Masters screamed, as his ball left the face of the driver and punched through the pine trees. It should have been straight, his swing had been slow and methodical, and the build up fine; but the small white projectile swung right with a heavy slice. Once again he had tried too hard and hit the ball, rather than stroked through it. The consequence of his impatience had been a ricochet in the trees and another lost ball.

"Bloody hell," yelled Ronnie Masters, his brother and partner. "He's been hit. Jesus Reg the bugger's been hit. Come on."

Both men were running now - toward a third man, who had just fallen as if pole-axed, ahead of them. Under the pines and through the bushes they were beaten to the spot by a fourth man who was sitting his partner up as they arrived.

"You bloody fools," he yelled as the brothers approached. "Couldn't you see us?" Then turning to his partner, who sat on the ground, asked, "How many fingers can you see?"

"Soddin' dozens," came the sarcastic reply. "Bollocks that hurt." He rubbed his skull with his knuckles. "That really does kick the crap out of you. Like a flamin' brick-bat, that could have killed me."

And that was when the idea came to him. A simple idea, so simple it hit home with the ringing clarity of a church bell on a frosty December morning. So simple in fact that it could be fool proof.

"Are you hurt?" asked Ronnie.

The man was shaking his head now, "Nope," he said. "It would take more than that to kill me," he joked. "A blow to any other part of the body could have been lethal; the head, nah." He laughed, "A great numbskull like me ain't so easy to kill." He rubbed his head again, as he replaced his cap. "Smarts a bit though and I think you've lost your ball. What's the rule on that?"

"I didn't see you in the trees or wouldn't have played. I'm so sorry mate." Ronnie took the blame for his brother's poor shot. Force of habit in their business had made him do the same thing, year on year. If Reginald cocked up, he, the younger brother, was always there to pick up the pieces.

"I should've hit my own ball a bit straighter," the man laughed. "Then I wouldn't have been poncing in a landing zone. Christ you must have given that one hell of a twatting."

Reginald Masters had arrived panting after the exertion of jogging. He was the older of the two men and had, by right, inherited the pole position in the business when their father died. It was not a large business but death paid well, if you had verve and could stomach the constant reek of formaldehyde. So far both families had lived well, even if Ronnie had a few more, "*on - costs*," as he called them, than his older sibling.

"Bloody hell," puffed Reggie, "you ok?"

"I'll live," the man was smiling. "Can't sit here on my fat arse all day though," he laughed, getting to his feet.

Then pulling another ball from his pocket he walked out onto the adjacent fairway, dropped it and slowly set himself up for the strike. It was perfect nine iron and left the club face with a singing whine as it headed straight toward the green. On the front edge it caught in the longer grass, skipped left and then rolled downhill toward the pin: It stopped two feet short.

"Great shot," Ronnie Masters called and made an applauding action. "Sorry," he shouted once again and turned away.

With a casual wave the other pairing was gone and the seeds of a crime had been sown. Ronnie wondered if it were possible as he returned to his own ball and Reg found his in the undergrowth.

The Masters brothers returned to their game. Both played a shot and walked back onto their fairway.

"Christ that was lucky," Ronnie remarked, "he's gonna have one hell of headache though, in the morning. He could have been a cabbage about now."

"I know," Reggie laughed nervously, "imagine if he had been

seriously injured out here. It's nearly two miles back to the club house. I could have killed him."

"Well how were you to know he was in those woods?" his brother replied. "And you nearly lost your ball too," Ronnie laughed.

"Hold on Ron I'm being serious here. I could have been in real deep doo doo."

"Well he's fine," his brother replied, "so don't lose any sleep about it. I'm sure he's fine. Look," he pointed to the pair, who were now on the green some three hundred yards off. "Jumpin' around like a gazelle, he's fine."

* * *

"I love it when you come inside me," Corrina Collins said, as Ronnie collapsed on top of her. "Sooo deep and sooo loooveleee," she panted into his ear, as he rolled onto his side. The front of his chest hair was soaked with his own exertion.

"Fuck you're good," he panted. "You," he laughed, "are gonna be the fucking death of me."

"I know," she giggled. "I'm a good fuck. Actually I'm a great fuck. I think I could fuck you to death."

He snorted, "That's true. Hell yeah, that's true."

"That is why, you," she started to lick the sweat from his torso, "love being with me." Long slow flashes of her tongue, caused him to shudder.

He knew they would have more sex and that the urgency would be replaced by a slow and painstakingly erotic build up. In about half an hour from now he knew she would have him hard again and then be sitting astride him as if she were riding a rodeo bull. And he, he would be so deep inside her that she would scream in delight.

"When are you going to leave the bitch?" she asked almost casually, without stopping her tongue action.

"Next summer," came his stock reply.

"What like last summer and the summer before that?"

He smiled a nervous toothy grin.

"You're a fucking shit Ronnie Masters. A fucking shit,"she exploded. "You fuck me and you fuck her too and all the while you are shitting on both of us. I warned you that I wasn't going to be hanging around forever. I'll just go off one day."

"No you won't," he replied. "You love the cock too much - my cock."

"Why you arrogant prick," she snapped. "Just because you bought this flat and everyone knows me as Mrs. Masters, that won't wash with me. How long do you expect this to continue?"

Ronnie Masters was sitting now, with his back to the woman.

"Aren't you going to answer me then?" she asked.

"I've got it all in hand. It's all going to be sorted sooner than you think. I've got it all planned out. This time next year you will be the new Mrs. Masters and I'll have enough to pay that bitch off too."

"Well you have one year and this time if it's not sorted. I'm fucking gone and you can get some other fool to suck that cock of yours."

"But you like it," he laughed, turning to face her fully erect.

"Wrong," she panted, "I love it."

* * *

"The thing is a golf ball isn't a just a ball. You have to know the type that's best for you. What type of clubs do you use?"

"Wilson DD 5," Ronnie Masters replied.

"Any offset angle?" the assistant in the pro shop asked.

"Nope," Masters replied again.

"So you hit straight?"

"Ish," Masters grinned sheepishly.

The assistant became serious, "There are loads of cheap balls on the market. And they're all crap. Solid, plastic, rubber, combinations. Then there's the steel inner with a liquid core, supposed to give better top spin; but let's be honest unless you can hit the thing like Tiger Woods it ain't gonna make any damn difference. Amateurs is amateurs."

Ronnie Masters nodded; he was used to the talk of the semiprofessionals. The ones who taught lessons and plugged away for a living on a daily basis because they loved their sport.

"We got these and they," the assistant paused to enhance excitement, "are superb."

Ronnie Masters picked up the ball and looked at it. It was round and white and dimpled like any other golf ball he had seen.

"Looks amazin' don't it?"

Masters wanted to reply with a comment which said it looked just like any other ball, but instead he said, "Yes."

"Solid steel inner wrapped in a fine weave nylon wrap coat and then covered with impact resistant oxymonoprypopolene."

Ronnie Masters had always wished that there was such a thing as a bullshit detector. Perhaps like Fozzie Bear of The Muppets, everyone who began to bullshit should waggle their ears.

"These," the assistant continued, "will give you twenty yards on a drive and more back spin from a nine-iron than a ricochet." He held one up to the light, as if he were examining a fine jewel through which the light might refract. "Poetry," he said, "absolute poetry."

"Steel inner?" Masters asked.

"Makes them hard, the best controlled ball on the market, but if one of these beauties hits you on the nut it'll be like being hit with a bullet."

"A silver bullet?" Ronnie laughed.

"Yeah and I reckon one of these beauties would pop a werewolf off too," the assistant replied, joining in with the joke. "Would you like to try a few?"

"I'll take three dozen," Ronnie Masters said.

* * *

Masters the undertakers had been in business since 1897. It was established by James Masters and then passed from generation to generation without the interference of death duties or family squabbles. James Masters' special gift had been to understand the changing fashions for burials among the nouveau riche and aspiring middle-classes as Victoria's reign came to an end. Glass coffins, solid lead and imported Italian Marble gave the business an edge in the market and one shop had rapidly become two and then three. The final boost came with importing specialist cheap pine coffins from Romania; coffins that looked expensive, but burned easily, as cremation became more fashionable. He also managed to create the ornamental ash casket which could be kept at home, buried or interred in a chapel.

His business acumen had been passed to his son and he, in turn, had made the business an even greater success. During the 1930's and 40's Masters came to dominate the market place; at the zenith of the Masters death business they ran upwards of over forty units. Unfortunately he got to sample his own facilities earlier than he thought he would, due to a weak heart and overwork.

Michael Masters the father of both Ronnie and Reginald had been rather less successful, but had managed to secure a marriage to a society debutante. A rather needy, vacuous and unintelligent woman, whose beauty was her principal concern; followed by her necessity to maintain it. As she grew older the business dwindled, aided by her need to preserve her social standing. Michael, her husband had slipped into habitual drinking and gambling and, in consequence, the once thriving undertaking chain had reduced to a few simple outlets.

The two Masters Brothers had inherited many things but neither had the tenacity of their forebears - while each had inherited their own special weakness from their mother. Ronnie, his love of risqué sex and wild women and Reginald liked a flutter on the ponies. Neither was good at either and, in consequence, selling the business seemed the most appropriate answer. Ronnie was all for it, dissolving all assets and living off the proceeds, while Reginald, the more sentimental of the two, was all for continuing. Neither man had children that were remotely interested in maintaining the family's commercial success. Many times the brothers had argued about whether to sell to the Matthews family. Reginald's principal objection seemed to be based on the premise that once Mitchell Matthews, a Gypsy no good, had worked for their father and after learning all he could, had set up in direct competition. The current Matthews was younger than both by twenty five years and a rapacious business man. The offer he had made for the Masters Undertakers chain was, by all accounts fair, if less than generous; and Ronnie knew that the offer would fall in overall value over the coming years, as their business began to fail. He was for selling the business now, rather than when the market had reached rock-bottom.

* * *

"It's not my fault mum," Ronnie pleaded.

"Well just whose fault is it then?" his mother asked. "If it's not your fault?"

"It just sort of happened,"

"Sort of happened?" she snorted. "What is wrong with you? Can't you keep your dick in your trousers? Like father like bloody son." She became emotional, "You're seventeen years old and how old is she?"

"Fifteen," the young man replied.

His mother, who stood in front of him, slapped his face and then promptly sat with her head in her hands at the kitchen table, her shoulders heaving as she sobbed.

"What the hell do we do now?" the boy's mother asked. "I hope to God that you haven't told your father – he'll go ballistic. Fifteen, my God, fifteen," she repeated. "Under the age of consent. What would the police make of that one eh? Rape?"

"But she consented," the young man blurted, "I didn't rape her, I would never do that."

"You stupid, stupid boy," she snapped. "Under the age of consent means rape in the eyes of the law. If her parents want to prosecute," she paused, "and wouldn't you? There might be a nice little cash pay out from a family like us."

"It's not like that," Ronnie pleaded.

"Bloody marvellous," she paused, "marvellous." She paused again, "Your father and your uncle will be ruined. Can you even imagine the scandal?" Her voice began to crack now, "You really are the most stupid boy this family has ever produced. Just look at yourself." As quickly as she started the emotion stopped. "Do her parents know?" she asked. "Where do they live? She saw you coming you bloody silly little fool. I bet the family don't have a bean but she got you hooked. Pathetic, typical Masters - think with your balls. One girl drops her pants and in you go and I have to pick up the pieces."

In the kitchen of 84 Langdon Road, Ronnie Carl Masters junior sat with his sour faced mother Carol. She was a woman whose countenance had seen a few cares and woes. Twice her husband had had an affair and both times she had stuck by him; principally because she abhorred the idea of solitude. She had once wanted him so, wanted children, but the last few years had seen the marriage disintegrate into a sham. Somehow she had managed to mentally transpose all of the blame onto her husband and his infidelity, without any regard for her own contributory conduct. Her youthful allure of sex had now been replaced by revulsion; her once chatty demeanour had soured and, in consequence, the pair became two people held together by the glue of financial circumstance. This conduct by her son had been one more tale in a catalogue of woe.

"She wants an abortion," Ronnie suddenly blurted.

"At least she's got common sense then," his mother replied, wiping the tears from her face. "And I suppose we have to pay."

"Well that way her father won't know."

"Wouldn't it have been better if we never got to this place?"

"Her father," he hesitated, as if he didn't wish to say, "is Vernie Matthews."

"What you mean, the, Matthews?"

The boy nodded knowing the antipathy between the two families, particularly his father Ronnie and Vernie, the son of Mitchell Matthews.

It was almost too much for his mother, "Don't tell your father," she said, "he'll go apoplectic. I'll give you the money, but I want to meet the girl first."

Ronnie Masters junior went white.

The logistical problem had been vexing Ronnie senior for days. How to propel a golf ball with sufficient accuracy to hit a target the size of a watermelon. The impact needed to be smooth, high velocity and yet precise. In his workshop, which doubled as second living space, come study, come garden shed, he had experimented. The last ridiculous idea involved fixing a golf ball to a hammer with tape and then striking. That idea had, like all the others, been abandoned. The tape traces would show up on forensic tests – he needed something more precise.

In an old arm chair he sat looking out of the window across the vast expanse of lawn toward the house. He could see the wife he despised, talking to his no-good son and his girlfriend, a pretty little thing he thought. Masters wondered what they were talking about; his wife seemed agitated and animated. No doubt, he considered, some crisis or catastrophe was about to happen and once again he would have to pay. Carol now bored him, both sexually and mentally and as a result, he had gradually created a haven at the farthest end of the garden. If he could afford the divorce he would gladly jump at it. Once the business had been sold he and Corrina could laze their days away in the Maldives. Find an island hideaway – somewhere warm; somewhere he could take back the lost years of undertaking and slide into disgraceful retirement. He imagined Corrina face down and nude on soft sand and an expectant shudder hit his testes. It would be a pleasant fantasy coming out of the sea like James Bond; drinking cocktails and having sex until he was replete and empty - he could rest and recover. Corrina breathed new life into him; made him come alive again.

For now he had to make do with the building hideaway, a log cabin style shed with a warm, low, flat roof. There he kept his tools, undertakers tools, tools of the trade which made Carol shudder; bottles of various preparations, and formaldehyde. Carol hated the smell of it and had made him wash his hands repeatedly when they first started dating, but she loved the money he made. Far more than other boys of his age and consequently, she had let him take her knickers off one night in the back of his car. It had been a sweaty fumbling which had ended in a rather inconclusive climax for herself and a grinning baboon like triumph for him. That had come to signify the nature of their marriage – inconclusive. Now he had his shed, with a TV, kettle and armchair and she had the house.

He could see the animation continue and decided his best course of action would be absence; a long absent walk with Charlie his red-setter. From behind his garden hideaway, he had access to a couple of fields which the family owned and from there, once across the bridleway, down a lane or two and he would be free. Free to walk the lake edge and chat with fishermen who chose to stay overnight in half closed tents, rather than spend more time in their matrimonial beds. He could see the solitude in their eyes, hear the disappointed dreams in their talk and taste their surrender in the air around them. They, like him, had found their own escape.

Try as he might he simply could not find the method of propulsion. An air gun of some sort – he had tried one of the kind used to propel ping-pong balls, but it lacked power. Then he thought of tennis balls and the sort of machines used at clubs to toss projectiles at practising, aspirational champions – nothing had worked.

As he rounded the far side of the lake he stopped to speak to a man long used to the silence. There was a black retriever bitch and both dogs ran as the two men exchanged pleasantries.

"Afternoon," the small man said, as Masters approached.

"Kicked out again?" Ronnie laughed.

"Listen my son," said the man, "I'd rather be fishing here than sitting with the fat cow and her family." He laughed. "That little half tent there," he pointed, "is all I need and the dog is better company than all of those bleedin' wastetrels in her family."

"Terrible though isn't it? Us grown men having to stay away from home to get some peace?"

"It's shit, but I'd rather be here than there."

The two men laughed together and Ronnie Masters passed a hip flask to the man.

"Try a drop," he said, "it'll warm the cockles of your heart. Put hair on your chest."

The man took a deep swig, "Whoo eee," he puffed. "That's some good malt you got there."

"I know, not for beginners though."

"Great bite."

"Caught anything worthwhile?" Masters asked trying to change the subject.

"Not unless you call a mirror, worthwhile."

"Big?"

"About eighteen pounds."

"Bloody hell that's big isn't it?"

"I've had bigger out of this lake."

The man turned to his gear and then with a catapult propelled a series of pellets into the water some forty yards off. Ronnie Masters saw the float bobbing and realised that the area around it was being baited. His mind shot into high speed overload as he watched the repeated loading of the catapult and the accuracy with which it delivered the pellets.

"Carp," Masters nonchalantly continued, "I ate that in Hungary, Hallas-Ley, they called it -fish soup."

"Christ I wouldn't eat carp. Might as well eat a goldfish. Same family."

"So you use the catapult to deliver the bait?"

The man nodded. Ronnie Masters was certain he had now found the vital missing link in his plan.

"I don't have time for fishing," Masters offered, as his mind raced across the possibilities which now lay before him. "Wish I did though."

"Listen if I didn't go fishing, I'd have killed her by now," the man replied. "I got a fat-arsed wife that ain't no good for nothing. Spends money like water, and ponces around with a bunch of her friends who all look like they ain't got a decent fuck in em. I'd be better off if I was single. Fifteen years wasted."

"You'd have been out by now if you'd topped her."

"I tell you what there are times I could do it too. Fat sack of shit that she is."

"Why don't you get a divorce?" Ronnie asked.

"Because," the nameless man replied, "I got kids that ain't worth a damn, and I ain't stupid. Those child support bods they'd have my guts strung out all over the place." He was threading a maggot onto a hook, "Then I might as well disappear up my own arse .You know like the oozoolum bird. Nope I'll wait my time and then wham. I'll be gone - home free. And she can get a job and look out for herself, fat lazy cow."

He flicked the rod and the maggot was delivered into the patch of baited lake.

* * *

Ronnie Masters was amazed by the sound which a golf ball made upon impact with a human skull. If he were asked to describe it, it could best be called a cross between a dull thud and a squelch. The corpses he had used in the chapel of rest had played their part as he experimented. All the skulls he had cracked were now cremated and ground to dust, and long since scattered. The evidence link was gone, and the catapult had been purchased fifty miles away where he was completely unknown. He had thought of steel, but in the end had gone for a plastic body and rubber propulsion. Both could be disposed of in a cremation. A small incision here and there, a couple of stitches and that too would end up in a furnace. Once the deed had been done it would be impossible to trace.

First there had been the old man. His head had cracked like a twig when the skull spilt but he had managed, by the skilful use of make-up, to disguise the abrasion. Then came the teenager who died on a motorcycle. His skull cracked like an egg on impact, but the ceremony was sealed casket and he hadn't needed to bother with covering the mark. The third time he tried it – he nearly made a fatal mistake. A young woman, who had died of cancer. First they wanted closed, then suddenly open casket and he had to slap a few hurried pastes together to hide the damage. He had said that this happened sometimes with cancer victims and the family had believed him, but for a while it had been touch and go. He decided it might be too risky to experiment for a fourth time. Especially when the family wanted to sue. He gave them a hefty discount and the greedy vultures had saved five hundred pounds, making £250 for each grasping child.

The optimum distance was three feet; that much he had learned. One clean pull on the catapult and then - bang. His biggest fear was that Reg might not remain still for long enough and that the ball might not quite hit the killing spot above the temple. It was risky but he needed to make sure that Reg stayed still. The only thing he could think of was booze. That could give him an excuse as well; the excuse for not getting back to the club house as quickly as he should.

Cigars, he'd get some fine Cuban ones too. Then they'd look like they were celebrating: Celebrating their decision. He rehearsed the argument for the police from the comfort of the armchair in the shed.

"Well we were looking for a ball in the undergrowth and I was behind a tree when suddenly my brother fell. At first I didn't know what was wrong, then I heard someone shout. I saw he had been hit and I took off for the clubhouse. I'd sat him against a tree. I'd left my mobile in the car, you see, club rules and all that. No mobiles on the course. I was going back to the clubhouse as fast as I could and then we got a buggy out to Reg, and, and." He wondered if he should cry. Perhaps that would be a step too far? An over elaborated lie. Liars like children always go the extra yard and the result is instant disbelief. He'd have to give that a little more thought. Perhaps a little research was still needed.

His mobile phone rang.

"Hello," he said.

"Hello big boy," a sultry voice enticed.

"Mmmm," he replied chuckling, "you dirty little bitch."

"Do you fancy coming over for a game of hide the salami? Bet I can find a place where all of it can go."

He looked at his watch, and the windows of his house, "I don't know if I can get away."

"I'll get you away," the voice said. "I'll take you to heaven and back."

His resistance was breaking down, "You really know how to get a guy interested don't you?"

"That's because I'm the puurrrrrr fect, little pussy," Corrina purred.

"I'll be over in an hour or two," he chuckled.

"That might be too late. Pussy might have gone to bed."

"An hour then?"

"Oh lovely, pussy gets her cream."

* * *

Ronnie Masters showered and splashed on Versace after shave. His wife Carol knew what that meant. It meant he would not be home that night. Meant that once again he was off for sex with some young floozy. She thought about the two brothers and on balance, Reg, despite his gambling, was, in her opinion, the nicer man. True he was not as sharp as Ron but at least he kept his dick in his trousers and not in the willing mouth of a young slut. She despised him; couldn't wait for the day when the kids had flown the coup; then she'd show him, get her own back, divorce the pig.

"I'm off out," Ronnie called to her from the front door.

"Ok," she replied from the kitchen where she was watching the television.

"I might not get back till late. Looks like a long job."

"Ok."

"Big crash on the motorway, lots of bodies to sort out."

She lowered her voice to a whisper, "Yeah and that's where you ought to be you piece of slime; spread all over the motorway. I hope you crash and die." Then more loudly she called, "Ok."

As he left the house and pulled the front door closed behind him he wondered if she had even the slightest clue as to where he was going. She was a dullard he reasoned; a middle-aged frump of a dullard who dressed in tweed and flat shoes, like some ancient old maid. He wanted youth and life and vibrancy; he was surrounded by death all the time and he had had enough.

In the Jaguar he flipped the CD player on and Corrina's

choice popped into the speakers: Snow Patrol - Chasing Cars. After a couple of verses and a Maldivian fantasy, he flipped to mute and called, "Matthews," into his voice recognition phone.

The reply was sharp, "Yep," it said.

"Vernie, you still want to buy us out?"

"Masters, you know I do," came the terse reply.

It was clear that neither man liked the other. Perhaps in another life or another time they would have made the perfect business partnership. Both were self-centred; both were egotistical; both mistrusted everyone and both had secret mistresses.

"Of course I want to talk about you selling," Vernie Matthews laughed.

" Loretta's coffee shop on Argyll Street," Ronnie Masters said. "Lunchtime tomorrow?"

"Does this mean that that brother of yours has changed his mind?"

"Leave the persuading to me."

"Fine, but I don't want to be wasting my time again."

"Listen," said Ronnie, "if you come up with the right cash offer then we can get somewhere."

"Cash? What no shares this time? No percentage? That's a change of heart then. What about all his sentimental crap, about saving the Masters name for future generations?"

"Look it's cash or no deal and we sell elsewhere."

"Really?"

"Really."

"What time then?"

"Two?"

"I'll be there."

Ronnie Masters punched the disconnect button and under his breath hissed, "Gypsy fucking cocksucker."

* * *

"It's a good deal," said Ronnie.

"What?"

"Matthews reckons," he played a short pitch, "8.3"

"That's not even half of what it's worth. Shot." Reg replied. He adjusted his stance, "That Gypo knows that he's on to a good thing. He's a piece of slime and besides," he pitched his own reply onto the green and watched it roll over the back of the 7th. "Oh sugar!" he exclaimed. "What are we going to do when there's no business left?"

"Fuck off on holiday?"

"No seriously Ron? What about the family and the kids."

"Look none of the kids are interested. Cigar?" He handed his brother a hand rolled Louis Rae.

"What's the occasion?"

"Celebrating."

"Celebrating what?"

"Freedom? Look you could play the gee gees. Relax a little and well" He handed his brother a hip flask.

"What's this then?"

"Dalwhinnie 15years old."

Reginald took a deep swig of the Voltarol laced alcohol. The pain killers his brother used for lower lumber pain. A strong sedative, easily dissolved and because of the prescription totally explainable if found during an autopsy.

"Nice," Reg said.

"I know," Ronnie Master laughed, as he placed the hip flask to his lips. Only when he did so, he covered the mouth of the pewter vessel with his tongue and after a mock swallow quickly passed the item to his older brother. "We could have this all the time; play more golf; have a few drinks and let the world drift by."

Reginald Masters drove on the 8th and by the time they had walked and played the 440 yards to the green most of the first hip flask was empty. Ronnie produced a second - this time even more strongly laced with painkiller.

As they set up at the ninth tee Reggie Masters was giggling like a school girl and his words were slurred.

"It's your honour," he said to his brother. Taking a deep swig from the second flask.

Ronnie Masters wondered why the pair behind them had not yet played through. The two must be very slow he thought, but at least they were not in sight and could not act as witnesses. He couldn't see them, but he knew that now was his one chance. He drove the ball straight into the dense woodland where only a few weeks earlier the idea for today had come to him.

"Oh, fuck me," he said.

His brother laughed, "That's a bit of bad luck."

"Ha fucking ha," Ronnie retaliated.

Reggie's shot was not much better and less than ten minutes later both brothers were scouring the leaves and detritus for their balls.

"I need to sit down for a moment," said Reg. "I think I'm a bit pissed."

"You silly sod," Ronnie laughed.

"I know," Reg replied, as he sat with his back against a tree.

His brother went to his bag.

* * *

The noise of Reginald Masters' skull cracking was like a soft boiled egg being dropped on a floor. A sharp crack followed by a sickeningly soft slap. For a moment his head jerked as the impact of the golf ball pushed his head to the left and then he slumped. Immediately Ronnie went to his brother's wrist - there was a pulse but a deep crimson welt had appeared at his temple and was spreading across his forehead. He was bleeding internally.

Almost casually now he threw his cigar into the grass and looked back up the hill to the tee. There was no one there, and at a leisurely pace he set off for the club house. He looked at his watch it was 3.03.

When he arrived at the club house he was puffing and panting and saying about how his brother had been hit. The clock in the bar read 3.48.

The barman was amazed; he had never seen anything like this before - two accidents in one day. First a broken ankle and now this, someone out cold on the course; hit on the head by a ball. One ambulance had just left and already they needed another.

***

Michael Stokes looked at the case file. He felt there was something wrong but he couldn't explain what. He was a Detective Constable; new, young and fresh faced, a young man with aspirations – an Essex lad with a thirst for more than white stiletto shoes and hoop earrings. He sat looking at Ronnie Masters – the interview tape running.

"So your brother was hit by a flying ball?" he asked.

Ronnie Masters nodded.

"Where do you think that came from?" the Constable asked.

"Well there wasn't anybody teeing off ahead so I reckon it was the pair behind us. We had gone into the woods to find a lost ball and I reckon they didn't see us."

"That is very possible."

"That must have been what it was," Ronnie Masters replied. He knew that at eleven the catapult was going to be cremated inside a child death. He had placed it there himself - underneath the pillow. That was the last link and last piece of evidence. Once that was gone all they had was guesswork. It was the perfect murder. He had committed the perfect murder. He Ronnie Masters had done it. He looked at the clock. It read 11.35. A sigh of relief silently left his lips.

"There's just one tiny problem with that," said the Detective Constable. "We checked the tee times and there were only two pairs out near or around at the time of the incident. Yourselves and the pair immediately behind you."

"Well it must have come from them then."

"In most cases that would be quite plausible. But we have a tiny problem."

"A problem?" Ronnie repeated.

"Well a little more than a problem actually."

The policeman smiled, a knowing smile, and a row of peg teeth, small and white shone at Masters. Consequently, Masters had the distinct notion that the whole of his plan had suddenly been exposed. His mind raced as he tried to think what he might have missed and how he would clarify his story - by muddling his story.

"I don't understand. There were some people behind us and we were in the trees and I saw them tee off. A stray ball must have hit my brother."

"You saw them tee off?"

"Well no not exactly, heard them more like. Do you play?" Stokes shook his head.

"It's a very distinctive sound, a solid tee shot." Masters continued, his confidence restoring as he spoke, "A cross between a whizzing rocket and a tin can being hit by a stone."

"Oh," said the investigator, "you heard them tee off then?"

"You know, as a player; the sound of the ball being hit."

Their eyes met and Masters produced a most innocent stare. He was calm and now totally unflustered. Stokes smiled again.

"Golf is a great game," Masters added. "Well it was for me until this happened."

"You seem to be playing a rather dangerous game I'd say," Stokes' face was emotionless as he replied.

"If you were a player you'd know."

"I don't," Stokes paused, an extra long pause for accentuation, before he uttered the word, "play." Then smiling again he added, "What did Churchill say? Something about spoiling a perfectly good walk. Mind you he always hated sports and the Scottish too; he really was a xenophobic toff."

Ronnie Masters was feeling relaxed, he had thought of every angle. The forensic evidence, the catapult and his excuses. He had repeatedly trotted out his reason for not having a phone; the distance to the club house. The fact that he had no way of getting help quickly. The policeman in front of him had listened intently and had been nodding, an understanding nod. Even the body language had been receptive to what he had been saying.

"You see, my problem is simple," said the Detective Constable with sudden clarity, "the pair behind you had an accident on the 5th. One of the men slipped over and broke his ankle. A very unfortunate event; a cruel twist of fate and totally unforeseeable. A buggy went out to him. So you see the ball that killed your brother could not have come from the 9th tee. Have you any idea where this golf ball came from?"

Ronnie Masters turned white.

"I've listened to what you say and it all makes logical sense." Stokes said, as he folded his hands under his chin in a cupping motion, with his elbows on the desk. "But it just isn't true is it?"

Ronnie Masters began to sweat.

the faith healer

This story is dedicated to A. H. - the last of the teenage idols.
1935 - 1982

I

First things first:-

What I am about to tell isn't really a story at all; it's more of an account. What's the difference? Simple, an account is as factual as it can be without being untrue, but, and here's the rub, it is only seen from one angle. There are no other voices in here, no alternate perspective. No narrator seeing the story from any other angle except the one you will be given. I make no apology for that, because what you read is what you get. I should know I'm a journalist.

When a critic read it they said it was a parable; a parable for the new millennium and I nearly choked with laughter. I hate, no that's too strong, let's go for dislike, dislike is better; dislike people who try to be pretentious about writing. You see them all the time, or should I say hear them all the time. They pontificate about what a writer really means, as if they know; half the time the writer doesn't even know. The muse comes and the muse goes - sometimes it's fruitful and others it is barren. Ask any artist what and how they create and they will give you the answer that they don't really know; you can't teach it, replicate it, unless of course you copy, plagiarise and then, well it is always a paler imitation of the original. Originality is the key. The critics said it was some kind of twenty first century warning about the perils of making deals with people that you couldn't really trust. And about the discovering of God and ways to return to a leap of faith ideology. I was so amused at that, bearing in mind that I am a total atheist that I laughed out loud. No mumbo jumbo for me, whatever the religion might be. No God or Devil, and certainly no vestal virgins waiting for me at the gates of heaven, should I decide to blow myself and anyone else for that matter, into small bite-size pieces. I had toyed with faith in my youth and finally had the sense to see that chaos was indeed the only answer. Chaos and chance rules the universe, there is no divine plan, no planned future for mankind, just luck. One big meteorite the size of the moon, or maybe a bit smaller, casually dropped into the Yucatan area and we would be enveloped in a mass of red rain that lasts for a million years. Hey it did the dinosaurs so it would probably do us, unless we evolved into worm-like things and burrowed into the mud.

Maybe that's all we are in reality, worms burrowing into the mud of a planet? What is Australia to an English ant, they are universes apart, oceans of time separate them, and why not us from other life forms? How arrogant would it be to believe that no where else in this vast expanse of black there are other life forms? Once you get over the enormity of that idea, think it through, you can easily see just how insignificant and worthless we actually are. Humans are just a spot of water on the windscreen of eternity and they can be wiped aside as easily as, well as easily as anything. Worship the sun? Why not it's as good as anything, and without it we and all our world ceases to exist.

Saying things like that has always endeared me to people, but I have long since given up taking any notice or giving a damn. Better to be hated and feared than loved and adored, isn't that what Machiavelli claimed?

Anyway I am telling this account to you, word for word, in exactly the same way that I would tell it to my mother. As true as I stand before you, or perhaps I should swear on the bible? This happened, it's all true: I swear by almighty God and would I lie? In God we trust.

Oh, I had best give you some credentials or validation or some such nonsense; maybe even chant some mantra to make you believe me, though why you'd bother you'll never really know, so why should I ? Look I am totally open minded, and totally cynical, so bear that in mind when things happen that don't seem right – and don't expect me to give you all the answers; you're supposed to be an intelligent human being , though that's an oxymoron anyway.

My name is Oliver James Dorothy, I am forty eight years old with a receding hair line and a passion for German Lubecker marzipan and yes, I have had people take the Mickey out of my name for as long as I can remember. I am overweight, and slightly red of face, like a man who likes a drink or two. Blood pressure you see – but I don't over imbibe. My real weakness is good food, well cooked and enjoyed with pleasant company. I have a snort or two sometimes; a good malt from the highlands, crisp and peaty like the land on which it's produced. But I don't get drunk - well not very often.

At school the children sang, "Follow the yellow brick road," in high squeaky munchkin-like voices with unfailing regularity. Or there were those who shouted, "Hey Dorothy, click your heels man," across the crowded playgrounds, and that was the pupils.

I'd come out of college with the idea that I could make a difference. I had a kind of evangelical zeal to make all children educated in the ways of English; after several years of verbal abuse I snapped and had retaliated, just as I had done as a child. Told this spotty chav boy precisely what I thought of him. I think I added something like, "The best part of you ran down the inside of your mother's leg." To be honest I don't totally remember, I was feeling too good at the time - lost in the moment.

Next day I was marched into the office of the Head teacher, by her goose stepping little side-kick of a deputy. "The Head wants to seeee you," he had extended the see so that it sounded like a siren's wail. Once upon a time I thought he was one. He held his hands in such a supine position every time he spoke, that I expected to hear the chant of, "Knit one, pearl one," as he spoke. I followed his slope shouldered back as he marched before me.

Once Uriah had departed, she immediately headed for the moral high-ground and talked of how we should, "Respect the children." That was a laugh, especially as she spent her days ensconced in an office surrounded by her group of acolytes. Small minded over sweaty men who managed to cram the word yes into every sentence much like a chav can use the f word. All I could do was look at her hair for distraction. A badly bleached mop - a top a rather dull brain and dressed in clothes which were style-less. That did always get me about teachers, their ability to encapsulate the fashion of many generations at the same time – she was no exception.

I thought of the 1980's Mullet hair style – three haircuts in one and all dreadful.

Her dress sense was dreadful. I marvelled at her Chinese print jackets, mock silk, combined with a skirt which hugged the apple shape of her body and enhanced the scarlet glow of her over scrubbed face. "Mutton dressed as lamb," was the phrase that kept bubbling at the back of my head.

As she droned I felt my mind start to wander. I saw myself pouring a cup of cold coffee over her head and asking her politely to get screwed. Instead I just listened and when she suggested I apologise to the child I declined.

"You see," she implored, "the child's mother has complained."

I shrugged.

"It seems you called the boy scum," she continued.

"Well he is!" I exclaimed.

"Mmmm," she considered. "Well the mother has spoken to the father."

"Single parent is she? There's a surprise. What is he one of nine? Ten? All by different jockeys? Does she communicate with him on her mobile? Funny that she even knows who the father is around here. I expect he was conceived in a whirling thrash of alcohol induced copulation." I really didn't care what I said now.

"Well the father is going to make formal complaint that you called him scum."

"Well the father is scum isn't he? He's been in the grubber and one of the boy's sisters is on the game."

"You called the boy scum," the Head teacher continued, "that is not acceptable."

"But he is," I confirmed.

"Well I've asked Dean to come to this office."

There was knocking at the door.

"Come in," the Head teacher called, and the boy entered.

"What's that piece of scum doing here?" I promptly asked, as his spotty grin appeared.

"Mr. Dorothy," the Head snapped, as she ushered the boy out again. "I thought we could settle this easily."

"We can."

Within two weeks I had turned to journalism, leaving behind me several years of the most memorable clap-trap I could no longer endure.

A small inconsequential woman, who had climbed up the greasy career pole, by being a truly dishonest and untrustworthy individual, was now looking at me as if she ruled the world. When I think of her now, my skin begins to crawl and a broad smile appears on my face. The over wordy American marketing speak and the superlative, have a very, very, nice day. That made me laugh. Don't just have a nice day, have a very, very nice day. What a crock! When I think of it now I realise just how absurd the place was and how, though I wanted to make a difference I didn't. The kids succeeded despite the teachers and not because of them.

And the trouble with the teachers? They moan. One endless moan after another. If the kids wore brown, rather than black shoes- they moaned. If the weather was bad - they moaned. If the heating went off they moaned. But, and here was the rub, when asked to actually do anything, like raise a complaint, they scuttled under the nearest log. So for my trouble I'd become the staff rep. Listened to their moans and voiced them. Now I was voicing my own.

I think my parting words were something like, "You can take your school and your scum kids and shove them right up your fat jacksy, or did I actually say arse?"

Either way it was the cause of my journalism on education and I had created many features about the state of the nation's schools, and my editor loved them. Well I say my, I was a freelance stringer, a ducker and diver, a digger-up of shit.

I developed a new strength to look at things as they actually were and not as people might want things to be perceived. I had a built-in bullshit detector and I put that to good use in my journalism. That's what being different makes you – it makes you strong. Education has nothing to do with learning; it's all about social conditioning. Learning to do as you are told. Learning to learn the rules and what you should regurgitate like some great Pelican. That's the real deep seated problem, if you teach someone to think, to evaluate, you have to accept that they might not reach the same conclusion as you. But the clue I'd thought, was the thought process. That's precisely what I wanted the kids to get to; some did –most didn't. Teach a person to think for themselves and you are home and dry. Once you've done that, the whole world is set in motion and once moving it's unstoppable. And that I suppose was why I was offered the assignment.

As the years passed the quips about Kansas and red shoe heel clicking began to diminish from my memory and I had become a fixture among the Fleet Street fraternity. Considered a cynic and hard-bitten, editors used me to get inside the darker side of humanity. There was no Mrs. Miggins cat caught up a tree for me, or fluffy white bunnies in some girl's pet corner. Nope, I got the "Jilted woman boils bunny," story, or "Corrupt politician caught in bed with a rent boy." I'd dug up the piece which made headlines on the masturbating chokers club. You know where people jerk off at the point of death. Only sometimes it goes wrong and people die.

Famous people too. Singers, MP's, and all sorts, even a guy that ended up in jail for manslaughter after his wife begged him to strangle her at the point of orgasm, because she came more deeply. And he killed her, actually killed her; the MP found in wardrobe with an orange in his chops and Michael Hutchence found with a belt around his neck. All the scum came my way, and I kind of liked it. The teaching evangelist had been knocked out of me and unlike others teachers not been replaced by well meaning masochism. I wasn't going to have to deal with the scum and now I could call them that: Scum.

Weird stories about weird scenes inside the gold mine, whatever slimy dirty story the world could dredge up, I usually got them; mostly after some smoother and more old school tie, knob head had either turned it down or messed it up.

Me I hadn't gone to Eton, or any public school for that matter. Hadn't even passed the eleven plus. You know, the test, where you had to fit shapes together to make a triangle. And on the basis of some flawed test your life chances were chosen for you, I couldn't see the point in that, but boy I could read and write. Read everything D.H. Lawrence had written in one summer holiday, including Lady Chat. I was fourteen.

When I got to university, despite coming from a secondary school background, I excelled. The toffs and those with a hot plum in their mouths disliked me; disliked me because I was ruthless and more clever than they were. I had to be, there was no daddy money to fall back upon. When they went home to their opulent families at Christmas I stayed in Halls. Usually because I had a job in a bar or a petrol station. Something that kept me working and gave me food, any menial job in fact so I could stay at university. That was when I hit the books. Late nights in the library working, studying, reading, grafting and that was why I got a first.

Summers I spent on the building sites, working to try and scratch money together for the next year. Up to my neck in filth, pug, muck and bullets I sweated my youth out through my pores. But I was not going to be held down, any obstacle I vaulted over, and as a result? Well .....

To the posh girls I was a novelty, a bit of rough with a brain, so I often did not sleep alone. Once I went off to Lincolnshire to this place, I'd been invited by this girl you see, and I was coughing all night. On the second night the lady of the house, the mother, brought me some medicine and herself in a tight negligee. Man she had hard nipples and what she couldn't do with her mouth. That was my introduction to the wealthy.

To the boys I was either ignored or deplored, unless they needed help with assignments. They lacked my drive, both in the bedroom and the classroom, and they resented me for being a member of the, "Nut brown working classes," a subject of derision. It was at university that I learned the real nature of prejudice. Not the overt, but the covert; the covert of whisperings and snide comments. They were probably the most important lessons I ever learned, and that includes some rather inspiring lectures; that was what made me an effective journalist. I learned quickly and didn't need to be told things three times. I could piece stories together. I could think.

February the 3rd, I remembered it well, as well as the day I lost my virginity, painful, and yet one of those times a person never forgets. My editor Marmaduke Fussly called me into his office and with a sweep of his pinned striped arm, with a fat pink hand protruding from his pin-striped sleeve, bad me to sit.

"What do you know about faith healers ?" he asked throwing a pack of cigarettes across the desk at me and pulling two dirty scotch glasses from the desk drawer.

"Not much," I replied as he poured.

"Me neither," He exhaled and a large plume of blue smoke rose into air. "But there's this American chappie, Lucus Cropier, he's causing a bit of a stir. He claims with faith he can give everybody ..."

"Oh Christ not another one?" I laughed reaching for a scotch which Fussly had poured in generous measure.

"This one's different Dotty."

He had given me the nick name when I started and it had stuck. I sort of liked it but didn't know why. It would have upset me years before and were I still at school I'd probably have busted his nose. Like I did that once when a kid attacked me for being, "different." You know like Piggy in Lord of the Flies.

"So what do you want me to do?" I asked lighting up.

"Find out about the guy. Where he comes from – you know the routine."

"Well that's easy enough," I mocked, exhaling a deep blue haze. "Bible belt somewhere in the mid-west."

"Well then? Off you jolly well go?"

"What to America? On expenses?"

"Absolutely. This chappie is coming over to the Albert Hall

in early April, Easter time, so you've only got a few weeks to dig up the dirt. So you'd better piss off and do your worst. There's a dirty little grubbling."

"I'll need some money," I replied, still slightly stunned by the sudden impulse for me to be given expenses. I usually had the slim pickings associated with the grubby underworld, not trips to the States.

"There," he said, "company credit card, twenty five thousand dollar limited. And before you think about pissing off with my money, just remember I'll have your bollocks pickled if you do."

"Why me?" I genuinely asked.

"Why you dear boy? Because you are cynical, and you won't be swayed easily by a confidence trickster. You know the kind that offers comfort to confused old ladies just before they enter the glorious kingdom. Provided that they have left their money to the right church. So get out there and root around in the mud of his past. You know the kind of stuff. Ex-girlfriend exposes, get them to tell you he has a passion for bum fucking. Or that he once drank too much and then slapped one of them about. Hey he might even be a queer – even better."

"You really are a nasty bugger," I replied laughing.

"Yep, ain't I just? But this is journalism." His face became serious. "Listen Olly I want everything you can find."

He never used my name unless he felt that a really serious story was about to break.

"Draw a thousand dollars from petty cash and get on a plane tonight. Get there hire a car do whatever it takes but get me my story." He hung his head despairingly in his hands

"What's wrong?" I asked, seeing his body language.

"Nothing," he replied, "I'm just considering the situation."

"Find out if she," he corrected himself, "he, find out if he, is genuine."

It was then that I knew the real motive for sending me on this wild goose chase. Marmaduke's wife Jennifer was suffering with multiple sclerosis, and she was now in a wheel chair. When I'd first met her I had been amazed by her striking figure and beautiful long legs. Twenty years his junior she had developed early on set and was looking worse by the day now. Poor old Fussly he'd spent thousands getting her care and to no avail, now he was sending me to find out if this faith healer was genuine. I knew he was probably just like all the others, a con. I realised that despite his cynical approach Marmaduke must love his wife a great deal, a very great deal. Love her enough to compromise all of his ideals and also to put some last ditch attempt at a cure in the hands of an evangelist faith-healer.

"Why didn't you ask one of your Old Etonians to do the job?"

"Oh Christ Dotty I want an answer which I can trust not some half-baked crock of pooh."

I smiled at his faith in my skills, "So you trust me?"

He nodded.

"So much for Eton then?"

"Bollocks to Eton." He lifted his glass in a mock toast.

"Bollocks to Eton," I added as our glasses clinked.

"Listen though Oliver I'm deadly serious about this. I want you to get over to the states and find out what you can. Birth, him as a teenager, anything. I don't want some spoon bender making chumps out of the British public. Listen, he claims he has touched the hand of God and that when he lays his hands upon someone that their soul belongs to him. That in return for the healing they must give up their soul."

"He sounds like a right basket-case to me," I replied, pouring us both another Scotch. "So I'll do a bit of research over here for a couple of days. You know British Library, that sort of thing."

His response was swift and angry.

"Not bloody likely!" he snapped. "You my old son; you will be on a flight to Dullas tomorrow. Mandy will send over the tickets first thing, first class. You'll be flying into Washington to attend his next great event, near to Arlington."

"What's he gonna do next then? Raise someone from the dead. How about JFK?"

"I don't give a rat's. But you better be on that plane or you'll never write another word in the UK, unless it's a letter."

The conversation then turned into something lighter and

altogether more pleasant as we drank another Scotch or two before finally going our separate ways. Me to my unmade bed, complete with unwashed clothes strewn upon it. And he to his crippled wife who he loved more dearly that anything. In fact Jennifer was the most precious thing he had and he didn't mind who knew it. He had said it often enough – that, "Jenny was his life."

Staring at the ceiling of my run-down flat, I watched the head-lights of the traffic as they danced across the patterns in the Artex, my mind wondering precisely what I was supposed to find. The fact that the faith healer was genuine or that he was not? That he could cure serious illness or he could not? I imagined that Marmaduke would be imagining much the same and hoping it was the former rather than the latter.

* * *

On the plane I was using my internet connection to find as much information as possible on the incredible life of Lucus Cropier and his meteoric rise to fame. Overnight he had become a phenomenon, though some church leaders particularly the Catholics had denounced him as a fraud, a small time magician.

I located him instantly and noticed immediately his looks, which were striking. Tall and athletic he was a beautiful specimen of mankind. Don't get me wrong, I'm heterosexual, but I could see the depth of his appeal to women. It was reassuringly fatherly, almost like Santa Claus in his full roundedness, but he was slim. Like Elvis Presley he had that voice in rich baritone, but there was edginess too; an edginess which spoke of sexual promise and danger. Like Count Dracula or Errol Flynn or Clark Gable there was that something, that star quality; that something which made everyone listen when he spoke. His hair was a lustrous black and his eyes deep, thoughtful and almost hypnotic, were dark pools which seemed to reflect thoughts. When he spoke I could feel myself being drawn into his world. His voice was soft and yet somehow commanding and when he raised his hands it was as if his stature increased thirty fold. Like Martin Luther King he had that indefinable something which makes a person listen. He certainly was one of the best orators I had ever seen in operation. But more than that he seemed genuine, gentle and caring and people responded. Men began to spontaneously cry when he touched them, usually on the shoulder, while women fell at his feet shaking uncontrollably. Young girls were burbling and giggling and if I didn't know better I'd say their reactions were almost erotic, almost pre coital. Many fell face down, but raised their pelvises, or crawled provocatively on all fours as if in preparation for penetration. Many cupped their genital area as if someone or something was attempting to enter them and they were seeking to deny access to themselves. Many were baying, long loud moans so provocative and sexual in nature that I could feel my own arousal, just looking at the pictures. Some howled and cried like wolves or bitches on heat, as if calling for a mate, while others tore at their clothes exposing their breasts and legs in a display of lewd abandon.

I watched as he manipulated large scale audiences into virtual hysteria and then calmly cured cripples by laying his hands on them. Those he touched thrashed and he made much theatre out of that and I wondered how many of the miracles were staged? If he was a magician he was excellent at his trade. I thought it was a kind of mass hypnosis that he administered; a kind of Hitler style rally abandon, coupled with chanting and wild promise.

I saw with my own eyes the contracts which were willingly signed by each person before they were cured. It was a simple contract which merely stated that the soul of the person, once a cure had been affected, belonged to Lucas F. Cropier. There was nothing more, and the souls he claimed, in the interview which was carefully spliced into the live footage, they were souls for his ministry and he was collecting them for a far better place than this earth.

At the end of the forty five minute laying on of hands he simply slipped from the stage as rapturous applause and crying broke out among the crowd. There were shots of him back stage, wiping his hands and face in a towel and taking a drink of pure apple juice, apparently he drinks nothing else.

"And why not?" he said for the camera, "for the apple is from the tree of knowledge and from that we should always drink deeply."

Then briefly he was back on stage bathing in the adoration of the crowd and then once again gone, this time in a plume of red smoke which rose around his feet. And I presume he then passed into a trap door and back to his dressing room. It certainly was a show. But for me the cynic that's precisely what it was a show, a carefully staged rock-star show. He gave the crowd what they wanted, a kind of religious infusion combined with entertainment.

Then came the interviews with those he had cured, hundreds of them. The lame who were walking and the blind that could see. I was completely sceptical. No worse, I thought the whole thing a charade, an elaborate charade designed to entice even bigger audiences. Yet there seemed to be no collection plate. I switched off and suddenly felt a huge surge of relief pound into my blood as if even the recording contained some attractant or hypnotic content.

Thinking about the performance I could see why people liked him. He had star quality, just like the great rock performers and he used every ounce of it to his advantage.

"Would you like a drink sir?" the trolley dolly chirped. "Red wine?"

"Thank you," I replied, my mind racing still. "What sort is it," I asked.

"Shiraz," she smiled a toothy American smile at me.

"Oh that's a bit on the sharp side for me. Do you have any white, a nice creamy Chardonnay? If you have I'll take that instead."

As I drank the crisp cheap wine there was none of the richness which I had come to expect. In fact it tasted bitter, dull, and as a result I left in unfinished.

I wanted to sleep so that I was ready to listen and watch the master trickster at his work when we landed, but I had to find out more. My lap-top started the trawl once again.

I started to seek background detail. The Cropier family had been resident in New Orleans, there were connections to

Lafayette. They came to prominence as lawyers in the civil war; one had been an aide to Robert E. Lee while another, a sibling, had been an aide to Ulysses Grant and a third had been a prominent patron of the arts at The Ford Theatre. They had moved to Washington after the war and came to sudden prominence in the world of politics. Lucus had been born the only son of this old French family, his grandfather had two sons, Louis and Francois and both had high political and military connections. Louis, The father of Lucus had been advisory aide to Joseph Kennedy during the Second World War. He had advocated appeasement of Hitler, but as the war grew his prominence waned. Whereas his uncle Francois had been a close friend and advisor of Patton; as the fortunes of one waned so the other waxed, that was until the sudden death of Patton after the conflict. With the election of the Kennedys to the White House the fortunes of the Cropiers rose once again.

Louis the father had been almost seventy when Lucus arrived and the scandal of his pregnant thirty year old bride was the talk of Washington. Louis however, had made much of his vitality and youthfulness.

Lucus had grown into the ministry of the church as a rebellion against politics. It was there that he had learned the art of oration.

I did a swift calculation. By my reckoning Lucus Cropier was at least sixty maybe even older and yet he looked like a man of twenty. There was no crepe paper skin, no dulling of the eyes and certainly no loss of physique. On his head there was not one single grey hair, and yet he did not have that ridiculous look of an old man trying to dye in youth. He still had it, and had it in abundance. He looked positively vibrant. In fact I would have said that despite the age difference between us he looked the younger man. Now that is never easy to say but like I told you I'm pretty straight. I have this thing about age too, so I don't want to admit how age is getting at me. You know the creaking and cracking first thing in the morning and how I don't drink after 8pm, just in case.

The interviewer looked uncomfortable on the screen. To any observer it could almost be construed as fear. Though he was asking questions he gave the impression of a wild animal ready to take flight at the first opportunity.

"Well my father was a man of principles," Cropier began.

The interviewer was looking uneasy.

"A man with a passion for life, a lust for life," Cropier continued.

Cropier was casually dressed; a non descript casual, the kind that does not draw the eye but looks strikingly smart nonetheless. I watched him as he spoke, tried to see some pattern in his movements; listened to the musical lilt of his voice to see if it had any special tone or hypnotic quality. As he spoke he drew me in.

I woke to the sound of movement all around me as people were getting ready to disembark. I had no recollection of switching off my lap-top, and absolutely none of stowing the item away in the overhead locker. The landing had been so smooth I had not stirred from my deep sleep. It was something I have never done before or since and to this day I can produce no rational reason for it. It just happened like that. That is the truth.

II

My hotel was a warm building which looked out toward a swathe of tall pines interspersed with deciduous trees, mostly Aspen, Beech and Maple. The lobby was clean and bright and despite being on the edge of the city it was easy to get a taxi into the centre. From Dullas airport it had cost me nearly fifty dollars and I wondered what Marmaduke would do, once he got the final expenses tally.

Lucus Cropier was reaching the heights of fame now. His latest venture was to be staged in the main drag between the Washington Monument and the Lincoln Memorial. The last major event I could remember taking place anywhere near there had been Martin Luther King's I have dream speech. At the foot of the Lincoln Memorial, King had voiced his hopes for a generation. Now Cropier was going to stage an open air faith healing circus and the government were going to applaud and sanction this absurdity. In the land of free and the home of the brave a magician was going to attain the same iconic status as a prime mover for civil rights; I marvelled at the idea - only in America.

I poured a large scotch from the mini-bar and switched on the TV. Adverts hit my eyes like a wall of solid rock, impenetrable, huge and repetitive. My body clock was thrown out of sequence and I looked at the clock to see how much time I had before the start of the event: Hours! I opened my passport and flicked the valuable press pass onto the bed. That was the ticket to get me closer to this man who had swept across America like a plague, and was about to enter Britain for the first time.

After a revitalising shower and a meal in the hotel restaurant, I took a stroll. It was mid - afternoon now. The steak I had eaten was best described as a Desperate Dan sized portion and I hadn't been able to finish it; the fries and chicken which had accompanied it were so vast that I genuinely exemplified the word, "full."

I walked down past the White House taking in the sites which I had known when working on the Washington Post. I crossed the park and slowly made my way toward the Washington Monument; the monolith which stands like a needle puncturing the sky, a vast accusing finger pointing toward the heavens. Then facing toward the Lincoln Memorial, I saw the circus which was the evangelical experience of Lucus Cropier. A white canvas tent faced me, the front open and covering a vast stage hung with red and yellow curtains; that stood between me and Abraham Lincoln, like some obscene carnival scene... A band of musicians were sound checking, a guitar and a piano and a set of drums. I could hear the sound travel up to the monument, a sound of rock music. To any ill informed bystander it looked like the preparation for some outdoor evening concert; there were lights and bunting and flags, American flags draped in long swags from tree to tree. There were ice-cream vendors, hot dog sellers and men whipping candy floss onto sticks. It instantly reminded me of the old style fun-fairs I had experienced as a child in England. The bright lights and loud sounds which were designed as an antidote to the post-war austerity of English rationing, combined with the glitz and glamour of the Catholic Church.

For some reason I thought of the inside of the Duomo in Florence. The huge painting of the Devil herding the innocent into hell and the monsters that were eating them there. This had the same colour, the same shock value to the eye. I tried to think of myself as a peasant coming into such a building and being overawed by the images I saw. Overawed by the gold and the incense, and the opulence of it all, and here Cropier was doing exactly the same thing.

I made my way down toward the stage, I ducked under a guy rope hoping to catch a glimpse of the architect of this utter madness, but as I approached two burly bouncers appeared as if from nowhere. They reminded me of Staffordshire Bull Terriers.

"Nobody goes under the rope," one said.

It felt like the old nightclub adage, "If your name's not down you're not coming in," only this was delivered with menace, while the second man made a sound which was reminiscent of a growl.

"I'm press," I said, "I've come all the way from England. Flew in today to interview Mr. Cropier." I tried the approach which had seen me in good stead over the years. It failed.

"Mr. Cropier doesn't do interviews," the first man snarled, "And besides he's not here. Won't be here until just before the show."

I stood my ground.

"So can we ask you to leave sir?" He lifted the guy rope.

Both men grinned, and I had the distinct feeling that both were full of impending menace and possible attack. Like two wolves they drew their lips back and exposed large white fang-like teeth, in a warning. One ran his tongue across his fangs as if cleaning them.

"Ok," I said, "but can I interview Mr. Cropier after the show?" I asked. "Give him my card and say that I am doing background research on him before he comes to England. That should make him interested."

I felt rather than saw a third man approach me, only this time it was from outside the guy rope. He was tall, thin and incredibly strong, for when he introduced himself as Mr Cropier's agent and shook my hand his grip was so powerful I thought all the bones in my hand would be crushed to a pulp. I couldn't now describe the man except he was dressed totally in black. There was not one speck of colour on him, though he had heavy rings of silver or platinum on each finger. I had not seen him approach and I had not heard him approach. Suddenly he was there; it was as if he had silently slid into position.

"Ambrose St. Helliere, manager," he said, "at your service. Without giving me breathing space to give my name, he continued, "So you want to meet our saviour?"

I found the use of the word rather strange, but carried on

with the charm offensive. "Absolutely, I'm doing an article on his extra ordinary gift of healing. I work for a paper…"

"Which one?" he interrupted.

"Well actually, I'm on assignment…"

"So you're freelance?"

I nodded, unable to continue with the game. For some reason I felt compelled to give the absolute truth. I thought of Marmaduke's sick wife and the possibility of a cure. Thought of how cynical I was and yet how some of the research showed this man to be genuine. My brain was bubbling with the idea of an exposé and yet now I was uncertain. I kept thinking: What if this guy is for real?

He, as if he had read my thoughts suddenly said, "Thank you, that is very honest of you," as if I had spoken my thoughts out loud. "I will arrange an interview after the show. Perhaps if you come back stage at the end of the ceremony we can whisk you in to see his Lordship."

"Marvellous, how do I get back stage?" I asked.

"Oh Ronnie and Reggie there will know who to look for. They're terrific at their job. They are so quick on their feet, though you wouldn't expect that from such big men."

I turned and expected to see them directly behind me, where only a second before they had stood, but they were now talking to a couple who had strayed under the guy rope at the other side of the perimeter, some 400 yards away. I could just make out the faces of the young couple as they were ejected; though the distance was great, I could see a look of abject terror in their expressions.

"So I make my way to the stage?" I asked.

But as I turned to face him once again I saw him striding off into the distance. I wondered at the cynical view the manager had exposed by calling Cropier, "Saviour and his Lordship," perhaps, I thought, there is tension in the camp and the manager might spill some beans for me. Perhaps the Prima Donna complex had started? Perhaps Cropier was going to do what all celebrities seem to do and disappear up inside his own rectum? Perhaps the rot had started? I vowed to get at him over dinner- once I had the interview with Cropier in the bag, or on tape. I'd have to get back to the hotel and get my machine, I thought, that would be fine. Get a few drinks inside the bugger and offt we'd jolly well go. Maybe there'd be a story of the ungrateful star, no longer in tune with his Svengali. A story of lust and groupies and money all made out of a trick and the whole damn thing would come down like a doll's house in a hurricane. Maybe I was going to get a real doozy at last. I could almost count the money, but in a way I felt sorry for Marmaduke, his hopes would be dashed.

I sat on the grass and lit a cigarette, then lay back and folded my arms behind my head to contemplate my next move. The warm afternoon drifted on the clouds above my head.

When I woke up it was getting dark and the crowds were beginning to gather, there were groups of people massing and my bladder was full. I needed to pee, so I made my way over to the chemical toilets which had sprung up while I lay sleeping. I couldn't believe that I would not have noticed their installation.

My mouth was dry and I needed a drink. No time to go back to the hotel now, I'd have to wing it and write it up later. I kicked myself for being such a chump and falling asleep again.

At one of the stands I bought a giant soft drink. It was red, so I assumed it was cherry or some such. It was synthetic and rather sharp with a slight bitter after taste. I drank deeply like a man who has come through a sand storm to a clear mountain spring, then suddenly stopped myself. "Berk, what if there's something in the stuff," I said aloud.

"Hey buddy," the vendor squealed in reply. He was a fat, pink-faced, man who clearly felt aggrieved at what I had said. "There ain't nothin' in ma drinks. That's a goddamn sweet mother of a cherry soda boy." His voice had a Carolina drawl, slow and soft like some new hidden language.

"I was just talking to myself," I protectively answered, in my prim English, whilst trying to walk away.

"You Australian?" he asked casually, as he flipped a few hamburgers which were grilling under his sweaty attention. I notice a tattoo on his left forearm – it read, USSS Nem something, he noticed my eyes and covered it.

"British," I said, noticing he had noticed my curiosity.

"Well you ou-tta' know betta' then boy. Mind ya mouth son," he concluded, as a small boy in a checked shirt called for burger, with onions. "You know what they say don't ya?"

I shook my head.

"Curiosity killed the cat," he paused, and slapped the saliva from the back of his hand as he passed the burger to the boy. "So don't you get too beaky boy, don't get too damn beaky."

As I made a rapid exit. I thought the boy reminded me of the children's character Howdy-Doody. It was a surreal moment. As the child smiled at me I thought I saw sharp white teeth. Pointed like one of the dolls which attacked Jane Fonda in the film Barbarella. Things began not to make sense.

The lights on the stage were shining brightly, and I could hear the breeze flipping the bunting back upon itself, making a whiplash slapping sound above my head. I thought for a brief moment that the flags were bats. I pinched myself, but did not know if I was dreaming that part too. Everything was wrong, nothing made sense.

Bats were circling above the whole park, or at least I thought it was bats and the ground seemed to be moving, undulating like some moving carpet or giant escalator. I had the most sudden fear of being trapped. In this open space I felt claustrophobic like I had never done before. The very air seemed to get thick and my breathing increased in speed – adrenalin was coursing through my veins and my whole being screamed run, run now: Start and never stop.

Suddenly a chord of heavy guitar struck out from the speakers like some great summoning bell and the crowd, into which I had melted, turned as one, and the performance began.

First came a man clad in yellow and green like some bizarre clown, a huge grin painted on his white face. Half clown half monster he strode about the stage rhythmically, to the beat of his own bright red guitar. The drummer, naked to the waist slammed roll after roll behind a bass held by a leering, tongue lolling, mass of hair which nodded to the beat. A spotlight shone on a keyboard player who stood rather than sat.

The sound was powerful, hard, but even now I cannot retain a single note or melody.

The band played and the crowd cheered which surprised me. There were so many age groups there, some as young as three were dancing and clapping as if listening to a nursery rhyme. The old men seemed to be jiving or jitter-bugging with the young women. Off the beat unless they were hearing something I was not. Older women were sombre and singing along, though I could not make out the words, but I caught the odd phrase which made me think Sinatra.

Old women were wailing and crying now, distraught in the knowledge of the sound. To each it was as if they were all hearing something different to the other.

I heard hard rock, others soft ballad but all seemed content. It took every ounce of will power to turn my gaze away from the stage, and as I did so a great chord erupted and the smiling faces I saw cheered.

The guitar player was at the microphone, "Ladies and gentlemen," he shrieked as the crowd went wild in anticipation. "Ladies and gentlemen, please put your hands together for the sensational Lucus Cropier."

The crowd erupted.

"Can I put my hands on you?" Cropier asked.

The crowd yelled again.

"Can I put my hands on you?"

Another cheer.

"Well can I? Can I make you feel? Can I make your body heal?"

The crowd began to chant, "Yes, yes, yes."

"Finger tips of holy fire," Cropier screamed, then raised his hands above his head. "I give you everlasting sweet desire." And with that he jumped into the crowd and began his ministry.

I had been moved by the grass carpet toward him, and suddenly there he was directly in from of me.

"And what can I give you?" he asked, looking into my eyes.

I felt a sudden shock shoot through me as if I had handled a wet plug socket with bare hands.

"Of course you do?" His voice pierced the crowd. "Of course you do." Then he turned his back and vanished ahead of me and try as I might to force my way through the crowds I always seemed to be one or two strides behind him. I felt like a man swimming after a beach ball which was skipping over the ocean surface in the wind. The more I tried to catch it, the further away it went, and the sea of humans was too strong to swim against.

I watched as he raised a man from a wheelchair and made him walk like an infant toward him. He tottered, smiled and stumbled, then I saw the man collapse in tears into Cropier's arms, only to rise once again and skip like an adolescent across the stage. As true as I stand here I saw a woman with such bad arthritis that her hands were twisted and knarled like old parts of a wind blown tree. He took his hands and placed each of hers between his, much as you would a sandwich in a grilling machine. Her screams rose above the crowd but when he released her from his grip her hands were straight, thin and fine, as if they were made of porcelain.

"Do you give your soul unto me?" Cropier asked.

The woman screamed, "Yes."

"Then you will receive back your life," Cropier yelled and the crowd chanted.

"Life, life, life."

I had seen him do this on the film footage.

"Louder," Cropier screamed, and the fever pitch increased.

"Do you want life?" Cropier asked the old woman again.

She fell to her knees with her face buried into her hands.

"Yes, yes I do," she answered meekly.

"Then get up," said Cropier, "stand up and face the world."

As the young woman rose her whole posture changed. Her spine straightened as her face, released from her own grip, was younger, revitalised. The crowd gasped to see the transformation. And I could not believe what I saw. The woman had grown young, grown young before my very eyes. This once arthritic old woman was now vibrant and in possession of the figure she so obviously once had.

Cropier turned to the crowd, "Let me put my hands on you, Let me put my hands on yoooooo," he yelled. "Give me your allegiance, give me your souls and I will give you salvation. I will give you the world and all that's in it. I will give you everything your heart can desire."

The crowd began to chant loudly, "Salvation, Salvation, Salvation now."

Cropier moved to a blind man whose eyes were black holes of emptiness. He placed his palm across the man's head and when he took them away two fine blue eyes stared out from under the covering.

"See," yelled Cropier. "The blind man sees. Believe in my ways and sign my contract. Give me the power to change your world. No more heartache, no more pain. I can take it all away. We can all go walking naked in the rain."

At that point the heavens opened and a rain fell upon the whole gathering as if on cue. People started to dance and young girls took off their clothes and began to gyrate naked and provocatively to the music which had started once again. These were the rhythms of life, peristaltic rhythms, and some were gyrating in front of groups of young men. Some were on all fours their legs spread wide and their heads down as men approached behind them. It was as if an orgy of animalistic sex were about to commence. Like a mass herd of copulating goats the audience laughed and bellowed and brayed. Cropier had vanished into the crowd and I had lost sight of him; I could still hear his voice which now had an undertone of menace woven into it. I wished I had my camera, or a recorder or something, anything, which I could use to make a record of what I was seeing. No one seemed to take the slightest notice of the copulating couples around them; most were in some kind of mass hypnotic trance. A young woman walked straight toward me and grabbed at my covered manhood. She clawed at me in complete abandon, fell to her knees and tried to rip open my fly, until I shoved her away. Then some other man lifted her over his shoulder and slapping her hard on the rump whooped as if he had collected her as his prize.

The crowd were in a state of hysteria, crying, yelling, howling, and Cropier had gone. My eyes strained through the crowd, but I had lost my mark. I had a terrible urge to move to get to the stage or get to the edge of the crowd - get out.

"Get out," I yelled. "Let me out."

"But you are out," a soft voice said behind me. It was the man himself. I had not seen him approach and suddenly he was there.

"Amazing isn't it?" he said, as the world around us became instantly silent. It was as if we were now inside a bubble, a sound-proof bubble and he and I were observing like gods or aliens. "The masses," he continued.

I was too dumb-struck to speak.

"The thronging huddled masses. Take a close look Dorothy this isn't Kansas is it? Home sweet home and all that jazz. Most of these specimens would sell their child for a dollar, and you know how much they profess to love their offspring? Just look at them," he paused, "and this is the pinnacle of creation? All they need is a little en-ter-tain-ment to keep them happy," he sounded the syllables in a Carolina drawl, "and a belly full of food and something to lick around at night and they'll sell you their soul. Humanity verses a volcano, humanity verses the sea, I wonder which I should bet upon?"

"How did you do it?" I asked. "Did you spike the drink or what?"

"Or what," he replied, sarcastically.

"Well some how you induced the whole crowd to do things which only the most base of animals would do."

"Precisely," he laughed. "And are these not priceless? Just look at them, a cosmic experiment doomed to failure. A rabbit walking upright, a dinosaur without scales. We should despise them all."

"So why did it not work with me then?" I asked. "What makes me special?"

"Me," he answered. "I make you special. I allowed you to see this. I wanted you to tell Marmaduke precisely what he wants to hear."

"How the hell?"

"O come on Dotty, hell has got nothing to do with it. Do you think you are the only one who can research? I have legions at my disposal and you? You are just a small irritation to me, like a small pebble in my shoe."

"A pebble in my shoe? What are you then Mafia?"

"Don't be absurd," he snapped. "I," he paused, "I am more powerful than you could possibly imagine. Take a look around you. I have the power to give you anything you desire, any woman, any job, any life; money, sex, fame, you can have them all. All you have to do is believe. And then your spirit will start to leave."

"Listen sunshine," I was on the attack. "That old woman wasn't old at all. She was just an actress. An actress who rubbed her make-up off in her hands when her face was hidden. And the hand thing - that was some sort of trick too. You must think I came up on a down train?"

"You have no faith?"

"Faith? Bloody faith! In what, a magician who induces crowds into hysteria? I've seen pop-stars do much the same thing."

"My you are cynical."

"And you Cropier? How do you say it Crop-ee-air? You are just a copier. A copier of cheap tricks and home spun miracles. A charlatan."

"You just come and see me after the show, and I will give you the one thing you desire – your interview." He laughed, a deep guttural laugh, "Now the show must go on."

When he stepped forward suddenly, I was at the back of the crowd and he was at the stage once again and person after person was approaching him for a cure. The music had gone and the healing had begun in deadly earnest. I tried to push forward but this time I could never seem to penetrate the crowd.

I could hear the chants, soft and mellow, as he gave them the religious experience that they all sought. Some went to rock concerts, some to political rallies, others came to events like these. Events where somehow the meaninglessness of human existence might be explained. He was right, this was obscene, but I could no longer see the obscenity. My eyes strained through the darkness to see the nude and the naked. I could not see any. I began to doubt my own sanity and eyes. Had I really seen copulating couples, and if I had who would believe me? Couples and groups of youngsters engaged in mass hysteria sex, and publicly to boot. Without evidence I'd be laughed out of any editorial office in either the US or UK.

All I could do now was sit on the grass and wait. And as I waited, I drifted; as I drifted, I lay back and placed my hands behind my head. The grass was dry to the touch, drought dry.

When I woke my clothes were bone dry and Ronnie and Reggie were standing over me with rather gleeful expressions on their faces.

"Mr. Cropier will see you now, sleeping beauty," they said in robotic unison.

"Jet lag, it's just jet lag," I proffered in reply.

I I I

"In the morning, don't say you love me," Lucus Cropier chirped as he sat in his dressing room. "Isn't that we're supposed to say? You know after we have taken advantage of someone? Twirled them around and stolen their pound, dropped their panties on the ground?"

He was mocking me, even using my currency of words, instead of the almighty dollar. And the panties, he knew precisely why he had chosen that word. I was onto the back foot already.

"You see I'm a poet and don't know it. Well I do actually, there's many a song lyric I've influenced." He looked blankly at the ceiling, "Oh Robert where are you now when we need you most."

I noticed the gaunt body, the black hair and the physique which was toned and muscular; he works out, I thought. Works out hard and eats well but not to excess. Here's a man who takes care of himself, and for his age he looks great. Much better than me in fact, despite being older.

"Do you like what you see? From what I know of you though, you like the girls don't you? Teenage girls to be more precise." He winked in the mirror as I watched his reflected face. "You all have your weaknesses - it's just finding out what they are." He paused and smiled. "Don't you agree?"

"I wanted to do an interview with you," I blurted. "I also wanted to talk to some of those you supposedly cured."

"Young and fresh and sweet?" he continued, almost taunting me, "like the first of the new corn?"

"I didn't come here to talk about me," I replied, trying to divert his uncomfortable prying mind.

"Really, how unusual. When people come to see me they tend to want to talk about themselves and what I can do for them. Human beings are wonderfully selfish don't you think? And marvellously stupid? But you're different aren't you? You think you are so clever," he paused, "and you are," he paused again and his reflected gaze caught my eye once again. "But, and here's the real question, are you clever enough?"

His ploy of going off at a tangent was excellent for interview diversion. The other, blunt instrument technique, is one that politicians favour – continually talking and not allowing anyone else a chance to get a word in edgeways. Cropier was more polite than that and far more cunning. A gentleman, to all appearances, made of softest fine velvet, but in reality a steel fist ready to strike anyone down. He was like a Scorpion circling with his armour up and his lethal stinger ready to be let loose. Warm and rich was the best way I can or could describe his voice. It had no accent at all, and yet it was unusual, not English, nor American and it was gentle, probing, insistent, like the fingers of a lover intent on gaining access to your intimate parts. Trying to worm his way into your thoughts like some bug which had entered your brain through your ear. He was hard to resist; but it was hard not to like him. He smiled a lot, and his eyes glistened. Refined, that's probably the best word I can find to sum him up.

My mind was drifting as if I were entering some soft dream, a trance; I felt as if I were in the half world between sleeping and waking. Suddenly I was snapped back as if released; as if his mind snare had suddenly been loosened and I was allowed to draw a breath, to live once more. If it was hypnosis I had absolutely no idea of how it was done. Maybe it was the tone of his voice or the rhythm of it – but the truth was it worked. Worked on me, the cynical hard-bitten journalist that I was.

"So you want to interview some of my cured congregation," he paused, and then laconically repeated, "just some, oh dear?" He puckered, as he removed the heavy lip make-up, which gave his mouth a full set of lips. "Why not all? After all you believe I'm a charlatan don't you? Otherwise you would not have used the word, supposedly?"

"To be honest I'm open minded," I lied.

"So have you done the research? Have you studied my school

records, my family background?" he smirked into the mirror so that I could see his reflection. "Have you looked into the records and wondered like the rest why I still look so youthful?"

"No," I lied again.

"Now that's not really true is it?" he chuckled. "You mean that you haven't even googled me? I find that hard to believe. I bet you checked me out on the plane on your way over. You see they say I am some kind of Warlock, Witch or Wizard. Let me tell you, none of those are as great as me, me I am far more. Does that sound arrogant? Alarming?"

All I could think was, "Yes you big headed bastard," but I said nothing.

He chuckled, "Your thoughts give you away," he said.

"You don't have any idea what I'm thinking."

"Oh but I do, I do," he replied in a very grave voice.

"Why the grave voice?" I asked, trying to unnerve him much as he was me.

"Grave, ah yes, what about the grave? The grave of the child that died? Have you tried that one?" He paused again, and then wiping a tissue across his skin, I could see that he had had facial surgery. His neck was far more lined than his face - the tell tale sign.

"What child?" I tried to sound unknowing.

"Oh my Oliver," he smirked, "you are a cunning little chap."

I wanted to answer but thought, you patronising little charlatan, who the hell do you think you are? Instead I asked calmly, "How did you know my name is Oliver?"

"Ticket, dear heart."

I flipped open my wallet and saw printed, one ticket in the name of Mr. O. Dorothy. How the hell he knew it was Oliver I could only imagine, maybe he played the percentages, after all poker players do. Olaff was unlikely as a Brit. Owen? More likely for someone from Wales, so maybe he just guessed. It's not like there are many names that start with an O.

"There is a grave in Lafayette Cemetery," he began, "that stands above the ground. Water table and all that. And on that grave there is, oh it's a child's grave, a name carved into the soft sandstone. The name is Lucus F. Cropier. Haven't you heard the absurd notion that I stole the name and made my identity from that grave? The fact that my father and mother are now gone? Isn't that rather obvious too? Obviously I killed them and became their son?"

I coughed

"I know it's ridiculous isn't it? I mean we Cropiers are a very select few. Most of my ancestors are in Arlington, just across the Potomac. In fact I'm going there tomorrow, just like I always do when I'm in Washington. There's no Lucus there though. There's one of us in the chair of my grandfathers, Pere La chaise. There are two in Lyon, one in Marseilles and three in your homeland. You see I've done my research too."

"I didn't realise," I replied.

"You see that's the problem isn't it. What people don't or won't understand they either destroy or worship or both. What about you Oliver. What do you want to do?"

"I just want to get at the truth."

"The truth? And what is that? The truth is what people make of it. It's the perspective from which you observe which gives the reality. Therefore not everything is as it seems. Was Hitler a bad man? He loved his dogs and he was a vegetarian, like me. Was Napoleon just compensating for his small stature? Did Lenin really care about the masses, did Frederick Engels and Karl Marx, or was it just an intellectual exercise - a bit of fun. Would the real Martin Luther King stand up? Perhaps a bad choice that, as the man had a tendency to put his stand inside anything young wet and willing. He really did know the meaning of the word to stand, and he did so frequently, and with relish. You see he was no saint, he loved women and women loved him, or his fame to be more precise. So he had what he wanted and the truth, your wonderful truth is suppressed. And why ? Because it's politically expedient. That's why! Don't talk to me about truth or justice or fairness or deserve, he who holds the power holds it all.

Even poor Old Lucifer was cast out of Heaven, the greatest of all the Angels, and why? Because he dared to be different,

237

dared to say, hold on a minute this isn't fair, this isn't," he snarled the words, "the truth."

"That's a very bold thing to say for man of your persuasion," I interrupted.

"Persuasion? What persuasion? Jane Austen persuasion? I more than any stand for the truth and look how I have been repaid. I am vilified; I am a charlatan; I am a fake holy healer; I am something to be feared and despised. What because I speak the truth? Because the truth is ugly? Because the truth is not some meadow full of sweet scents and fluffy clouds. No! The truth is wet earth and musty rot and green flesh and decay and for what - salvation? Or is salvation just a holy game? An experiment? Salvation or salivation, are they not one and the same thing to the observer of an experiment? What about Nietzsche? What did he really think before it was all taken away in a masturbatory haze which drove him crazy? You see there's safety in the post coital bliss, that's why he was at it five, six times a day. Unbalanced, different, difficult to put into any category. Much better to be in a hazy self-induced bliss?"

"So is that you?" I asked.

"For your help and before I come to your beautiful country, and for the sake of Marmaduke's wife I will tell you something that no other human has ever found, or known in their ridiculous research on me. Why? Because they are stupid, gullible and week, suggestible, flawed and above all else cruel. I will give you the truth. It is ugly, bare and foul, much as the truth really is. I will let you speak to the people I have laid my hands upon. You will get your story and what a story you will get." He paused as if recalling an old story and then began again.

"At the back of Old Crofton Church, near Titchfied in Hampshire lies the grave of Lucus F. Cropier, and his two earthly parents Marcel, a Frenchman, and Lucrezia, an Italian, a dark and sultry beauty from Verona. They came to England in 1590 and something, the precise date is not known. They were fleeing the oppression of the French state and found asylum in a small village which was within the estate of the Earl of Southampton.

Now the Earl of Southampton was known as a patron of the arts and Marcel had proved himself to be a fine poet and playwright. He was employed by his benefactor to teach the children of this nobleman French, Latin and the Classics, and in due course he taught others in the village of Titchfield - for free, in his own time. Are you following this?"

"I wish I had a note pad to take this down," I replied.

"There's no need, I'll make absolutely sure that you remember," he said, before continuing. "Marcel taught the Earl's children well, conversed with William Shakespeare, of whom the Earl was also a patron. Met Christopher Marlowe and penned a few words which Marlowe added to his own work. Perhaps you have heard them before. Marcel wrote them for Lucrezia. He began to recite:

And I will make thee a bed of roses,

And a thousand fragrant posies,

A cap of flowers, and a kirtle,

Embroidered all with leaves of myrtle.

In time there were seven children in all for the Earl and his Spanish bride, and Lucrezia made a name for herself as an apothecary. Skills she had learned in Verona and brought to England with her. Shakespeare stole that notion too and used it in Romeo and Juliet. Lotions and potions were created and dispensed to the whole of the locality and as a result health improved. She made soap, as only the Italian monks could. She used the shells of nuts to make exfoliating creams for those with skin disorders. She dispensed a perfume which acted as a flea killer and made a form of shampoo, from lamb fat, salt and herbs which killed head lice. The people of Southampton were some of the healthiest in the Kingdom. Lucrezia pioneered the use of fresh water from the Meon River. She filtered hers and boiled it and allowed it to cool before it was used in the home. That was what her Roman ancestors had taught her, and she was fastidious in that one matter. She persuaded the people to dig midden pits, and stools were left to rot well away from homes. Pots of urine were not casually thrown into the street, but were poured into drains which ran through a series of gulleys out toward the sea.

Infections decreased and mortality expectations improved. Indeed the Earl had even mentioned to the Queen, the skills this apothecary had. So much so that Lucrezia was asked to London to treat the Queen's teeth, which she did, quashing the pain; removing those that were rotten and having a set of false ones made of wood and moulded with silver and gold.

The fame of these two people spread far and wide among the nobility. In time they had a son Lucus. A small boy also with extraordinary intellectual and healing powers. Do you recognise the scenario?"

I nodded, "And he was your name sake?"

Cropier had finished removing his make-up now and was resting his chin upon his folded hands and gazing at me through his reflection in the mirror.

"It's a rather a strange coincidence," I continued. I was genuinely intrigued. Why had no other journalist ever found this? Why was I being told? My whole assignment was being given to me verbatim in a conversation. I could hardly believe my luck. If this could be verified in research I could have my link to getting a front pager prior to his English visit. My luck was in and I'd been taught never to look a gift horse in the mouth. I decided to be as receptive as possible and not interrupt whatever, Cropier felt this was most important to his cause, and peoples' belief in him, so let him continue.

"Please carry on," I begged, "this is totally fascinating. The boy?"

"The boy Lucus had even greater powers than his mother. Women in childbirth sent for the boy and his laying of hands on their abdomen removed the pain. The Earl's wife, who he loved with all his heart, could have died at the birth of her third child, there were complications; she was haemorrhaging badly due to difficulties, but when young Lucus came to her aid she sent everyone else away and the boy delivered the child, almost painlessly. A seven year old boy delivering a baby. It was rumoured that he opened the women with a knife and delivered the child through her abdomen. A kind of caesarean section - much as the ancient Romans had done. The mother was ill and required nursing, but she went on to have more healthy offspring. All of those were completely without further complication.

Lucus cured broken bones and set them in splints. Cured fevers by drawing out the puss and infections – much as an Indian does the venom of a snake. There were no bleedings and no leeches, but there was laying on of hands. All in all he helped to make miraculous cures the like of which had never been seen before. People came to him like an old widow woman of the mountains, full of reverence, full of respect, full of awe.

Of all the Earl's sons, that boy delivered by Cropier, he was the strongest and rose to the greatest political prominence. His eldest brother died of some alcohol induced seizure, while the elder fell from his horse and broke his neck whilst hunting. All of this of course happened after the Cropiers had gone."

"But where did they go? Surely the Earl rewarded them for their efforts?"

"Oh, he did. Rewarded them handsomely, with a house and an income. But the priest or vicar, or whatever you'd like to call him, hated the family, hated their prominence, hated them with all the pious Christian virtue he could muster. You see the Cropiers never attended church and he claimed that they were a power for evil in the village. Said they were in fact foreign Catholics, sent to blight the lives of good God-fearing Christians or worse, that they were worshippers of the Devil. And the stupid sheep of his herding actually began to believe that God had cursed them. Lucus F. Cropier became an outcast, something different, something to be avoided, unless a serious illness forced people to him covertly. Like all rebels before him he was shunned. Remember the archangel Lucifer? The first of all the rebels, oh how he was vilified, hated and despised, so too was Lucus F. Cropier. "

"But he wasn't a rebel," I interjected, "he wasn't Lucifer, he was just a small boy."

"Now do you see?"

"See what?"

"The nature of being human is not to question, but to accept. Isn't that the basis of the leap of faith? You don't need to understand, you must never question, but above all never ever challenge. Blessed are the cheese-makers for they shall inherit the earth."

"So what happened next?" I asked.

"The following summer was exceptionally wet and many crops failed due to blight and mildew. And as you know people are amazingly superstitious and stupid. Do you avoid walking under ladders or make the sign of the cross in the path of a black cat? What about salt? Now there's a good one. If spilt, spill some more and throw it over your left shoulder. My, my what would happen if you used your right shoulder? The whole of your world would collapse. Ridiculous? Absolutely! But that is what people, nasty little humans are like. They kill what they don't understand and what they do understand they abuse. The power in the splitting of atoms and what do they make? A bomb. A bomb so dreadful that it could start a thermo-nuclear reaction so devastating and so awesome that this whole planet could be blown into pieces the size of a cup cake. Now that is advancement." His voice was filled with distain and loathing and his eyes became glazed as if he were drifting into his own imagination or entering some trance-like state.

I tried to pull him back, "What happened next?" I asked rather sheepishly.

He responded, "Cholera broke out across the south and the villagers, like all good Christian people, had to find someone to blame. A scapegoat was needed and there he conveniently was. The fact that Lucrezia Cropier had been correct about filtering the water was ignored and people died; died in their droves as a consequence. You see she had seen it before in Italy. If the water was clean then Cholera ceased to spread. It was not based upon her medical understanding but upon the application of intelligence and observation. Hence she told people to boil their drinking water. Had the villages done so, then they could have beaten the disease - which incidentally we now know is waterborne."

"She must have been a very intelligent woman?" I proffered.

"She was," Cropier replied. "A truly kind and gentle spirit and…"

"You seem to speak as if you knew her personally," I added.

He ignored me and stared into the mirror before him. His eyes were moist and there seemed a deep longing within them. A longing brought about by his experience of pain and disappointment in humanity. I actually began to feel pity for him.

"One night," he recommenced, "the Cropier family were visited by the villagers or townsfolk or whatever you'd call them. Marcel was swiftly beheaded and his heart removed. Lucrezia was disembowelled, as they tried to find the demon inside her," he paused. "Can you imagine what that young child saw and felt?"

I shook my head and agreed with him.

"They disembowelled the woman. Slit her from vagina to chin," his voice trembled, and he gave a slight cough, "to find a demon." He stopped again.

"Times were different then," I offered.

"Were they?" he asked, his voice heavy with sarcasm. "Really and what do they do now? Burn Jews in ovens? Pack thousands of skulls in walls of a tomb? Humanity is a disgusting aberration. Don't you think there are people out there who would not do the same to me? And we are in the twenty first century. Even the most base of animals does not take such pleasure in the killing of their own kind. Killing is such sport."

Again I could sense the real bitterness in his voice as he imparted his mixture of history and philosophy to me. To be honest I actually agreed with him. I hated those wealthy socialists who knew how easy it would be to live without money; but none of them were prepared to release their greasy grip upon it. He was right the world was patently unfair and everything was just luck.

He caught my eye. "The best thing in life is free," he sang, "but you can keep that for the birds and bees - just give me money. Money that's what I want."

"The boy what happened to the boy?"

"The boy? He was crucified."

He replied as if inside a tunnel. His emotions completely shut down.

"He was nailed to the front door and while still alive the building was set a blaze. The lovely villagers stood and watched as a boy was cast back to hell."

"Jesus Christ," I whistled threw my teeth. "Didn't anyone do anything?"

"The priest did," Cropier continued, "he chanted some exorcism incantation, even when the boy's screams could be heard over a mile away. The priest of course said it was the devil returning to hell that made the boy scream so."

"What happened next?" I asked.

"Well at first the whole of the village remained in conspiratorial silence and then finally one half-wit boy blurted out how the holy priest had told them that Cropier was the son of the devil."

"And?"

"He was executed."

"Who the witness?"

"The priest of course."

"So that branch of your family was simply rubbed out?"

"Burnt out, and their bodies are buried in a small corner of the cemetery. Time forgot them, but I remembered, and others who have looked have not found. That is because the parish records have been removed, altered, sanitized. You see the victor controls the past and history controls the future. That is the Christian virtue which speaks of love and forgiveness. It's obscene, just because the boy was different."

Now I was beginning to understand the man. Actually I began to fear him less and understand him more.

"Didn't you do an article on the very same thing?" he asked suddenly.

"When?"

"I believe I read it in Harpers. Or was it Men Only?"

I knew he was taunting me, throwing my emotions around like a rollercoaster; I was also stunned that he had read something by me. How could he know I was coming to interview him?

"Your piece on 1066, the battle of Hastings? Harold and the arrow in the eye. Yours was an intelligent exposé. Harold and his brothers being killed by knights on horseback. What did you say?" He paused as if recollecting, "Oh yes, I remember. The lance through the chest and his head and leg being hacked off. Then the discovery centuries later of a one legged body under Bosham church. That was what you said? Buried on the coast to forever guard these shores against invaders. I enjoyed it very much and it was spot on for accuracy. You see you are a very clever journalist. You found things that no one had found before."

Once again I was astounded that he knew so much about me, and the more we spoke the more I began to admire his intelligence, his wit, and his charm. This was no man to be feared, but one who perhaps deserved the adoration he received from his adoring public. There was definitely more to him than met the eye; more than the normal spiritual healer man.

He sighed heavily, like a man leaning on a garden spade after turning the soil. "Just because I'm different the persecution continues. The power to heal is a miraculous gift. You want to meet the people I have cured? Meet them because you do not believe me, or believe them? Then come to Arlington, to my family graves tomorrow and ask all your wretched questions, see what you can dig up for the sheep that bleat; or are they wolves that bay for blood?"

I could sense the bitterness returning to his voice again and wanted to ask more questions, get more answers, but he had obviously concluded. I actually began to feel sorry for the man. He seemed so genuine and different one to one. Not at all like his stage persona. Maybe he was like his British counterpart and it was we who had not progressed since 1590. Maybe we were still like sheep easily led into the path of wolves. Maybe the wolves were in fact the sheep? It all began to fall apart in my reasoning. My mind felt like sponge that had absorbed too much and was now sodden and useless.

The two hell hound body-guards miraculously appeared as if summoned by a silent bell. The interview that I had wanted so badly I now had, and Ronnie and Reggie led me back through a maze of tunnels and walkways out into the front of stage area.

The crowds had dissipated and the lights on the stage were out. The razzamatazz had gone and the debris of a human gathering lay scattered on the ground. I kicked my way through empty cartons, cups and food wrappers and then disappeared through the perimeter tape and walked.

I walked aimlessly at first, digesting his ideas, his show and what he had told me. Eventually I was back at my hotel and as Cropier had predicted I remembered every detail.

As I transposed the story into an e mail, which went to Marmaduke twenty five minutes later, I actually began to believe that Lucus F Cropier was, well I couldn't say what he was, but he was different. He was without doubt the most different person I had ever met.

After a few minutes, for some reason, I sent a post script. It was almost as if my hand had a will of its own. I wanted to be cautious, because I still felt uneasy, but I felt compelled to write. Involuntarily I hit the send button and the message simply read:

Oh my God!!! Think he might be genuine – will confirm with detail when witnesses and others seen tomorrow. The man is amazing!

IV

Arlington Cemetery just after dawn.

A grey mist hung over the Potomac; a mist which swirled and clung like the hands of wailing women to the feet of an ascending soul. The sound of birds in the dawn chorus was as sweet and melodious as the taxi driver who brought me was gruff and unimpressed. I wondered if he was up early or to bed late. Either way he was clearly not enjoying the current situation.

I passed the Jefferson Monument and was impressed by the choice of the neo-classical for the remembrance of a man who clearly was a giant of humanity. I could visualise the man, belting out those famous words, "We hold these truths to be self-evident that all men are created equal." I wondered what Cropier would have made of him, had they met. Maybe he would have dispelled Jefferson's truths as lies and destroyed any faith I had left in their possibility. I thought of Lincoln and knew that something had gone wrong between the two monuments, and that something had set brother against brother, black against white.

I passed the Kennedy flame and moved out past the rows of white flags standing testimony to the cost of freedom being buried in the ground. There was something eerie about this place, something like the Belgian battlefield sites; something of business not quite done and a generation lost in the mire of time; the more I thought the less comfortable I became. The lost artists were here, alongside writers, poets, inventors, all were here, cast aside in the turmoil of human stupidity and nationalism. They had paid the cost of freedom and their payment was the soft moist body of mother earth; uncomfortable would be too subtle for what I felt. Emotional turmoil would be far more accurate. My heart was racing, pounding in my chest.

Walking without a map, as if drawn to a specific area of the graveyard, I made my way across the grass to a small knoll and there they were. Six people, including the man himself, standing like stone statues, head bowed, before a small mausoleum. The stone of the structure was yellow and worn and no inscription at all lay upon it. To the layman it would be passed and ignored as a relic of the past. Something which once had significance but now was gradually being forgotten. Around about were the graves of the civil war – the markers of the lost generation. It was a sombre, sobering place to be.

As I approached Cropier spoke, though he still had his back to me, "This is a fearful place isn't it?" he said. "A place where the sense of loss is most profound."

"I thought it would be difficult to find," I admitted. "But I found it easily, and I left my map back at the hotel."

"Every time," he continued, "every time I am in Washington I come to this place. It keeps me grounded. We all must know that our feet are forever in the clay. After all that is what we are." He turned to face me, "this is Harriet, do you recognise her?"

I shook my head and a youngish woman in her twenties raised her head from the reflective pose and came to meet me. As she approached she smiled and a set of white teeth appeared in her face. The remaining four mourners stood stock still as if in prayer.

"Hello," the woman said, and reached out a gloved hand to mine. "I was at the healing last night. Perhaps you saw me?"

I shook my head.

"I had a horrific accident when I was young and my leg was shattered into so many pieces doctors thought I would lose it. Instead it grew stunted and twisted, but Lucus healed me. He is a marvel." She threw open her coat and stood before me. I looked at the woman who had the most perfect set of legs that I have ever seen. Her thighs were balanced, with a beautiful bowed shape and her calves were straight and symmetrical. The balance between the two was highlighted by the tight-fitting, figure–hugging skirt which she wore. Her knees were perfectly aligned and she could have been a model. Save for a set of small hairline scars above her right knee she was perfection. She closed the coat.

A second person rose from contemplation and came forward, a dark haired man, who, he claimed, had been blind from birth. From the inside coat pocket he produced a medical report and pictures. A passport which clearly showed his ailment; but he stood before me with the most intense and seductive green eyes imaginable.

A third man whose hands had been disfigured from birth came forward and shook my hand, his grasp was firm and yet as cold as death to the touch. Another man came forward to explain how serious burns on his face, which no amount of skin grafting could cure, had been cured by Cropier. The more closely I looked the less able I was to see any scars.

Finally a second woman came forward to explain the serious curvature of the spine she had endured as a child. She showed me pictures of a curve which had the shape of violin. The X-rays showed her back as she explained the pain; explained how the faith healer had laid his hands upon her and her back had straightened.

Then to my utter amazement she dropped her coat and stood erect and straight before me. There was no curve and no clothing either. She turned her back to me and I was given full view of the most exquisite shape and form. Just like the woman with the legs she was perfect. The faith healer had given her the perfect body. I could see why everyman would want her and every woman want to be her. Her skin was without a single blemish and completely hairless. It was as if she had been air brushed.

With a casualness which was borne out of acquired confidence she bent from the waist and picked up her coat. Her legs slightly parted she gave me a brief and fleeting glimpse of everything she could give to a man. At that moment I thought I had seen a glimpse of heaven. She was the most beautiful female I had ever seen.

"You see," said Cropier, "I just gave them their hearts desire and all I took in return was a pledge."

I was stunned. Only he and I remained now, standing in the enveloping mist. The others had quickly disappeared, each to five separate points of the compass. Only he and I stood together at the centre. It was as if we were at the point where time commenced and ceased – infinity.

"Have you seen enough?" he asked me.

"My God, she was the most beautiful thing I have ever seen."

"Yes, she is, but God made her deformed and twisted, no doubt he had a divine plan for all her suffering - all I did was make her whole. There is no virtue in torture and why should one person be born perfect and another so ugly that dogs bark at them when they pass." He was smiling, "And," he continued, "she has the humility to know what it was like to be shunned, so she is beautiful on the inside too. That is a rarity in beautiful people, but she has learned. I have simply taken all her ugliness away," he paused and laughed. "And she could be yours if you desired. All you have to do is believe."

"How?"

"I'll introduce you. She is truly everything you could ever desire. I made her that way. She is your perfect woman."

I could not think. Was I being bribed? Was I being duped? Or was this man truly some kind of miracle man?

"When I come to London I will bring Victoria along with me. She has never been."

Instant jealously rose in me.

"No I have never slept with her, nor will I," he chirped before I asked. "I think she is a woman, a person not a thing," he paused once more, "and she works as a secretary for me, not a whore. Maybe you can't understand that with your background, but I can."

"I wasn't going to say anything," I blurted in self protection.

"For all I know she is probably still a virgin; she is only eighteen and she has only just begun to come to terms with her beauty. Sometimes things are more difficult to accept than you can ever imagine."

"You'll bring her to London?" I asked.

"Yes." He looked at his watch, "And now," he stated blandly, as if nothing at all were of any consequence, "you need to catch your flight, and you have an article to write. We don't want to keep the story waiting now do we?"

A large black sedan pulled up only feet away and as the mist cleared I could see the tarmac road which wound through the endless graves.

"Get in," Cropier motioned. "It's your lift back to the hotel. Please accept it with my compliments." And with that the vehicle started to glide, so smooth and fast that I thought there was no contact with the road.

"As we drove back, I was convinced. This man was no charlatan. He was a healer. Somehow he had a gift. A divine gift. Where it came from I had no idea but it was a gift so special and so unique that I could understand the worship he inspired. I admired him. He was the kind of man to whom respect could be given. What is more I believed him to be genuine. If he placed his hands on Marmaduke's wife could he cure her? I was convinced he would. I was also convinced that if the object of my desire, which had been dangled before me like a prize, came to London, she would be mine. Cropier had told me as much and I actually believed him. Call me gullible, call me stupid, but that interview was the most intense and emotionally draining experience of my life. Cropier had offered me more than I had ever been offered before. To be offered a dream is enticing and I understood in the instant what those who had been healed gained. Cropier had offered the same to me; and I too, shallow selfish me, could have the one thing I'd always wanted. It was too much to comprehend.

He was The Faith Healer.

V

The flight home had been uneventful and the article I'd been commissioned to write flew onto the page without any difficulty. Whatever I wrote just made sense and the style was open, honest and quirky. Never before had the words come so easily and never before had I used all of my persuasion to support an act. I believed the man: He was genuine, and I was about to tell the whole world so. I relished the power which I had and the fact that my article would help people understand the strange and yet awesome world of …

I toyed with a title - the headline. That had not been so easy, the hook was the thing upon which I could hang my bait, and that bait had been Cropier's final parting phrase to his ensemble. Finally I came up with: Let me put my hands on you? I thought it was good, but at the last minute changed it to: Hands of Healing.

Marmaduke changed that to: Hands of the Healer.

So there it was completed, my piece on the man and my investigation.

In print it caused a stir and some colleagues became rather scathing of my efforts in the persuasion department. All except for Marmaduke, who, unbeknown to me, promptly had his sickly wife flown to America for a personal interview with Cropier, on the back of it. Cropier was by all accounts pleased by what he read and even thanked my commissioner for sending such a diligent and open minded reporter, rather than the rapscallion, as he called them, booze-sodden, once again his words, cynics that frequented this business. Gratefully the healer man had laid his hands on Jenny and to my, Marmaduke's and everybody else's amazement her recovery had been swift and miraculous.

Her hands regained their shape, and gone were the twisted and knotted fingers; in consequence, she painted her nails a bright pink; wore jewellery again, and smiled. Her legs once again became lithe and strong and she stood upright and erect with raised breasts and rounded hips. Her eyes sparkled with sexual promise and Marmaduke showed her off like some fine art piece of porcelain: His trophy.

It was a perfect ending.

I continued with my freelance work which came in rapidly, so rapidly in fact, that I forgot my encounter with Lucus Cropier, or should I say that it dulled into a memory. I was making hay while the sun shone and what hay I was making. Finally I was getting the recognition I deserved, and as my fortunes waxed so too did those of the faith healer. His first London tour had been an extensive success. People had travelled from miles distant to reach him; some from as far as Russia and other far flung parts of Europe. The prime reason was always to be healed. And Cropier had obliged, by getting them to sign away their souls in allegiance to him. As a result whole families joined him and extended families too. Nothing breeds success like success, and Lucus Cropier was rapidly becoming a world – wide phenomenon. He had suffered the condemnation of the Catholic Church, and other religious groups who feared his growing influence. He was rapidly becoming an icon on a par with Marilyn Monroe; James Dean; Elvis Presley; the Beatles and Michael Jackson.

There had even been assassination attempts by some religious sect members - Opus Dei I believe. Some ancient society pledged, as an arm of the Knights Templar, to protect the rights of Christ against the demons of the underworld. One man had lunged at Cropier with an ancient dagger and punctured his upper arm, twice, before being bundled to the floor by onlookers.

Cropier had not sought medical treatment, despite the intended injury and had continued with his ministry as if nothing had happened.

When I tried to find the assailant for an interview he had vanished. Vanished as if he had never existed, no body - I mean nobody seemed to know his whereabouts. No police officers seemed to know where he was being held, and I felt the heavy hands of obstruction at work, blocking my every path. Eventually I gave up. The fickle public didn't care either way and the man, whoever he had been, just vanished.

Posters were created, tee-shirts, documentaries, fashion accessories, biographies, in fact all of the paraphernalia associated with twenty first century stardom could be purchased at the high alter of capitalism, but Cropier remained aloof. And the more aloof he remained the more adulation he received, such was the nature of his fame. He gave no interviews, sanctioned no official merchandise, though other entrepreneurs quickly cashed in. Meanwhile he simply continued to work his magical healing: That I found exceptional. Never before had I known, "a star," to be so down to earth. It was almost as if money did not interest him, and as for women, well he did not have the appetites of others. As far as I could ascertain neither was he homosexual - in fact he was almost as pure as the driven snow. There had been no dirt to dredge, no long lost skeletons falling from the cupboard and that had been refreshing. I remembered his and my discussion, or I thought I did, about the value of fame and money and the masses.

On one occasion Cropier's official car had been blown to pieces, killing everyone inside. Apparently a small child had run toward an open window and tossed in a hand grenade, Vietnamese style. The explosion had killed everyone, including the bomber, but Cropier had fortuitously been riding in a smaller, less conspicuous, car to avoid the adulation of the crowds. Luck or judgement had saved him on that day: And he always seemed to be lucky.

I seemed to recall how Cropier took no more than he actually needed and only wanted people to commit their souls for the future. That I found to be a genuine price for such magnanimous works for the good. In short I was impressed; especially as I did not believe in, "the soul." Every time I think about it I am forced back into a university tutorial with Volger Berghaus, a rather austere Swiss/German who made us examine the theology of

Mary Shelly's Frankenstein and poor Victor's demise at the hands of a magnanimous God. The same God who dropped the roof of a church on a hapless, worshipping congregation in the deep south, killing and burying all of them. No doubt they screamed hallelujah throughout the ordeal.

The belief in the soul did not come easily to me and that made me scathing of Cropier's bargain. To me it seemed like money for old rope. A devil's bargain so to speak and one I would have entered into with consummate ease had I been ill, or someone protecting my family.

I decided to make an impromptu visit to Mr. Cropier to follow up on the Washington interview. A surprise visit to his last London show of that year: It was the 4th of April and now virtually nine months since I had seen him last. I remember it well. Remember it? I shall never forget it.

Oh I forgot to add that Victoria came with him and he did introduce us. We hit it off immediately; she was a perfect match for me, just as he had said she would be. She seemed to like everything I liked, was a perfect cook, and hostess; she charmed everyone she met and despite every man and his dog chasing her, she was 100% loyal. In the bedroom she seemed to know me better that I knew myself and she was a virgin. I was in love, am in love, and we are due to be married when she gets back from Idaho, where she is visiting her mother. She wants to carry on Cropier's ministry and to be frank, I think it's a good thing. She was, is, the best thing that has happened to me in a long time. Not only is she beautiful to look at she is beautiful in character too. I must sound like a right chump but if you had seen her, you too would be as captivated as I am: I am lucky. I am in love.

* * *

It had been cold that year and the ride in the black cab had made me feel chilly despite the onset of a mild spring. The air was damp and stuck to the collar of my shirt and jacket like a fine light mist. In fact all of my clothes were damp, lightly dusted with a sugar rain, not wet but uncomfortable enough for it to be unpleasant. I wished we were in a warmer Washington.

The cabbie, like all London cabbies was chatty and generally in good form as we sped around and through the small side streets which only those with, "the knowledge," really knew. It amazed me that he could dart from area to area like a small black beetle scuttling on scented walkways.

"This bleedin' we'ver," he snorted, "all the roads gets clogged up." He seemed to be making excuses for the route. "Good job I knows the way eh?" he laughed out loud.

"I don't mind," I replied. "As long as I get there."

"Well I bleedin' well do," he retorted. "Ev'ry time it rains it ain't pennies from 'eaven. It's more like a warning from 'ell. An' us lot," he paused, "the dumb smuck cabbies," he paused, as he concentrated, before darting ahead of another car whose horn sounded, "we gets the blame."

"I know, any sign of bad weather and the whole country grinds to a halt. Wet leaves, ice, snow."

"Ain't that the truth? You know there ain't enough gritters to be worth spit in the centre. But the council never gets the blame it's just us. Hyde Park last winter was like a bloody ice-rink, nearly two days to get the bloody thing sorted. Every main frog is jammed," he continued in his broad cockney accent, "and the security around Olympia for that daft Yank is crazy. You'd think he was Kennedy the way they go on. Bloody faith healer."

"You don't believe in him then?" I asked, as I was thrown first to the left and then to the right, as he manoeuvred through the chicane of parked cars.

"Na!" he exclaimed. "It's all a gimmick. A bit of the old s,h,1,t, if you ask me. How can anyone be a healer? He ain't bleedin' Jesus now is he? "

"No, but he never said he was." I could almost feel myself becoming defensive.

"Too right if he says that, then they'd 'ang 'im. Stuff 'im up like a right kipper. Bullshit baffles brains. "

"So you don't believe in…"

"Listen gov'ner, I might be a cabbie by I ain't stupid. I ain't sayin' I'm a mastermind neither, not like old Fred Hou…" He stalled, as if trying to get a name from his memory.

"Fred Housego?" I offered.

"That's the chap," he chirped, "he was a cabbie but not dumb like me."

I was patently aware of the mistake I had made, as a young reporter, in assuming intelligence by the job someone did. Big mistake. Life gets in the way for some people and they end up doing something which they perhaps had not been destined for. Just take my school friend who had ended up getting a girl pregnant at sixteen. He had been as smart as me, only he'd been better looking, so he got to do the deed. What a mess, especially after both sets of parents set up a shot-gun wedding. There and then his life was flushed straight down the toilet. I wondered what he was doing now. I was a reporter and he well…

"I do the crosswords though," he smirked in the rear view mirror. "Done The Times in less than twenty minutes once." He triumphantly announced.

"Really?" I replied, less than interested. I knew how they were compiled.

"Yeah, anagrams I do them too. Any puzzles in fact. Especially when work is slow. It's like combat really." He gave away his military past. "Drivin' is like that, periods of intense work interspersed with naff all, and boredom. So I do puzzles, some guys read, and some even got a mini telly in their motor."

"Anagrams?"

"Yeah, like people's names. You know Mr. Mojo Risin, being Jim Morrison. Lots of stars do that, they take the letters in their own name and then they create another. It sort of helps give 'em ideas - and it helps to exercise the old grey stuff."

The man was interesting. Cabbie or not he clearly had an intellect and was unafraid to use it.

"What do you think of Lucus Cropier?" I asked.

"One letter short," he laughed in reply.

I nodded, but had not the least idea of what he was talking about. The cabbie caught my eye in the rear view mirror and sensed my confusion.

"He's one letter short of the perfect anagram," he snorted again, as we pulled up at the Olympia destination. "That's twelve pound forty, gov," he demanded, as he flicked a switch on the meter.

On the pavement I suddenly stood clutching a receipt for my expenses as the taxi sped off into the distance. The whole place looked desolate and dark, but I knew Cropier would be there. His show complete the final few stragglers were making their way out of the complex and into the London darkness. I just wanted to see him once again, to try and confirm my original thoughts about him. In the last few months he had reached super stardom, become a pin-up on the front cover of a variety of magazines; he truly was a phenomenon, the phenomenon. I wondered how long he would last. A man who could heal the sick and make a brave new world, surely he was destined for immortality.

I weaved through the thinning audience and skilfully avoided the minders Ron and Reggie, who seemed distracted by their efforts to clear the auditorium. I slipped, unseen, into the maze of walkways which serviced the backstage dressing rooms. For no reason other than curiosity, I examined my receipt from the taxi driver. To this day I do not know why. On the reverse he had scrawled, "A rose by any other name," and "anagram away to find an answer." Why would a cab driver take the time to write something like that down? Unless he was no cab driver at all? I shuddered and wondered if I was under surveillance? If I was, just who was watching me and why? I was lost and had no idea what he meant, save the reference to Shakespeare. I stuffed the receipt into my pocket and thought hard. Lucus F. Cropier? Was that an anagram? If so I could solve it. But first I wanted talk to him once again; wanted to check my perceptions; wanted to know if I had been fooled, duped or if Cropier actually was some kind of saviour.

Quickly I made my way down the maze of the long corridors, searching for his dressing room. Then to my amazement there it was, a single dark- red, or was it black, door?

I listened carefully, half hoping that he was there alone. I could hear no voices. Without knocking I burst in and as I called the man's name I noticed them. The sharp teeth which protruded over his lower lip and the two hooves as clear as day where there should have been feet. His face instantly turned toward me, his eyes a flame red and I fancy he snarled at me. He sat imperially before the mirror where he was removing his make-up.

"Well, well," he laughed. His voice seemed to have dropped two octaves, "So you've come back again. Why? Don't you believe what you saw last time? Back like a bad penny, or irksome reporter, you turn up to make my life a misery." He dropped a towel over his hooves to disguise them, but it was too late I had seen. Ronnie and Reggie suddenly appeared behind me in total silence, and I sensed rather than saw their presence.

"I just thought that..." I blurted.

"Thought that you could what?"

"Continue from where we left off."

"And just where was that?" he asked sardonically. His tongue flashing like a serpent's out of his mouth. I thought I could hear a faint hiss.

"Well in Washington you told me..."

"What did I tell you?" he interrupted.

"You told me you were a collector of souls?"

"Correct."

"But I saw your feet!" I blurted.

"And what did you think you saw?"

"Hooves!" I could hear myself yelling as one of the minders punched me in the kidneys and I fell to the floor, a small trickle of urine leaving me as I did so. The pain was excruciating.

"You should have stayed well away," Cropier chuckled, as the second guard kicked me in the lower stomach barely missing my testicles. "You really are a tiresome little man aren't you?"

And with that he stood up and stepped toward me, and I saw, once again, the clumps of horn which passed for feet. They were less than a metre away now.

"Yes?" he continued, "you didn't think I would do all this for nothing in return, did you? All I wanted was a few souls and for that I gave a life time of bliss. A very small price to pay for your heart's desire. You should have taken the chance when I offered it to you, Victoria did."

"I don't understand," I spat at him.

"But of course you don't, you silly little man. Did you think you could fool me? I can create Kings and Emperors so a troublesome journalist should cause me no problems at all."

I was shaking my head, trying to make sense of what I had just seen. Already I was beginning to doubt my own sanity: I was in shock. I was spluttering, as more kicks hit my back and shoulders, "What the hell are you?" I screamed.

He stamped his hoof loudly against the floor boards with a resounding crack.

"Isn't that obvious you silly little thing?" he mocked.

"Oh damnation," I was screaming now.

"Precisely," he scoffed. "I think our guest wants to leave," he said to Ronnie and Reggie. And as they lifted me to my feet I could have sworn that his eyes turned to those of a snake. "I will see you later," he laughed.

The fear I felt within me was like nothing I had experienced before or since and the circulation of my blood almost ceased. The smell of his breath was all pervading. Like the smell of rotting compost, mixed with the blood of a butcher shop; the smell of death. I almost fainted.

"Who are you?"

"But you know that," he laughed back at me. "I wanna be rich and I wanna be famous, I wanna be, I wanna be."

"Souls? You're collecting souls?"

"Absolutely!" He stated emphatically. "The more the merrier don't you think?" He was laughing now, "Anagrams, anagrams, life is full of little anagrams. Your little cabbie might just be right. Lucky for you he was who he was or you might have had a nasty accident on the way here. Raspberry jam in cab or a bomb that might have been ironic. Victoria is gonna miss you, miss you, she sure is; miss you, miss you," he teased in a chant. "But don't worry she'll be perfect for someone else. All she needs is a briefing, or should I say a debriefing. I wonder who will be playing happy families inside her next."

I could hear myself scream. Deep gut wrenching screams which would have pierced the very silence of eternity.

* * *

In the asylum they gave me sedatives and waited, waited nearly a year, or so they told me, for my mind to recover and only now have I had the nerve to write this down. I don't know how to end this account; I don't even really know if it's possible, or whether I am crazy. But I do know something happened to me, something unearthly.

Lucus Cropier, I wrote the name down on a sheet of paper - then played with the letters. They give you paper here, drawing is therapeutic you see, like art.

Nothing came.

I re-wrote it: Nothing.

I wrote the name again, this time in full: Lucus F. Cropier. And there it was the missing letter: The cabbie's missing letter, the one little, "f," in the middle. The letter that made the whole thing suddenly possible.

Intelligence is a curse, not a blessing as they say. I saw through the whole stardom of the man. I completed the anagram, before dropping the pencil - my fingers trembling uncontrollably. There on the page was his real name – simple and utterly terrifying.

The problem that I have, is that he is still out in the world. Victoria who I thought loved me, never did. My editor thinks I have lost my marbles and he has no idea what his Jenny has signed away. I can't get a damn thing published and Cropier's soul collecting continues unabated. Maybe I am mad after all.

sugar b,
sugar p

L.amond

For Zsoka - who fought and won

Sugar b, Sugar p

"When he woke the pain in his rectum had not gone. The burning sensation was travelling into his brain and he felt sick and hot. When eventually he was forced to go to the toilet, he used the corner of the space which passed for a cage; he could see blood on the floor, even though it was dark. His hand went to his back passage and the blood stood black on his palm. In the daylight it would be crimson.

He felt up to his face - it was puffy and sore from the blows which the men had rained down on him whilst he had been aboard the boat; his lip was swollen and the gums of his mouth were cut and his nostrils hurt. There was some blood there too.

He had become used to the abuse when it came; he would have liked to fight back, but they were too strong for him and the tugging on his nose made him submit.

The men laughed at him, taunted him, kicked and then inflicted even greater pain, as he squealed in his resistance. The more he resisted the more they seemed to like him. Had he learned to be compliant they would have either killed him and thrown his corpse overboard or left him alone. As it was he had not learned to temper his spirit and the sadistic torture continued day after day until the auction drew near. Other boys had submitted more readily, and in consequence, were troubled less. It had been as if his captors wanted to make him docile. They beat him, raped him and threw him from man to man like a parcel, a rag doll.

He was 12 years old and had he grown to manhood among his own tribe he would undoubtedly have been a warrior. But fate had intervened and he had been captured by the Deli-deli, a neighbouring tribe. They had promptly allocated some of the adult and young adolescent females of the Waggotsi as breed mares or sex slaves, or both. They slaughtered the male prisoners and sold all of the children to the next available Arab trader that was prepared to pay a good price for human flesh. The result had seen 76 children sold into slavery; transported like cattle to the West Indies to work on sugar plantations six or seven days a week, until they perished like livestock. When they would simply be replaced by new slaves. Sugar and Rum were big business, and like all major empires slavery played a vital part.

The captured children had been chained together at the neck, approximately two feet apart and then marched forty miles across open brush land. Those that could not, or would not keep up, had been whipped and beaten until either they did or they died.

Sold on the dock-side for supplies of ammunition, alcohol and glass beads, the new owners became the transport traders – Arabs.

Then came the boat. The huge three mast boat which stacked them in racks like drying fish on a Gold Coast afternoon. Once a day they were taken aloft to walk on the deck, if those on that duty cared to, and to watch the open water in which the vessel bobbed like a cork. Many times the human cargo remained below decks, amid the stale stench of urine and human excrement. Time froze and the boy could not really remember whether it was day or night, or how many days had passed.

When he did get taken to the decks, his eyes were stinging and weeping from the bright light and salt. Bodies were thrown overboard and some of the slave cargo was tied and dipped. A practice by which some had their hands bound and were then thrown overboard – only to be hauled back onto the deck almost lifeless and gasping.

Occasionally the sharks took one, or part of one and the remainder was thrown back; but mostly the strongest survived. Five times the boy survived this cleaning regime.

These Arab sailors used whom they pleased, woman, girl, and child; took them against their will, while spectators laughed. The actions of one oppressor often incited others to do the same with another hapless victim; some were chosen for the sheer sport they could offer, or their fighting spirit: That was always broken.

In that short space of time he had learned more about the cruelty of human beings one to another than ever before. He had witnessed things and had things done to him that most human beings would never endure; but somehow he survived.

Some of the girls had suffered such rapes that once unchained for a repeat of the activity they threw themselves into the ocean to avoid any repetition of the act. Some suffered multiple assaults and were pregnant with an unknown mixed-race child before their feet even touched the shores of the Americas. Others were beaten so hard that flies laid eggs in their open wounds which festered until they were thrown overboard as delirious shark food.

When the boat finally landed they were herded like cattle amid the noisy hubbub of a trading port. Chained and shuffling they were placed in open sheep pens. Less than half of the children had survived the journey.

Then came the auction. Every captive was stripped naked; some were sold in lots, others, mostly girls, were sold individually; and the Arabs who inflicted pain went away with money. He was dragged to a cart, his feet flaying out at the new men. Cruel men with clubs that came down upon his shoulders until he was too weak to fight; too weak to lift his arms to defend himself. These new men kicked him like a dog. Kicked him until one of his teeth flew out and his ribs were sore and his breathing shallow. Then they dragged him to a water butt and held him face down until his lungs felt as if they might burst. Every time he resisted he was plunged into the airless fluid until he became quiet.

He learned quickly.

In the early hours he was allowed to sleep, after he had been fitted with an iron collar that is. A collar so heavy that it weighed his neck down as he lay. From the collar hung a chain and on the end of the chain hung a lock which was fastened by a heavy black key.

The man who held the key, also carried a club; and the boy learned that if he could not work out the man's language and gestures quickly the club was brought down upon his arms or back or head.

Learning was effective and quick.

The law of the club taught him everything he needed to know about his captors."

Paul Collins closed the book from which he had been reading. His voice had been slow, deliberate, designed to upset and yet enticing the listener into his world: The world of his imagination.

* * *

"Oh my God, how can you read this? It's so inhumane. It's disgusting."

"Because it's the truth, and the truth is often ugly," he smiled, "and my job is to educate you," the lecturer paused, "to educate you, Michelle?" Paul Collins answered. "Now that is something and nothing..."

She didn't grasp the irony.

"Educate yeah, but this is bloody sickening, boys being raped and..." she snapped. "Why don't you give us something not to be horrified by?" Michelle Ward asked in reply.

"Because," Collins answered, yet again, "the past is horrific, people are horrific and the truth is ugly. Life is in fact dull, brutish and short. What would you like me to teach you? That everything is pink and fluffy and everybody lives in a nice place? That love exists and that everything has a happy ending? When I was young like you, I thought that love would last forever: I was wrong. Just be thankful that you can determine that much? Can you choose whether to live or die? Wear whatever - pink is great by the way."

"Like chav heaven," a boy at the back piped up. "A big pink heaven where the gold hoops grow on trees, like spaghetti."

The room erupted in laughter, and Michelle Ward went scarlet. It was clear that she was the butt of the joke, primarily because she was wearing pink.

"Bollocks," she yelled, without turning around and raised a single finger salute as her accompaniment. "I still think it stinks."

"Of course it does," Collins the lecturer concluded, "Life isn't fair. The moon is not made of cream cheese and nobody believes in Santa."

A bell rang somewhere in the distance, he was not sure, maybe it had been the striking clock and Paul Collins thanked providence for the welcome release from his class.

* * *

"On the other side of the barn he could see his sibling - a sister. She was curled in the foetal position nursing her lower abdomen and sobbing softly; only weeks before they had been running through fields of maize on their parent's farm. Now they were here, caged like animals and subjected to the most hideous acts.

She was 11 years old, pretty and yet her youth had not deterred her new masters from using her. On the boat the men who had traded them from their village destroyers and slaughtered their parents, used him for sport. Now it seemed to be the turn of his younger sister, whose puffy face showed the signs of a beating. Her nostrils were bleeding from the device which had been hooked onto her face to make her arch her back for a more convenient presentation. There were marks on the back of her neck like the bite marks of many animals.

He had heard her crying and sobbing and choking as something was being stuffed into her mouth and down her throat against her will. He had heard her retching and begging and the sounds of three or four men laughing and grunting gutturally amid her pleading squeals. It was as if these men focussed on her, as the previous men had focussed upon him. He heard one man laugh and utter the phrase, "The darker the berry the sweeter the juice;" and had heard his sister beg and then after perhaps an hour it had gone silent. All around the smell of fear clung to the cages which housed the slaves.

Each night the men came to her, pulled her from the cage and dragged her into a corner of the barn he could not see, and each night she cried once they had gone. Occasionally one man would come and pull her from the cage in the day and grunt over her squeals of objection."

Paul Collins sat in the staff room of the college and wondered - wondered what those around him thought. Did they even know and if they did know did they care? He knew that the old maids of the staff did not like him and the new breed of thrusting executive types were no happier. He had long realised that education was about enforced social conformity and adherence to "the rules" and it stuck in his gullet.

"Ah Paul," the principal said, as she approached.

Collins knew the tone.

"This module that you are delivering?"

"Which one?"

"I think we know?"

"Oh do we?" Collins was sarcastic in the extreme. "Has Medusa started to encourage the students to make more complaints? What is it this time? Let me guess the module on Byron and Lady Caroline Lamb and the illegitimate child with Augusta?" He paused and pulled a cigarette packet from his pocket.

"You can't smoke in here," the principal quickly chided.

"I know that," Collins replied. "No smoking in Colditz. We don't want any bombs to go off, now do we?"

The principal's voice began to show signs of anger, "You see, the problem is, you are a bit," she paused as if searching for the right word.

"Truthful?"

"No."

"Honest?"

"Graphic," she concluded. "Lots of detail which some people might find offensive."

"Graphic? An interesting word choice. Graphic?" he repeated.

"One or two of the students are upset by the choice of detail, on this thing you are doing on American slave literature. About the rapes and the," she lowered her voice, "sodomy."

Collins raised his voice, "Sodomy?" he virtually screamed, "not Buggery?"

"I would have thought Harriet Beecher Stowe might be more appropriate than the ranting of Richard Wright. I mean do they need to know all of the sordid detail? Couldn't you tone it down a bit, a little bit," she qualified. "That way your ideas might not be so..."

"Powerful?" he interrupted.

"Shocking?" she urged.

"Hey, yes um miss, I's a good nigger, I doose as the mistress say. Ain't I just a good Uncle Tom?"

"Mr. Collins please don't use that word," she said indignantly.

"What word is that? Uncle Tom?"

"No the, n, word."

He knew precisely what he was doing and saying, but had absolutely no interest in her indignation, "That's fine coming from someone who doesn't know the difference between buggery and sodomy. I'm going for a cigarette. That is if you've finished?"

The principal shook her head, "Paul," she was toning down, "all I'm saying is that I'd like you to consider what you say," she paused once again, "carefully."

"What you want me to do is sanitize history. Make it palatable for the white middle-class? I mean what if we upset members of the board and I ..."

"All I'm saying is be careful. I think you're an excellent teacher. Too good for this place but you're a walking time bomb. Just look at you. You drink too much. There are some rumours going around about one or two of your female students."

"One or two? Just one or two?" he was becoming indignant. "I thought I was a wicked lothario with the soul of some socialist demon?"

The principal continued, "Look you're a writer and a damn good one and you teach the art better that anyone, all I'm trying to warn you of are consequences."

"Consequences?"

"Precisely, consequences."

"There are no consequences? And what would they be? Life throws you a breath and you catch it and when your time is up," he paused, "and some of us," he paused again, "oh hell, what's the point? There is no point."

With that he jumped to his feet and made his way out into the open air. He didn't really want to smoke. In fact he had been giving up, or at least trying to, but there seemed no point anymore. There were many things he was trying to give up; many things he should have given up.

* * *

"June 10th – the day we were sold to the Codrington family. Some women came in fine dresses to look at us in the cages as if we were horses. One or two of them were laughing, joking. One went to my sister and told the man that she would make an excellent house girl. She could work at the Ballinger house, cleaning.

I was sold as a plantation worker. To work the crushing machine. I was small and nimble and I could get inside the workings of the windmill as the great crushing stones pulped the cane stalks. Once I had become too big for that I could be used for the back breaking work out in the fields loading the sugar onto the carts which would pull cane from sun rise to sun set. Sometimes I would get to be inside the raking rooms where the sugar syrup was laid to let the moisture evaporate, until eventually it could be raked and loaded into earthenware cones to dry."

Paul Collins continued to read. His class listened.

"June 12th- I have just endured the most hateful experience I was branded today. A red hot iron was used on my right shoulder blade, a large letter, P. My sister was branded with a, B, and cried for nearly an hour until an old woman came and placed some sacking over the burn after smearing the whole area with butter.

In the afternoon we were loaded into carts and transported to a place named Betty's Hope. A large plantation owned by the Codrington family, sugar growers and refiners from England. The house was a fine house and I thought that was where we were to go. Instead I was taken to a village of wattle and daub huts with banana palm leaves for the roof. I was given a meal of millet porridge and shown where I was to sleep."

"Branded? My God that is awful," Michelle Ward was the first to speak.

"No it's tragic," Gail Sommers added. "Foul and tragic."

"There are still families who have a respectable business built on the misery of slavery," Paul Collins was at the stage where he didn't care anymore. He was saying as he pleased, after all what more could they do to him now?

"Yeah and one of them sponsors this college," Michael Yeates was the boy behind the voice. "Isn't that so Mr. Collins?"

"Totally correct," Collins answered, knowing full well that his response would be, reported, to the principal. "Nice to know that your family fortune is based upon the misery of others. The overriding principal of capitalism my boy," he put on an affected accent. "To shit on others before they shit on you. And thus you see the whole world is built upon a premise of shit."

His students roared. They loved the anarchy of the man. He knew that the result would lead to some form of disciplinary action. Some sort of hearing with those that fancied themselves as guardians of the young. Now he simply didn't care anymore. Nothing really mattered, in the end.

"The sugar barons who still run the family businesses? All this built on slavery - disgusting, depraved. Such are the fortunes of the great and good. These are the same people who would educate you into what to think and do?"

Collins stopped discussion and continued to read from the diary account.

"Morning and I was suddenly awake. I could feel moisture falling on me and I thought for an instant that I was back in the rack on the boat. That I had dreamed the open air and that urine was falling on me, somebody else was urinating on me. In fact the tropical rain had blown in and the meagre grass hut was leaking and the rain was landing on me.

It was still dark and I could hear the sound of others in the hut breathing as they too felt drops of water hit their faces. They tossed and turned on the matting which served as mattresses. There was a cover under which I slept, a brown cover which had once been a sack; in all I had four of them. In the corner of each, three words were printed: Codrington Sugar Antigua. The material was not warm, nor soft, but it did, it was all we had..."

Paul Collins suddenly slapped the pages of the text together. "Right," he said, "You have a flavour of the text now. So the assignment."

There was a collective groan from the students.

"I need you to read Jane Eyre and Wuthering Heights with a view to examining the use of the idea of slavery within the texts." He paused, as if deep in thought, "Just how does Heathcliff make his fortune? Is he a slave trader? And," he paused again, "What does Edward Rochester do in Jamaica? Is Bertha Mason white? Or a mulatto?"

Michelle Ward smiled as she spoke, "I thought she was a dark beauty?"

"What does dark mean? Define please?" came Collins' reply.

"Well it could mean many things."

He smiled a broad toothy smile, and then raised his voice, "Hit the books people, hit the books. Oh and have a good weekend."

"Some weekend," he heard one of the students remark as they left, while he packed his briefcase for the last time. Then turning to the door he opened it and before stepping out into the corridor he mouthed the words, "Last words, last words, out." He flicked the lights off and left the building.

* * *

Paul Collins sat at the computer trying desperately to draw together the stands of the text he had been writing. He had to finish it. He tried to separate his mind from the terrible dilemma of his own life. The continuing story of the black African boy who had been taken as a slave to Antigua. Those he taught had no idea that the text was based upon the shady history of his own family. A family that had disowned him, because he felt the injustices and had been open enough to talk about them.

He wanted to write about the way in which the boy's sister had been abused until finally she died in child birth. A thirteen year old raped and torn apart for the sake of money. Wanted to make his statement about the misery some inflicted on others; talk about the use of live children inside the crushing machine. But his fingers refused to move. For an hour now he had sat staring, staring at the blank page which was his computer screen.

"Hopeless," he mouthed, "totally hopeless. You've got to get out of this place. What is- is. Nothing can be changed."

The bell rang and he lifted the receiver to the intercom.

"Paul?" a female voice said.

"Come on up," was his reply.

He buzzed the bell and the main door opened allowing entrance two flights below.

Michelle Ward walked into his hall after using her key and kicked off her boots. She smiled and jumped toward him throwing her legs up around his waist as he caught her. She was planting a firm kiss on his lips as they stumbled toward the bedroom.

* * *

"Why don't you go through the daily routine?" Michelle Ward said. "You know the sort of thing. How about one man gets killed in the crusher, or one gets kicked by a horse and the owner shoots him like a lame dog, rather than expend the money on medical care?"

The room was dark now and the young women slipped her warm hand to the man's spent testicles.

His body reacted to her touch.

"Or you could have a woman come and check the weight of these," she said "to see if he might make a good man slave. You know for mating all the girls. You'd have to make him grow up a little, so these," she manipulated his testes with her hand, "so these were nice and full and heavy."

"What like a stud bull?"

"Precisely," the young girl giggled, an infectious giggle which gave him encouragement. "You could call it the," she paused, "Mandingo!"

277

"Mandinka?" surely.

"Who cares as long as you write about sex and all that going on?" She was making circles of the hair on his chest now, twirling and fluttering her eye lids provocatively. "A sort of Lady Chatterley, between a slave and a mistress."

"What with forget-me-nots replaced by chains?"

She laughed, "You see, you get my drift. Anyway you set my assignment, Mr. Heathcliff."

"How long are you here for?" he asked.

"All night," she giggled again. "So we can act it out if you like? I'll be the lady of the house come to buy a man for her female slaves, and you can be that man. I can test you out."

She giggled again.

"I want to write about the women in the sun, working, and you, you, little minx want me to write something to titillate your sexual urges."

"Yep!" she exclaimed. "And the deeper and more intense the better."

"Shameless, totally shameless."

"Absolutely," she replied.

"Are you hungry?" he asked.

"Starving," she answered.

"Chinky?"

"Great."

"Is there anything you want?" he asked casually.

"Duck, pancakes, and anything you choose. I want to take a shower. Is that ok?"

She kissed his cheek and then rolled to the side of the king size bed. Planting her feet firmly onto the floor, she stood erect in one fluid movement: Her body was perfect. Her hair was dark, raven dark and her skin pale. One of his former girlfriends had said that he had a deep seated Snow White fixation, now he almost believed her. The shape of that bottom was precise, as if drawn by Renoir. The hips, the small line of her spine in the centre of her back, everything was perfect. Her breasts were pert, high and firm, the nipples formed like small mouth – sized treats. The skin was smooth and fine and the aroma which rose into his nostrils was like some delicious Arabian sweet meat. He watched her as she oozed across the room and then followed her to the shower.

When the Chinese food arrived they sat in front of a TV screen with cartons on top of a small coffee table. She giggled as she ate, and laughed at his fears for his place at the college. She told him that he was too intelligent to be working there anyway. Too strong to waste his energies on some mad improvement scheme or other; that he would be better to write. She playfully flicked his ear with her nail and bit his shoulder the second time they made love, and finally she curled next to him as they spooned into sleep.

* * *

"Cutting the canes his back was aching. Aching like someone had beaten him. He wanted to feel warm rum on his skin, the warm rum made from the sugar which he had carried to the cart. He knew what the rum was for - dulling the senses of men who had been pressed ganged into service of the crown. Dulling their senses so they could not taste the maggots in the stale hard tack, or feel the biting agony of wounds and infection."

When the juice of the canes had been extracted, the soft sugary mass was raked in the sun; then finally transferred to the earthenware cones from which the dark molasses sugar dripped ready to make the liquor. Like blood it dripped, his blood and the blood of generations before; dripped into the vats which were distilled to make Nelson's rum. The same rum in which Nelson had eventually been pickled after Trafalgar."

"Is that true?" a nameless voice asked as he read.

"Absolutely," Collins replied. "The Admiral's body was preserved from putrefaction, by rum. Not a drink to take lightly." He paused then attempted to shock his class even further, Michelle caught his eye as he did so. "I believe the men drank the rum after they were back in Portsmouth, such was their need."

"No way dude?" a different voice exclaimed in disbelief.

"Way dude!" Collins instantly replied. "And as we are in the realms of surfer speak. Antigua is not a surfer's paradise. Though they do drink a lot of rum on the beaches. Where was I? Oh yes.

It had been five years since his younger sister had died. The last known link to his past died giving birth to the second child which had been forcibly placed inside her. No sooner had the first, which had been a still born, died, then a second was growing within her. Once again the overseers had used her, and once again her midriff began to swell, only this time slightly more quickly."

Collins paused to take a mouthful of water, and sneak a quick look at the clock. This might be his last lecture. Twenty five minutes – he had just twenty five minutes. It might be the last twenty five minutes.

He coughed and then began again.

"The night his sister died he made a vow of vengeance and tonight as he drew the cord tight around the man's neck he was laughing. He bit his victim's ear as he, returned the complement, "The darker the berry the sweeter the juice." He pulled tighter as the kicking increased. Harder and harder the man kicked as he struggled against the rope which was restricting his air and forcing his eyes out of their sockets. Then all struggles with life ceased.

Quickly the young slave found the keys which held the throat collar in place and released the shackles which bound his legs: He was free.

Stripping the corpse he pulled on the dead man's clothes and stuffed the pistol and knife into his belt.

At the entrance to the slave quarter he stopped. Stopped as two large dogs bounded toward him. Two large mastiffs approached with teeth exposed in a bared grin. They sniffed at him and on recognising the scent of the overseer on the clothes he now wore they let him pass and trotted back to their positions of vigil.

Over the outer compound fence he leapt and vanished into the night: He was free. Free like he had never been before. Free in a land which he did not know, free in a place he had never been before. As free as a dead man."

Paul Collins' mind drifted, back and forth across the narrative, the hospital and his life.

Collins had looked at Michelle Ward, and smiled as their eyes met. He had wanted to tell her, that much she deserved, tell her before it happened. In the end she would just get everything and that should be enough. As he looked he realised that he loved her; a deep and intense love, something which he had never felt before, and now would never feel again. She had been his muse, a dangerous one at that, but he wanted to tell her everything would be alright. Tell her to move on and find someone else.

Secretly he hoped she might cry, at least for a while, but he knew that time did heal and ten years after he had gone she might remember him in a different way. A gamble is a gamble, some you win and some you lose. In some cases you don't even get to choose.

He continued with the narrative. "On the first night he walked into St. Johns and stole a pie. It was the finest pie he had ever eaten and he ate it all. Ate it with wrists which were not shackled. At the back of Mitchell's tavern he stole four bottles of beer to slake his thirst after the salted meat. The first he forced open easily, the second was more troublesome and by the third his balance was going. The fourth remained unopened where he left it in the goat shed of Able Turner's farm.

In the morning he woke with a headache and milked the goats before the maid could arrive. When she did she could not understand how such prolific milkers could dry up overnight. By the evening they were once again full to bursting.

On the back field of Turner's he caught a chicken, snapping the neck like a twig. He stole six eggs which he stuffed into his pockets before venturing out across the sugar plantation and up toward the hills."

Collins checked the clock – ten minutes.

"Once the bird was plucked he roasted it on spit. The eggs he pierced at one end and lay upright in the embers of the fire. They blackened quickly but cooked to perfection. The meat he ate hot and greasy, the juices of the bird running down his chin and melting onto his chest. That night, the second, he slept in a shallow cave, while the tropical storm washed away the remnants of his footprints in the soft earth of the plantation over which he had run.

At daylight he headed east. First to half-moon bay, there he walked a full mile along the edge of the surf, obliterating both his tracks and scent. Stripping naked he swam, swam like a dolphin released, he ducked and bobbed and finally emerged a full half hour later, only to find his clothes gone and the last remnants of hard egg had been devoured by some unseen creature. He cursed his stupidity. "

Collins stopped, shutting the book. "That concludes it," he said. "It's over."

"The hell it does." A loud voice screamed from the back of the auditorium. "You can't leave your hero like that. Naked on a beach. What happens next? Does he live or die? Who tells us that then?"

"You do!" Collins exclaimed. "You are the reader, make it work. I only had a few minutes left."

"But you are the writer, so write us an ending. You can't just leave your hero like that."

"And just why not?" Collins replied, into the darkness, shielding his eyes from the spotlight which shone upon him. "And who's to say he's a hero anyway?"

"You've got to finish it?" a second voice pleaded.

"Call yourself an author?" a third voice now joined in.

"Look," Collins spoke with complete sincerity, "what would you do when the end comes? When the demon of despair hits you like a ton of bricks? Where would you run? When there is nowhere left to run to. You'd make your hero run? You'd make him fall in love and be safe and free in the arms of the woman? I suppose you want me to do that too?" He sighed heavily, "I was in love once you know. " He corrected himself, "No, no, I am in love."

There was a long silence before he spoke again, "Well not all stories have a happy ending and mine is one of those. It just ends." He paused as if reflecting, "Sometimes life just ends. Sometimes it's an accident; sometimes it's murder and sometimes," he paused again "sometimes it's just luck. Good or bad."

"What just like that?"

"Just like that, as Tommy Cooper used to say."

The audience tittered at his makeshift humour and philosophy.

"Well that's shitty." The same voice replied, a woman's voice.

He started humming, and then singing, "Don't get strung out by the way I look, don't judge a book by the cover. I'm not much of a man by the light of day; but by night I'm one hell of a lover."

"Well I still think the story should end- decisively."

"How decisively?" Collins replied into the darkness.

"That's up to you," the voice from the audience yelled. "You're the writer."

"Precisely." He yelled back.

Paul Collins reopened the book. Looked at the clock - four minutes. He started to read.

"That morning their lovemaking had been more intense than ever. Michelle had done things which he had not expected from one so young and his explosion had rippled into the day."

"Finished? Have you finished now?" the audience voice asked.

"Well and truly," Collins had replied.

"So what happens next?"

"We all come into this world naked and naked we go," he said. "We bring nothing and take nothing too. A strange irony for a society built upon the acquisition of riches. Did you know that the Bedouin chiefs give wealth to their subjects and keep nothing for themselves? The American Indians did just the same. The greater the chief, the less they owned. Strange that."

"Just tell me what happened to that naked boy?"

"The same as happens to every naked boy. He runs as fast as he can until he turns into the gingerbread man."

Collins lit a cigarette.

"Please don't," she pleaded.

Collins stubbed it out.

"He makes his way to the north and chewing sugar cane he gets enough energy to keep going. He is hunted by packs of dogs until eventually he is captured and ..."

"And then what?"

Paul Collins voice became sombre, "He runs until he reaches the very edge of the island. The place where the devil's bridge spans the opening of the land that leads to the open ocean. And then knowing he is only a short distance away he starts to swim, swimming back to where he came from. Swimming in the tepid water over which the boat came with him shackled. He swims until the water swallows him; swims until he starts to breathe the fluid and feel no pain."

**

"Mr. Collins?" the nurse was waking him.

"I need a shave," he said, in sudden reply.

"It's time for your morphine."

The nurse was preparing the needle, as the woman walked in. The nurse shook her head at her.

"It isn't fair," the woman said, "he didn't deserve this."

Collins spoke calmly as the needle point punctured his arm, "Deserve, deserve has nothing to do with it." His face was smiling, a broad grin. "I wanted to go swimming with you one more time; wanted to slide under the waves like the boy." His speech began to slur, "But time got in the way and Michelle ..." His eyes closed, "It was...

"How long does he have?" Michelle Ward asked.

The nurse looked at the notes, "A few hours max. I'm so sorry."

"Do you know he never said a word to anyone? Not a damn thing. He just quit his job, and took off. Hid himself away until I finally found out last week. All that pain and all that medication and he never said a word. And he was finishing his book. He just poured out everything into that book. It's all about him and me and the story of our love affair."

"I know," said the nurse. "He's been talking about Antigua.

I was born there, did my training there and then came here in 1967. I know the places he was talking about. Betty's Hope, and the Codrington sugar company." She smiled, "You're Michelle aren't you?"

There were tears running down her face in the silent response.

"He loves you, you know." The nurse lowered her voice, "He told me that so many times." She looked into the young girl's eyes, "You are his one you know."

"Can I stay with him?" Michelle asked.

"Of course you can," the nurse replied. "Of course you can."

order 410

For those who know - love never dies

Order 410

On the eastern edge of Southampton there is a park. Not an opulent park with running deer and fountains, but a municipal park. An area owned by the city council, a place planted with shrubs and a walled garden; a place where people go to walk their dogs and build snowmen, which happens about once every twenty years.

I live near the park and I try to walk through it from time to time. I especially love the spring, when the flowers start their early push. It is a place where the air is clean and sometimes I walk through the avenues of trees and down to the only stretch of beach in the city. Today, as I do nearly every day, I was walking my dog alone, when I spotted a man in the distance.

The man was tall and slender with a skin which seemed elegantly pale; the sun of that pale winter afternoon gave his skin a translucence which made him look almost opaque. He was, as I remember, strikingly handsome. The pale skin accentuated both his eyes and his dark uniform. With shoes polished so that they gleamed, he stood erect and thoughtful at the end of the road which had once led to the house. I was certain he was observing me as I walked toward him and taking in all the detail I had about me.

He was dressed in naval uniform, an officer, I think the rank bands donated, though to be honest I was not sure, the rank of commander I think? There was something very attractive about both his demeanour and his dress, very attractive indeed. He had the majesty of a man used to giving orders and having them obeyed; confidence that was what he had, pure confidence. His walk was fluid and almost gave the impression of him floating over the cobbles and tarmac as he moved. Immediately I thought of a dancer, he had that look; the Fred Astaire look, slim, athletic and proud. I could see him advancing with his hands in his pockets the way Astaire used to when approaching Ginger prior to a big band dance number. The tilt of his head and the slightly sheepish approach, confident and yet reserved; his hands in his pockets. They didn't seem to make them like that anymore. These days they were too worried about saying the wrong thing or being non PC, and I hated that. I wanted to see more men on chargers with their gleaming armour showing through their shirt buttons. My friends laughed at me, teased me, when we had our girly nights out.

Gloria my best friend had said, "They don't make men like that anymore. And anyway they are fantasies. You'll have to settle you know, one day you'll have to settle."

We had joked about it. "Well I want a real man," I'd growled in reply. "I don't want a baby boy, nor some toy," they whooped at me, "I want a real man." I was drunk at the time. "Someone to sweep me off my feet and carry me upstairs and ravish me."

"You're drunk and horny you silly slut, you need a man between your thighs," my friend Jenny had said. "Cock a doodle do, any cock'll do," she crowed. She was drunk too.

We all fell about laughing. Why I was thinking about that now I had no idea.

He was smoking a cigarette and standing looking at the bowling green as I approached. I had butterflies in my stomach - why I had no reason to think: I just did. Once upon a time there had been a house on the spot where the greens now stood. A display on the wall gave a miniature potted history of the location. And I had often imagined what the place would have been like in its heyday before it fell into ruin. Chandeliers hung with candles as they danced Viennese waltzes; men smoking cigars in the garden and fine furniture everywhere.

The house had been built in 1859 by renowned architect Richard Wright, and he had lived there until his death in 1892 when the property had been sold to Lord Radstock; Radstock subsequently sold the property in 1937, and it was demolished in 1957. The house, or where the house had been, was now replaced by a huge bowling green. A flat raised structure which would have been the area of the original ground floor slab.

The naval officer was standing in front of what would have been the front entrance. I had seen photographs, old sepia photographs, which showed a portico under which the old Victoria carriages would have disembarked their cargo. Or Edwardian early cars would have noisily parked, coughed and spluttered before wheezing to a halt away from the stables. I had imagined the taffeta and lace dresses and the silk top hats and the black silver - topped canes. I often wondered how I would have fared had I been born in those times. A close friend had once said I would be a servant, a governess; I replied by saying that I would be the lady of the manor – having married well. We had laughed about it at the time, but I knew that what my friend had said was most probably correct. I had delusions of grandeur.

The naval officer's hair was dark and smoothed close to his head, perhaps Brylcreem; it reminded me of the forties movie idols. A young Larry Olivier, a Heathcliff without his Merle Oberon.

I, on the other hand, must have looked a complete mess. Walking my dog in wellies, my hair was unwashed and tied back in a pony tail, my make-up nonexistent and I cursed the missed opportunity which had suddenly presented itself. I could hear my mother's voice in my head telling me, "Never go out in public unless you are properly dressed. You never know who or what you might meet." The clean underwear syndrome, just in case you did get that bus run over you. Now I wished I had taken her advice. Not that my underwear wasn't clean. Crikey.

Perhaps I had best explain. I'm a school teacher and have been one for the past eight years, so you can guess at my age. I am average to look at, and have average intelligence. I work, or should I say babysit, children between the ages of eight and twelve. It is not an environment which is populated by the kind of man a woman likes; well not the kind I like anyway. Most of the men I meet are dishevelled, with poor dress sense and obsessed with education and I would like someone who is obsessed by me. Most teachers moan constantly, and the men are riddled with anxiety, not performance anxiety, but a notion of maleness, anxiety. I always imagined a great love affair with a man who treated me like a fairy tale Princess. I always wanted to be Cinderella.

They say that every girl wants to marry her dad, and my dad was terrific. Confident, kind and just the sort of man I have never met. He was good looking too when he met my mother, the ice-maiden.

"What a great dog," he said, as I approached him. "What breed is it?"

He turned toward me and smiled. I instantly noticed his captivating green eyes and immediately saw the Celtic link in his features. His shoulders were manly and his voice deep, resonant and voluptuous, like satin being slid over cotton. Irish, I thought as I detected a slight accent, not broad and jarring, but sophisticated, soft and almost mesmeric.

I felt my tongue sticking to the roof of my dry mouth, "Weimaraner," I stated.

"German?"

"Yep, a hunting breed. Jagerhund," I said in German.

"That's interesting, have many of these got here now then? Must have been before the war? I don't think I have ever seen one before."

His voice oozed at me and I felt my knees tremble slightly. The hair on the back of my neck stood on end as his eyes went straight through me. This sounds totally stupid but he made me shiver; I actually felt a tingle up and down my spine.

"What happened to the old place?" he asked. Flicking his eyes over my shoulder.

I felt as if he had released me from an intense grip.

"There's a thingy-me on the wall, it tells you all about the history," I burbled.

I offered to show him and he followed me to the side of the club house facilities. There he stood and started to read a brief history of the building. It was then that I noticed the lapel pin, it read Penelope. It had one slight chip in the enamel as if something had struck it.

"Is that the name of your wife?" I asked, wishing I had not, as soon as the words left my lips.

"Oh no," he laughed at my stupidity, "I'm not married and never likely to be, now. Those chances are long gone. HMS Penelope was my last posting."

"Do you have a girl?" I blurted again.

I felt like a schoolgirl asking someone to go out with their friend. What an embarrassment to myself.

His face became sombre. "I did once, Florence," he said, "and I said I'd come back for her. Said I'd come back from Naples."

"What happened?" I had to ask, he had become so melancholic.

"I suppose," he paused, "I didn't make it back in time?"

"And?"

"Well she married someone else. She had a couple of wonderful little boys. She brought them here once, before they were grown up."

"Did you love her?" I cursed myself for asking such a personal question; I'd only just met the man.

"With all my heart and soul," he said. "She was the one thing on all this earth that I prized the most."

"And she married someone else?"

"Yes."

"Oh my God, that's a really shitty thing to do."

"We saw each other a few times after she was married and I knew she still loved me and then one day she just stopped coming."

I could have wept at the way in which the stranger relayed the pain of what must have ripped his soul apart, to me, here by the old Bowling Green that had once been a house. I wondered if this had been a special location for them. The romantic in me came to the fore and I saw him as an Edward Rochester deserted by his Jane. Left to wander and wonder at what he had done wrong. Conversely I felt relieved and rather comforted by his obvious pain and I wondered who the woman might have been that killed the affection inside him. Whoever she was, she needed her head examined, he simply was gorgeous.

"It was such a place," he said.

He seemed willing to talk and that was half my battle. Perhaps, my mind was saying, you, you could put him together. I could see the muscles ripple in his chest as he sighed and I knew that if I could manage to seem intriguing then there might be a possibility of meeting him at another time, when I had a chance to put on my war paint. I could heal a damaged man and make him whole again.

"It has been a long time since last I was here," he said. "The world was full of gaiety and joy then. There were dances you know, mostly for those who had made it through the old Victoria Hospital."

"I'm being very rude," I interrupted. "Let me introduce myself. Veronica Clay." I offered my gloved hand and he took it. "That is Sally my bitch."

He patted the dog's head. "John Waldegrave," he replied. "Commander John Waldegrave RN," he corrected.

"Are you on leave?" I asked.

"Leave? Yes, since the 18th February, but only a short hop this time I'm afraid and then it's off to Naples and Italy. Order four hundred and ten; order four hundred and ten."

I wondered what order four hundred and ten could be. It was obviously very important; perhaps it was some sort of top secret mission? Maybe this Commander was a real life James Bond? He certainly looked the part.

"What part of Ireland are you from?" I asked lamely, trying to engage him in deeper conversation. I wanted to get to the exchange of phone numbers.

"Castle Town, Queen's County, Ireland. Well that's where my family are from."

"So why are you here?"

"So many questions. Haven't you heard that gossip costs lives?"

My God I thought, he already thinks I'm a talker. I can't let him think that. I could feel myself being drawn to him and I had a terrible urge to hold him and cuddle away what seemed to be the melancholy of some ancient pain which clung to his voice. I wanted to tell him that I could make him happy. I checked my own ridiculousness.

"Sorry," I said, and then suddenly blurted, "it's just that you seem so unhappy. Perhaps I could give you my phone number." There I'd said it. I might as well have kissed him there and then.

I reached into my pocket and drew out a note pad; and then as I fumbled for a pen he produced one from his top pocket and passed it to me. I tried to click the top; he smiled and taking the item back unscrewed the top and the fountain pen was ready.

I scribbled the eleven numbers of my mobile and ripped the top sheet from the perforated edge and passed it to him. He folded it carefully and placed it into his breast pocket.

"Now yours," I said, a little too eagerly.

Once that was done I screwed the top back onto his pen, handed it back and stuffed the prize winning number into my pocket. All the while I was thinking that this could be the most wonderful opportunity. This man oozed romance, it was as if he was made of love. As if everything about him, the air around him, was constructed of pure love. Never before had I experienced anything like it. It was like some heady perfume wrapping around me as we spoke. It was as if I was naked: Totally naked and open, not physically, but mentally. His eyes did things to me that I cannot explain and don't really want to. I think it was love at first sight-though I never believed such a thing existed.

"There was an avenue of Beeches," he said, snapping the spell. "When last I was here. Great majestic trees. Over there I think it was."

"That's still there," I said, I paused, "but aren't you cold? My place is not far from here and we could have coffee?"

There I'd said it. Thrown my cards on the table like some wanton slut. I might as well have told him he could have my knickers off if he liked. Knickers off in less than thirty minutes; I couldn't believe what I was saying or doing.

I don't want you to get the wrong idea. I'm not some sort of hussy you know. It's just that if you had met the man you would probably be just the same or worse. There was something which made me act irrationally. I can only say it was love. True love like some great force of nature – unstoppable, unsinkable.

He smiled, and his teeth were perfect. "I'm always cold," he said, "In this line of work you get used to it; the sea is a cold place to be. But a drink of tea might be nice. It's so long since I've had a nice cup of tea."

The headiness of the moment was shattered as Sally saw a squirrel and suddenly disappeared into a deep dense growth of Rhododendron bushes. I called and she didn't return. I called again, and still she refused to come back.

"Excuse me," I said, "I'll have to go and get her." And with that I toddled off to where she'd gone.

I couldn't have been gone for more than a minute. When I returned the man had gone. I looked in every direction and could not see him. Either he was a fast walker or he had run.

"Shit, Veronica," I said to myself. "You stupid slut you messed that one up."

I put Sally on her lead and wandered around the ornamental gardens, in the vain hope that I might see him; that he might have decided to continue his stroll.

After half an hour I gave up, cursing my own stupidity. Then it struck me I had his number and had even managed to give him mine. I'd call him. Where was the harm in that? I mean? I'm not a crazy bunny boiler, but sometimes you have to take a chance - don't you?

***

After that day things sort of went a little bizarre. Let me explain. I walked around for bit and Sally chased a few squirrels. I met old Mr. French, who knows all about the history of Southampton. He's one of those old chaps who love to talk to children and he has often come to our school to talk about the past. I ought to get a tape of his stories before they vanish along with him. Once he spoke about the Spitfire factory down on the banks of the Itchen River. He had a model and everything. The boys loved that. He had photographs of the old church at the bottom of the town, the night it was on fire, after a bombing raid which was obviously designed to get the factory. The German bombers missed and set the town alight instead. Virtually all of below bar was alight that night. He has a spaniel named Freddie and he, well he dives into bushes like they are water. If there is anything alive in the undergrowth he can catch it.

I spoke to him for about ten minutes on the likelihood of him coming to school to talk to the children about the women's land army. That had him hooked and I thought that he might know someone who had worked at that. Something for the girls I thought as the dogs frolicked about, chasing each other in turns over the flat grass and around the majestic oak tree.

Then I blurted, "You haven't seen a young naval officer on your travels have you?" I asked.

"What him? Is he back again?" he replied as if he knew the man.

"Do you know him?"

"You must be about the tenth pretty girl who has asked me about him." He was chuckling in a knowing way, a knowing way as only an older man could.

"I met him today," I sheepishly said.

"Did you?" the old man smiled. "Good looking boy. Took after his mother, my God she was a dark beauty. And Florence, she waited for him to come back, a real lady she was, but he never did. It broke the old man - nearly killed him."

I spoke without thinking, or should I say I was thinking aloud? "He's not so ugly himself." Instantly I wished I hadn't said it. I felt rather stupid. Rather stupid? I felt very stupid. I went bright red in a blush, but secretly liked the notion of Mr. French considering me a girl. That was a wonderful choice of adjective too. However, I was too embarrassed to pursue the matter and disheartened by the number of women that asked after him. I reasoned not to ask any more questions and decided to make my way home. I made a rapid exit and started to walk.

The winter sun was dying and that February I felt more alone than ever. Another Valentine's Day had passed and once again I was alone. I had visions of me being an old maid living the life of the spinster teacher. Like Mr. Chipping I'd be saying to people that all the pupils I had ever taught were my children.

A vague excuse for being a relationship failure - like me. You see I like men and they like me, but after a while they get bored. Bored because I'm often tired; tired? More like exhausted. Just ask any mum and I have thirty of the little darlings every day. Perhaps I'm not exciting enough? I try to be, but being a teacher is tough, though most people think it's easy. After all, everyone went to school - how difficult can it be?

Without thinking I reached into my pocket and found the note pad. There on the front page, in a perfect copperplate hand, was his number: Castle Town 410. That convinced me, I'd been given the classic brush off. That was why I stopped going to clubs and bars, it was the standard way to avoid being harassed. A false number and a quick disappearing act, I used it too. Sneaky I know, but it works, and now I had had it done to me. Disappointed I stuffed the notebook into my pocket and started to think about the marking I had to do and the coming week.

**

February drifted into March and try as I might I could not get the image of the smoking sailor out of my mind. Daffodils had pushed their way into the warming sun, and the Camellias had started to bloom in the ornamental gardens of Mayfield House. Even the Cedar tree, in the middle of the round lawn was greener: Life was returning to the soil and then I realised in what a beautiful location this house had been placed.

At times I thought I was an obsessive. I even walked Sally to the same spot where I had met him; not once or twice but every day. When I got to the entrance of what once had been Mayfield House I felt a sad sense of regret. Like an opportunity had been missed or a chance scattered. For some reason my mood changed and that was when I told Millie.

Millie was my oldest friend; she had the brashness and self-assurance I lacked. In fact at times she was a little too – bossy. As I was taller, than average, she was shorter; as I was softly spoken, she was louder. A blonde, that's her, and a brunette that's me. We were total opposites in every way, but we always laughed when we were in each other's company. It had been like that since we had been at school. Sometimes I wondered if we would be friends, had we met as adults. She had a slightly superior air, some said snobbish even, but I knew that was really a front, a bit of bravado.

Amelia Oldham, Millie to her friends, had come down from London for the weekend, and as we walked Sally I told the story of the sailor. Millie listened, that was her skill, she had gone into law and me teaching. I sometimes wondered if our careers should have been the other way around.

Then she said it, "Haven't you googled him yet then?"

"No, I'm not some kind of bunny boiler."

"Look," she laughed, "You can find out all about him. I bet you didn't even try the number did you?"

"It's only got three digits. How crap is that?"

"Ireland? You said he came from Ireland?"

I nodded.

"And you haven't even tried the number?"

"I thought it was a spoof number."

"You thought? And you didn't even check? You chump." Millie was laughing, "Sometimes I wonder about you Veronica. You're like your name, clay. A lump of clay."

I blushed, that's what I seemed to do often these days, when I think of men.

"Where's the predator in you girl?" she mocked. "You've got to get out there with your noose and snag you a man. We better get weaving on this: Get ready to be a cowgirl."

"What?"

"A cowgirl!"

We burst out laughing. Laughed right there at the front of Mayfield House.

"You're a right smutty bitch Millie Oldham," I said.

"Well, when we get back let's get on the internet and find your prey. We'll cut him out of the herd and you can drag him down and devour him," she laughed. "You said he was a Commander RN and you know his ship? Easy then. " She made a guttural sexy growling sound and clawed the air around her.

"Come out, come out wherever you are," she continued. "He can run but he can't hide," she purred.

We were both roaring at the whole lunacy of it now.

Then she starting skipping, skipping off down the path that led to the ornamental gardens, "We're gonna find you," she was singing. "Come out, come out, wherever you are."

That was Millie to a tee. Mad, bad and thoroughly funny to know.

***

Millie was sitting in front of my lap top.

"What's his name?" she called to me.

I was in the kitchen.

"John Waldegrave."

"Nothing," she called again.

I arrived with the coffee and biscuits.

"Commander RN? Let's try that," she paused, "nothing. Let's try the MOD site." She typed his name into several sites and each time she drew a blank. "Are you sure he was Navy and not merchant marine?"

"Oh he was Navy alright."

She typed again, "What was the name of his ship?"

"It was on his lapel, a girl's name. Penelope."

Millie nearly dropped her drink in astonishment as the screen filled with the image of a cruiser. HMS Penelope. It was steel grey with a red under hull and looked like some ancient airfix model.

"Oh my God!" Millie exclaimed. "This can't be right."

I was behind her now looking at the screen.

"What a bastard," I said, "he lied."

Millie was reading from the drop down menu, "HMS Penelope, nicknamed the, Pepperpot, a cruiser, sunk off the coast of Italy 18th February 1944. Torpedoed by a U boat." She scrolled down, "Two torpedoes starboard and the ship was listing badly, then the U boat fired two more at the portside and the magazine was hit. The whole ship was blown in half and went down in six minutes. Two thirds of the crew died, including the Captain and several senior officers."

"What a cock," I said, "why would he say he was on that ship when he wasn't? What a knob."

"It gets worse, look."

Millie had the crew list up now and there he was: The Hon John Montague Granville Waldegrave. Died 18th February 1944.

"Right," she said, as she checked out the full name. " Oh my God," she bit her lip. "John Waldegrave was heir to the title Lord Radstock. He was the last male heir. He would have been a Baron."

"Why would anyone pretend to be a Lord who died in the war?" I asked. "It's nineteen ninety seven." I did a quick calculation, "That's fifty three years. He'd be about eighty five." I was astonished.

" There's a link." Millie clicked on it. "Look," she said.

At that point my knees buckled and I thought I was going to collapse. There was a Times article from 1944. And there was his picture.

"That's him," I squealed. "That's him."

"It says that John was heir to the Queen's County Fortune - Castle Town Ireland. That they, the Waldegrave family had a home at Mayfield House, which they had allowed to be used as an extra nursing facility under the jurisdiction of the Royal Victoria War Hospital at Netley Abbey. The ship Penelope was torpedoed by U boat 410 just before the Anzio landings."

"That's the number he gave me 410, and he said he had an order 410," I shuddered.

I wasn't listening to the sound of the words anymore. I could see the picture of the man in the paper and it was identical to the man I had seen. Absolutely identical.

My heart was pounding now trying to make sense of the whole situation.

"Hey, look at this." Millie had moved sites. "Mayfield House was bequeathed to Florence Wright, by Lord Radstock."

"I thought Lord Radstock was John?"

"No this was his father, Montague. He bequeathed it in 1953

when he died, to Florence and Malcolm. Florence it seems had lived in the house since 1944 with her husband Malcolm Wright, and their two sons."

Now I was beginning to actually feel frightened. Who was this strange man I had met? Was he some sort of obsessive lunatic? I'd even given him my number, and it wasn't a fake one.

She carried on reading from the old newspaper now shown on the computer screen, "Apparently after the Duke."

"Lord," I corrected.

"Whatever." She continued, "Lord Radstock had one son, John who was engaged to Florence Stockton, and after his son was killed at sea he took Florence in as a daughter. She married this Wright chap and they lived in the house with the old duffer until he died in 1953. Then after his death," she scanned down, "on the 4th of October 1956 there was a terrible fire and both parents were killed in the blaze. Lord Montague Radstock had two surviving daughters though, both younger than their dead brother. They took both boys to Ireland and the ruin was left to Southampton City Council and finally demolished in 1957. They claimed the place was haunted and refused to have anything to do with a restoration or rebuild."

"So who the hell dresses up to pretend to be someone who died years before?" I asked.

"There are a lot of sick people out there," she replied. "Hey shall I try to make the image bigger?"

I nodded.

There on the screen was the man I had seen. John Waldegrave Commander RN - the man I had spoken to. His hair, his face, everything was identical, right down to the lapel pin. I looked closely and noticed it was damaged in exactly the same place. As I stared into the eyes of the image I was mesmerised. Those were the same eyes, of that I was certain, only in this picture he lacked the deep sadness of the man I had spoken to. Everything made sense, all the names and the dates tallied; but nothing really made sense at all. Florence saw him? He saw Florence? But then she didn't come back anymore? She couldn't come back, she was dead.

"Bloody hell," Millie exclaimed, "there can't be two men who look that good, can there? He's bloody lovely. No wonder you wanted him, or even the chap pretending to be him. I'd shag him myself." She paused and to defuse my anxiety added, "Hey, I'd shag them both." She was laughing now, "At the same time too. I've never done that before either. Does that make me a slut?" She paused and smirked. "Ok, ok," she said, "I'm a slut. But that would be fun wouldn't it?"

The tension was broken and we were both laughing. Thank God for a friend like Millie Oldham, that's all I can say.

"The problem is Mill," I replied, "nobody's going to shag anybody. We're looking at a dead man. A man who's been dead since 1944."

"Do you believe in ghosts?" she asked.

"I never did before but he was not like a person, he was like a raw emotion. It was like he was love itself. This isn't making much sense is it?"

Millie was shaking her head.

"It's like the love between Florence and him was embodied in his being."

"Oh my God," she laughed, "romantic or what?"

"That's the thing though, love, true love, never dies it becomes something else. Maybe a child or a person or him? I felt it all around him and I don't care what you say he had come back and he was looking for her. His love would not let him rest."

There were tears in Millie's eyes. "I wish I could find my John Waldegrave," she said, "I'm really quite lonely."

Minutes later both of us were sobbing, though why we had no idea, maybe it was for relief, for self-pity, but I like to think it was for love.

skin deep

Lamont 2010

For anyone who can enter the garden of delight

Skin Deep

"Chuck the damn things in the back," the man yelled, "never do any damn good. Just take up space. We'll get some more from Marks and Sparks, they're cheap as chips. Bloody things just sit there takin' up space, and stinkin' up the place."

"Will do," came the reply, from the garbage collector, as he lifted the plants, complete with pots, onto the lid of the bin, which he then wheeled away. At the side of the vehicle he placed the small plants inside the cab, there were six in all; six small dishevelled plants with pale yellow leaves and a series of roots, which clung to the bark and moss of the transparent pots which enclosed them. Then returning the bin to the house, he watched as the man fired up the engine of his Ford Focus and disappeared into the traffic.

The yellow truck moved through the small back streets like a snail, crawling from stop to stop; the three man team emptying the wheelie bins into the back of the steel maw. Some of them spoke and some reacted with hand gestures; reaction to the constant horns of – late for work workers – that had lost patience, waiting to move through the chicanes of parked cars.

This was just another dull winter day; February the seventh to be precise, and a fine drizzle had begun to fall. A full soaking drizzle which gradually crept down the collars of the working men and penetrated their waterproof overalls. Although the garbage of Christmas had now been cleared, there were one or two bare Christmas trees still languishing in the front gardens of the Victorian terraced houses. The red-clay bricks shone as if polished clean by the weather and the mullions of stone were stained by the grime of the city; all in all it was a depressing sight. But one of the men, the man who had placed the plants in the cab, whistled as he worked; a perpetual smile painted across his winter-cold face.

The bin men moved methodically, almost languidly at times; pulling the items to the throw bar which raised and then tipped the bins into the belly of the truck. Then the hydraulic scoop pulled and constricted the items into the tight dense rubbish, which ended up in the vast burial mound of land fill. The contents of these trucks was used to fill in the land reclaimed from the sea, and Portsmouth was further ahead than most in creating new land masses. Fifty years from now, the methane of decay would have been burnt off and the top soil, now piled so high, would long have sunk back down, much as a grave does once the coffin collapses around the corpse. In a matter of years the building programme would begin and new houses would be littered over the once drained mud flats and river silt.

Once the Romans had taken their war craft deep into the harbour, now the water was only three feet deep at high tide and no vessel could get to the once thronging Portchester Castle. Children scampered like mudlarks, in the summer, over the flats at low tide and men with metal detectors found the odd Roman coin or artefact lost overboard. The world had moved on, but the accumulation of human detritus continued. Once in corrugated aluminium bins thrown upon the shoulder, now with the wheeled bin - the rubbish; the flotsam and jetsam of humanity continued to build.

"Christ, how many more of those soddin' things you gonna collect?" said one of the operatives, who watched his smiling colleague retrieve another spent orchid from the crushing jaws. "One of these days, you'll lose your fuckin' arm. Yu'll get the thing caught and before we can help ya, you'll be tore to bits like a fuckin' rag doll. And what for? An old fuckin' plant? A piece of worthless shit."

"These are not worthless plants, they are young plants and they, like all things, deserve life or a chance at it at least. I will save as many as I can find and with some love and care they will bloom again. I've got loads at home. Nature's wonderful, it endlessly surprises."

"Fuck off; you sells 'em don't yer?"

"Nope I don't sell them, I care for them and look at them.

Sometimes I give them to people who like them," he paused, "but I never sell them. The scent they produce is beautiful and it's the breath of life to see them."

"You're fuckin' nuts. They're all shit and they don't even look nice, that's why all these bastards chuck the fuckin' things away." He waved his arm in a great sweep across his horizon. "Just look at it, it looks like shit. All the flowers are dead, the stalks are brown and the leaves ain't much better. Chuck the thing in the bin."

"Look," the smiling man replied, hiding his face as pedestrians passed the garbage wagon, "you take things out of the bins too. All these plants need is tender loving care. Just like people they need to be loved or eventually they die. Just because something is bashed about a bit, it doesn't mean they are good for nothing. "

"What like you?" the younger man laughed. "What's that on your face? Psoriasis ain't it? Looks fuckin' disgustin'. Looks like a pizza, all chopped up. You look like shit, cut up shit and you talks bollocks, complete fuckin' bollocks. The stuff I gets I sells. Everythin' needs to be loved? Yeah like the biggun I had Saturday. Hey Harry?" He called to the third man who was driving. " That bird on Saturday, the one with the big tits. What was her fuckin' name?"

Harry shrugged in reply.

He had touched on the smiling older man's two most vulnerable and exposed nerve endings: Scars and loneliness. A skin so deeply pocked and scarred, caused him to hide his face from passers by and members of the public. He had seen them when he came to empty their bins. Seen them try to avoid looking, but look they did nonetheless. Just as men looked at huge breasts in conversation with the possessor, even when they tried to avoid them. Like his uncouth and stupid bin dumping partner, to whom big breasts were the most important thing on any woman.

Since his late teens he had avoided people and people had avoided him. He was intelligent and clean, kind and well spoken. A man who never swore and a man whose lust for life was boundless. When he had gone to interviews often the scars on his face broke out and wept like sores, the stress making his affliction worse. The consequence was always the untrue excuse of unsuitability. At times he wondered whether he would be the same as those others, had he a face to admire. Would he spend his weekends trying to bury his face in the mounds of soft of female flesh, chew on the pert nipples of humanity which brought them back to life. But nipples never came to his lips, not since the unremembered slaking of childhood.

Consequently, he had avoided girls, or they had avoided him and he lived alone. Not once had another living soul reached out to touch him. But he was not bitter – instead he focussed on his work, the only work where a torn face did not matter: A refuse collector in the early hours and a breeder of flowers in the afternoons.

He, in reward for his kindness, had spent much of his life alone and had learned that orchids repaid the tender care given, with a devout blooming. Once he had even thought of shows; he knew he could win, but the face, always the face held him back. He'd even thought about a mask or make-up, but in the end his reluctance drew him back to reclusive solitude.

One thing he had learned from solitude was that human beings were in the main utterly selfish and reluctant to even look at anything different. Once he learned about a parrot that had escaped from a house and how the owner had pursued it to no avail. A few days later the poor escapee was found dead, mobbed by crows and seagulls until eventually it simply expired. That was the same trait he saw in humans. Children in the playgrounds and on their way home from school, taunting the unfashionable fat kids, or those with ginger hair. Like being different was some kind of affliction. Parrot or human the same fear of difference made them attack. Then he reasoned what the main issue of aliens landing would be? The primary concern for humans, he deduced, would be how to kill it, them, they, rather than communicate; and the more he saw the more he despaired. But still he smiled; smiled, because he had discovered true beauty. He knew that once retired he would become a recluse and devote his time to orchids.

He kept a dog, who, like all animals, failed to see the issue of the broken, bleeding skin and instead would lick his face with her soothing antiseptic tongue. She loved him, as he did her- unconditionally. His scars did not bother her, it was his personality which caused her to adore him. Not once had he struck her, even in the course of training. Not once had he taken a stick and beaten her for an indiscretion on the floor.

She knew his love and she chose to repay it with devotion.

"Them plants ain't no good," the younger man chided, spoiling to create an argument to counter the sheer boredom of bin collection.

"You say that every time I collect one. It's getting rather boring. You do what you want to do and leave me to my plants." His voice was neither aggressive, nor placatory, it was simply bland - bland and accepting. "But they are beautiful, just as nature intended. And when they are healthy again, I give them to people who'll care. "

"So we should all collect the fuckin' things?"

"Well we should all collect beautiful, useful things."

"Yeah, useful things." The younger man laughed, "Like that bird, the one with the big tits, they're useful; or things I can sell on ebay or to the car boot sale people. Then I can spend the money on me. Not like you – you berk. If you can't fuck it or flog it ain't worth a wank. You tosser. Look what you gets? Bloody plants. And not even good ones at that. Old ones, fuckin' old ones with no fuckin' flowers. And then after all the work you gives 'em away. Pratt!"

The younger of the two men was scornful as he spoke; scornful as only a younger man could be, when faced with an older man who was disfigured. He was firm and healthy and women loved him. Only last night one of the girls from the council pay offices had bucked and moaned underneath his weight; squealed like a stuck pig when he had thrown her around his bedroom. He had even paid for the taxi to get her home-he was generous like that, he bragged. Had found her knickers in the morning, in the bed, and laughed at her stupidity in leaving them behind. She was even stupid enough to want to stay the night, but he had given her the heave-ho once his selfish deed was done.

* * *

The motorcycle roared into life. A welcome sound which drowned out the endless existence of his misery. Many times he had wanted to take the bus. But he knew what the average passenger would do. Many would actively avoid sitting next to him, just in case. They feared contagion, so he settled for the anonymity of the helmet. The anonymity of loneliness, the anonymity of pain.

Ten miles from the town he turned into the gravel drive of the two bedroom bungalow which he had bought fifteen years earlier when his mother had died. His father went first and now, even though in his late forties, he felt like an orphan. There were no siblings, no brothers, and no sisters; there were some distant cousins in Canada but he had not seen them for over twenty five years; and since the death of his mother, communication had reached the impersonal Christmas card only stage. He knew they too were embarrassed by his face, embarrassed to invite him to their continent as they had once done when his mother was alive. Now he was consigned to the easily avoided. So he tended his many greenhouses, walked and played with his female spaniel Emma and waited.

In his diary lay the despair of his utter loneliness; the details of his feelings scribbled onto the page with his most intimate thoughts. Complex thoughts; thoughts on love, life, would have beens, orchids and beauty. There were sketches too, fine pencil studies of orchid blooms, and poetry. Intense poetry which spoke of loss and life alone. Poetry which no other living soul would read. To anyone who read them it would seem he carried the world's guilt upon his back.

The grounds to the bungalow were spacious but the accommodation was meagre. He kept a study which held a vast array of books and horticultural magazines; many of which published his articles on orchid husbandry. The study had a desk, computers and an examination table. Here he studied plants and shunned society. Here he undertook the cross fertilisation of plants which had created his finest triumph: His very own orchid.

To the rear of the house lay the main bedroom which opened onto the vast expanse of lawn, shrubs and borders. In the summer the warm scent of buddleia and lavender swept into his nostrils. Adjacent was a small bathroom with the variety of lotions and potions he applied to stem the nagging itching, and soften the skin which his fingernails often tore open in the night. Emma slept near the foot of his bed at times, but like all trusted companions she managed to find her way onto the bed at night. She accepted him and he accepted her. It was a bond which neither would willingly sever.

The rear gardens were surrounded by secluding trees and his greenhouses held his finest prizes- his orchids. Like the one he now placed on the kitchen table, he had recovered them all from a variety of bins across the city. The orchids which carried the care instruction to "destroy," once the flowering had failed. He had seen them in the supermarkets when last he had gone, but now he had groceries delivered. Delivered to save face, delivered to hide.

Flicking the switch on the kettle to on, he retrieved the post and sat looking at the plant. The leaves were yellow but he knew his preparation feed would enable life to come again. He looked and thought purple phaelenopsis, after a few more seconds he revised his opinion to white.

As he sat drinking tea he flicked the post open and on the third letter dropped both the opener and the letter as if startled or stung.

* * *

The door bell rang.

After the third ring and Emma's incessant bark he walked down the hall and pulled the door open with a scowling tug.

"Mr. Stephen Jenks?"

"Who wants to know?" he replied, pulling his dog back by the collar.

"I'm sorry," said the woman, "just little old me."

She was tall, blonde and athletic - beautiful and softly spoken. Her dog sat next to her, dark, sleek and implacable. Emma ran about him but he did not move; his crisp harness of black and yellow with the long handle, which rose to her left hand, stood like a hoop of iron which held him fast.

"I'm so terribly sorry to bother you," the woman said. Proffering a container in her right hand.

"I don't understand?"

"We're collecting for the guide dogs. I know it's a bit of a liberty but perhaps you might like to contribute to a worthy cause."

It was then that Jenks, the man with the hideous face, noticed the vacant stare and the yellow harness of the Labrador. The woman had not flinched when he opened the door. Had not, as others had done, tried to run away, made banal excuses and left with the speed of a gazelle. This woman stayed, looked, but evidently could not see.

Stephen Jenks thrust his hand into his pocket and produced a two pound coin which he dropped into the collection canister she was holding. Then as he fumbled for more whilst trying to read her identity card for a name; he was stunned by her sudden remark.

"Two pounds, that is rather generous of you," she said.

"Erm, well here's a little more," he smiled at his own ridiculousness, and wondered how she knew what he had put in the box.

"I heard it," she volunteered without request. "You see when you are a blind beggar your hearing gets very acute."

"But you're not a beggar," he retorted. "I mean you are just collecting."

"Just collecting?" she laughed. "Well isn't that what beggars do? They just collect?" She did not wait for him to reply. "I get sent to collect all over the place and today I've been sent here."

"Well you can beg from me at anytime," he stupidly said, and then as quickly regretted it. "I mean, I don't mind putting money in for a pretty cause, I meant needy cause." He paused and stumbled over his words, "What I meant to say was that I don't mind giving money to people less fortunate." He stalled and spluttered, his words were all coming out wrong, twisted by his own tongue.

"So now I'm less fortunate?"

"No that's not what I meant to say, I mean?"

"What did you mean then?"

"Oh Christ," he floundered. "I just meant to say that I'm sorry you're blind." He was feeling decidedly uncomfortable.

"Sorry? There's no need to be sorry. Fate makes us what we are?"

"I just wanted to…"

"When you have fallen down a hole," she continued, "the first thing you should do is stop digging."

His face was red, though she could not see it.

"Thank you," she said, and began to turn to exit the doorway.

It was then with a sudden unexpected flurry that Emma the spaniel crossed behind the woman. It was unpredictable, and rather impetuous of the dog, so impetuous that it broke with her normal character. Jenks would later think how, "She'd never done that before." The fall was sudden, sharp and shocking. Her hand left the handle of the guide dog harness and she lost her footing; fell onto the gravel at the side of the step.

Stephen Jenks was out of the house, his arm grasping her under the shoulder. Lifting her to her feet and she was whimpering and complaining about her wrist.

"You'd better come inside," he said, taking command of the situation. "I've a little brandy and we can take a look at that wrist. If it's broken we may have to take you up to A & E."

"It won't be broken," the woman said. "But a little sit down would be nice and Charlie could do with a drink. That's my dog."

Helping the woman into the kitchen Stephen Jenks sat his guest at the table, while he wrapped a cold soaked towel around her wrist. It was then that he noticed how cold her body was; her arm was stone cold as if frozen. As her dog lapped at the bowl, Emma lay totally still as if only she and her master were in the room.

"My God," he blurted, "you're freezing. I think you must be in shock. I'll turn the fire on."

"There's no need. I'm fine," the woman said. "I always run cold I've been like it for years. No amount of heating will do anything for the pains I have had to endure. There are many things which I have seen that I would rather not and many things I have felt that I would rather have not seen."

Jenks was bemused by the cryptic answer, but there was such a sadness surrounding the young woman that his heart began to beat rapidly in response to her sorrow.

"Let's have a look at that wrist again," he offered.

She obligingly lifted her hand and arm so that he could wrap a small bandage around the now bruised area.

"I still think that we need to get you to x-ray," he said.

"Oh don't be so silly," the woman laughed, "the fuss you make you'd think I'd been crucified."

The remark to Jenks seemed totally absurd, at odds with what he might be thinking. Never in his wildest notions had he thought of crucifixion. In fact that had never even crossed his mind.

"I think it's lovely the way you care for those plants," the woman said, "just like you are caring for me, right now. That is so rare when these days everyone thinks they need to behave like a pit-bull. There are just a few people who can see the beauty of creation; sadly I'm no longer one of them. There are so few people who care. I think that special orchid you have developed is marvellous. Beauty and the chance to give it are a special kind of gift. Rather like life."

"How did you know about my plants?"

"Well, it's rather a local legend isn't it? Your special orchid?"

Stephen Jenks shook his head. "That plant, my special orchid you called it? That orchid I call T after someone I knew, someone special. No ones knows about that. It's my secret."

"Oh don't be so coy," said the woman, "everyone knows about you. What was the name of this woman Theresa?" She pondered, "Yes that was it Theresa."

"How do you know so much about me? I have never told

any living soul about Theresa," Jenks blurted, suddenly disturbed and unnerved.

"That's easy – all you have to do is look and then you can see."

"But you, you're blind."

"I see said the blind man – when he didn't really see at all," the woman laughed.

"But that doesn't explain it."

"Explain, no. Understand yes. Oh the name's Mary by the bye. We haven't been introduced," she paused and smiled, "but there now we have. I'm Mary and you're Stephen."

"How did you find these things out about me?" Jenks asked. "I try to keep my life private. Nobody comes here."

"Someone does."

"Who? I don't know your someone."

"But he knows. He knows you Stephen. Knows all about you. Knows everything there is to know. Theresa told him, told him everything."

"Don't be bloody ridiculous. Theresa died, died in a car crash over thirty years ago. I should know I was the driver of the car that killed her. How can he talk to her? She died, died right next to me, trapped, we were both trapped and she died. He couldn't know that, no one around here knows that. I don't believe you and I think you should leave now."

"Well you might not believe it but it's true," she replied, without making the slightest intention to move.

"Jesus Christ am I under surveillance? Who's watching my house? I don't appreciate people snooping on me. I don't want people to be around here; this is my space; my home and I don't want your someone around."

"But I thought you might like to be..."

"I don't want anyone around here. I don't need anyone and my orchid, no one knows about that. So what the hell is going on?" His voice was rising in volume.

"Does that matter?"

"Of course it matters," he snapped in reply. "Everyone is entitled to their privacy." His voice was raised fully now, "I'm sick to death of this, this, this."

"I'm sorry if my interest in you has caused you concern."

"Caused me concern? It's made me livid. I made the most beautiful orchid in the world. Beautiful like my Theresa; even nature, or Jesus Christ himself couldn't create something like that and you talk as if you've seen it."

"Fine blood red, with a white heart and stamens of pure gold. You're right it is beautiful. Just like you, Theresa agrees with me, she thinks it is lovely that you named the new variety after her. And that is why we have come to visit you Stephen."

"You've been snooping, no one knows about that orchid. No one. We, we, just who the hell is we?" He was animated now, sweating.

A sudden pain hit his chest as if he had been punched and a large lead weight had been placed upon him, or a knife twisted into his heart. Pain shot down the length of his arms and his breath became short. His eyes lost their focus and he desperately needed to stem the pain, which had now increased in intensity.

"I need to sit down," he said meekly.

"I know," Mary replied.

At that moment there was a loud knock at the door.

"I think that's my someone," Mary smiled. "I'll let him in, shall I?"

Stephen Jenks face was turning blue, lined with total fear; fear of who this person might be; fear of what these strangers were about to do to him. Fear of what they might know. He was finding it hard to breathe now and he wanted to shut his eyes as he threw his head back and gasped for breath as the pain increased.

* * *

Stephen Jenks stood talking with the man who had come in, he suddenly became calm. The pain in his chest had vanished and Emma lay prostrate on her bed. Despite the presence of the stranger she was totally calm, either she had not noticed him or she was dead; he couldn't quite decide. He studied her and she seemed to be totally still; he wanted to go to her and see to her but his whole body felt intensely heavy- too heavy to lift. A glow began to emanate from the stranger's whole being as his voice poured into Jenks' ear like warm Olive Oil. He began to forget why he was angry and he could sense the calm of the afternoon now descending. Emma was at peace, he could see that and the stranger was telling him too.

"I've been watching what you do for a long time now Stephen," the voice said. "It's the orchids I'm interested in," the stranger continued. "What I have seen is marvellous, beautiful. I need a new gardener to design something extra special, something breathtaking."

"I agree, Mary added," her eyes a new translucent blue. She smiled as she spoke and Jenks noticed she was now looking directly at him. There was no vacancy, no stare just a deep lapis blue, like the lagoon blue of his childhood.

"Why don't you show us how you did it? How did you create something so exquisitely beautiful?" she asked.

Stephen Jenks, as if commanded, walked into the kitchen. The heavy weight which bore down upon him was immediately lifted; in fact he felt light, almost carefree. The voice followed, seemed kind and sensitive and as they passed the over mantel mirror Jenks saw his own reflection: That was still seated in the armchair. That part of him didn't seem to matter now and the orchid he held was glowing radiantly as if the sun were back lighting the gold of the stamens. The plant danced in his hand like a collection of childrens' laughing faces. The petals glowed and the blood red colour drew a warm smile from his face.

The man's voice continued to pour out words, words which he could not recall, nor remember.

"It's time," the voice said.

"Time?"

"Time for us to go; time for you and Emma to enter my garden," the voice continued. "Look," it said, "Theresa's waiting."

And Stephen Jenks gazed into his reflection in the mirror once again. The reflection he now saw was him, but it could not be him, he was young again, standing next to the stranger looking at a reflection of a young man. The face was wrong too. There was no deformity now, no scars, no broken skin, and the seated deformed man was smiling with his eyes wide open. It was just him, Emma and the stranger and the new reflection.

"It's time," the stranger repeated, reaching out a hand to Jenks.

It was then that Stephen Jenks noticed, for the first time, the scar. The scar of a round hole of a wound in the man's right hand. He had not seen it before and only now that he was standing had he finally noticed it. In the middle of the palm was a distinctive mark.

"How did you do that?" Jenks asked.

"Stephen that's another story. Shall we go?"

The voice had changed now, changed into the voice of the long gone Theresa, and the hand he saw before him had lost the scar and become beautiful. Fine nail polish appeared bright crimson and the fingers tips glowed with a fine gold edging. The skin was white and yet strangely translucent. Emma was frolicking at his feet, jumping like a puppy once again. Her old, dull and opaque eyes were brown and bright once more and the winter day had become a sparkling spring morning. She was running ahead now as she had always done. Light was streaming through the open door, birds were singing and the scent of fresh mown grass penetrated his nostrils: It was like he was young again; young and vibrant and ready.

Theresa was leading him now; leading him toward the open door into spring, asking him to follow. He could see her clearly; she was wearing that dress, the dress she had worn when they were driving that day, but the blood had gone and her hair was vibrant, free and blowing in the slight warm breeze. It was as he had imagined it would be.

Stephen Jenks smiled and held out his hand to grasp hers, which was offered to guide him, and his eyes widened as he stepped into ecstasy.

who killed
santa claus?

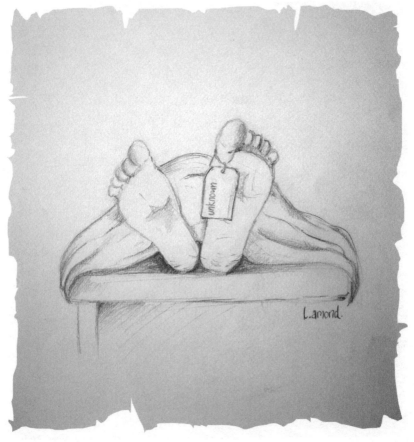

For my mother
who loved Christmas
&
My father who was Christmas

Who Killed Santa Claus?

"When he comes out, you pop him good, right? You make sure. You hit him real hard. I don't want him to pull some heat and start blasting. "

"A gun? Jesus Will, you never said he was packin'. We aint gonna get shot at are we?"

"Why? I don't care and neither should you. It's all the same to us. Long as we get the money. If he tries any of the smart stuff you can do 'im."

"Hey, I didn't want this," the younger man replied, his tone now very serious. "What if he's, you know, the real Santa? Perhaps we get the wrong guy? I don't wanna shoot Santa. You know like a mistook identity thing? All the kids will be wanting their toys and ...." His speech was slow and deliberate, as if each word demanded a heavy degree of thought. "It's nearly Christmas and he's probably got..."

A slap from the older man resounded in the darkness, as a well aimed palm struck the speaker's cheek.

The blow provoked a response. "Ow," the receiver yelped, "what you do that fur?"

"To wake you up you numb nuts. You really are a smuck aren't you? Dumb as a donkey now. Half a brain?"

"I aint no donkey," the young man replied, rubbing his burning cheek. "And sides that weren't right, to do that." His voice was loaded with indignation.

"Yeah? You are soft in the head? The real Santa?" The older man's voice was full of mockery, "So what we been doin' for the last three days then? Waitin' for Elves and such? Countin' goddamn sheep? It's him alright and I ain't standin' here waitin' for the sky to fall in, or for him to drop us a little penny or two. That bullet scrambled your brain. The real Santa?" Once again the voice was loaded with sarcasm, as he continued in a chant,

"He's makin' a list, he's checkin' twice, he's gonna find out who's naughty or nice." He stopped suddenly and then said, through gritted teeth, "And boy oh boy aint he gonna know? It's gonna snow tonight and I don't wanna be froze up out here. The real Santa? How many nuts in a Santa suit do you know? Listen Larry boy," he continued, "how many people gave a damn about you after Vietnam?" He did not wait for a reply, "I'll tell you how many none, zip, diddly squat." He paused scanning the darkness through the lightly falling snow, " Me I'm makin' a stand and then bam bam it's goodnight Vienna and we, we take a little bag of money and go relieve our own need. The man's a fruit, runnin' around givin' parcels of money to people. You gotta be craz-eee, to do that."

"This ain't right Will," the slow considered reply came, "he's Santa. He's one of the special people. He's Santa! What about all them little kids? "

"You soft head. You aint turnin' all wide eyed and weird like them other chumps are you?"

"Nope."

"Well just see you don't, the guy's got loads of money and he gets his thrills from feeling good. He feels good by tryin' to be Santa. He aint Santa. He's just got more money than sense, ain't that the truth, givin' all that loot away, he could do with a good crack on the skull. Hey, it might knock some sense into the dumb ass. It's like he thinks he's some kind of super hero who dresses up like god-damn Santa Claus. And all the people love him ah." The man made a sound like the ah of a twee granny addressing a small child. "He's a crazy with money that's all. All those lovely middle class arses, they don't care, it appeases their conscience, makes 'em feel kinda warm inside. Bullshit it's all damn bullshit. They're all the same them do-gooders; makes 'em feel kinda gooey and good inside and the rest of the year they'd sell their grandma for a sixpence. You never see them lessen they want you to clear their garbage. Christ they make me totally sick. They make you feel like you should tug your forelock and say, yes sum, master, like you're some nigger, some kinda animal. They might not say it; hey they're toooo genteeeel." He made a mock curtsy, as he stretched his words, "But black or white we're all the same to them. They toss you a bone or two like a dog and you gotta be soooo grateful." He voice became loaded with hatred, "Well I aint no animal and I ain't no dawg. I'm done with being kicked." His eyes were bright now; his voice was sharp and spittle flew from his lips in anger. His pure hatred was there for all to see. Only in the back alley, wrapped as the men were in thick overcoats, no one saw them, and no one cared.

The older man was stamping his feet to ward off the cold and the redness around his eyes was complimented by the sheer terror of his younger accomplice.

"Look at us Larry? Just look at us," he mocked, "we're dressed in rags." He started to sing in mockery, "Land of the free and home of the brave." Pulling a cigarette from his pocket he lit it quickly. "Look at you, you're so messed up you can't even remember your name sometimes. And who apart from me gives a damn?" He started singing again, "This land is your land, this land is my land, this land is home to you and me. Bullshit, it's all a bunch of bullshit. Look we fought for our country and look at us. Stuck in a rat hole alleyway. We ain't had a decent meal in days. Bullshit man, it's all bullshit." He drew deeply on his cigarette. "They send us half way round the world to fight someone; it don't matter who, Vietnamese, Cambodians, Iraqi, Afghans. Hell they'd shoot us up to the moon if we was dumb enough to go . Go and fight some damn aliens on some sort of bug hunt. But hey man when we come back, what do we get? What we got? This shit alley and some garbage bins to scrape around in. You can't think straight and I got the shakes. Well me I'm sick of eatin' out of garbage cans. I want my meals on a white tablecloth with one of them silk napkins to wipe my face. No more chow in a trash can. I done my time. I ain't eatin' shit no more. No sir, no more."

He threw the cigarette to the ground and blew on his hands.

"But why we gonna shoot him, Will?"

"Can't you remember?"

"I forgot," Larry replied, sheepishly.

"Cos I ain't gonna let nothin' stop us now. I ain't doin' time and I ain't havin' no nosy cop shove his beak into my life neither. "

"But we ain't gonna shoot him are we?"

"Who?"

"The cop?"

"What cop?

"The cop you're talkin' about."

"Listen you numb nuts. Any cop, any cop that shoves his nose into our business." He fingered the small automatic he constantly carried. "Hey man I might be a bum, but I ain't goin' down without a fight."

"Right Will, yeah right."

"You really are a dumb bastard ain't ya?" Will asked.

"No," came the sheepish reply. "I just don't wanna kill Santa Claus."

"Holy shit, ain't you got that yet. There ain't no such thing, he don't exist. What the hell did they do to you in that POW camp? Half your damn brain ain't no good anymore."

"But we're waitin' fur him?"

"Yeah, but Santa Claus don't exist, this guy just dresses like him, right?"

The younger man was nodding now. Nodding automatically as his dull mind struggled with the concept of the existence of Santa Claus. As a boy he often wondered how the fat man in a red suit got around town and up and down the chimneys until eventually his brain gave him a headache. Now he struggled to remember the concept of precisely why he and Will, his old orphanage buddy, were there. It was cold and he wanted to have a warm drink like some chocolate with marshmallows in it. His mind attempted to concentrate on what he had been told to do.

"You ain't gonna shoot him though are ya?"

"Larry, you just leave the thinkin' to me. It ain't Santa Claus though, remember that."

* * *

"Would you look at that?" asked Michael Andrews as he passed a newspaper across the boardroom table to his boss

Andreas Sophanopullos. "He's been out again. That's the third year in a row now. How much has he given away?"

"I've no idea," Andreas Sophanopullos replied, as he glanced at the headline. It read: Just who is Santa Claus? "He's just one hell of a nice guy, wouldn't you say?"

"I'd say he was crazy," Andrews replied. "Throwing all that money away on down and outs. All those pieces of scum that drift around our city. Hey, I see them huddled in doorways when I go to the opera. Stinking, lazy, lowlife scum, they need to get a job. Junkies and alchies most of them. What a waste of resources and taxes. I'd have the lot rounded up and shot, or better still make them do some kind of hard labour."

"Yep, much better if they could work," added Mike Lazarus, senior sales negotiator as he entered. "Waste of time givin' that kind of scum a chance. Put them in the old workhouses and set them working everyday, all day, that'll keep them off the streets. Or prisons put them in the prisons. Rags to rags in three generations, if you leave them as they are. Most of them drink too much, have kids like rats and don't know how to bring them up, or should I say drag them up." He laughed loudly and poured a coffee and then sat poring over the quarterly sales record. "Not bad," he chuckled, "not bad at all. This is gonna be the best Christmas sales record we've ever had. I'm lovin' it."

"The only real thing you care about," Andreas laughed, "is your fat Christmas bonus. Where exactly are you going this Christmas?"

"Antigua boss."

"Mmm, nice, warm, and beachy."

"Yeah and somewhere where there aren't children. I hate damn kids, clogging up the world. Every time I see the parents I hate them more. It's like they got to get to the front of the queue because they got a kid. On the planes and at the airports and then I got to listen to them, squawking , squealing, running around and makin' a nuisance of themselves. I want sun and sea, you know somewhere young girls can get their bikinis on and…. "

"That's fine talk from a guy who sells games to kids," his boss laughed.

"Just because I sell them the stuff, don't mean I got to like the scum. But this phantom Father Christmas is good for business. We sold more toy Santa dolls this year than ever before. What is it he does?" he lifted the newspaper and began to read: "He left two thousand dollars in a kid's shoe. Some kid in an orphanage. Some worthless kid writes a letter and he gets two grand; now everyone thinks that Santa Claus exists, what a load of crap, but good for business." He rubbed his thumbs and fingers together making the universal sign for cash, and winked.

"Sorry I'm late," Polly Small excused, as she entered, she looked dishevelled. "Bit of a problem at home."

Sophanopullos looked at the woman. Her hair needed a style and her shoes had seen better days. She worked as a note taker and part time secretary, but her life held little joy as far as he could see. He wondered what she did when the lights of the office went out. The New York apartment she shared was meagre and her sick mother was a drain on her resources, he imagined her on a warm Antiguan beach and noticed for the first time her delicate figure. A figure made more delicate by the inadequacy of her diet. To the outside world she was thin, fashionable even; but he somehow knew she would love nothing better than returning home to a two inch thick steak and a bottle. But she said nothing and simply ploughed on, trying to balance the need for medicines with her own simple wants. He wondered what she did when she was not caring for her parent, or cleaning, or working for him.

"That's Ok," he said, "we were just having a chat about holidays and this Santa Claus thing in the paper."

She was hanging her coat up now and seemed a little less flustered. Sophanopullos noticed the thread bare sleeves and the worn cuffs. It was a coat that needed replacing and the lining was torn too. She tried to hide it in the folding but his eyes were sharper than the other men in the room.

"I know it's great," she smiled back; "I wish someone would be that kind to me."

Sophanopullos smiled at Lazarus and he in turn shook his head.

"They say he gave two thousand dollars to an underprivileged child. I think that's lovely. What a shame there aren't more people like that in the world," Polly sighed.

Mike Andrews waited for the explosion from Lazarus but he simply dismissed the remark as one coming from the people he despised the most - women.

* * *

"It's cold Will."

"Yeah I know."

"Ain't we gonna go inside and have hot chocolate now?"

"Jesus Christ, what is wrong with you? You been kicked in the head? What are we doin' here?"

"Waitin'?" Larry answered.

"Yep we're waitin', but what we waitin' for?"

The younger man screwed up his face and for the first time anyone, who had heard their previous conversation, would have realised that his mind was not as sharp as it should be.

"Santa," he suddenly blurted.

"Yep that's it, got it in ten - great," said Will. "We're waitin' for Father Christmas. Waitin' in the cold. Waitin' for our chance to get some dough."

Willy Eckstein studied the young Larry Fogel. Larry was as dumb as they came but as loyal as any guard dog. Once when they had been boys together in an orphanage, a Lutheran orphanage, they had gravitated toward each other for protection. Larry because he needed someone to help him with letters and such and Will because his need was friendship. Then when they reached sixteen they had been thrown out onto the streets and together they joined the army. There they learned basic life skills and then were sent to fight; fight anyone they were told to. Larry finally caught some shrapnel to his head and once in a while the pieces caused a short circuit and he had a fit. Willy Eckstein, hard as he was, intemperate as he was, could not watch his friend as he lay frothing on the ground like an epileptic dog and so here they were. Larry was fine until he lost control and then people, "Let him go," because he was an embarrassment, and they simply could not be bothered. Everybody loves a cute puppy but an injured dog? Nobody wants to see an injured dog. So they shunted from town to town; one aimless job after another. Ten years had passed as they shunted back and forth from city to city, but always they ended up back on the bottom rung. To Will it always seemed like one step forward and three back. Often he wondered how the others had survived. Those boys he had once hated so much now seemed like a distant memory of recalled childhood; a jaundiced memory of things gone by; a foreign country once visited and now forgotten. Only Larry remained and together they had become the losers, the forgotten and the forsaken.

In the frost and the dark of their chosen alley they stood huddled and stamping against the cold: Both were pitiful; both were cold.

* * *

"So Polly where are you off to this vacation?" asked Sophanopullos.

Polly Small, laughed nervously, "Oh nowhere, I've got my mother to look out for and my kids, but I expect they'll go to their dad's in Florida. He's got a good job down there in Article Marine."

"How long do they go for?"

"A couple of weeks, so it's just me and mum. I'd love to go to Florida one day and stay in one of those fancy hotels. In one of those rooms with two toilets."

"Two toilets?"

"Christ, she means a bidet boss, what a dumb broad," Mike Lazarus laughed.

Polly Small's face went scarlet with embarrassment.

"Mr. Lazarus here," Sophanopullos added, "he's off to the Caribbean."

Polly now had her head down and was ready to take notes, clearly unwilling to continue any conversation.

Two further men and a suited woman joined the group and

within seconds the conversation turned to the December sales figures and what might be needed to punch the turnover that bit further. Andreas Sophanopullos was a self made man, a millionaire of Greek origin, who despite being raised in an orphanage had managed to claw his way into the toy market. Not having grown up with many he had developed the knack of hitting the market with precisely that which was the "zeitgeist," of the moment. He had made a fortune out of playground obsessions; first it had been pogs, meaningless bits of plastic which could be a badge or a button. These carried the faces of the latest cartoon characters or sometime teen stars; here today and gone tomorrow. Then he had created the butterfly cards; cards impregnated with a mixture of Henna and Indian ink, which, when soaked in water could be placed on the hand or arm and leave a visible, if indistinct, mock tattoo. Then came the fake lip ring. A clip which sat over the lip and looked, to all intents and purposes, like a real live piercing. This had been a real winner when combined with the fake smoking cigarette - guaranteed to get any teacher livid.

He laughed and joked about his ability to produce crap and make it a hit and in turn make millions. The stupidity of children had never ceased to amaze him and the gullibility of their parents shocked him even more. He wanted to get involved in the pop industry next; there was a real place to make money out of garbage.

* * *

Mike Lazarus stood in front of the bathroom mirror, studying his girth. He had told everyone he was going to Antigua over Christmas, wouldn't be back for at least two weeks. He was flying out on the 26th, Boxing Day, to London and then back across to St.John's. It was the most reliable method of travel and cheaper, he had told everyone; staying at Coco beach; no phone, no cable, and there he was, " Gonna screw and drink and eat some pussy," he bragged. "I got this girl, wears a bikini so small makes her tits look like two little puppies fighting in a bag." He had laughed with Andreas Sophanopullos, about how he'd, "Have one of those with a pink nose, and give it a little stroke."

In truth he was staying in New York, he had plenty to do and at last he had the cash to do it. He could spend his cash on his indulgences, enjoy something wild and totally unexpected.

He walked to the window and studied the streets below. His apartment was warm and plush and there in full view were the street walkers, the girls who plied themselves into the night. He wondered what each of them might do for a thousand dollars. In his hand he cupped a glass full to the brim with Talisker, a ten year old whiskey from the Isle of Skye. It gave him the courage he needed to ask and also get on with the thing he sought the most. To others it might seem perverse, but to him it had become addictive, just like a drug or alcohol. For the last three years he had told lies about where he was going and what he was doing and each year had been better than the last.

Outside he could see the down and outs and those less fortunate sitting in the doorways. The frost was beginning to make the breath of those below crackle in the night air, but he was warm in the blue light which bled from the TV screen. A huge smile was growing on his face and a confident warmth in his belly: It was nearly time.

* * *

The story of the mysterious Santa Claus was being used as a media novelty item. Often his sudden gifts and antics closed the local TV news report. It was now the 24th and several times the man had delivered surprises to the needy. As in previous years the gifts had become more and more lavish the nearer to Christmas it got. Everyone was talking about whether they would get, "the", Christmas gift this year.

There had even been some political commentators who speculated on whether Father Christmas existed and whether this guy possessed the true spirit of Christmas.

In the Bronx two nights ago he had walked through a

neighbourhood posting fifty dollar bills through doorways. He had handed out twenties to kids playing ball and they had not taken them or thrown them away, thinking the whole thing a hoax, until the news report said he had given away twenty thousand dollars in one night.

Reporters had speculated that he was probably a millionaire, with some deep seated guilt ridden tendencies, while others just said he was a crazy. Someone even said he was a kind of vigilante – like batman. Only he combated crime by giving kids money. Some wealthy socialite from the Hamptons was calling for his apprehension, because the kids would be spending the money on drugs and drink and the crime rate would rise.

The last part of the report had some seven and eight year olds talking about how they posted a letter to Father Christmas last year and they had the stuff they asked for.

"Father Christmas, lives at the north pole," one little girl had commented, "but near Christmas time he comes to our city, to help people," she added.

Lazarus smiled at the report and then sat in his favourite TV chair and flicked through the channels.

* * *

In the dining room of the New York Ritz, Andreas Sophanopullos sat and ate a small meal. It had been a long day and the 24th always was a long night. The firm, his firm, had closed down for the Christmas holiday. The employees, even Polly Small, had received their special bonuses and now it was time for Andreas to check and counter balance. Time to get down to some real work while others were out of the way.

"Tomato and Basil with Pesto sauce," he ordered. "Is the Beef Wellington good?"

"Superb," the waiter replied.

"Ok, I'll have that then, with the artichoke hearts and some asparagus."

"Potatoes?"

"You know Joe, that I never eat those hideous things."

"I know sir, but I have to keep trying." The waiter laughed at his own joke.

"I've lived in this hotel now for how long?"

The waiter evaluated, "Three, no four years," he corrected.

"And I bet I've not eaten more than half a dozen potatoes in that time?"

"But I have to try?"

Andreas laughed at the man's tenacity and then simply closed the menu.

"Champagne I think," he said. "Bollinger?"

The waiter nodded, "Special celebration?" he asked.

"Yep, it's another Christmas and we're still here. Can't be bad."

The waiter nodded, "We do have this amazing dessert, a new creation by Giuseppe."

"Oh ice cream," Sophanopullos sneered. "Why do Italians always go for ice-cream?"

"No this is based on a traditional Hungarian dessert, something called, Shomloi Galushka. It's sort of biscuits and alcohol and trifle and rich chocolate and cream."

"Mmm sounds nice, have you tried it?"

The waiter nodded, "And it's absolute heaven," he added.

"Ok I'll have some of that it'll keep my strength up for the night ahead."

The waiter smiled and made the assumption that a man with money would spend a night with some eager money earning female. His assumption, as with most people, was based upon his wants and desires and not those of others. Sophanopullos knew only too well the curse of the self – obsessed; these were the people who purchased their desires, without thinking about what present a recipient would like. That classic mistake had made him a millionaire, a millionaire by manipulating public desire. He often bragged that he knew what the public wanted, before, they knew it themselves.

* * *

"He ain't comin'," Larry squeaked.

"Of course he's comin'."

"How can we be certain?"

"Cause this is where he lives, you dumb schmuck. Don't you remember? We followed him back here?"

Larry shook his head.

"Will," he said rather pathetically, "ain't we gonna get a drink. I'm cold?"

"No we ain't and we ain't goin' no where till that rich bastard shows. Shows up in his Santa suit and then we follow him again to make sure it's him. And when he goes to make his big drop we take the lot."

"Santa always comes on Christmas Eve, don't he?" Larry asked again.

This time Will had run out of the passion to argue, "Yep," he replied. "And tonight is Christmas Eve."

"See I remembered," Larry Fogel grinned.

That night for the first time in twenty two years and as if to order snow began to fall. Already there was a light dusting on the sidewalks and the sound of the traffic had changed; changed to the more muffled sound which snow gave a city. Cars had begun to park up and by morning the snow would be crisp and deep and even. Larry Fogel looked up into the sky and felt the soft flakes fall on him like the soft dusting of icing sugar on a cake. He was smiling like a child and stamping foot prints into the soft white covering.

Willy Eckstein was watching the apartment window, when the light went out his senses went to red alert. He checked the three dollar watch he wore, it was 11.30pm.

"Come to daddy," he whispered, as he blew on his fingerless gloves and pushed Larry between two large dumpster bins. He had calculated that the man they sought would be passing directly in front of them in about four minutes. His fingers reassuringly found the automatic in his mass of pockets and he drew in a hushed breath.

"Don't you say a goddamn thing," he exhaled at Larry. "Not one thing, got it?"

Larry Fogel nodded.

In the Irish bar on Maple and 3rd, Mike Andrews was downing his third pint of Guinness and casually looking at his watch. She was late and he knew that she'd probably not turn up.

"Long day Michael?" asked the barman, as he placed a fourth pint on the bar top.

"Yeah long enough for me to down this."

"She's not coming," he continued, with the sage wisdom barmen exhibited to all drunks.

"I know."

"It's Christmas Eve, and she's married."

"I know."

"And she'll have things to do." His accent was heavy now and pure Boston Irish; third generation Irish with a Massachusetts drawl. "That's the trouble with married women they have commitments."

"I know."

"She's probably got to go to some party or something."

"Listen," Mike Andrews snapped, "save your home truths. I know."

The barman was already moving out of earshot to serve a couple of new customers who had just entered. Andrews began to wonder if the man was right. Barmen usually were; they listened to the ravings of drunks and fools for a living. He was neither, but his idea of a nice Christmas Eve was not drinking Guinness in a New York bar or waking up alone in his cold bed on Christmas morning. He wanted more than that and she was what he wanted for Christmas.

Once he had asked her to leave the man, come and live with him. She had made an excuse, a good excuse, one based on family loyalty and he had hung around like a spare prick at a wedding - waiting. One year had drifted into the next and now she was so sure he loved her, she could do as she pleased. Even the barman knew it.

"What a wicked game to play," he said into the glass, which was now virtually empty. "Next year." He looked at the clock it was getting close to the Santa hour and he needed to go if he had any semblance of making things happen.

As he left he heard the barman call, "Merry Christmas buddy." He waved a response and walked out into the cold night air.

* * *

In her cheap apartment Polly Small opened an envelope which had been slid into the mail box. The buzzer had gone four times before she had lifted the intercom receiver. She thought it was carol singers or kids playing a prank.

"Hey lady?" the unknown voice said, "delivery."

"I didn't order."

"Look lady I got a prepaid order for delivery here. What do you want I should do then?"

"It must be for someone else."

"It says Small on the box."

"Ok I'll come down."

When Polly Small arrived at the front lobby a large box had been left. It had taken her less than a minute to arrive but already the delivery boy had gone. It was one of the things she hated about New York. The self – interest, the lack of any waiting. She looked at the box. It was sealed with heavy duty transit tape and someone had written Small and her address on the top flap.

Back inside her apartment she placed the box on the kitchen table, and then flicked open the flaps with a knife. Inside were cartons of Chinese food and tucked between them was an envelope. It was brown and basic but as she opened it, her heart stopped. Inside were large bills: $25,000 in mixed notes and a card with a smiling Santa Claus image.

Ho Ho Ho - Holiday, was all that was written on it. It was ten minutes after midnight.

* * *

In an alleyway at the back of Montague and Murray, two men

were standing in front of a man holding a gun. Officer John Fowler had seen it so many times in the neighbourhood. Two men mugging one of the more wealthy people who were stupid enough to take a short cut through this alley.

Without a sound he flipped the gun from his holster and dropped his cap to the ground. Then with the stealth of a stalking cat he melted into the shadows to get closer.

John Fowler was an old fashioned kind of cop. The kind that would rather make a clean arrest, than end up with a group of body bags to show how great he was. In his late forties, with just a little time left to do before retirement he had volunteered to do the Christmas shift, so the younger guys with kids could be at home. Christmas Eve was usually a good shift; cold, but usually without incident and his wife liked to bake. When he got home at around two he'd have warm mince pies and Port while she would have a Bailey's Irish. Sometimes they'd go to late, late mass, or if he was on till four they'd stay up and go to morning mass.

As he made his way down the alley through shadows he could hear voices.

"Where's the money?" a voice said.

"There is no money," came the stilted reply.

"Of course there's money."

"Who do you think I am Santa Claus?" the man laughed in reply.

"Don't be a smart guy, everyone wants to be smart guy," Will Eckstein mocked. "If you're dressed in red you ain't the devil, or the tooth fairy. We just want that damn money."

"Look I don't have money."

Suddenly Larry Fogel spotted Fowler and yelled, "The cop."

Will Eckstein turned and fired several times into the darkness. Nothing found a target. Fowler was down and returning fire.

John Fowler fired and watched as two men fell. The third was sitting, screaming loudly as he approached. Holding his weapon cocked in readiness, he advanced gingerly should any more firing start.

In the white dusting of Christmas snow William Eckstein lay dead, his chest bubbling as the last throws of life left him. There was one clean and lucky bullet hole where his heart should have been and another in his liver. His eyes were open but the opaque glare of death had already overtaken them. A small smattering of snow was already landing on his face.

Huddled, screaming and traumatised between the dumpster bins sat Larry Fogel his arms were clutching his knees and he was rocking like a small scared child. His face was totally white as if he had seen something so fearful that his mind had collapsed in a paroxysm of fear and imploded in one last effort at self protection. His voice was chiming repeatedly, "Here comes Santa Claus, here comes Santa Claus, here comes Santa Claus, Santa Claus, Santa Claus."

"I need an ambulance," John Fowler called in. "I've got one suspect under arrest and two people down."

Some distance away a man lay face down in the snow. Fowler could see a set of heavy black boots and a long black coat spread out like the wings of a bat. The man was still and silent. Fowler picked up Eckstein's pistol and advanced toward the prostrate form, a gun in each hand. A squad car appeared at the end of the alley and two further officers ran toward him.

The light from the patrol car headlights lit up the bright red of the Santa suit, which had been shrouded by a black overcoat. Fowler turned the man over.

"Jesus Christ almighty John," one of officers said, "look at his face."

"Face?" the other whistled through his teeth.

"You must have hit him loads of times and," he paused, "he's smiling."

"It's Santa Claus," said the second.

"I couldn't have done it," John Fowler replied, "I only fired twice, check my weapon guys?" He handed his weapon to the men.

"He's right, two shots."

"See, two in the dead guy and none on this other guy," Fowler affirmed.

"The other gun shows five empty," the second officer confirmed.

"And I bet ballistics show five bullets in the wall behind where I was."

"Well beats me," said the second officer, as he stood erect. "But something sure as hell killed the blazes out of Santa here."

Larry Fogel was dribbling now, his rocking motion had increased and his face was in a state of sheer terror. His words were clearly audible, "Santa Claus, Santa Claus," he kept calling.

"What happened?" Fowler asked him, but the rocking response and chant continued.

One patrol man was back at the squad car now, his voice crackling as he called for an ambulance and the coroner. The second was standing behind Fowler as they man-handled the traumatised Fogel from between the bins and back down toward the black and white.

* * *

"Ok buddy," said the paramedic. He spoke to Fowler with long breathy gasps. "It aint even funny; quit the horsing around huh. Aint it bad enough that we gotta pull this shift?"

Fowler was confused, "What are you going on about?" he asked.

"The second body? Is this some kinda practical Christmas joke? You cops, aint you got better things to do?" He was smiling broadly.

"Up there, a guy dressed as Santa Claus," Fowler pointed.

"Yeah, yeah," the paramedic's tone was mocking. "Right next to the sleigh packed with sacks of toys and magic reindeer."

"There in the shadows. Dressed in black. Laying down in the snow."

"Not red then? What was he doing taking a nap? Drinking his milk and eating a mince pie? " The paramedic snorted, as he hopped into the ambulance. "I expect you want me to believe that Rudolph came and whisked him away?"

"Where the hell is the body?" asked Fowler.

The paramedic shrugged, "Beats, me," he smirked.

He turned the ignition key and the ambulance engine roared

into life, "Ho, Ho, Ho," the driver chuckled, as the vehicle began to back away out of the alley. Fowler thought he heard, "Merry Christmas John," as the siren burst into life. Saw a gloved hand give a joyful Royal wave, a brief flash of white and red and then the vehicle was gone. He also thought that for a brief second he saw a beard and a broad smile.

Fowler was running now, running back to the spot where the body had been. His heart was pounding and his mind confused: The body of Santa Claus was gone.

fighting dogs

For the small, the greedy and the cruel.

Fighting Dogs

"Listen to me Partridge. I don't care what your objections are. We're not interested in your pinko-liberal views. You're supposed to be a cop, a thief taker." The man paused, his face reddening as he spoke. "They're bloody Gypsy scum. Bleedin' Irish tinkers, Pikeys and rogues every bloody one and I want this nonsense stopped before someone gets hurts." Spit flew from between his clenched teeth. There was real venom in his voice. A venom created in the prejudices of his past.

"That I understand sir," came a reply from within the gathered ensemble; the voice belonged to John Partridge, nicknamed, "the turkey," by his colleagues. "But do we have to use terms which are so racist or anti-ethnic? Can't we just refer to them as travellers?" he asked openly.

"Listen son," came the terse reply. "I don't run a charm school here. We nick villains. I expect you want me to refer to their wives as ladies of the night too?"

There was massed muttering from the gathering of men.

"You call them what you like," he continued, "but in my book they're, tramps and prossies. You call them trollops or whatever polite term you want. I can't think of a polite term for a whore."

"But they deserve respect," Turkey replied yet again.

"Oh my Christ, I've heard it all now," Inspector John Macfee continued. "Let's hold their little hands all the way down to the station and talk to them nicely and get them to stop. Then," he scoffed, "they'll all go home and take their dogs with them?"

"Well at least it will give them a chance to abide by the law before we nick them," came Partridge's voice from the crowd, though the resolve within it seemed to have weakened.

"You really are a turkey," Macfee continued, "you be nice if you want. You hold their little sweaty hands and tell them not to do it. And while you're talking to them they'll have your car up on blocks and one of their sticky-fingered kids will have nicked your boot laces. Try talking to someone who's been a victim and then see if your viewpoint might change? I don't know what they teach you boys up at the training school these days," he paused. "A series of airs and graces, all that political correctness bull. But down here in the real world the truth is ugly. That's why they call it the ugly truth. And these Gypsies are ugly: They are scum."

There was some suppressed laughter from others listening.

"I'm sure we can impress upon them the need to desist," Partridge retaliated.

"The need to desist? The need to desist?" Macfee repeated sarcastically. "The only thing that will make a Gypo stop is a truncheon up his arse, or a boot on his neck. This is not rural Hertfordshire where people play country games like tip the cow, spot the stranger or stone the idiot." The room erupted into raucous laughter. "These Gypsies have been holding fighting sessions. I wouldn't mind so much if they were beating the living crap out of each other. Hey I might even buy a ticket or two myself. That I could stand, put a couple of them in a cage and let them beat each other to death. But this is dog fighting, and it's flaming barbaric." He paused again, "Putting two dumb animals in a ring and letting them fight till one kills the other, that's bloody disgusting."

"Well I'm sure there is a something we could do," another new voice continued.

"There is," Sergeant James McCormack interrupted as he stepped forward, "I'd shoot the lot of them. The dog owners that is." He was the police dog handler brought in to advise. "A dog is the product of training. The owner is the real culprit. Those dogs are teased and taunted until they are so violent that they attack virtually on demand. The problem is that these dogs also attack people, people who are walking their placid dogs in the park. That's the real problem, these types," he refrained from using the word Gypsy, "these types, give all dog owners a bad name. Just look at the way they keep horses chained up on common land. Why on earth would people want to keep horses in a city environment in this day and age? It's a scandal. Last month this happened."

McCormack flicked a switch and an overhead projector whirred into life. "This," he said, "is the result of two pit bulls attacking an innocent walker in the park. Not a pretty sight."

On the screen there appeared a picture of a Doberman. A brown and tan male with the loping legs so much part of the breed. It was a dog with stitches to the neck and several puncture wounds on the lower legs.

"The owner, a woman, had been bitten as she tried to help her dog during the attack," McCormack said. He showed her forearm, complete with stitches, to the camera.

McCormack flicked the remote and a second image appeared. This time a child, a girl of maybe three or four appeared. A pretty little girl with blonde hair, or she would have been if it were not for the facial scars. One ear was missing.

"Not very pretty is it?" he asked the assembled officers. "We're not sure what did this, it could have been a Staffordshire terrier, but I'd say a Pit Bull."

"Bloody hell," exclaimed one of the policemen on the front row. "Christ where did that happen?"

"Mayflower Park," McCormack replied, as he flicked to the next image, and then the next, and the next. "I won't go on. Seventeen incidents and not all by the same dog or dogs. The worst one was a Labrador which stood its ground against a Pit Bull to defend the children of a family."

A fresh voice piped up from the crowd, "What happened to that dog?" it asked.

"The Lab was killed, killed in front of the children it was trying to protect and the Pit Bull was shot: Armed response unit."

"Thanks Jimmy," Macfee added, as he interrupted. "So you can see we have a problem. And I want it sorted. Fully sorted. I want you lot to get out there on the street and find me these villains. I want the dog fights stopped and I want these dogs found. Somebody out there knows what's going on – find me that person. I don't care what you call these scum, be as nice as you like, or as evil, but if we don't get this stopped a child is going to get seriously hurt, killed maybe."

There was a general muttering from the officers being briefed.

"I don't care about the dogs, they'll have to be put down. But I want the men who are doing this. I want their arses in court and I want the whole operation shut down before some kiddie gets it." He had repeated the concept twice to drive home the notion of a dead child. Macfee was less than politically correct, and not concerned with niceties; he was old school, firm but fair, harsh with the criminal and yet deep down there was a heart of gold which wanted to make a difference. He set his own standards, which he had learned the hard way – experience. "So can we stop the pussy footing around and get these Gypos caught. Oh I might add that when the woman with the Doberman was attacked the owner of the dogs gave a false name and address."

The room fell silent as further instructions were given.

"I want the Wallingford estate combed. Every house gets a visit and I don't care that it's a bow and arrow district. Go in pairs. The Pattersons live on that estate and the Hendersons too and both families are upset by what's happening."

An officer in the front row raised a hand.

"Yes son?" Macfee said.

"The Patterson and Henderson organized crime families?"

"That's them. They'll sell you coke and get you a woman but they assure me that neither family has involvement here. And strange as it may seem I actually believe them, you see both of them have greyhounds and they might not like you or me but they love their dogs, more than they love money and that's saying something. If they get involved we're going to see some bloodshed, and I don't mean animal blood. Dog fighting is the kind of gambling that they don't take part in. You see they have that old school thing called honour among thieves." He paused, "They'd top you and drop you if they had to, don't get me wrong here, but," he paused again, "we have some new faces on the manor and the families are just as pissed about it.

You see this gives them a bad name and if some kid gets killed it's bad for business. They might just get more than they bargained for. It's a strange relationship between them and us I know, but we have to assume they might be able to help us here."

McCormack butted in, "Remember that sometimes these people can be good allies. As long as we get what we want, everyone comes up smelling of roses."

***

Finny the Turk was a thin man who sweated a great deal. His hair was dull and rather greasy which gave him the look of being older than his years. Clothes that could have done with a good wash clung to him like they were one size too small and ten years too old. Garments, his, seemed tired and lacklustre, the colour having faded and the dullness being augmented by food stains which would never be removed, except by fire.

Finny was sitting in The Giggling Sausage cafe when the two police officers walked it. It was a cold day and a warm cup of tea would have been nice at anytime but today it was especially gratifying.

The two officers sat at a table near the door and as the place cleared Finny became more uncomfortable. He started to shift nervously from buttock to buttock; when the cafe owner went out to the back the female officer of the pair spoke quietly.

"At the Obelisk, thirty minutes Finny, be there," was all she whispered.

Finny the Turk left.

"Hey Joe?" the male officer called.

The burly Irish owner reappeared from behind a curtained entrance.

"What can I do for you Officer Stokes?" he asked softly. His accent was soft, southern, with a rounded lilt which was shrouded inside a rich baritone.

He was a man who looked confident, the kind of man who would not tolerate interference in his life. That much he had proved when one of the rival protection gangs paid him a visit in an attempt to persuade him to take out insurance. He had declined and delivered the two bully boys back to their boss via a skip. He had also said that if anything happened to his business the retribution would be swift and decisive.

One evening a fire started. It was put out before any real damage could occur and that same night Polly Patterson was found tied to a tree in the middle of the city park. Her hair had been cut, her clothes removed and her skin painted red with the word whore on her back. Alfred Henderson was found the next evening, again naked, sitting in shopping cart with his testicles shaved and blue paint poured over them.

Both families received a letter in the post, both with the victim's hair enclosed; both families understood the message. There had been no need to wrap a fish in newspaper - this message was loud and clear.

Joe O'Neill was a man who had contacts, some said with the IRA. His brother James ran a scrap metal business and many of the local lads scoured the scrap vehicles for spare parts and tyres, before they were cubed. The sound of revving engines and loud boys graced the yard but the brothers were well respected in the criminal fraternity. Some even said that the families left them alone because they were scared of them. Whatever their contacts were, they were of sufficient weight to scare others away. Both the Pattersons and Hendersons were aware of the IRA implication and as a result, the cafe, the owner and his family, continued with their business uninterrupted and the scrap metal yard thrived.

Constable Michael Stokes asked the question, "Joe, do you know who's involved in this dog fighting racket? You have your ear to the ground. You must have some idea? " Stokes was an Essex lad who said it as it was. He knew the lay of the land and to all that witnessed him at work they knew he was destined for higher things. He was the kind of officer who took hold of a case and shook it like a rag doll. Tenacious and yet very fair, even the local likely lads liked him.

The burly Irishman shook his head.

"Just a name Joe? Any. Or a location? I mean these Gypos, they trade with you guys."

"I don't know what you mean," he replied.

"Scrap metal?"

"But I don't deal in scrap metal do I?" he replied. "I just fry sausages. Metal that's my brother."

"Well your brother might know some of them?"

"Go ask him then."

"Come on Joe," Stokes was asking, "you know all of the villains. They come to get their breakfast here."

"Do they?" The Irishman's answers were getting shorter and more terse.

"Just one name?"

"Do you want some more tea officers?" he asked casually, in reply. It was clear that he had no intention of continuing further.

"Just one?" Stokes persuaded.

"The Turk knows, why don't you ask him? Or try Merryweather," he finally relented without looking up.

Michael Stokes knew all about Daniyel Merryweather. He had once asked the boy's mother about the spelling of his Christian name. They as police officers had often joked about it and wondered if the Registrars of Birth and Deaths had a private bet on to see who could get the most absurd name spelling registered. Mary Merryweather had been married to Josh a part Romany with some very dubious connections; he had been illiterate and she was hardly better, but she had been a beauty, dark eyes and dark hair which glowed an almost blue-ish black in the sunlight. Josh had been a beer sodden lump who had been repeatedly arrested for drunken disorderly. Mary had been the kind of woman every man wanted and the mix of the two, had been like petrol and a flame. One day in a state of abandon Josh Merryweather had fallen through the scaffolding on a local site and disappeared from view hitting every putt-lug on the way down . His death had been no great loss to the world and secretly the police and local community heaved a collective sigh of relief. The Health and Safety Executive had pronounced alcohol as the cause of death, which no one contested. The employers had been absolved; the lawyers had grown fat on the legal aid fee, and the police and local community were glad to have seen the last of him. In life he had been a nuisance and in death even more so. However, his son, complete with his stupid phonetically spelt name, had rapidly grown into his father's shoes. As time progressed his feet were getting too big for even those shoes and it could be quite plausible that he was involved in the dogfight business. Daniyel certainly appeared to be cruel enough. One of the older local residents, who had known him since his childhood, had been heard to remark that an apple doesn't fall very far from the tree.

Daniyel Merryweather, an objectionable, rude and aggressive boy, had transmogrified into an ape like man, only more rude, more violently aggressive and more hairy. The only aspect that was lacking to make the Edward Hyde illusion complete, was the fact that his knuckles didn't drag on the ground and that he had no Dr. Jekyll side at all. What you saw was precisely what you got, and what was seen was never very pleasant.

"Thanks Joe," Liz Jordan, said to the cafe owner as both officers left to the sound of the jangling door bell.

Joe O'Neill spoke softly under his breath, "Somebody's got to do something about those dogs and that little scam. We can't afford to have the police nosing about everywhere. If we have the filth digging they'll put everything in jeopardy. "

"They didn't see me did they boy?" Came a terse reply from his older brother, who appeared in the doorway behind the counter.

"No, Jimmy," Joe O'Neill, replied casually. "We have to sort this lot out once and for all or they're going to mess everything up for us and that we can't afford that. What we have here is nice and sweet. I don't want some greedy little bastard getting things all hot and unnecessary."

"I'll speak to Mickey Sullivan," was all James O'Neill hissed in reply.

"Good idea."

The obelisk was a local landmark, a landmark which had once stood in the grounds of a fine manor house. The manor house had long since gone, demolished as death duties had stripped away a family fortune. The obelisk remained a white smooth finger, pointing heavenward in defiance - a monument to the politician Charles Fox. Erected by his friend Tankerville Chamberlayne it remained a bleak reminder of the political connections the house once had; now it was as inconsequential as the politician it represented. It remained in the corner of a municipal recreation ground, a naked reminder of a powerful friendship and was disregarded - except for the graffiti that appeared on it from time to time.

Trees had grown around and behind it, though part of it could be seen from the field where local football teams played in Sunday leagues. Every weekend boys played and gradually grew into fat middle-aged men who swam in their own regret. Many thought that they had a talent: Most didn't. Others dreamt they could have been a Bobby Moore or a Bobby Charlton, the problem was that most went the way of Jimmy Greaves. Hit the bottle or knocked up a local girl and then married. Their dreams shattered they played at being footballers now; some even trained local boys' squads so that the dream perpetuation could continue. For most they had no other viable option except perhaps building site labourer, thief, or maybe the forces. There they could be marched into the line of fire and then once buried could be forgotten before the next consignment arrived. For those, there was no obelisk, no marker for their passing. They came, burned briefly and then simply went out. The final con came in stealth tax every Saturday night as they watched the silver eye; here a set of bingo balls rotated until six were chosen and the lucky number match gave a £1 million payout. The dream of winning wealth was their last chance at escape, a vague chance dangled like a carrot before a donkey.

Life for those in this community was less than an aspiration. Selling drugs, selling people, selling themselves, they would do anything at all to get the dream. They wanted to be, "Living the dream," whatever that might mean - some voyeur idealism of red carpets and fast cars, loose women and boozy orgies; everything the silver eye told them was necessary. The problem was that most failed and failed abysmally as they lurched ever closer to the pit of oblivion. The girls pumped out children like the shucking of peas and the boys eventually turned inward and gave up, propping up the bars and talking of might have beens.

The Warhol dream of everybody having fifteen minutes of fame had now almost become a religion, a nightmare vision of the future. The notion of fame had been the altar upon which many had sacrificed themselves. Luck was the only answer, the chance of being in the right place at the right time. Most were in either in the wrong place or in the wrong time and consequently their talent went unnoticed.

Michael Stokes knew exactly what he was dealing with - Liz his partner did not. She had grown up in a comfortable suburb of Winchester, with a dog, a father, who provided and a mother who read to them at night. She had made trips to the library at weekends, and earned her pocket money by tidying her room. Michael Stokes had grown up in community like the one he now served and patrolled. A community which spent most of their time in open conflict with any authority figure. A community which blamed others for the failure within it. A community which was nothing like the word implied; in fact it was just a rag-tag and bobtailed group of misfits that happened to share the same space of air and ground.

His mother had been a teen mum too and his father a drunk, at the very first opportunity he had made his dash for freedom. His launching pad had been education but he also knew he had been born lucky; he'd been born with a brain and some teachers had recognised that. That was his only chance and he had taken it; nothing came his way except hard work. The school had given him every chance and he had seized the day, "Carpe Dieum," as his old school motto had said, and he had done just that. He had succeeded because he had wanted to and not because someone else had wanted him to. His great strength had been in his character and that he had not fallen into the trap of blaming the world for not providing him with a living. There were no people holding his hand, he had learned to stand on his own two feet, forcefully and quickly and he had. Sometimes he wondered what had become of his parents, but his self-preservation instinct was stronger than any possible romanticised attachment to his past: He succeeded alone.

Michael Stokes was smart enough to know that his life, his career, was nothing more than a glancing blow against a great steel drum of eternity. A hollow drum which rang in his ears, delivering an apocalyptic clang – like a death knell. He knew what the locals knew – that nothing really mattered. His thoughts were tumbling like dice, or as he saw it dominoes.

As the two officers walked behind the shelter of the wooded avenue leading to the monument they could see Finny in the distance, he was rolling a cigarette, which was more likely a joint. He seemed nervous, and twitchy. Stokes could only muster two words in his mind - poor bastard.

"Allo Fin," said Stokes as he approached.

"Listen Mr. Stokes I don't know nuffink."

"Mmm, double negative," Liz Jordan replied. "If you don't know nuffink," she mimicked his accent, "anything, should I say? Then you must know something?"

Michael Stokes liked her. She came from a completely different background to his own. Privileged, middle-class, she had gone to a "nice" school out in the valley. A place where the children said please and thank you and didn't take everything that wasn't nailed down. She also had the most marvellous legs which reached up to a perfect backside but never met in the middle. There was always that heavenly two inch gap of seduction at the top of her thighs which he wanted to explore with his tongue, but had never managed to even see, let alone touch. Sometimes he had wondered whether a Brazilian or a Hollywood was her preferred option. He hoped it was a Hollywood, that would suit her general appearance and his likes. At times he could imagine her smooth softness on his tongue tip and he loved the fantasy. Her virtue, however, unlike the girls of the community they served, was a little less easy to invade.

Finny became smilingly nervous and shifted from leg to leg as if he needed the toilet.

"But you don't even know what I'm going to ask?" Stokes continued.

"No, no that's right," he grinned back.

"Daniyel Merryweather?"

Finny began smoking nervously, "Yeah?"

"I want you to find out something for me Finny," Stokes requested.

"Like what?" he replied. His tone was bordering on the insolent.

"That's not very nice, not very nice at all," Liz Jordan interjected. "You should learn some manners Finny."

There was a noise which seemed to be ejected from his lips, a sound which made a "Puh,"

Suddenly Liz Jordan angrily slapped the cigarette from his face. "Listen!" she exclaimed. "You might like to smoke a joint in front of us, but you shouldn't have any crack on you should you?"

"That weren't no joint," Finny pleaded apologetically.

"And I suppose these aren't yours either?" She reached into her pocket and pulled out at least ten packets of white powder, which she held by the corners and shook at him. "Finny you've been a really naughty boy this time."

He started to blub, "But they aint mine I never seen them before," he squealed.

"Oh, dear. Now that's not true is it? You see your finger prints are going to be all over these little bags."

"I aint touched them."

Liz Jordan shot a sideways glance at Stokes. "Well you're going to."

Michael Stokes was pulling leather gloves over his fingers.

"No Mr. Stokes," he said, "everyone knows I don't deal in crack. I do a little dope and pills everyone knows that. This aint fair, it aint right. I don't deserve this." He was almost crying now.

"Well it looks like you've upped your game then?" Stokes replied.

"And deserve has got nothing to do with it," Liz Jordan laughed.

"This aint fair," his voice raised in pitch as he looked from person to person for a solution.

"Look Fin we wants some information." Stokes added the local dialect superfluous, "s," the pluralisation made him sound villainous.

"No one's goin' to believe that crack was me?" he almost squealed.

Liz Jordan put the packets into her breast pocket and buttoned her tunic. Her reply came as almost a whisper, "It'll be my word in court against yours," she said, "and who are they going to believe?" she paused, "I wonder?"

Finny the Turk shot a pleading look at Stokes, who simply shrugged. "I didn't see nuffink," he said.

"This aint fair, I don't know..."

"No?" Stokes continued, "That's why you're gonna find something out for us."

"But I can't Mr. Stokes," he lowered his voice, "the families will..."

"I don't need to know about them. Merryweather Danny? I want to know if he's involved in this dog fighting racket."

The look on Finny's face was relief, sheer relief. He had always disliked the boy when they had been at school together. Merryweather had bullied him mercilessly, bullied him because he had contracted Polio when he was a kid and Finny had trouble with keeping his balance, because he had suffered paralysis down his left side as a result. Merryweather had tripped him in the corridors, pushed him and then he and his mates had laughed as Merryweather mimicked his shuffle. Merryweather nick named him, "Superspas" and it had stuck. His relief was intense now.

"Oh he's involved alright," Finny answered quickly.

"How ?" Liz Jordan continued.

"He's got a mate, who's got a farm and they have this barn with a pit."

"Location?" Stokes asked

"I don't know," the Turk replied.

"That's not much use," Liz Jordan persisted.

"Honest I don't know," he replied, looking pleadingly from officer to officer. "But his mate's called Richard Parker."

"What Parker the dairy people?"

Finny shrugged.

"I want you to find out more," Stokes said.

"But I can't. You don't know that Merryweather. He's a total bastard. I can't."

"Do you want me to get a message to Gill Henderson.?You know that you're selling crack on her patch? I don't expect she'll like that very much? She might pickle your balls," Liz Jordan interjected.

"I can't Mr. Stokes."

"Or we could get your old mum's benefit stopped?" Liz Jordan added.

"You bitch," Finny exploded. "You scum!" It was clear he was angry. His eyes looked aflame and spittle stood on his lip.

Michael Stokes slapped his face. "That's no way to talk to lady now is it?"

Finny the Turk shook his head in reply. Immediately he resumed the supplicant attitude, an attitude which he always used for self protection. Since his schools days he had learned that melting into the background was the best protection. Those that fought back either had to be tough mavericks that were aloof and resolute, or work as a mob: There was neither option open to him.

"You got three days Finny or we stuff everything up for you," Jordan said.

Just then two small boys came around the corner of the open field and seeing the police uniforms took off at high speed.

"Let's hope they didn't recognise you eh Finny?" Officer Stokes snorted. "Now piss off and get me something I can use."

With that it was as if Finny the Turk had been released like a greyhound from a trap and he immediately disappeared and blended into the trees behind the monument and was gone.

"I didn't know you were going to pull that one?" Stokes laughed.

"What one?" Liz Jordan replied.

"The crack?"

"Oh that's not crack, that's talcum powder, unscented of course. Handy little accessory, a bit like the policewoman's lippy." She was laughing as she spoke, "Seems to have done the trick though. I thought I heard his sphincter slam shut."

"Bugger me," Stokes stated, "is that what they teach you at those convent schools in the valley?"

"Listen you bigot," she smiled back, "it was an all girls' school, but we had our little bits of fun. And it wasn't a finishing or charm school, you had to learn to look after yourself. Survive on your wits."

"I bet you bloody did. That was a stonkingly good bluff. You had the poor bugger nearly shit himself."

"Nearly?" she smirked. "From the way he smelt I thought he had."

"Yeah he does get a bit high when he's excited."

"A bit?" she laughed, "he could be bottled and used as a rodent repellent."

"Imagine what he's like with his clothes off?"

"I'd rather not," she replied.

"He had a crap life as a kid too. First he got Polio, then the dad scarpers with some young piece of skirt; his mother, gets paranoid and keeps coal in the bath so it doesn't get lifted. He wasn't brought up - he was dragged up. He's a poor little bastard really."

She side stepped the social issues. "Well at least now he will be a little more active," she replied. "Fear is a great leveller and," she paused, "if he knows anything he'll get back to us."

"Let's hope you are right on this one. I know he has some information and it will be interesting to see if he spills the beans or if he runs for cover. He's scared to death."

"I really don't care what he does," Liz Jordan said coldly. "The question is who is he more scared of the Hendersons, that shit Merryweather, or you and me?"

"Maybe the bugger is right?"

"About what?"

"About you my dear," he was chuckling as he spoke. "Maybe you really are a bitch of the first order?"

"Don't be a total prick," she mocked in response.

He laughed in reply, "If you're right we should have the detail in the next couple of days."

***

Richie Parker's farm was an old dairy establishment which had been delivering milk since the time of his grandfather. There were also acres of land turned over to fruit and vegetable fields. There had been a full bottling plant, which employed forty men and a five hundred strong herd. Now the family and the dairy had been gradually dismantled and some of the land sold off for building.

As a business man he was a failure, as a man a total failure. His ideas on investments had faltered and he, in consequence, gambled and began to make acquaintances that left him open to police investigation. Parker also had a passion for young girls which these new acquaintances used for their own ends. In physique he was a large boned man, clumsy and awkward, in character he was small, greedy, barbarous and cruel and the introduction to Merryweather had enabled him to feed both his addictions and his desires.

The latest scam had been to bring into the country a series of girls from Romania. These girls were brought into the country to work on his farm, mostly as fruit pickers. Many spoke hardly any English and worked upwards of twelve hours per day. The youngest and prettiest he traded.

The girls once they had arrived in England began to realise that the streets were not paved with gold. Whilst they had often left one room hovels they found that what was on offer was a little less than they expected. Work in Parker's fields was hard and long and he did not have to persuade too hard or too long that a better life awaited those who "married," one of his, "clients," or did some dubious adult filming. The introductions paid well, with some clients paying as much as five figures for a "wife." The Parker side-line was lucrative and so far not one single case had been brought to court. The girls who declined to be, " traded," either remained working in the fields until exhaustion found them or excuses were made and they were rapidly shipped back home. There were always more willing to make the trip and take a chance.

Parker provided the transport from their homelands, clothing, introductions and pocketed a fat finding fee, whilst giving each girl the princely sum of £5000 once any transaction had taken place. The profit margin worked out at 80% per girl, and he estimated that nearly two hundred women had passed through his farm cottages or workforce in less than four years.

The key to his success was that these women were not sold as if they were cattle; they were willing participants in all phases and saw the opportunity to marry in the UK as an advantage. For some it was a dream come true, for others an abusive nightmare. Parker knew several farmers all over the country who had done the same with the Poles and the Bulgarians when they joined the EU. The police were unable to prosecute him because none of the girls were forced or sold, they were introduced, a technicality in reality; but of sufficient worth. A technicality large enough to keep Parker out of jail and make him wealthy. It was far better than scratching around for the various EU subsidies which he could get if he were prepared to bow and scrape. In his life he had done enough of that with his own father and he wasn't about to do that again with a bunch of nameless bureaucrats in Brussels or Whitehall.

Once he even held a girl auction. Fifteen girls were catalogued, with their consent of course, as if they were beasts. During the venture he liked to think that some of them actually enjoyed the idea. On offer was a short term night of sexual pleasure; a quick way for the girls to earn extra vital cash. Each stripped naked, voluntarily, and then they ran in a ring before being herded into pens and sold as individual lots. Parker took 75%, proving once again, that the marketing was the key rather than the product. Though it had been entertaining, the gross profit yielded had been no more than the one to one sales. Some girls had made a ridiculous price as the men vied to out bid one another, while others had not reached the original estimates. Parker had felt like some Roman auctioneer selling Nubian slave girls; it had excited him and Daniyel Merryweather had provided several clients and protection from the rival gangs. There had been no trouble and no real necessity for Merryweather, but he had been thankful just in case. In turn Parker had agreed to find another location for the dog fights; his farm it was the perfect place.

***

"You bastards don't give a damn do you? Just leave me sittin' out here while you drink you cups o' tea I spects. I wants you to do summink."

The woman was screaming at the Desk Sergeant. Who began filling in a large blank form in front of him.

"Missing person is he?" The officer asked.

"Missing? My Finny 'ee's gawn. Sumbody done 'im. An you don't care do ya?"

"Mrs Camekeskou, you'll have to give me full details. For the forms and such. You know, his age, a description of what he was wearing at the time of his disappearance."

"Give you 'is age? Age? What the hell do you think this is a circus? He was dressed like he normally dresses - cloves. E 'ad on a lever jackit and a tee-shirt wiv mota'ead writ on it. And some shoes. Them white ones wiv a tick on the side."

"Trainers?"

" Corse they was trainers. Oh an 'e 'ad green laces in 'em. You know like the glowy ones what you buys in the market down town."

"Florescent? Green you say?"

The Desk Sergeant was smiling broadly.

"This aint bleedin' funny. Finny's gone. Not been 'ome for three days and I know who's done it too."

The Desk Sergeant knew the family, knew the woman before him, knew she could not read and write, "You'll have to fill in this form," he said. He turned the clipboard to which the papers were attached toward her and lifted a pen as if to pass it.

"Can't write," she said.

"You can't write?"

"You heard me you bastard. You knows I can't write nuffink down. You don't give a damn about my Finny. You get that Stokes bloke out here and let me talk to 'im. He's the reason fings aint right. And that bloody sour faced cow that he's on the beat with; looks like a bitch lickin' piss off a nettle most the time. Don't know her name but I know her type. Stuck up cow."

"PC Jordan? Elizabeth Jordan?" The Desk Sergeant enquired.

"If you say so."

"I'll see if she's here," he said, and left her to stand as he went out to the cells area.

Mrs Camekeskou stood and waited.

***

Mickey Sullivan was holding Richie Parker's left eye in the palm of his hand and watching as the attempted screams were muffled by a piece of thick hessian. Parker's hands were bound behind his back but his feet were lashing out in all directions. Half yelling and half trying to run he was desperate to get to his feet; Sullivan repeatedly kicked him at the back of the knees forcing him back down to the floor. Around him the white walls of the fighting pit obscured his exit. A large circular concrete pit with walls seven feet high and over a foot thick, with a drain in the centre - it was a totally enclosed 30ft space. This had been the old bull ring. The place where cows were brought to be mated, before artificial insemination had taken over. The hose which Parker had using to wash away the blood from the nights entertainment was still running and now his blood was mingling with that of the dead dog and his own urine. The other dog had been taken away and some were now in the old horse stables, secure and licking their wounds.

Fear was causing Parker to collapse and he knew the man was after money. The entrance doors were shut and he had not seen his assailant as he struck him on the back of the head. It had been as if he had approached in the shadows like a ghost.

The man had brought him back to consciousness; he had forced the hose into his nostrils and the lack of air had him awake instantly Mickey Sullivan asked him questions but none of them seemed to be about money, or the safe, or the girls. Then Sullivan dug his eye out of the socket with a spoon as he screamed in terror. The pain had been intense: He had passed out.

"Now I want you to understand exactly what is going to happen to you," Sullivan said as he spoke. "Do you understand what I'm saying? You nod if you do. "

The terror in Parker's face was most apparent in the one remaining eye he had left. He was nodding as if possessed.

"Do you know what you have done you little sack of shit? Let's get this straight somebody doesn't like you," he paused, "and why? Because you are messing up their trade and you and your dumb bell partner are bringing more and more plod into the area." He paused again. "That is not good news for a blind man now is it?"

Parker was still nodding.

"This business with the girls that we can let pass, that didn't cause us any problems. I mean plod and his silly little ways is one thing and everyone likes a nice piece of tail, but this." His voice rose in pitch, "This little bear pit, well it's drawing attention to this little quiet town. Attention draws the police, and we don't want any more police around here. We'll have animal rights campaigners next, or the anti-blood sport league. Next thing you know this town will be in the dailies. You see some big nosed copper is going to find out what we do and that is bad for business." He paused and lit a cigarette. "So now here we are. I have one of your eyes and you are here all alone in the dark with me. That's where you are gonna spend the rest of your days unless you are very lucky. In the dark."

He flicked the eye into the air as if flicking a coin and casually tossed it into the path of the water which washed it down the central drain grate and out into the slurry tank.

"This is one silent barn," Sullivan smiled, "nobody's gonna hear you scream out here. Hell I could cut your balls off and stamp them flat under my heel and no one would know. That eye, sorry about that, but I had to be certain you understood I was serious. I think we see eye to eye now don't we?" He chuckled as if he had delivered a great joke.

He held his cigarette in front of Parker's remaining good eye, and blew astringent smoke into the orifice where the other had once been. "How many fights have you seen in this bull pit?" Sullivan blew on the read end of the cigarette. It glowed in the gloom. "It's getting dark soon we won't be able to see a thing and then where would we be?"

***

Michael Stokes was very calm, "When did you last see him?" he asked, his pencil poised.

"You really are a bastard aint ya?" Finny's mother replied. "You asked him to find out about that Daniyel Merryweather and he did that and now look what's happened. That Merryweather's done 'im in."

"We can't know that for certain now can we?" Stokes was listening carefully. "So when then?"

"Two days ago."

"Where?"

"What do ya mean, where?"

"I thought the concept was self-explanatory?"

"Eh?"

"I just wanted to know where he was last seen."

"I seen 'im in the Giggling Sausage. We was 'avin a breakfast an then I was goin' up the town to get a few fings."

"So Finny was there?"

Stokes wrote a note.

"Yeah he was and we had a tea and then I left. He says he was goin' to see you about Merryweather; he said he knew where the fights was done and he had to tell you before all the shit hit the fan, and now he's gone. I never seen 'im again. You made 'im ask around and that bastard Merryweather's found out aint 'e and you, you shit, you don't care do ya?"

"So you had breakfast in the cafe?" Stokes was remaining clinical.

She nodded.

"Then you went to town. And you left Finny sitting in the cafe?"

"Yeah he was talkin' to that big fat Irish bastard when I left. The bloke what owns the place. Fat ignorant pig he is. There weren't no one else in there."

Stokes made more notes. "Girlfriend?" he asked.

"Course he aint got a girlfriend. Who'd want a wreck like 'im?"

"And you are his mother?"

"But I aint blind, and fore you say I aint got a good word to say about anybody. That's 'cos most people are shits. My Finny he's a nice boy but look at 'im. He aint boyfriend material is 'e? He haven't got a decent shag in 'im, poor love. He can't walk most the time let alone do the love jog."

"I'm just trying to see where he might have gone?" Stokes continued.

"Gone, you best go and see that bloody madman Merryweather. He's the one you're after and 'is twisted mate. The one that sells the girls."

"Sells girls?"

"Bloody hell aint none of you got a brain? Richie Parker owns that farm on the A 42, with the red brick gables. Rosewall farm - luvly 'ouse. Shame he aint more like 'is dad was. A real gentleman he was; mind you he liked the ladies but 'e always was a gentleman, he always paid. Not like that son of 'is. He brings in girls and then he sells 'em. Right bleedin' pig he is. Them girls come from," she paused as if trying to think clearly, "Youain, or some such place and pretty most of 'em are."

"Ukraine, in Russia?"

"I don't bloody know." She snarled, "You really are a right clever little bastard, or at least you fink you are."

Stokes did not react.

"One day someone's gonna pop you and you won't even see it comin'. Big-headed prick that you are. Serve you right an awl."

Stokes remained calm, "So Richard Parker's involved in the dog fighting?" he asked again.

Finny's mother nodded.

"How?"

"Finny told me that they got some sort of bull pit or somethin'. It's in one of the old barns a long way from the road. You get to it down an old track off Causeway Lane and Parker keeps some dogs out there. Only he's got the real dangerous ones, the killers. There's some old sheds out there too. It's miles from anywhere. Finny was scared that if he found out ..."

"Who found out?"

"Bloody Daniyel Merryweather. Aint you been listening? So my Finny found out some stuff for you lot an now you got what you wants 'e's gone and disappeared."

"Well he hasn't spoken to me about all this. Maybe he has just gone to ground for a while?"

"E tol' me in the cafe. That's how I knows."

"Like I said maybe he's gone to ground – we haven't seen him," Stokes replied, a slight tinge of apprehension in his voice as he spoke.

"More like in the ground and iffen 'e 'as, I'll top Merryweather myself if I has to. You mark my words they'll fine 'im one day - wiv 'is froat cut.

***

The blow that was supposed to split Mickey Sullivan's skull like a walnut missed and hit him on the collar bone with a resounding crack – that broke like a dry log. Sullivan's reaction had been instinctual as he plunged the knife into Daniyel Merryweather's neck. Once, twice, three times with lightening reaction speed. It was semi-dark and he did not see who the attacker was, but had heard them approach; in the split second that realisation had saved his life.

Merryweather felt the first insertion deep into his windpipe as his vocal chords were severed; the second had torn a hole under his jaw and the third had punctured the jugular. Blood was spraying everywhere as he tried to fight back. Mickey Sullivan's knee broke his nose as he pulled the man's head forward.

The pain in his shoulder blade was intense and Parker was scrambling like a crab with one claw, as he tried to get away. Sullivan kicked his legs from under him and he fell on the gargling Merryweather.

"You little piece of slime," Sullivan hissed, "I'll dig your other eye out."

Parker lashed out with his legs in an attempt to ward him off, but missed his mark. Sullivan retaliated and Parker's testicles exploded with one kick. Instantly he vomited and starting choking. Sullivan was kicking him now and his breath was coming in gasps and wheezes. As he rolled across the floor he felt two of his ribs crack and the pain in his chest became unbearable. Sullivan was kicking and kicking and he seemed unable to escape the onslaught.

Mickey Sullivan suddenly sat, unable to kick the wretched mess that had once been Richie Parker any longer. The pulp that had once been a head was bubbling but he thought the man dead. His partner, Merryweather, lay on the cold bare concrete like some form of zombie. The pool of blood, in which his face was drowning, was slowing down and Sullivan knew that death would not be long. It was a macabre picture like a man slaking his thirst beside a river bank, face down and drinking – only this drink was blood. He felt the wound to his shoulder. The skin and flesh had hardly been broken but he knew the collar bone had been. He had felt this pain before when he had played rugby for London Irish. It was exactly the same as then.

Now he realised he had a problem. There was morphine in the boot of his car but he hadn't anticipated having to lift two bodies, that would now be impossible. He pulled the mobile phone from his pocket.

"Joe," he said, "I need some help, I've got two bodies and my collar bone's been done in."

"Just leave then," came the reply, "make it look like a robbery."

"That's not so easy," he was breathing heavily now, "I haven't got the keys to the safe." He was gasping. "I need to get some pain killer or I'm going to pass out."

"You're supposed to be the revolutionary. Ready for everything. Now you say you might pass out? If they find you there then we're all in the shit. I'll come now."

Mickey Sullivan was sitting in the front of his car when the van arrived. Both O'Neill brothers were in it and he smiled and raised his left hand. His right hand would not work.

"I took some morphine," he said, "and a couple of snorts of dynamite just to keep me up and running."

"This is a right bloody mess Mickey," Joe O'Neil said.

"I've done the safe," he offered in reply. "Found the key in Parker's jacket pocket, the toot is in the boot. I'll have to lay low for a bit. Maybe get back over to Clare and hide up in Bunratty."

"You'll have to get that fat arsed sister of yours to look out for you Mickey and make a broth. She was fine lookin' gal was she not, when she was younger?" Jimmy O'Neill was laughing. "Still those two are dead are they? We'll leave them there. See how long it takes for them to be found.

"Go take a look if you like," Sullivan puffed. He was finding breathing difficult now.

"Nah," Joe O'Neill snorted, "we know you're good at your job there Mickey."

"Let's have a look at the cash, how much was there?" asked Jimmy.

Mickey Sullivan got out of his car and walked with the two bothers to the boot, and as he lifted it, a revolver wrapped in a towel exploded in a muffled puff behind him and his lifeless body, minus the face tumbled into the car.

Night had set in and the O'Neills worked quickly. Within minutes they had set the barn ablaze and were driving both vehicles back to the scrap metal yard. There were no dog walkers or hikers and virtually no cars on the road, and their return was completely uneventful.

Fire fighters worked through the night to bring the blaze under control and some voyeurs, who fire watched, had heard dogs screaming in the stables and sheds as the fire spread. The fire crews had tried to save some but had been so badly bitten in the process that they gave up. All in all in was a newsworthy piece of arson which was attributed to kids at first and then gang warfare thereafter.

At the scrap yard gates they drove both vehicles in, used a crow bar to pull the number plates free from Mickey Sullivan's car. The windscreen Joe O'Neill smashed along with the front head lights before his brother stopped him with a finger to the lips which implied too much noise. The tax disc and money from under the lifeless body of Mickey Sullivan were retrieved. Surprisingly, there were few notes which had been stained in blood and Mickey had been prepared enough to place the cash into two holdalls. Jimmy O'Neill estimated almost £100,000 - a staggering amount. The blood stained notes were burned on the pot bellied stove which ran day and night to heat the site office. That accomplished they left as quickly and as silently as they had come. Once again they were lucky, no one had seen them and those that had passed in cars saw nothing unusual. The O'Neills kept strange hours and often there were delivery vans coming and going at all hours of the day and night. Vans carrying boxes. Coffin like boxes mostly. Boxes of machine parts.

**

It was the heavy rain that woke Finny; somehow it was dripping on his head. Water had got into his bed, only he wasn't in bed; couldn't be in bed - he was inside a box. Only it was metal. His left hand was working and he could feel wet carpet: He was on the floor, but the carpet was wet, very wet. Then he felt the sharp edges of metal. The roof was leaking. The sound of the rain was heavier now and the pounding sounded like the rain on a tin roof shed. His eyes didn't work in the dark – he needed to switch the light on. Where was the switch, he needed to find the switch.

He wanted to kick, but his legs weren't working properly. They did not respond to the commands he was giving them. There was something else in the dark with him and he didn't know what it was. He didn't know how he had got there. Didn't know where he was and couldn't remember.

The cafe, he remembered the cafe and then everything went dark. His mind went blank after his mother went to town and Joe O'Neill gave him that free tea.

Then the room was swaying gently and he could hear the sound of machines. The puff of a diesel engine and the slow and awful sound of screaming - metal screaming. His mouth wanted to yell for help, help to pull his legs out, help to let him out. And then suddenly he was plummeting down, like jumping off a diving board and he landed with a bump. The lid of the car boot flew open and for no more than a few seconds he saw the sky and felt the rain on his face. Saw the lifeless co passenger next to him, and realised what the lump was, where he was, and what was about to happen. His mouth tried to scream but it would not work something was wrong. He needed to pull himself up and out but his arms were useless. Rain hit his face and with a little more time he would manage to ...

After that the great jaws constricted the space he was in. The metal began to scream around him, scream for survival and the body next to him began to get closer. Too close, he wanted to push it off. He was finding it harder to breathe and things were beginning to burst. His head felt as if it were in a vice. And then the space got smaller still and the darkness set in and all the while the rain poured and washed away the anti-freeze, the oil, and the blood.

***

Michael Stokes knew he was right.

"Finny just vanished," he said to John Macfee. "It doesn't make sense govner."

"Why?" came the terse reply.

"Well he goes to the cafe with his mum. They sit and then she goes off and he's never seen again."

"So? They topped him and I don't know, fed him to the dogs?" The Inspector was less than interested. His caseload was high and he knew there would be time enough to stumble across Finny's body at a later date."

"I reckon those Irish are up to something," Stokes remarked, almost as if he were thinking aloud.

"And I suppose those two are Irish gun runners for the IRA? What they sell the scrap and get it made into shooters?" Macfee was being heavily sarcastic, and Stokes felt like a little boy with an obvious theory. "And you want me to sanction you going down there and feeling their collars?"

"Well we could just do a routine sir?"

"Alright," Macfee acquiesced, "but don't take Liz, I've got something much tastier for her. Our little flasher chappy has started up again."

"Oh she'll love you for that one."

"I know," Macfee laughed. "Take Partridge with you. He loves all that ethnic correctness shite. He can talk to those tinkers and get a feel for their lives."

"Yes sir."

Michael Stokes turned on his heel and cursed his luck as he made his way back to the central office. On the way he got Partridge to get a car organised and find a description of Finny and what he was wearing when he disappeared. Then he went back to tell Liz the good news.

"You're on the flasher case," Michael Stokes said, as he returned to the shared office.

"Oh you are kidding me," she replied. "He does it on purpose just to taunt me. He really is a complete chauvinist pig. Just because I'm a woman and I might be offended by a nutter in a raincoat I have to go out chasing him. It's not like I don't get to see enough pricks in this office is it?"

"Well it's not exactly a laugh a minute for me either," Stokes replied. "I know that there is something wrong about the O'Neills. They just seem too smug. They are never bothered by the Hendersons, or any of the rival gangs and families – why?"

"Because they are decent blokes?"

"No there's something wrong. They have a hold over those others."

"Or the others are scared of those brothers?"

"Perhaps they are," Stokes replied. "You see you should be on this case with me, instead of the turkey."

Now it was Liz Jordan's turn to mock. "Life has a kind of karma don't you think? A turkey looking for a Turk. An irony really?"

"Well I reckon there is something going on. Does the IRA still exist?" Stokes asked

"Woohah," Liz Jordan replied. "Go steady there. That is an anti-terrorist action. What do you think they are up to then Colombo? A bomb factory? Maybe they make exploding sausages instead of cigars."

"Ha bloody ha, don't take the piss."

"Novel though, the next great terrorist attack. I can see the headlines already. Minister slain by exploding sausage, thought to be the new cunning threat." She was sniggering.

"How about money laundering through the two businesses. Or using that yard as a drop site for weapons." Stokes was smarting and looking forlorn as she worked her sarcasm.

"You've seen too many films," she remarked.

"Well I know they're up to something."

"Well everybody's up to something. The question is, is it legal?"

"They're doing something and that much I know," Stokes replied.

"And by know you mean sort of guess?"

"Ok I guessed, but even you think there's something wrong." He paused before continuing, "Come on you know there is something not right too, that's if you're honest."

"Look," Liz Jordan continued, "they've probably got some fiddle or other on the go and the last thing in the world they want is a nosey young plod like you sticking his beak in."

John Partridge stood in the doorway. Michael Stokes wondered how much he had heard and how he might react as they explored the scrap yard. He had never worked with the man before.

"Right I'll see you later," Stokes remarked with a big smile, and a wink of his eye, "for drinkies and nibbles? Perhaps a little game of croquet on the lawns."

"Oh that'll be spiffing don't ya know," Liz Jordan replied, completely understanding his reference to her upbringing. "I'll get my favourite flamingos out. Should one dress for dinner or can one come in ones skivvies?"

"You can come in your underwear, or posh bint outfit. In fact go with the first choice."

Liz Jordan threw a note book at his head but missed.

***

When the two officers stepped out of the squad car the rain had begun to fall as heavily as it had done for the past six days. The oil soaked earth of the yard had become slimey and the petrol and other fluids were making rainbow patterns as the water worked upon it. It gave the whole place an almost supernatural feel. It was the blade runner feel, some science fiction movie of twisted metal and rust combined with perpetual rain. The scrap yard looked like some great alien space station perched in some distant corner of the universe; a transition point between the present and the abyss.

The O'Neills had made good money from the scrap metal business, more money than anyone at first could imagine. Enough money to buy houses at first. Rows of terraced houses which they rented. At first it had been migrant Irish, when they moved on, the Asian families moved in. The community was poor and the O'Neills had managed their affairs well; apparently they were fair landlords. The properties were well maintained through their links with the Irish building fraternity and they had expanded into the cafe business. There were two, but the real wealth had come from the scrap.

John Partridge was the first to speak, "Blimey what a place, it's like a vision of Hell."

Cars were stacked four deep, the seats and tyres removed. They too were in large mounds like some awesome tower of Babel waiting for collection and recycling. There were two large flat back Lorries in the yard and Jimmy O'Neill was working the huge electro magnet which was lifting and stacking the cubed cars ready for transportation. Once gone the cubes would be delivered to furnaces where the slurry of rust and debris would be burnt away and the pure molten ingots of steel would once again be formed into the panels of the new cars. It almost seemed like a life cycle. The cubes like cocoons full of rancid liquid would once again rise as brief butterflies, only to be cubed once their turn in the sunlight had transpired.

The second lorry was being stacked with tyres and two young boys covered in black stains were struggling to load them, while a lorry driver was standing at the office door drinking a mug of something. The boys looked young, no more than sixteen and they were wet. With bedraggled hair they toiled and the policemen felt, rather than knew, how wet their clothes would be after the exertion.

Jimmy O'Neill jumped down from the cab of the crane-come-electro magnet, immediately he noticed the police car. One cube was hanging suspended above the truck ready to be loaded. He raised his hand in recognition to the officers and made for the hut-come-office, as he did so, he made a drinking mime to the boys loading tyres and they ran for cover.

In the office the kettle had boiled and Jimmy O'Neill arrived panting. The two boys were stripping down to their underwear and drying while the driver was puffing on a cigarette. As the police arrived Jimmy O'Neill was spooning several sugars into his brown syrup which was pretending to be tea.

Michael Stokes took off his cap as he entered and shook the water from his shoulders.

"And to what do we owe the pleasure lads?" O'Neill asked. "You'll have a brew I expect?"

"Thanks," Partridge replied.

"Tis a filthy morning," O'Neill continued. His accent was warm and broad with an Irish lilt despite his many years in England. "Pissing down and not a good day for the work. But there we go. We are all waterproof underneath eh lads?" He nodded toward the two boys who were now dressed in dry clothes, "Drowned rats," he sniggered. Their wet and discarded ones dripped from nails on a far cross beam. They came to collect their tea. "Doughnuts in the box," he said. "I'm sorry it's not the cafe, or we'd all be having bacon sandwiches right now. Mind you I expect he's sittin' in the warm with his feet up."

Michael Stokes was straight to the point. "We're looking into a disappearance."

The two boys were eating heavy mouthfuls of doughnut and the driver had his chair propped against the wall, the two front legs raised, like some indolent school boy might do. He had learned to distrust authority at school, and that distrust had never left him in adult life.

O'Neill gave no reaction, made no enquiry.

"Finny Camekeskou?" Stokes questioned.

O'Neill shook his head.

"Finny the Turk most people call him. He's gone missing."

O'Neill still gave no reaction.

"He was last seen in your brother's cafe?"

"Ah well you'd best have a word with Joe then. I think I know who you mean. Little weasel type. He tried to sell us some scrap cars once. Only they were stolen and I sent him off with a flea in his ear. I don't want any funny business going on in this yard."

"Well he went missing, at about the time of the fire up at Parker's farm," said Partridge.

"Sad business that, them two lads dead in that fire," O'Neill replied.

"Well we wondered if you had seen him about?"

"No," O'Neill replied. "What about you two lads. Have you seen him?" He turned back to the policemen. "He sells them dope you see," he continued. "They think I don't know but they smoke that muck here and then one day they'll have an accident. Be like the raspberry jam in those doughnuts, only they'll be laughing. Why do you think they got the munchies now?"

"We aint seen 'im," one of the boys added, his mouth loaded with doughnut.

"Jimmy do you mind if we take a look around? He may have crawled into one of the old cars. Especially if he ran after the fire or was injured," asked Stokes.

"You look all you like boy," O'Neill nodded. "Only don't go climbin' in them cars they are likely to topple over. Oh and watch out for Satan he's out the back but he's chained in the kennel."

With the rain running down their necks the two officers made a sweep of the yard. As the office had been untidy the outside area was organised. Cars were stacked prior to cubing and the metals sorted into piles ready for sale and collection.

"He's not here is he?" Partridge said, as they moved through the towers of wheel-less cars.

"Of course not," Stokes replied.

"So why are we here?"

"These Irish chaps have got something going on. I don't know what it is but I know, I can feel it in my gut." Stokes was working on instinct

"So that's it is it? Gut reaction. And what if your gut reaction is just a curry or a piece of fish not quite right?"

"Ha bloody ha. Look the last place Finny was seen was the cafe?"

"So shouldn't we be going there then?"

"We will do but I want to unnerve the bastards a little bit. They're far too cool for my liking. And besides..."

"And besides that we're getting soaked?"

When they returned to their car the loading had restarted and the lorry with cubes, that once were cars, was about to leave. Hand signals were given and the puffing of the electro magnet ceased. Jimmy O'Neill was climbing down and coming over to the police car. As the lorry passed Michael Stokes saw it. A simple thing. A thing so simple that it would assure him of a rapid promotion - though at the time he was unaware.

A small simple thing, that confirmed he had been right to trust his instincts. There it was as clear as daylight. A thread of bright green, fluorescent green, a flash of instant colour which stood out from the drab brown of rust. In one cube he could see a line, one fine line of green like a painted splash of colour on white paper.

At that point he knew he was right and using his radio he called it in.

casanova's mask

L. amond

For my friend Edmundo Jim

Casanova's Mask

That year it was cold, colder than anyone in England could have imagined. Snow lay all about, deep and crisp and even and it wasn't even the feast of Stephen.

Bohemia is a cold place and by that I don't mean the act of being Bohemian as being cold. You know starving in some attic, throwing another chair on the fire or hunting for that last elusive shilling, or should I say zloty, for the meter - all for the sake of art. Slopping paint onto canvasses in the vane hope that years after the artist's death people would suddenly realise that they missed the best groundbreaker alive. That he died alone - unloved; died embittered and full of the notion of his personal failure. Sounds a bit like Vincent, now there is a very sad tale of a man born before his time. Bohemian doesn't describe what his mind was or his work. It wasn't until I'd see his work, in the flesh so to speak, that I got it.

I could write and that was why I was chosen for this job, rather than living like some bum completely consumed by the overriding need to produce some major text of earth shattering import. That was my weakness - I was lazy; perhaps I lacked courage and maybe, I had no drive. That single-mindedness which makes the obsessive compulsive artist made me line things up in straight lines. That was my contribution to the debate. Instead of trying to produce something unique I was prepared to settle for mediocrity, and the result, I'd missed my window of opportunity. I had squandered my youth, frittered away a substance more valuable than gold and diamonds: Time. There were no meals in prizes and if you did get one, most people didn't give a damn. Like the school certificate, at the time it seemed worth the effort but later experience shows it is not; not worth more than a meaningless piece of paper. Least of all to all the people I cared about and those that were supposed to care about me. What I meant was the place - it's cold. Germany, Austria and Czechoslovakia are freezing places to spend a series of dark nights in mid winter.

Darkness, however, has always been a friend to me; in it you can hide, murder, die or simply sit and reflect, and I had done lots of that. The Castle of Dux, now known as Duchcov Castle was more bitter a place than most – and I was more bitter than most.

That winter I had taken on a plum of a job, though some people would see it as a bore; I was cataloguing the artefacts which had once belonged to Count Joseph Karl von Waldstein. He of Beethoven's Waldstein Sonata, friend and patron to Voltaire; Goethe; Mozart, and my real reason for being at the castle, Giacomo Casanova. Yep he of the womanizing and endless golden copulations fame. Giacomo Girolamo Casanova de Seingalt had lived and written his final memoirs in this very castle. Here he had exploded the myths about his life, here he wrote his, Histoire de ma vie, that's autobiography to you and me. Though he died before getting any further than 1774. I imagined him sitting in the library, isolated, alone, scribbling down the encounters he had had with so many women. His words spoke to me from the scribbled notes and text and we both knew the pointlessness of it all.

Let me explain, seven years ago I had the messiest divorce of the century. I thought that I had been one of the lucky ones. The kind that marry early and then end up staying with that person for fifty odd years until eventually they sent us both off, virtually together, in some swirling crematorium black plume. I was a romantic; I use the past tense now because I have learned my lesson and what a lesson it was.

My wife had managed, over the long years, to be indulging in all sorts of liaisons; right from the start she had been infatuated with some politico, who to be frank, was nothing more than a foil for others. I as "the chump," believed her whines and moans about all the things I could not be. She told me my failings regularly and I, being in love, actually believed her. Believed everything she said that was wrong with me, including my tastes in the bedroom. Apparently, I was too dominant, too willing to try things new - the truth was I would have tried anything to get a sex-life. I was young, vibrant, in love and I wanted to make love to the woman I loved. The only problem was she didn't love me. And I, fool that I was, had been too blind to see it.

The arguments had been fierce and personally very painful to endure until eventually we hardly spoke at all. But as they say what doesn't kill you always makes you stronger. We spoke little save for a sort of grunting, lack of discussion - that became the norm. In the end the whole of her presence began to weigh down upon me like a heavy weight being placed upon my chest crushing the air out of me.

On reflection I think she had very deep seated issues, so deep and so obscure that I could not fathom them. I was too young, too stupid and at first I thought the problem lay with me. Am I too sexually demanding, maybe couples in their twenties only do have sex once a month? We went months without the simple pleasure and warmth of each other. I certainly would have liked more - she however, would have liked less and she told me so. So the once a month became once every three months, and that turned into rarely and that in turn became almost never, and only grudgingly if an argument were created. In the end I couldn't be bothered to argue and let the matter lie.

I am ashamed to say that once, just the once, I employed the services of a young lady who managed to enjoy my entry into her, or at least that was what she told me as I paid her. She had even given me a few extras along the way and shown me the true meaning and capacity of an oral orgasm, mine. The explosive climax she had imparted had ripped me apart; it had been a steep learning curve - not just physically, but mentally too. The guilt I experienced was absolutely appalling. The consequence, I never visited her or any of her kind again. I began to become sullen and withdrawn as our marriage had become a dilapidated sham.

It wasn't until years after we had tied the knot that I realised her true feelings gravitated toward the same sex. But, and here was the rub, her father, a man of the cloth, often spoke of his aberration of homosexuality. Maybe he sensed, or maybe he even knew that she had a real urge which no marriage could change. A man of his generation, a man of his time, perhaps he thought that she could be turned back toward the path of heterosexuality. The problem was that his wonderful daughter hated me , despite the children she bore me; despised men and has now set up home with some grotesque who acted like a male at all times.

Now as the dust settles and time heals over the wound, I realise she was just as unhappy as me. Time and dishonesty destroyed any chance of her happiness, and her unhappy predicament ripped up mine as well. But much water has passed under the bridge, and I now realise that the opposite of love is not hate it is indifference. Hate requires passion and an interest in another human being, as time passes I find that I simply don't care enough to expend any more energy in that direction. I am not bitter; I am not sad; I am not even vengeful; the truth is I just don't care anymore. The past is a foreign country and I don't live there anymore. That was why I got this job – indifference; cold, calm and calculating indifference.

There is a popular saying that what does not kill you makes you stronger and now I was rising from the ashes. Having been told I was, "shit in bed," and a "selfish pig," time and a divorce had allowed me to meet a guardian angel. This angel slept with whomever she wished and told me so. She never once made pretensions of love, but when we were in bed she put me back together. To her I am eternally grateful. Unlike my wife, who hated the act of physical union, this woman adored it. She understood her body and mine better. When in the afterglow we talked, she told me of her divorce, of how her ex had blamed her and I realised that she too had been maligned. Most worthy of all she told me that I was good in bed, that I made her orgasm, made her have multiple orgasms. And this woman wasn't afraid to scream if she reached one or dig her nails into my flesh to express her lust.

I withdrew from the mess of marriage and post marital

trauma and now had taken a job working in the vast library of Waldstein; doing the job that had once been started by Casanova himself. I was hoping to learn the art of seduction, the art of sex in fact.

Oh the marriage? Eventually my wife took time to avoid me and I did the same of her. If we had had no children I think the marriage would have been over many years earlier, and I didn't realise just how unhappy I was until it all fell apart. I had clung to the useless notion like a man possessed, as a drowning man clutches at straws. I think mostly because my parents never managed to hold it together for more than a few years.

I remember how she would rush to bed to avoid being awake when I ascended the stairs. Or if I decided to take an early night she would dilly-dally for over an hour, purposefully waiting me out. As for a sex life that stopped ages before the communication stopped and the divorce started. There is nothing quite as insulting to a man as a woman wiping her genitals post copulation with the words, "Err disgusting stuff," coming from her sneering post-coital mouth. Temper that with a sucking through the teeth or a look of disgust, similar to the face one might show after the sucking on a lemon and I am sure you, the reader, will understand.

I hope there are not too many out there who have experienced the dull ache and pain of rejection on this scale. If so I can only say – leave now, run, run as fast as you can.

It matters not a jot if you are male or female, run, run in every direction and hope in the chaos you run into something nice – I did. My freedom and there I found myself.

* * *

"You're going where?" My friend had asked; when he heard of the assignment I had taken.

"Czechoslovakia," I had replied.

"What Prague?"

"Nope I'm going out to the middle of nowhere. A castle – Duchcov Castle to be precise."

"Right," he had been dubious. "What the bloody hell for?"

"Cataloguing," I had given as a guarded reply. "I need some time to get my head back on straight. I'm done with all this crap."

"Right," he had answered again, his voice full of sarcasm. "That's what you do that's your job isn't it? So, I didn't think you were going there to shoot a porn movie. Though," he pondered, "some of those Czech girls are lovely. You could buy us a couple and bring them back."

"You really are an exploitative bastard aren't you?"

"Yep." He raised his left hand to show the absence of a wedding ring. "Free as a bird and not all screwed up like you." He had paused, "So spill, what's the crack then?"

"I'm going to catalogue some of the stuff belonging to Count Karl Waldstein. He was very influential in the arts during the nineteen century. Mozart and Goethe and Casanova all had his patronage."

Jim had burst out laughing at that. We called him Jim, because he called himself that. I think it was because he had such an old fashioned first name that he settled for the middle one. Anyway he was laughing - laughing at me.

"There are some diaries and all sorts which Casanova left behind after his death; they have only just come to light. And there is something better letters to Lorenzo Da Ponte, that's Mozart's librettist to you. Apparently there are some ideas which seemed to have been incorporated into in Mozart's Don Giovanni."

He seemed unimpressed, "How long do you reckon on being away?" he had asked.

"Six months maybe a year?"

"Holy shit, what sort of cataloguing are you going to be doing?"

"Going through several trunks of letters and other artefacts. Things that had been stored for years."

"What sort of things?"

I had shrugged because I didn't really know. That had been eighteen months ago and so far I had only scratched the surface.

To be honest I hadn't really kept in contact and I had not even looked at a Czech girl in that time. I had done with women and they had done with me. To be honest I was kind of glad, it released me to think about other things and to get my head back together.

I remember the day as if it were yesterday - April the 4th. I had been sifting through a lot of papers when I found a small leather bound notebook with some of the pages missing. I had seen this kind of book before but in Florence rather than Venice. The pages looked as if they had been worn by use. I knew at once it had been Casanova's; knew his hand which was small and pinched, not at all like his extrovert character. The words and letters seemed introverted and introspective and he was writing in Italian, and not French. In fact it had the feel of a Bronte story book, a Gondal, the writing was so small. I read it from cover to cover: It wasn't a continuous text, more the random jottings of ideas, phrases and notions which gave insight into the man's character. As I read it I began to fully understand the psyche of the myth.

At first I thought it was random, but as I read there were what seemed to be recurring themes, incantations and, as I thought, spells within the pages. I knew Casanova had been accused of occult activity because of some of his lucky medical prognoses and the fact that after the fated duel he had such a bad injury to his left hand that physicians advocated amputation. Casanova however, had healed himself, with a combination of strapping, garlic washes and a variety of cleansing purgatives and bleeding. Bleeding I thought would have weakened him, but Casanova had bled the wound and not his whole body. The result: The infection and puss had been cleaned away by the flow of blood and miraculously his hand had been saved. True one or two of the fingers were bent, and the scars were pronounced but in the main he saved the hand and confounded medics at the same time. Their reasoning - he was a devil worshipper, a man in league with the dark forces. This diary proved he had been involved in some way, shape or form in some ancient society and I was the first to find it. Find it at the bottom of an old trunk that had probably not been opened since the Lothario's death.

One word kept reappearing in Casanova's notes – Rosenkreutz.

The book also contained some sketches. Mostly of buildings and locations in Venice. Locations associated with the Carnival. There in the middle was a very detailed sketch of a mask - a carnival mask. I had seen one like it before. They were all over the markets stalls of Venice, but this one had something different. The expression was strange, neither jolly nor frightening, but there was something about it, it had an eerie look.

I thumbed through the pages delicately. There were references to other works which were not known to me, but they must have been known to him – to Casanova. It was as if, in his duties as Librarian, he had indexed and collated his research. The name Christian R appeared, and a strange design of three balls over a crucifix entwined by a rosebush. It was as if Casanova were playing with an idea, a notion, and a design.

There was no one to tell and no one to involve. I was alone and for a brief moment I felt connected to the past through the words which the man had written.

The more I read the more I began to understand. His notes made it clear that he was a man of conquest and by that I do not mean he was a rapist or some form of bondage and sado-masochism freak. His conquest harked back to the knights of old or at least to a romanticised concept of chivalry. Like Goethe, the German poet and inventor of Romanticism as a style, he saw sexual conquest as a manner of protection.

I was enthralled now and I read his notes aloud. "First the man must rescue his damsel in distress. Have a genuine hand in helping her. Then he must show that he cares for her by protecting her; then as is only natural with women they will reward him for that service. Most will reward by the giving of themselves and therein lay the conquest. After all what greater gift can a woman bestow upon a man than to allow him to enter her. Allow him to experience the ultimate and intense pleasure that there is, by the mingling of his fluids within her. "

It seemed to me that Casanova understood the inner workings

of the female soul. "Never," he had written, "should a man confound and confuse the art of dutiful reward with words of love. The art of seduction," he continued, "is one in which the mistress takes a more than active part."

That I found very strange. Words of love were seen as a weakness? Most women, Casanova claimed, did not respond to them, they liked to be rescued?

I shut the notebook and pushed it into the thigh pocket of my cargo pants. I must have done so without thinking, an almost subconscious act. I carried on sifting through the papers. The more I looked, the more I found, pictures of the same mask, drawn from several different angles.

There were also accounts of the role of the Chamberlain to the Emperor. Casanova's notes on the Chamberlain's policies for the Emperor. It made for an interesting read about Casanova the man, as opposed to Casanova the myth. In truth he was a bit on the dull side, though his natural good looks and confident temperament made him the target for women.

Week followed week and eventually the cataloguing began to draw to a close and I felt I had achieved a great deal. Twenty four months of work had helped me to heal, and I had learned so much about women without ever having been involved with a single one. My confidence had increased and I thought that the next Venice carnival would see me in attendance.

* * *

"And this one," the shop assistant was saying, "is 187 Euro."

"But the one I am after looks a bit like this." I drew a rough outline on the tissue paper laid out on the counter before me. The drawing was crude and lacked the finesse of Giacomo Casanova, but I think it sort of had the notion of the expression.

The assistant was shaking her head and shrugging her shoulders. It was clear that the drawing was not quite as good as I thought it was. If truth be known it was pretty dire.

That had been the fifteenth or sixteenth shop I had entered that day, and to be honest I had lost count; my luck was running low and my patience even lower. Casanova's mask looked unique. There were many which looked similar but none had quite the same look. If I try to explain in words I probably won't be able to. The only way is to see it for yourself and try as I might I could not find one that looked the same as it.

I had started at the Rialto Bridge and gone through Campo San Bartolomeo; stopped at the statue of Carlo Goldoni, to get my bearings; then continued walking down Merceria di San Salvatore into San Zulian toward the church. I stopped every few feet to study the masks for sale. There were many, many with the likeness of the devil, or some ancient courtesan, but nothing like the sketch I had seen, and I had done my homework. I had looked up and researched the order of the Rosy Cross, Rosicrucianism to you and me. Freemasons, The Knights Templar and all sorts of strange organisations had been crossing my path, each one with a secret or some form of bloodshed in their history. The more I researched the less happy I became. It appeared that this group, to which Casanova belonged, believed in alchemy. But they also had other views on life, Christianity and the universe in general. They were like the Freemasons, but not, only more secretive, but not, and it was from them that some of the Masonic rituals were devised, or altered, or subsumed. This mystic philosophy seemed to have its roots in the Luneberg area of Germany around Braunschweig, the point at which the ideology of Nazism derived or was perverted. It was true that all things were interlinked, but the more I found linking the less I liked.

I was beginning to wonder more and more if the Casanova mask even existed at all, that was until I entered a shop on Campo Specchieri. There a fat woman with chubby hands greeted me and immediately began the ritual of attempting to sell me a mask. For some reason, still unknown to me, I showed her Casanova's original notebook sketch rather than my own interpretation. The book had been my constant companion since the cataloguing. I know what you will say – that I stole it? Well if I did I never intended to do so. At first it remained in my pocket. Then it went onto the bedside table, for night time reading at the castle and then when Hildegard, the maid, had packed my things she must have placed the book in my suitcase thinking it was mine.

A simple mistake. Once home I simply forgot to send it back. Foolish I know but at least truthful.

The reaction was instant. The fat woman looked over my shoulder as if to check there were no further customers behind me and raised a single finger to her lips. I was stunned by the immediate reaction which the drawing created. Her face was beaming and her eyes were shining; for a moment I thought she was aroused. She certainly seemed excited. Then she wrote an address on a piece of paper which she kissed and then slapped it into my left palm. The Rosa House, Palazzo Zorzi, and then she was half ushering me, half pushing me out of the door; like some lover who had covertly done the deed I was now dismissed and standing totally bemused on the ancient cobbles. Once fully outside she immediately shut and bolted the entrance making the closed sign to any new customers. I looked back at her through the glass and she appeared petrified - she flicked the back of her hand at me as if shoo-flying me away. Then the blinds fell, but I thought I could hear her laughing.

That was, to say the least, the strangest part of this tale. She was a chubby Italian mamma, but she had the look of a wanton harlot in her eyes the minute I had shown her the drawing. I cursed my stupidity in not showing the drawing earlier, but her attitude is what struck me the most. She ushered me out as if she might not be able to control herself if I stayed a moment longer. Her eyes had sparkled with a glow which increased the size of her pupils. She was feeling sexy and she knew it.

Outside the shop I dug into the rucksack I was carrying and found my map. Quickly I gauged the series of left and right hand turns I would have to make to reach Palazzo Zorzi.

Then I was off, marching through the alleyways and over the small bridges which spanned the canals, checking once or twice that I was in the right place. I estimated no more than fifteen minutes. Several times I had to make detours because I could not cross where I wanted to. The result was confusion. Despite the map I was never sure if I was in the right place at the wrong time, or the wrong place at the right time. What should have been a short hop turned into a three hour marathon. Whenever I thought I was there, I had to change tack and walk back over my route. Anyone who knows Venice will be aware that there are little courtyards and alleys and walkways everywhere. On that afternoon I think I travelled most of them.

Then after turning endlessly left and then right and back again and losing my sense of bearing, I saw a sign which I instantly recognised. It was a plaque on a wall. A crucifix wrapped in thorns and rose blooms with three globes suspended above it. It looked old, tired and weather beaten, an ancient symbol built into an ancient arch. There was no shop front though, just a grim narrow alley which appeared dark and threatening even in the full daylight. Alley might not be the right word - tunnel, it looked like a tunnel. I took a step forward and the tunnel seemed to open almost instantly into a courtyard entirely obscured from view and fully enclosed.

Bright pink blooms clung to terraces and balconies and everywhere the scent of rose hit my nostrils. Wisteria climbed high against the walls and the colour combination of pink and blue set against the red terracotta of tiles atop grey stone was stunning. Stunning enough to almost take my breath away. It was the most beautiful little courtyard I have ever seen. Equal to those I had seen in Florence or Rome and typically Italian. I thought I could hear Puccini somewhere in the distance, a tenor; Pavarotti perhaps and there was water running from a fountain, clear blue water like a mountain stream spewed from the mouth of a gargoyle into a rock pool. Light fell into the place, and the contrast to the forbidding entrance astounded me.

In the far corner sat a man, clothed in pure black. His hair was silver grey, long but full and his hands looked old, gnarled and twisted like the roots of an ancient tree; he was working on some delicate matter, it appeared to be a carnival mask. As I drew closer he began carefully laying gold leaf onto the face of the eyeless form. Light bounced from the object, and it was truly beautiful. I recognised the face, but could not give it a name. Like some long lost friend recognised at a glance, it was known but unknown at the same time.

The dark stranger spoke without raising his head. "You've come for your mask I suppose?" he enquired. "It is finished, there."

The stranger lifted it to show me. It was beautiful, possibly the most beautiful thing I had ever seen. Red and gold embroidery adorned the paper base while bells hung about it and the pure gold glowed with vibrancy. There were diamonds at the hair line and pearls around the neck. I could only guess at the value of it.

"Err," I stumbled, "well I suppose I have. Is that one for me?"

"Do you have the ledger?"

"The ledger?" I asked, confused.

"The book, the one you stole, the one with my drawings in. You should have left it where it was. It was safe there. I knew where it was, even if it was stolen. But oh no, you had to meddle, meddle, meddle, meddle. " His voice was angular, sharp and piercing like both his eyes and his hooked nose. "You know what I mean; if you want this mask you will have to give me the book."

"I have a picture," I offered.

"Not good enough," he shrieked like a wailing seagull, "not enough."

"I can get you the book," I offered.

"And I can make you a mask; a mask to get you any woman you desire, but first the book."

"But why must I give you the book?" I asked.

"It is mine, I want it back," he affirmed.

"You could have taken it back at any time," I said, "if you knew where it was."

"I knew where it was," he replied. "And Casanova knew where it was. Knew it was safe in that place. A place where I could not go. He knew that." The dark man smiled at me and I stepped back. His teeth were sharp and pointed and the canines were long and extended. I could swear he growled like a panther under his breath. "Now you have stolen my book from that filthy little thief, I want it back."

"How do I know it is your book?" I asked in a ridiculous manner.

"Because I say it is?"

"Even then why should I give it to you? I didn't steal it, I found it."

"Because," he paused, his lips concealing the teeth once again. "I can get you a date with Hedy Lamar, Marilyn Monroe in fact anyone you choose. I will trade that with you for the book. Once you wear your mask you will be able to see what each woman wants and by providing it, she will be yours. The mask will give you powers like those that were given to Casanova himself. I can give that to you. I did it once, I can do it again. Every woman that sees the mask falls in love with the wearer. This will be the most valuable possession that you ever acquire." His voice changed and became threatening, "Besides that book is my book. It is full of my incantations my alchemy and my ideas. Your little friend Casanova stole it from me and now I want it back. "

He rose and stood before me and the air around me began to thicken and I found it difficult to reason. The heat, the perfume, the conversation all became too much. Excess, sensual excess are the only words I could use to describe it.

"Where is Casanova's mask?" I asked.

"He destroyed it."

"Why?"

"That you will have to find out for yourself," he laughed.

"What you are offering me, you offered to him didn't you?" I blurted.

"And he wished for that so much, so much, so so much, that he got it. I made his wish come true. So too do you."

"But he destroyed it - why?"

"Do you believe in God?" the dark stranger suddenly asked. "Casanova did. He believed in both heaven and hell and we had a bargain. Only that thief broke the bargain and he stole my book. I gave him all those women, all that beauty and he stole from me." His voice deepened and the words became snarls. "Give me my book," he demanded.

"If it's yours why don't you take it?" I asked lamely.

"You must give it to me," he snarled, "of your own free will or the bargain is not a bargain. I am not a monster - I am a trader. Trade with me? The ledger for the mask, one simple exchange and we shall all be happy. We Venetians are all traders."

He was passing the mask to me now with his left hand, while my right had released the note book from my pocket. That persuasive voice was leading me and I could see no reason as to why we should not trade. The mask was beautiful and as I touched it I could almost feel a surge of confidence hit me like a shot of adrenalin.

His right hand grasped the notebook and the exchange was complete. The bargain struck.

"Perfect," he finally said, after leafing through the book to check all the pages were in tact.

I nodded.

"It all seems in order in here," he said, his relief absolutely apparent.

"I have not damaged it, nor torn any pages out, if that is what you are suggesting."

"Did you see the sign above the gateway?" he quizzed.

"Yes," I answered, "but I thought it was an arch, a tunnel."

"But look at all this beauty, is that found at the end of a tunnel?"

I shrugged, looking carefully at the mask.

"Well you should know that is my sign," he stated.

"And just who are you then to have such a coat of arms?" I asked.

"That is no coat of arms," he replied.

"Then what is it?"

"That is the sign of the most powerful of all angels. I give you what I gave to Giacomo Casanova."

"What?"

"Knowledge, dear boy, knowledge. For fifty years and one day the bargain will hold."

I looked at the mask and as I did it changed and the face became demonic, distorted and gnashed teeth at me like a living creature. For one brief moment I thought it might actually bite me.

"You have fifty years and one day," he laughed, "and then we shall meet again. Try your new face," he motioned. "Look at your new visage in any looking glass and see what you have become. What you were has gone and what you are will," he paused smiling, "remain."

As I did what he asked two beautiful women appeared at the entrance to the courtyard – both saw me and giggled impulsively beckoning me to follow.

erotique fantastique

For those that can,
&
For those that do

Erotique Fantastique

"Pass the sugar Tin Tin, there's a good chap," Michael Stokes barked. As he made a nodding motion with his head. "I need something sweet to warm me cockles. That bloody wind is brass monkeys. Christ what a place?" He looked around the drab interior which was brown and greasy from the long lack of decoration. "Who the hell would want to live in a dump like this?" He continued, without pausing for a reply, "Smells like death. I bet the owner lives over the shop Christ it's damp and dreary, what a place to spend your life."

"But the food she is good no?" came a reply, through a mouthful of food.

Inside the café the air smelt of cooking fat, sweat and a disinfectant which reminded Pancardi of the smells in Zoos when he was a boy in Italy. Briefly his mind hopped back into his childhood; a world of warm summers, innocent frog catching and the rich odour of newly mown grass. Tuscany and the tall larches, which swayed in the gentle winds that ran down from the mountains: It was a home he would always cherish. As a boy he had known dry summers pungent with the scent of lemons and the leathery feel of ripe olives. In this place now, it seemed a lifetime away and Stokes, his companion, was not averse to voicing his strong opinions, which though often funny, did make him think of home.

Stokes was the kind of man who would fearlessly stand in the middle of a crowd of black shirt fascists and claim he was a mulatto homosexual with a resounding belief in socialism. He used offence as a weapon to disarm; and, as he had told the Italian, "Get the bastards angry, it gets them unnerved and when they're unnerved they make mistakes. Usually whopping great bigguns, which we can use to good effect."

Stokes was old school, a man with an evaluative mind. A

maverick, someone who hated sycophants, bullies, liars, thieves and the other assorted, rag-tag and bob tails, as he called them, that made up the flotsam and jetsam of humanity. He was cynical, truthful, sharp, decisive and above all principled. The thought of corruption appalled him and the "new man," now entering the police force made him yearn for retirement.

He studied the men who scrabbled to be seen, even if they made little discernable impact on any investigation; called them empty vessels, but this Italian he liked - liked a lot.

"What a servant am I then?" The dark-haired man in the gabardine raincoat replied. He was slim, dark eyed, with a swarthier skin than Stokes'. His teeth shone as he grinned, "You want a slave? Get one of your own lackeys and not Pancardi, he is no slave." The man spoke with a slight Italian accent and in the third person, as if making comment upon a stranger, but passed the sugar anyway.

"On this case you are here to observe, learn how to be an excellent copper. Got it? I haven't got time to ponce around with false niceties. Could you possibly pass the sugar, if you are so willing etc. Besides I want to be out of this cold country as fast as possible." Stokes was not a believer in small talk and unnecessary politeness.

"Well," Pancardi pondered and grinned, "I may be a foreigner here, but how do you say? Kiss of the arse?"

"Well you got that wrong you garlic head." Stokes was smiling back, "It's kiss my arse. You can kiss my arse."

"And that Pancardi he would never do. Kiss the arse of a man whose arse she is like the rook's nest. How do you say? All shit and sticks." Stokes was smiling broadly as his own sage words were repeated back at him. "No you will never have the kiss of the arse from Pancardi. For that, one of your minions you must get, one of those boys." He nodded toward two uniformed officers who were now huddled over their cups of tea as they warmed their hands; clasping the china mugs as if they were precious golden chalices.

Giancarlo Pancardi looked at the man from Essex; studied his manner, his bravado and the way in which he ate. His knife and fork flashed across the plate, rather like a bulldozer bucket shovelling earth; eternally hurried like a man willing a heart attack upon himself. Only in this case it was bacon, eggs, hash browns, mushrooms and black pudding which the bulldozer demolished: The classic fry up.

"The food she is good no?" he asked a second time. He too was enjoying the greasy weight, and the feeling of satisfaction which was hanging heavily in his stomach. Since being in Britain he had learned to love the simplicity of a good breakfast, and although he didn't yet know it, it was to become one of his favourite indulgences. An indulgence he would advocate to all of his Italian colleagues and anyone who worked with him on a future case.

Stokes nodded. "Food's great," he mumbled as he ate.

"So why do you hate this place so?" Pancardi asked, as he lifted a morsel of runny egg and ketchup to his lips.

"It's the bloody weather Tin Tin, and it's the bloody weather," Stokes replied. "Who the hell wants to live here? Certainly not you lot. You don't see Italians clambering to get into the highlands and islands. Nope, you lot have got it right, sit in the sun and drink wine and eat ice-cream."

Pancardi nodded in reply and wiped his face on a paper napkin. The only indulgence to manners in the Smokey Joe café.

Stokes continued, "Half the time it pisses down and the other half it's fog. And when it's not rain and fog, it's dark - it's a miserable place."

"But the scenery is nice, the lakes and the mountains..."

"Oh really," Stokes laughed, "scenery? You want to talk to me about scenery? Just take a look at those two." He nodded once again toward the two uniformed officers. He pointed with his knife, which he held in his right hand as if he were conducting an orchestra and about to bring in some woodwind section. "They're so bleedin' cold that if they were made of brass their bollocks would clang every time they walked."

"Well I think the scenery she is beautiful. There is space here and places enough for a man to breathe. I would like to walk in the mountains, in the heather."

"Oh my God, it's all yokels, ploughs and animal shit up there. And they're not mountains they're foot hills. I've seen bigger bumps on a Brick Lane tart's chest." Stokes was a city boy through and through, and his language showed it. "Half the time they play spot the stranger and the rest is taken up with stone the idiot, or tip the cow. Even the pubs are empty, that's if you can find one. Maybe there's one called The Slaughtered Lamb, you know, for the odd bit of nocturnal lycanthropic activity. It's like Briga-bloody-doon. That's if you can find the place in all the mist and don't step in the sheep shit first."

"Sheeps?" Pancardi replied.

"Sheep," Stokes corrected, grinning.

Pancardi smirked, he knew that Stokes was frustrated, as frustrated as he was, frustrated by the lack of progress in the case. "We must solve of the case then; then we can go home to the warm south, no?"

Pancardi's English was getting better. He had now spent nearly six months in Britain working alongside some of the best that London could offer. The officers had nicknamed him Tin Tin, because of his accent and the small white dog which went everywhere with him. A small Bichon style terrier, hardly a mans dog, as they frequently told him. But Mostro as Pancardi named him was precisely that, a monster; he was fiercely loyal and most certainly able to assert himself when necessary even against the big police Alsatians. As they ate Mostro sat beside his master, resting and waiting, though the Italian let a few scraps of bacon fat and a whole sausage be eaten from his fingertips. The English in their typical xenophobic manner had lumped Belgians and Italians into the one simple bracket of "Johnny Foreigner." Pancardi spotted this early and pushed his difference into their faces. On every occasion he could, he ate the most heavily garlic laced sausage he could find. Then he had found the most amazingly aromatic Parmesan cheese and grated it into an oregano, basil and mozzarella salad. After that he sat and ate it while Stokes began his lunch of plain cheese or corned beef and pickle rolls.

Stokes respected the Italian for his blatant disregard of

authority. Respected his spirit and balls and the original terse business relationship had become warmer as a result; and now, after only a few months they were firm friends. Friends that drank together and had lunch at home with Stokes' wife. This Giancarlo Pancardi had proved himself a worthwhile copper - Stokes trusted the man. He was good at his job, hated sycophants, just like he himself did, and he thought carefully. He never dismissed a thing, even the smallest or crazy ideas from junior or uniformed officers he considered, and Stokes liked that too. It was a genuine humility, which only those who were good at what they did could afford and Pancardi had it in spades. Not once had Stokes heard Pancardi be dismissive and already the men on his team respected him. Foreigner or not he had won over the team and as a result the jokes and badinage had been lively and fun rather than serious. They were beginning to say that he had a sixth sense, a sense like he could become the criminal; step inside their brain. Especially murderers – those he was almost related to.

"The bloody thing is Carlo, this Lord's son disappearing?"

Pancardi loaded his fork, "Perhaps there is a connection, we have missed?" he offered.

"Christ I hope so because we've been all over the place and if it hadn't been for the cameras on the road we'd never have been up here. Lucky for us the silly bugger was speedin' really."

"The others they have vanished in cities, no?"

Stokes nodded. "Two in London; one in Reading another in Southampton, that's four and now this chap, in ruddy Scotland. Scotland of all places. The MO is the same. Car found abandoned, no note, no blood, no struggle, just vanished."

"Aliens?" Pancardi chortled.

"I'll give you aliens you bugger," Stokes smirked. "But it might as well be bloody aliens for all we know. How can so many men can just vanish and us have nothing?"

Pancardi considered again, "They must be linked in some way," he said, "some way that we have not yet considered. We've missed something."

"Bollocks," Stokes chirped. "We've been over and over this

and I'm now beginning to think they are all unrelated. Or we have a first class bonkeroony nutter on the loose." He reloaded his tea with more sugar, "Coincidence? I know it sounds crazy but these things do happen."

"No they do not," Pancardi replied coldly. His black coffee was weak and clung to the cup like an invalid. "This is awful," he said.

"Tell me about it."

"Not the case, the coffee."

Stokes let out a laugh which the uniformed officers reacted to. They too were beginning to doubt the wisdom of the search around Scotland.

"Right Tin Tin what's the score? What the Christ have we missed?"

Pancardi's voice lowered and he replayed for the twentieth time the facts as they knew them.

"The men they were all professional? One was an artist, one a doctor, one a lecturer in mathematics, the other a nuclear scientist and now this one." He paused, "The son of a Lord no less, pretty as a picture and as daft as a brush. Handsome but, how do I say?"

"Thick, typical landed gentry," Stokes offered.

"These we have in Italy too. More money than sense. The fashionistas."

"So what's the connection? Something binds them?" asked Stokes, as he fed bacon scraps to the small white dog that now appeared at his feet.

"That's the problem," Pancardi replied, "there doesn't seem to be one. At first I thought it was intelligence. That is until this last one. Then I thought age, but they are spread between their late twenties and early forties. They did not know each other, they are not related. The only things they have in common is the fact that they are men and eminent in their chosen field."

"Not much to go on is there?" Stokes replied.

"But," Pancardi continued, "they are missing. Oh and they have families, children. Apart from this last one he is single and childless. This is the one which, how do you say, upsets the apple cart. Until him I would have said someone is collecting these men for a purpose. What that purpose is I cannot see."

"Right, all of these guys vanish. Nothing taken from their bank accounts. No note, no struggle, nothing missing, no body, no DNA in the cars. It's just like they've been lifted, spirited away."

"So it must be aliens then?" Pancardi laughed.

"Fuck right off," was Stokes' intellectual reply. "Look," he continued, "there's got to be a motive, only we're not seeing it. There's got to be a link. It's probably something so simple that we just don't want to see it. Ockhams Razor?"

"Si Marco Aurelio no?"

"Precisely. The simple answer is usually the correct one and all that."

"So why is his car here in Scotland?" Pancardi was asking rhetorical questions of himself now. "Simple, if you know the answer."

"Well done Sherlock!"

"Phone records?"

"Nothing."

"Notes, letters?"

"None."

"Nothing at their offices?"

"Nope."

"No struggle?"

"Nope." Stokes was following along the pathway carved by Pancardi's thought process. "So they must have known their attacker? Or the link is so meaningless as to be random."

"But what if there was no attack? What if they went willingly?"

"Come on Carlo, nobody just walks off and drops their life. This is not viable. One maybe but five? Nope it just can't be that. That's like a turkey voting for Christmas."

"Religious sect? They could have been met by someone who persuaded them to drop their life and start a fresh one. Like that guitar player Jeremy Spencer, you know from The Fleetwood Mac."

"That has got to be the dopiest solution I have ever heard. And anyway he didn't vanish he joined some happy clappers. Some Jesus freaks got hold of him and messed his head up and everyone knew where he went. And it's Fleetwood Mac, not The Fleetwood Mac. "

"See people do this all the time?"

"No they don't, only fuckwits and people who are all messed up in the head with LSD do that. You know the rock star who's all messed up because they got fame and fortune too early or when they least expected it. Then they're all messed up because they begin to believe their own PR bullshit. You know, destiny and all that shite, when just like everything it's chaotic luck. The one in how many sperm are there? And only one gets through and so everything is chance, that's the law of the universe. There's no order, no big idea, no omnipotent being with a map of your life which links with mine. It's all fucking chance. Scares most people to death just to think like that. You know, the person that gets killed by the bus that blew up because they left the office too early or too late. There's an old saying," Stokes paused, "if the dog hadn't stopped for a shit he'd have caught the rabbit. Now that's what the universe is like. One minute you're in café drinking coffee and the next you walk into something just because it's there. Only that something's got a gun and you get shot. Lights out, game over and all because of chance – it's a bunch of bollocks really."

Pancardi could sense a storm brewing in Stokes' and just let him get on with it.

"It's like the blues thing, Slim Harpo," the Englishman continued, "Robert Johnson, Muddy Waters, Skip James and all the others, bashin' out tunes on beat up guitars - getting paid peanuts. Keith Richard said Muddy was painting the ceiling at Chess records trying to earn an extra buck or two when he first met him. Then along comes Chuck Berry and Richard Penniman, that's Little Richard to you, and they make a few quid; but even these guys are not superstars, not like, The Rolling Stones. You see the blues became a white boy phenomenon and Eric Clapton became God. He just played the guitar louder and with more power than the delta bluesmen. In fact those bluesmen never really stood a chance, intelligent and unusual and talented - but black. And me I loved them all, every blues band going. But I could still see the way things were going."

That was what Pancardi loved about Stokes, his skewed logic. He loved the music of the black Americans, the jazz and the blues, but he hated foreigners.

As the café cleared, the policemen realised that the whole investigation had stalled and they had to admit that the jaunt to Scotland had yielded no results.

Mostro, Pancardi's small white dog at Stokes' feet, sat bolt upright as two women entered the café. Both looked dishevelled and both were dressed identically; not as much like twins but in clothes of the same style and era. One was in her mid to late fifties while the other was late teens or twenties. Pancardi struggled with trying to assess whether they were mother and daughter. There seemed to be no family likeness.

As the women came into the café they called to the owner who promptly came out to collect the basket of eggs which they were obviously delivering. They were dressed in long skirts which were almost ankle length, floral and bold in colour. They wore sandals, but their feet were wrapped in thick woollen socks. On their heads they had woollen berets, and around their necks scarves of what looked like scrap wool. Multi-coloured and long and wrapped in great swags which tumbled over Afghan coats.

They smiled as they talked with the owner and looked every bit the part of 1967 and the summer of love, only this wasn't sunny California; this wasn't phantastic LA. This was Scotland - and it was winter.

"How's it going ladies?" the café owner asked.

"Fine," the younger woman laughed. "Mary's pregnant again and Jilly wants a baby too."

"I thought there weren't any men up on that commune of yours?" he replied.

"There aren't."

"So who's makin' all these babies then?"

"Wouldn't you like to know?" the older woman chortled. "There's plenty of men around who want to give a donation to us. You know to make the world go round?"

"And you never know," the younger of the two women smiled, "maybe we'll ask you for a donation one day. Mind you the way you are, it would have to be hand delivered. If you know what I mean baby." She winked at the man and seductively licked her lips as if she were about to deliver a deep languid kiss. Then finally she pouted a deep soft-mouthed kiss.

The café owner's face reddened and his tongued became thick and unwealdy in his mouth.

Pancardi watched as the two women collected their payment for the eggs, while Stokes buttered some more toast. As both women passed, Stokes hissed the word, "Prick," under his breath. The younger woman heard and shot a long look at the police man before breaking into a bright-eyed smile. In her eyes Stokes could see unborn children and a fecundity which spoke of passion and raw sexual power. He had seen that look behind the eyes of very few women and he knew in an instant that this young girl could do things to men, him included, which only fantasies could fuel.

Pancardi had seen it too, and the uniformed officers too. "Charisma," he said almost inaudibly once they had left the building.

"Sex appeal," Stokes replied, as the two women closed the café door behind them. "Christ she's got it in spades," he continued. "Marilyn had it, and that girl's got it. She could make a man want her even if she was dressed in a sack."

Pancardi nodded, "See it?" he said, "you can taste it in the air around her. Whoever finally gets her will be a very lucky man. You see my friend." He turned to the café owner, who was now standing sorting his eggs. "She is one of those women who can have their pick of the men. Not beautiful, well not classical, but raw and lovely and wild and untameable."

Stokes spluttered into his tea, suppressing a laugh.

"She is what we Italians call a man-eater; and you and me my friend she would chew on and then spit us out."

"She could chew on me any day," one of the uniforms said.

"Bloody hippy traveller or not. She could chew on me, but I'm not so sure I like the spitting out bit."

"No I'd rather she swallowed," the other officer chimed and the room flooded with testosterone and laughter.

"They aren't travellers," the café owner added. "They're from the commune."

"Commune? What is this commune?" Pancardi asked, suddenly side tracked.

The café owner paused and realising, what the officers already knew, that there were no other customers left, apart from the police, he walked over to impart his gossip.

"About fifteen years ago a group of them hippies bought an old farm and barns up in the high valley. About twenty of them there was, mostly women. Well there were some fellas too but there was an accident and two of them was killed fellin' trees. Then a third dies in the winter and, I think but I'm not certain, one or two of the others just took off."

"So what's the problem?" Stokes asked.

"Well," the café owner lowered his voice, "they started off doing farm work and some of them did cleaning at local houses, and the pub. Spud harvests, berry picking, and all the jobs that the locals didn't want to do. Like the Poles that we got now. They worked like crazy and rebuilt the house and the barns and made the place very presentable by all accounts. Lots of the local lads and some city boys worked up there and the rumour was they was getting' paid in kind, rather than cash. One guy used to come in here regular, told me some of them was so keen on gettin' a belly full of arms and legs that he could hardly get no work done some days. He told me that he shared two of them," he flashed his eyes from detective to detective, "drained his balls seven times in four hours."

"And because they fuck some bragging nipper half to death you believe the silly rumours? That's pub talk, some bullshit bragged in a pub because one of the guys was lucky enough to get laid," said Stokes unimpressed.

"Then one by one they all start to get pregnant." The man wiped his greasy hands in his apron.

"Ah ha, Aliens," Pancardi piped up. "Is the little commune called Midwich?"

Stokes was laughing now, picking up on the John Wyndham reference Pancardi had kicked into the air for his benefit. "And no body owned up to the fucking? Would you? Go home and tell the Mrs that the girls on the commune fuck like rabbits on heat?"

"That's the point, most of the men around here are spoke for," said the café owner.

"And there's all these pretty sticky girls without men, working at survival and," Stokes looked at Pancardi, "getting their naughties?"

"So all the local women they think their men are doing of the fuck?" Pancardi interrupted. The word fuck sounded slightly ridiculous when delivered with an Italian accent – comical almost.

Stokes corrected Pancardi's grammar. "So the local boys were going up there and fucking? And the women around here didn't like that too much I expect?"

"One of the council people," the café owner continued, "went up to check them out. And the DSS too. Turns out they was no men there. And the council thought they was running a whore house. But they couldn't prove a thing, even after the serious crime squad was called in."

"So are they?" asked Stokes.

"Are they what?" enquired the man.

"Running a bloody brothel?"

"Well no one can prove nothing but there's plenty of babies up there and the DSS are looking for the fathers. So far no luck."

Stokes was laughing again now. "Would you own up to it? I mean who's going to own up to fathering a child? What with the Child Support Agency on your tail?" He became thoughtful, "Anyway a standing prick has no conscience. Here end-eth the lesson. If they don't want their men drifting," he was considering his words, "and I suppose your local girls don't like other girls that fuck? On their doorstep so to speak? Well they ought to make sure that their men have no need to go."

The man was wiping the table tops with what could best be

described as a filthy rag now. "Mind you," he said, "there are some real beauties up there. It's like a chicken coop full of fat hens."

"Then we, the foxes," Pancardi joked, "will pay these fat hens a visit? As part of our enquiries of course."

Stokes and the uniformed officers were all laughing raucously as the door opened and a pair of middle-aged women entered and ordered two cups of tea.

"You sly old latin," Stokes whispered under his breath.

Pancardi winked, and gave a wry smile in reply. "Ah my friend, in the ways of women and of love the Italian he is the best in the world." He turned the conversation back to Stokes and his blues, "How does Bo Diddley say? I may look like a farmer no? But I am a lover. "

"Yeah and you can't judge a book by looking at the cover," Stokes automatically replied.

"You see even from Pancardi you can learn something."

"I thought it was a Bo Diddley song?"

"Ah but Pancardi he can make the sense of it, no?"

"I reckon you're nearly as daft as a …"

"As an Essex boy?" Pancardi quipped.

"No, I was going to say door knob, but in this case knob will do just fine."

* * *

At the High hills commune Giancarlo Pancardi got out of the car to open the gate, and stepped straight into some ripe animal dung. As he pushed the gate back, to let the car pass, Mostro, his small white companion, leapt forward to be greeted by a large powerful Newfoundland dog that sniffed him attentively. There was no noise, no barking and once Stokes had parked the car all four stood on a cobbled surface that had once been a stable yard. Mostro had the air of an Alpha male and the other dog seemed to sense the regal intelligence, and sheer guts of the small Italian Bichon. Pancardi knew what dogs seemed to know, that there were two groups, those who would fight and those who would flee and the bigger animal knew that Mostro was a fighter.

"Anyone home?" Stokes called loudly.

The silence was deafening.

"Doesn't look like much of a working farm to me," he commented, turning to Pancardi.

"It depends upon what you call work, no?"

"Yeah, and it doesn't seem like a brothel to me, either. There'd be blokes and cars everywhere."

"I agree," Pancardi confirmed. "The scent of sex would be everywhere."

The two men and the small dog, accompanied by the larger animal, began a small sweep of the various outbuildings - most were empty. One contained hay, another bags of animal feed and a variety of implements including rotivators. In one on the far side of the quadrangle they found two sows with litters and on another aspect three steel cages and a variety of freezers and storage facilities.

"Can I help you gentlemen? This is private property you know?" A soft, siren-like voice sounded behind them. Geraldine Singleton, stood erect and yet strangely languid. Her body barked at both men and she oozed as she walked with the ease of slowly poured treacle. Her whole being oozed sex appeal, and she knew it. Knew precisely what effect she could have on a man - them included.

Mostro barked.

"He's a better guard dog than old Pilot there," the woman said.

"Ah and you are?" Pancardi quipped.

"Jane Eyre," the woman laughed coquettishly; her voice soft and warm like pure Demerara Sugar. It ran into a man's ears like sweet molasses syrup rolling across the tongue. "And I suppose you are Tweedle Dum, and your friend there is Tweedle Dee?"

Stokes suddenly became formal, "Actually Miss Eyre," he flashed his warrant card, "if that is your name? We are Police officers, investigating a mysterious disappearance."

"Pigs? You're pigs, wow, how novel." She read the name,

"Detective Inspector Stokes, most impressive. A detective no less." She paused, "Oh don't tell me the local villagers have been saying that there are strange things going on up here again. People are strange, when you're a stranger."

"Faces look ugly when you're alone," Pancardi chimed.

"Yes and women seem wicked when you're unwanted," the woman continued. "Do," the woman continued, "Do you like the Doors Mr.?"

"Pancardi, please call me Pancardi, Giancarlo Pancardi."

"An Italian, from Rome." She read his warrant card, "And what are you doing here?"

"Officer exchange," he replied. "One of the Met. is now sunning himself in my lovely city, while I am here."

"I wouldn't have thought you old enough to remember The Doors," Stokes added tangentially.

"Oh I don't but that doesn't mean I don't like their music. And couldn't you just love Morrison - Mr. Mojo Risin," the woman retorted. "I like music from the 1960's"

"So we're pigs? But that phraseology also went out with the 1960's didn't it?" Stokes asked.

"I notice you have not got so many pigs here yourself," Pancardi said, trying to bend the direction of the conversation. "Three empty cages?"

"Oh those aren't for keeping pigs, those are for mating. We made a few pounds last year. Pig sells well. You said you were investigating?"

"Yes a young man disappeared some time ago," Stokes replied. "We traced him to Scotland near to here in fact and then we finally found his car, abandoned, in the car park of Nine Wells Hospital."

"Sorry, Nine Wells Hospital?"

"Dundee."

"But that's 70 miles away."

"Yes but we had his car last seen in this vicinity, caught on a speed camera in fact. The image of the driver was blurred but the number plate was clear."

"We only have the one vehicle here; an old VW transporter."

Pancardi wondered why anyone would volunteer the fact that they had no vehicle available. "Where is everybody?" he asked casually.

"Planting out."

"Planting out?"

"Planting out Inspector, root vegetables and young cabbages."

"Pancardi please, call me Pancardi."

"Well Pancardi, we plant and grow and feed ourselves with good food, and any surplus, we sell in the market in Pitlochry that way we have a cash income. We keep sheep and weave our own wool and make our own cloth. We sell that too, and some of the girls do cleaning and housework. From Aberfeldy to Ballinluig and across to Kirkmichael we even do dry stone walling, do you need any done?"

"Afraid not," Stokes replied. "You don't get much call for that in the city of London."

"And where are the children?" Pancardi asked, almost casually-too casually.

"The children are all in the fields too, they have to learn, and some are at school, and the babies go where their mothers go. So it's just lil'ol'me here for now, and that's because I have to start to get the food ready. Do you want to know what we eat too or shall I save that for another time? Oh and my grandfather wore blue underpants when my mother was conceived, but I believe he took them off at the time. Is that it? Or do you need to know what colour I'm wearing? Maybe I'm not wearing any at all?"

"Babies like in Africa, slung over the mother's back?" Pancardi snorted. He could sense that her irritation levels were rising and he tried to turn the conversation away from a systematic grilling.

"Precisely."

"What is your real name then?" Pancardi continued.

"Jane," came the curt reply.

"Jane what?"

"Jane Eyre, that'll do."

"Do you not have a real surname? Something that is not fictional?"

"I do, but I don't really remember it here. You see I'm not some piece of property which has to be tagged. I'm my own person and nobody owns me. Jane will do, that's the name I was born with. It's not he or she or it that I belong to."

Michael Stokes thought that a very strange reply and was just about to ask for the name more firmly when Pancardi interceded.

"Bob Dylan too, nice reference. They told us down in the Smokey Joe's that there were no men up here," he said with a broad grin. "And now we are here I can see that's true."

"Did they tell you we were all gypsies, tramps, whores and thieves too? Though that café owner wants to fuck many of the younger girls, he's always trying his hand. He put his hand up the skirt of one of the younger girls when she was delivering eggs once. Now we only go to the shop in pairs, it's not us that's the animals. That's the problem, the men in the village think we need fucking and their wives and girlfriends think we drop our panties."

Stokes' mind flashed at the use of the word, "panties," and as she spoke he knew she had chosen the word to titillate, to entice. For a brief second he wondered if she wore any, or if she shaped her mound of Venus, or went 1960's au naturale.

"And do the deed. Some have even had the police up here saying we're running a brothel. Listen, we don't need inspecting they do. They ought to keep their men on leashes, because we don't want them sniffing around us like we're bitches on heat. Just because we're a group of women doesn't mean we need servicing. We're quite capable of being on our own thank you."

"But without men how do they become of the pregnant?" Pancardi asked.

"That Inspector is absolutely none of your business. We are not whores and we can fuck who we like when we like. That is not a criminal offence. My cunt, my choice, I don't ask you where you put your cock now do I? And as far as I know fucking for babies is not a criminal offence. So it's none of your business."

Once again Stokes considered her choice of words. Not, prick, willy, slong and then to use the word cunt. He could see she was very confident and knew exactly what she was doing to both of them. She even pouted as she spoke and licked her lips continuously and he sensed rather than knew she was very sexually experienced. He wondered if in some previous incarnation she had worked as a whore or in the porn industry. She lowered her eyes too as she spoke and she set a glare upon him which made his spine tingle. This was a woman who could be described as sex on a stick, and she knew exactly the effect she was having. She even glanced at his fly, but for one second more than was decent and he could feel a slight tightening in that area as she spoke. It was the same reaction he had had to the egg selling girl in the café. To see one woman with raw sex appeal was one thing, to see two in the same place was unusual and he sensed more than knew that there would be others like her in the commune.

"Absolutely right," Stokes smirked as he replied. He was wishing more girls had been as easy in his youth. He had been all for free love, but the girls he had known hadn't. It had been one of those popular myths that girls in the 60's and 70's just screwed when they liked, with whoever they liked. It was one of those long held media myths that the riotous 60's was universal; when reality placed it in a few streets in London, a small canyon in Los Angeles and some remote cafes in Paris and Amsterdam. Reality and myth had become confused and this girl knew that much.

"If I want to take my panties down I will do." She was staring directly into Stokes' eyes and he could feel the hairs on the back of his neck stand to attention. She had the "it" factor and she knew it. Knew the one simple truth that men just wanted to explode inside her. It was something she had known since she was thirteen. Something she had used ever since to get precisely what she desired.

"Of course," said Pancardi sensing his partner's unease. "You may do as you please."

"And I will Inspector," she said, before finally releasing Stokes from the grip of her gaze. She turned her attention to Mostro, "What a cute little dog," she continued, "he's a Bichon isn't he?"

"Si," Pancardi replied.

She rubbed his ear, "Oh what a little darling you are."

* * *

When the remains finally emerged from the soft waters of the Tay River they were hardly recognisable. Both Stokes and Pancardi had long since departed for London and the investigation had stalled. For over six months one or the other had been back and forth looking to find answers to the missing man, now there was a body, or at least part of a body.

The young boys who had been fishing were shocked by what they found on the shore line. It looked to them, at first, like a beached seal. Pink and grey and bloated, but as soon as they discovered that the gelatinous lump had fingers on it they were on their mobile phones. Within minutes the Tayside police were there.

"Body of a man, about the right age Carlo."

Stokes was speaking into his office phone to the Italian who was out and involved in a possible homicide or suicide. A man found totally alone in his house, both he and his dog dead. A man who collected orchids and lived the life of a recluse. The body had been in an advanced state of decomposition when finally entry had been forced. His dog had been found at his feet that too was decomposing.

"Must have been a pretty sight, all those flies and all. Mine's no better, I think it might be our young aristocrat, or part of him, but we'll have to wait for the DNA results to get a positive." Stokes continued, "The local plod reckon he's been dismembered, either by a boat propeller or machinery. I'm going for an axe though. Looks savage."

"This case she is strange too," Pancardi replied. "The man he is dead at precisely the same time as his dog, very unusual no?"

"Well he could be a basket case, there's loads of them about." Stokes chuckled, "You know what they say one in four is a kook. Think of your three best friends, if they all seem normal, you're it."

"But maybe this man he was not a kook? Maybe it was made to be a look like a kook?"

"Well we need to get up to Scotland yet again, so put Sergeant Allinson on that case, he's a good man, and we'll check out the body. He's a solid bloke and if there's anything to find he'll find it. I need to get a few things together and so do you."

"Why?"

"Because if this is our man we are going to be up there for a few days. What about we meet at City Airport and then we can fly up. I'll get the chopper organised. Might be nothing, but at least we can check it out."

"Whereabouts was the body found?" asked Pancardi.

"In the water. River Tay. Well, washed up to be more precise."

"And do we have a cause of death?"

"Axe, like I said" Stokes lied, hoping his guess was right.

"The airport in two hours no?" Pancardi looked at his watch. "The time now she is 1.30. By 3.30 no?"

"Make it three," Stokes barked, "and no dog."

"Si," Pancardi replied.

Stokes knew he was not listening and that the command was unheeded. The small white dog would be at the airport sitting with his head cocked to one side giving a quizzical, whimsical look at him. Pancardi would do as he had always done since joining the team - do as he pleased.

* * *

Rachel Black pulled back the opaque sheeting which covered the chunk of raw flesh and bone that had once been a man and laughed. She had one of those laughs which announced her arrival and everyone knew her chirpy character would lift their spirits. The roundness of the tone was inviting, friendly and a sheer joy to hear – like the trickle of cool spring water in parched mountains. She was not laughing at the dismembered corpse, nor the unfortunate individual upon whom she was staring, but at simple joke involving roller skates and cars. A joke told by one of the police officers who rode the body in in a plastic bag.

"Jimmy Macpherson, you could be the next Billy Connolly the way you go on," she chuckled. "I mean those three getting cars and such based on how good they've been in not having affairs. And then the woman goes by the Rolls Royce on roller skates, and her husband inside the Rolls Royce. How do you think them up?"

The pungent smell of rotten flesh stung their noses. Rachel Black was used to it. She had lived with it virtually all her adult life. She had spent time as a nurse after leaving school and then had moved rapidly through the ranks until she had been noticed by a doctor who, after breaching the walls of her defence, had moved on. She, in turn, had learned the ways of men and become a pathology assistant. Now, after her initial heartbreak, the dust had settled and the bridges of her life, which had been swept away in the storm of his departure, had been rebuilt. Occasionally she heard from the man, as he expressed his regret, but that was long ago and many a beau had passed between her legs and senses since. She took a perverse sense of pleasure in torturing the man who had once meant so much, knowing his sense of regret had consumed him and ruined his career.

Now the man was a drunk and a hollow shell of his past. No longer a doctor he had fallen as she had risen, and Macpherson, the stalwart policeman had taken his place. It was a sort of Karma. Mac, as she called him, was not as intelligent, not as amusing or challenging, and not as wild in bed, but she could control him and he liked being controlled.

"Bloody hell," Mac exclaimed, "that looks awful. Can a propeller do that?"

"Nope," Rachel replied. She had seen many boating accidents and this was not one of them. "You know I'm not supposed to give a diagnosis. I'm not the doctor. But I reckon," she lifted a flap of flesh around the shoulder blade and a small crab fell onto the stainless steel examination table. The scuttling of the small feet and claws echoed into the air, accompanied by an overpowering smell which made Macpherson turn away. "Well this chap has taken a real pounding and not from a propeller. I'd say it's," she was now irrigating the flesh to wash away residual sand, "a chain saw."

"This is like something out of Jaws," Mac quipped.

"Well it would be if there were ever sharks in the Tay. But this is most definitely a wound caused post mortem. You watch when the pathologist gets here he'll confirm it. This is a victim of dismemberment. And what's more I reckon they'll be more bits found along the shore line."

"Well they got some specialist cops coming up later today. They been looking for a missing man for some months now."

"Well it might not be your man then."

"Why honey?"

"I'd say he's been dead less than 8 days. Been in the water perhaps five. If he'd been in there longer the crabs would have eaten the corpse down to the bone."

At that moment the double doors of the pathology department swung wide and the familiar call of, "Have no fear Mr. Mountjoy is here," was accompanied by the backing singer giggle of a couple of blonde trainee nurses. Rachel Black looked at the man, her superior, who always managed to pick the sweetest and most receptive assistants.

Macpherson knew that they received special attention from this doctor and he could smell the necessity for adulation in Mountjoy's hair jelly, which shone like a beacon on an ancient hillside. He wondered if the girls told him how wonderful he was and that his dick was the biggest they'd ever seen. And that he was too big for them to handle while he pumped his fluids into one or both. Briefly he wondered if they came as a pair or were busy trying, one to out do the other.

"What have we got then Rachel?" Mountjoy asked, his voice booming into the empty room.

"Male, dead eight days ish I'd say. No identification." The crab scuttled and Rachel washed it from the pathology table into the sink. There it scuttled desperately to climb the sides until eventually it settled into the prone defensive position.

The first girl had now turned green and stepped well clear of the partial corpse.

"Hums a bit, looks like decomposition has been slowed by the cold water. The wounds are post-mortem," Mountjoy remarked.

Rachel looked at her boyfriend and then at the second blonde whose lower jaw was now wide agape. The stench of death clung to the air and Rachel began to wonder how long the two would survive before one vomited.

"This is interesting," Mountjoy was lifting the same flap of flesh which Rachel had examined earlier. "This is no boat propeller; I'd say it's more like a saw or a grinding implement. Perhaps a wood chipper." He looked again, carefully examining the area close to the bone, "Chainsaw most likely."

Rachel Black was nodding, and the two trainees had backed almost to the door.

Mountjoy toyed with them, "Come and have look ladies," he said, beckoning them over. The slightly darker one left immediately to the sound of her own retching. The other stepped forward but immediately changed her mind and dashed out behind her colleague. "Can't get the staff these days eh Rachel?" And then laughing Mountjoy asked, "Can you finish up here? I'd better go and see to those two. If you do the write up I'll sign it off later OK?"

Rachel nodded.

After the doctor had scurried off behind his two would be concubines Jimmy Macpherson smiled at his girlfriend. "What a tosser," he said in disgust, "what an arrogant prick. Does he believe he's God's gift to women or what?"

"Oh he's alright really just a bit up his own bum."

"A bit. My God he's so far up his own arse, I can see his eyes behind his wisdom teeth. What a plonker. How can you work with such a berk?"

"Easy really. I get left to do the work and he just confirms later. That way I get lots of freedom and he doesn't try to get his hands in my pants."

"Well he better not try," Macpherson replied with indignation.

"Why would he try me when he's probably getting all he wants from those others and next year there'll be more interns? It's a good system and it works. He leaves me alone. I leave him…"

"Well I still think he's an absolute tosser."

Rachel Black removed her surgical gloves and threw them into the flip top bin, "Well it's a job, my job. Come on let's go and get a coffee."

Jimmy Macpherson nodded, "Well you are welcome to it."

Rachel Black flicked a switch and the room plunged into darkness, except for the light from the corridor which came through the obscured glass of the door.

The pair left and the room fell into virtual silence, with just the scuttling of the crab on the stainless steel as the only sound in the eerie dark.

* * *

"The body could have been dumped into the river much further up," Pancardi remarked, as he pored over a simple road atlas. "Look at this," he pointed to a spot called Gellyburn. Stokes leaned in and hunched his shoulders; to any observer he looked like a man laden with the cares of the world.

"Six bloody months of nothing and then suddenly a body turns up. Last man to vanish, first to be found," he said.

"Speeding on the M 90 just past Balvaird Castle on the way over the Friarton Bridge, that's where the camera shows our man." Pancardi was excited, his eyes were lit up and a whole new level of intensity had appeared as he spoke. "And now the DNA matches, we are absolutely sure we have a piece of our man. Where is the rest of him?"

"Probably scattered to the winds like that bloody Brave Heart bloke, what was his name?"

Pancardi chipped in, his mind refused to be side tracked, "Then again on the A9 just past the Caithness Glass factory here." His finger tracked the route, "He was really speeding now, in a hurry and then he vanishes. Where?"

"Right," Stokes replied, "where was he going again?"

"Aviemore?" Pancardi replied.

"So our toff with more money than sense is speeding up the A9, goes through a couple of speed cameras. Then he does a prompt U turn and ends up in Dundee. Parks his car in the hospital car park and the body part eventually turns up in the Firth of Tay near Invergowrie." Stokes was talking through his ideas, "It's a smoke screen, a red herring. If the body had not been found it would have washed out to sea, never to be seen again." He paused in detailed thought, "Carlo how about this for a theory? The guy gets lifted and held somewhere, for some reason, that's the thing, there's no bloody motive. But eventually the car is dumped and the bit of torso found to move us in on Dundee."

Pancardi took up the narrative, "Then the motive we must find and quickly. Why move the look for him to Dundee? So after he is killed the body he is dumped in the river somewhere?"

"But what if they wanted us to find the body?"

"Then where has he been for all the time. It is like time has stood still."

"It's in the motive," Stokes chirped, "Someone held him for over six months and then he turns up dead. Look the pathologist said he had been dead for a few days, not a few months. So why was he held?"

"Ransom?" Pancardi was swift in his reply, "and we have not been told of this?"

"So while we are busy trying to tie this into the other disappearances the whole thing becomes an illogical mess?"

"Maybe this is an individual murder and has nothing to do with the others? We are seeking in the wrong place all the time. Someone has told of us the lie. This Pancardi hates. To be made of the fool."

"And they had to have some privacy to cut him up. So being out here someone knew where he would be and how to lure him. After the ransom demand goes wrong maybe they dump the bits in the river and by chance we find one piece. What if there are other pieces somewhere, along the length of the Tay River? Then they take the car and dump it in Dundee?"

"But here is the real issue, no? Why were we not told of the ransom?"

Stokes considered, "Toff pride, Tin Tin, bloody toff pride."

On his radio Stokes issued orders for the whole length of the

River Tay to be checked and searched. "They can drag the whole thing but it's going to take time and we will have to do some leg work," he said. " We've got to tie this Lord fellow into the area somehow. Find out why he was here? There's something totally wrong. I can smell a real stink and it isn't rats. I've got a queer feeling about this."

* * *

When the car carrying the detectives, and their little white side-kick Mostro was once again out beyond the five bar gate and bumping back down the lane. Gilda lifted the pillow which had muffled the possible cries of Alfred Singleton 14th Earl of Strathmorton. Geraldine looked up to the window overlooking the cobbled quadrangle and called, "They've gone."

Across Singleton's lips was a piece of heavy grey gaffer tape and his hands and legs were bound to the head and foot boards of a Victorian iron framed bed.

As the detectives had begun to search for evidence among the out buildings he had rattled the bed until two women had made that impossible by adding their weight to the structure. Geraldine had then immediately gone to speak with them after giving instructions to keep the Earl silenced at all costs.

Gilda Morgan had taken hold of his flaccid penis and told him, by gently whispering into his ear, she would cut it off if he continued to struggle. Consequently, he had gone as limp as a boned fish. He knew what these witches could do; had seen them garrotte a man like some Gaelic warrior in a Roman auditorium. The man had tried to speak, tried to fight back, until they had cut his throat with no more thought than slaughtering a pig: He knew exactly what they were capable of. He had witnessed a murder and now here he was unable to move, bound and helpless. Half an hour after the detectives had left he was dragged out into the barn, yet again, a chain around his neck and his testicles tied with a cord. His body was cold and naked and he knew what that meant. Like an obedient bull he marched to the tune of the young women tugging him forward.

The first time he had tried to pull away, tried to fight, the result had been a tug on the testicle cord which was so severe he had vomited and passed out, only to be revived by a bucket of cold water once he was inside the cage.

The barn had been warm, heated, with the glow of dimmed lights and the women had reached through the bars to touch him. He could not resist, could not move. One hand had been insistent and had gently stoked his genitals until he became hard, another cupped his testes and moved them gently within its palm. He could see the nakedness of young girls in front of him. Young girls posing for him just a few feet away. Girls spreading their legs and parting their labia and despite his reluctance, the insistent hands continued and his erection strengthened. He tried to fight against the sexual arousal, but he could not. The dancing, posing girls, were giggling and using obscenities to encourage him, urging him on. The hand on his penis became faster and his power to resist began to disintegrate.

He was on all fours and trembling in his attempt to resist and then the hand became even more insistent. The stroking became uncontrollably intense until suddenly he ejaculated. At that point something was slipped over the head of his penis and the sound of a machine filled his ears. It was a soft sound and he could feel a pulsation on his penis which was working in unison with his muscular contractions. His ejaculation was strong, deep and heavy and seemed to empty his whole being into something to which he was attached. The whole operation had taken no more than five minutes but he felt exhausted as his muscles finally relaxed.

Instantly the floor show ended. The mechanical item was disconnected and a flaccid calm returned to his being. A few moments later the lights went out and he was left in silence. He could smell pig.

* * *

The road to Aviemore was long and dark and despite the winding turns Alfred Singleton had made good progress until he came to the sheep blocking his path. He had been on the way to meet some friends for a party and thought that he might pop in and see his older sister on route. The party was on Saturday and then on Sunday he could spend some time skiing, but he had Thursday and Friday to spend on the commune.

He and his older sister Geraldine had never seen eye to eye with the 13th Earl and she had run off many years before. Run off to the United States to be with some group of surfer bums. Now he was the only member of the Strathmortons who knew where she was. This would be his second visit and if it was like the last he was going to enjoy his two day sojourn immensely.

On his last visit Geraldine had explained that some of the girls were desperate, "to shag," as she put it, and he was only too willing to oblige. He had been passed from girl to girl like a sex toy and he had lost count of the names and times he had had sex. On the Friday, his first full day, he had not even dressed and the girls brought him meals in bed between the sessions: It had been heaven. Now he was on his way back for, hopefully, a weekend of much the same treatment and his groin was expanding in anticipation as his Porsche slowed to a crawl up the bumpy lane to the commune. Had he not inherited the vast estate from his father he could easily see himself being a stud bull to this commune of cows.

Fate had intervened eventually and the old man had contracted cancer. Mother disowned the old goat and so the servants cared for him. Sally the house maid spent many long hours with him. She was no spring chicken herself by this time and he had found it hard to chuck the old girl out when she had been such a good worker. But his mother had been adamant and she had probably been right - a new Earl needed younger fresh staff. So Sally and the other servants got their marching orders; including Marchant the butler, who his mother detested.

Suddenly he had become free and heir to a large fortune. Without a wife or heir himself the next person to inherit would be the closest male relative. A cousin who owned a farm in Nova Scotia; a strange black sheep of the family who supposedly had weird ideas on lots of things, especially politics. He had never met the man, who was also childless, but Geraldine had. She had visited the man and found him, "strange." His father had said that the best thing that Geraldine could do was produce an heir and that she ought to, "get fucking." He even intimated that Geraldine might have "done" the strange cousin, whatever that might mean, in his convoluted thinking.

* * *

"Hey Gerry what we gonna do?" the girl spoke with an accent.

"We're going to keep him here for a while and save his spunk for our supplies. Then we're going to get you pregnant with his sperm. Make sure you get the canisters labelled properly. We don't want any mix ups. You know what happens when we get mix ups?"

"The baby gets the wrong father?"

"No."

"What then?"

"If you put two different types of semen in the same womb they fight. There is a war, so the strongest semen gets to the egg. We don't want any of that do we?"

The girl looked bemused, and clearly did not understand the idea of semen inside her womb at war.

Geraldine Singleton had been a Cambridge girl and had worked in human embryology for some years, until her bullish and domineering father had declared it was time for her to get married and reproduce. Bully that he was, she had tried to resist and reason, her younger brother Alfred had supported her. He had been crushed by their father. But that was primarily due to his reliance on cocaine for solace. After the prison sentence father had scolded him and threatened to write him out of his will. Geraldine was put under severe pressure to mate and produce a male heir so that her father, the 13th Earl, could have the "decent" male heir he needed. Mother had been no support and had long since turned to the bottle for solace.

Geraldine had then been marched like a prize breeding mare before some of her father's choice eligible suitors. A group of more vacuous half-wits she had never seen. Most wanted to be huntin', shootin' and fishin'. The one common denominator they seemed to possess was an absolute submission to "The Earl." At dinner they dulled her mind with inane chit chat, whilst looking to her father for approval. In bed they lacked drive, energy and expertise; so quietly she had squirreled away a small nest egg before eloping with herself one moonlit night.

The men of the surf did not care who she was and her time in LA had forged her personality, until the private detectives came close to finding her. Then she had found out about the commune and once again vanished. Alfred had told her, "Father's furious, don't ya know."

"Fuck him," she had said in stark reply.

"You see Monica," Geraldine continued, "Humans are mammals just like the rest. So survival of the fittest comes into being. A man, who feels under threat by another male fucking his mate, starts to produce killer sperm which cut down the competition." She was searching for an analogy, "It's like an American Football game, with offence and defence blockers. Every little sperm has its role, while the quarterback storms through for the touchdown."

"I think I understand,"

"The other technique is like Mallard ducks. Females, they just fuck every thing and that way the male does not kill the chicks."

"That way then," she pondered, "the chicks could be his or any male could be the father but that doesn't matter?"

"That's it."

"All the males protect all the chicks?"

"Yep. And to make it even more unsavoury they rape."

"What?"

Geraldine Singleton was relishing the position of intellectual command, "They rape. In the parks of England the cute little brown ducks are being jumped upon by the green headed males. The kids feed them bread and mothers casually say, "Look at that Susan, they're playing." She mimicked a mumsy voice. "They don't say, hey look at that Susan that group of male

Mallards is playing hide the salami in that poor unsuspecting little brown female duck. They're group fucking her, against her will." She paused, "So don't get any of that semen in the wrong place or we may have a terrible upset."

Monica was overawed by the knowledge of Geraldine and was unafraid to voice that fact. "You know so much about this," she said, "I find it fascinating."

"It's one of the benefits of a public school for girls, where fucking was the main topic of conversation." She laughed, "You put a group of women or girls together without a cock and even a one eyed window cleaner with a face like a Rhino's arse seems shagable. Cock-a-doodle-do, any cock'll do."

"Well I went to a reet Geordie hole," Monica replied, with her guard down.

"You shouldn't try to cover up that accent you know," Geraldine encouraged. "You probably do it for men," she paused, "and don't even know that. They'll fuck you with or without an accent and you can't talk with your mouth full of cock can you? Well that's what they'll say as they force themselves into your throat. Most men don't give a shit about you, or if they hurt you as long as they come."

Monica laughed, "You don't like men very much do you?" she asked.

"No," was Geraldine's frank reply. "Thankfully with this semen bank we'll have enough spunk for fifty years and then the little boys we create can breed with our girls and we will have a true community. One based on peace and love."

"You make it sound so lovely," Monica replied. "Where I come from it was awful.

Our mama got beaten by our pap. Every Friday he went booozin' and when he come hooome she took abeattin'."

"Men are monsters," Geraldine agreed. "You know I was about ten and one day I was supposed to be in the gardens doing some drawing but I went back into the house. I saw my father bend one of the maids over a table and fuck her like a bitch. She was crying and he was forcing her. He didn't see me through the part open door, but I saw him."

"That's terrible."

"Just like ducks in the park. He had her uniform skirt up to her waist and she was crying. Sally her name was, lovely girl. He had hold of her hair and was pulling it back, and all the while she was saying, "No, don't please don't." But he didn't listen he was forcing himself into her, pushing her down with his other hand in the small of her back to make her arch up. I can see her face now and hear his grunting, grunting like boar servicing a sow and all the while she was crying. He was calling her a good girl and pushing and pushing. I just stood there watching, and then suddenly he grunted and pushed in deep one last time and stopped thrusting. She made a long ahhhh sound and then he let her go."

"Didn't she do anything?"

"I don't know I ran out into the gardens."

"No I mean did she tell your mam?"

Geraldine considered, "I don't really know. But she was at the house for a long time after that, I expect she needed the job. She used to light the fire in my father's room every morning and she had to do lots of things for him. I remember that much, sort of secretary come maid. He used to send for her when he was in his office. To run errands."

Monica was cutting, "And we both know what errands they were? Pap just hit our mam. I never saw them fucking but I could hear her some nights. Muffled and him grunting and her well, I don't know what she was doing, but there was always lots of little brothers and sisters. Our mam had eight before she stopped."

"Well when we have enough milked out of this man we'll get rid of him like the others. I'm sure Gertie and Hetty will do as they have always done in the past."

"It's amazing what a pig will eat," Monica replied.

"Out in the orchard and our man can be prime fertilizer for the apples. And to make things even better there'll be no forensic evidence anywhere."

Geraldine Singleton switched off the light to the storage room and the pair walked across the cobbles to join the others for a meal.

"So you see Monica," she said, "the milking machine we use has to be spotless so that the sperm is of the highest quality and so it doesn't get contaminated by a different set, or the man we have will start to produce attack sperm and that will cut down the fertility rate."

"Geraldine you know a lot about this too, but that man is your brother?"

"Yep and he's a total shit just like our father. In fact give him a few years and he'll be even worse. Then he'll be coming up here expecting to fuck whoever he likes whenever he likes."

"I suppose you're right."

"There's no suppose about it. Anyhow I'm hungry, so let's have something to eat, give him a couple of hours and we'll have another go."

* * *

"There's something odd about that place Carlo," Stokes said as they bumped down the track and onto a piece of tarmac. "The place is completely run by women and yet all those babies? Why?"

"You can never work out the ways of women," Pancardi offered. "This I know, I once was with the woman and you, you are the married man."

"No it's not that, it's like they go out and screw and get plum duffed. Who does that? And then it's supposed to be the local guys but none of them were sniffing around. If this commune or whatever it is was a knocking shop there'd be blokes everywhere. Word gets out."

"Knocking shop?" Pancardi asked.

"Yeah euphemism for fuck stop, cat house, brothel, shagging palace."

"This Pancardi he must remember, knocking shop," he repeated. "A good phrase. My English she is getting better no?"

Stokes nodded, "One day I'll teach you all sorts of cockney rhyming slang and that'll really fuck you up. Apples and pears, drum and hat, frog and toad. One day but," he paused as he checked the car speed on a roundabout, "but not today."

"We have this in Rome too. As you teach me I will teach you, no?"

Stokes ignored the remark about being taught. "So there's no blokes around and yet how many were pregnant? Five, six? That's a lot of babies to feed. I just got a sort of feeling, can't really explain it, but I know that there is something wrong. I can smell it in the wind."

Pancardi nodded.

The car swung onto the main A9 and Mostro barked once as Pancardi reached into his pocket for a treat. "Mostro he is ready for some food now, and so too am I."

* * *

The four days that followed the discovery of the partial corpse saw a methodical investigation of the Tay River and estuary. Progress was slow, Pancardi and Mostro combed the banks as they moved through various thickets of undergrowth and three boats dragged the river with Stokes barking orders at the teams of frogmen.

No further evidence was found and slowly the euphoria of the discovery of a body part began to fade. Even the Dundee Courier moved on to more banal local stories. The Italian specialist, photographed against the backdrop of the statue of Desperate Dan slid into the local bins and the investigation stalled. Michael Stokes became frustrated as other cases came and went, while this case dragged on.

Life on the commune resumed and the girls who wanted a pregnancy had one. The bank of semen was used to great effect and the birth rate doubled. Both boys and girls were born in the twelve months of "the trials" as Geraldine labelled them, but she reserved the "special" treatment for Monica, the small blonde Geordie girl.

The bodies of the unwilling sperm donors had been digested by the resident pigs and their manure had long since washed into the cool earth of the orchard. The single chunk of Strathmorton, which had fallen from the outdoor pig enclosure, nosed under the barbed wire by an over zealous boar, had slid quietly down the river bank of the Tay. There it hung unnoticed, close to the water's edge, amid a cloud of flies until a heavy rain slid it quietly into the water where it bobbed and floated until it reached Dundee. Now this final and only part lay preserved in the mortuary at Nine Wells Hospital.

* * *

When Monica Stephens gave birth to a baby boy it was a moment of clear joy for Geraldine Singleton. This had been the third girl inseminated by her with her brother's semen. One had not been successful and the second produced a girl. But Monica, poor, stupid, hapless Monica had been a willing breed cow for the commune and she had produced the 15th Earl of Strathmorton; had squeezed the muscles of her womb to eject Geraldine's passport to fortune.

The 7lb boy was healthy and a clear DNA link would be established, but Monica needed to be silenced, removed as the final piece in the puzzle. True there were others who could say certain things, but none to honestly say they saw a murder. Yes, men had been abducted and their semen forcibly removed but the only real accomplice had been the rather stupid Monica. What would the others say, that they had abducted men and aided in their semen removal to get pregnant? No one would believe them.

The fine long needle was sticky with blood and Monica was convulsing now as Geraldine twirled the item which she had forced into Monica's left nostril and up into her brain. It would be painful and slow, but it would look like a haemorrhage, and at post mortem nothing would show except for the brain cavity being filled with blood. Hopefully the pathologist would be lazy and the matter slip by in a routine examination. An experienced practitioner might deduce murder but most would opt for a stroke.

Monica Stephens' eyes grew wide and then began to glaze. Geraldine Singleton smiled as the point of death arrived and then slipped back to her room to leave the infant crying for a feed to arouse others. She smiled at the thought of one of the others girls wet nursing the mewling infant; wet nursing her key to a vast fortune.

The plan had been perfect and come to her in a flash of inspiration. The luring of her brother to the commune in pursuit of sex had given her the perfect chance. The first visit had resulted in no pregnancy and she had feared he might be infertile. After a semen analysis on Monica she found live little swimmers and then the plan struck her like a thunderbolt. If she were careful she could get everything, and that she had reasoned, was no more than she deserved.

It had been easy to lure the man to her lair. There they extracted all the semen she needed. Then all she had to do was to regularly inseminate a gullible receptacle - Monica.

Finally she needed to turn up with the infant, saying it was Alfred's, get the DNA confirmed and she could be the guardian aunt. It was so simple. The passport to her wealth lay in one simple further act of murder. Her mother needed an accident, perhaps a drunken fall or an overdose of sleeping pills. That would be so easy – simple in fact, once she had made contact again and won her trust. Her mother would probably be glad of the company and support now her vile husband and rather exasperating male offspring were deceased. Each stage of the plan had worked and she was convinced this would too.

* * *

Doctor Michael Richardson was a rather portly and inefficient man who loved an easy life. The result was a post-mortem which confirmed an internal brain haemorrhage or stroke brought about by the stress of childbirth. There had no fuss, no police involvement and no suspicion of wrong doing. The simple cremation and scattering of the ashes, as encouraged by Geraldine Singleton, under the trees of the orchard, was the final removal of evidence in the disappearance of Alfred the 14th Earl.

"Monica loved this orchard," Geraldine had said of Monica. "Loved to let the animals roam around free, as she was herself now. And it was only fitting that Monica should have this beautiful place to lay in peace."

There had been tears from the other girls and a scattering of flowers and then Monica and the evidence were gone.

Pancardi and Stokes had stalled, though from time to time the Italian did attempt to pick up the pieces. It galled him that he and Stokes had been unable to piece together any substantial leads. There was something troubling him, but he was unable to say precisely what it was. He had a feeling, a hunch, but could not actually say what that hunch was.

Others, including Stokes had told him to let it be. Set it aside as one of those dreary cases which could and would never be solved. Stokes had called it his Black Dahlia case, and as the months drifted past he left Pancardi to ponder and re-assess the evidence. Each time less and less sense could be made of it.

The partial corpse was interred in the family mausoleum and the Strathmorton Earldom passed to the Nova Scotia cousin. That was until the discovery of a male heir and the reappearance of the Earl's elder sister.

Gradually donor semen supplies depleted and Alfred's, corrupted accidentally, had to be destroyed. Then after years of exile on the commune, Geraldine suddenly decided to leave: Leave with the infant that Monica had conceived.

There were no tearful good byes and wringing of hands, Geraldine simply left at night with a note for the others explaining that she felt it was time to move on. Like her chosen fictional namesake, the exit was swift with just a note. A note that she was taking the child and she hoped no one would wish to find her. There was something about freedom and being, "her own person," which nobody took any notice of. There were babies to feed and animals to tend, and the child did sort of belong to her in a round about way.

The semen supplies had gone, the machines had been dismantled and the whole experience faded from memory as more traditional methods of insemination began to be employed by the communal residents. Girls brought home boyfriends from the local schools and the boys started to seek work out amongst the community.

The cages were used as they had originally been intended for pigs and the freezers were now full of frozen items to see the commune through the winter. One year passed into another and as the infants grew and time passed Geraldine became a memory.

The file made its way into the unsolved crimes unit and there it sat, gathering a thick coating of dust. A thorn in the memory of both Pancardi and Stokes. This was their, second one that got away; this was their Jack the Ripper. Now they had one each. The Whitby vampire for Stokes and the Ripper, albeit with a chainsaw, for Pancardi. As quickly as the abductions had started so they ceased. The random, motiveless and seemingly unconnected had confounded them. To Pancardi it was as if this was the case that was to be his nemesis, but from time to time he played the scenarios in his subconscious or in that dream world before the onset of sleep. The place where the mind sorts and sifts to make order and logic, by the use of the illogical.

* * *

"Look in the obituary column," Pancardi said excitedly.

"The line's awful," Stokes replied, "haven't you bloody Italians got a decent phone network? I can hardly hear you. And anyway what are you phoning me for garlic breath?"

"The Times obituary."

"And, haven't you noticed we're retired, finished, washed up, put out to grass. Soon nobody will even remember our names. How are you my old fruit?"

"The unsolved case," Pancardi chirped.

"What the Whitby vampire? I am beginning to think that bastard really was a vampire. Strange as it may seem it could, just could, be possible."

"No you old goat, the Strathmorton Earl. The body in Scotland in the River Tay."

"Oh Christ, not again. We've been over that so many times I'm sick of it. We're never going to find out the truth. And just for starters those other men. Gone never to be seen again. You might be right about that one too - abducted by Aliens."

Pancardi's voice became serious, "How many cases did we leave unsolved?"

"Two, just the two," Stokes repeated the number.

"That is a record no?"

"No," Stokes replied, "Sherlock bloody Holmes got them all right."

"But did he?" Pancardi was chuckling, "he was fiction, we my friend, we are the real thing."

"Like bloody Coca Cola I suppose?"

"Yes like this we are."

"You'll begin to believe your own bullshit soon Tin Tin."

"If I am the Belgian sleuth then you my friend are Capitan Haddocks no?"

"I'll give you Captain Haddock you garlic munching ..."

"Mike, I think I have a lead at last."

Michael Stokes froze, in all their time together Pancardi had never used his Christian name.

Pancardi continued, "The mother of that Strathmorton Earl. She has died in a fall at her home."

"So? Loads of people die, some are accidents."

"She was a drinker no?"

"Yeah, so she was probably so pissed she fell. How's Rome these days?"

"Warm," Pancardi sharply replied. "There is something wrong here."

"Oh Christ, not again Tin Tin."

"No this you must check out. I was reading The Times in the Borghese Park. I saw the article and I know there is something wrong. I can smell of the rat. There is a young heir, a son of the missing Earl, there have been DNA confirmations. When we investigated this do you not think it strange that we never found or heard of a woman. Then that this woman she was of the pregnant."

"You and your hunches. That case has been closed for over ten years. There's nothing left to say, we're retired, why can't you enjoy it? We went through every angle and still you won't let it go. The man was chopped up and we aren't going to find out how or why are we?"

"No listen, there is the long lost sister," Pancardi continued, "she has reappeared and the boy he is her…" The line crackled and some words were lost, "do the favour for me Michael…" Pancardi said.

Michael Stokes knew that the use of his Christian name a second time meant the matter was very serious. Pancardi using his Christian name, that was not his style. To call in a favour was even greater confirmation of the anxiety within Pancardi.

"I'll have one of the chaps go to check it out," he acquiesced.

"No!" Pancardi snapped, "You must check it out. We must check it out."

"Oh Christ why?"

"Call it a hunch?" Pancardi replied. "If you will not go then I must. I will fly over to England and be in Heathrow tomorrow. I will go to this Northampton place alone if must be, but with you if I can."

"Jesus bloody Christ," Stokes replied, knowing he had lost the argument. "I'll tell the Mrs. That you're coming on a visit for a few days. You can stay here. But, and it's a big but, we have no warrant cards and we'll have to tell someone trustworthy if we find anything."

"Allinson," Pancardi said swiftly, "your sergeant."

"He's Inspector Allinson now," Stokes replied.

"Him, he we must trust," Pancardi barked. "I will find out about the flights and call you later no? Then I will have someone look after Mostro. He is old and weary, but there is a young girl who likes him, and she helps me out some times."

"Bloody fine," Stokes replied. "You old Latin lothario, don't you ever give up?"

There was an immediate click and the connection died.

"Stupid bloody wild goose chase Italian," Stokes spoke into the receiver knowing Pancardi was no longer there. "Bloody great waste of time and effort."

Later he told his wife that the Italian was coming over for a few days and that they, that was Pancardi and himself, were off to Northampton. Her reaction was instant and she knew, as Stokes knew, that the case of the missing Earl was the reason for the visit. For the past thirty years she had lived and breathed the cases which her husband worked. She had listened and recalled the names of those involved in murder, fraud and embezzlement and knew as well as any other human being the detail of the cases. Pancardi and Mike had one or two which stuck in their throats, stuck like unswallowable fish bones and Pancardi was coughing again to shake one loose.

* * *

At the gates of the ancestral home of the Earls of Strathmorton a small car carrying the two retired detectives pulled up to the wrought iron gates which sealed the Northamptonshire estate from the world. Pancardi wondered how many men had been employed to build the vast wall which surrounded the estate. A natural stone wall set twelve feet in height and topped with sharp edged decorative flint. The Strathmortons would have used glass set into the mortar, if the present Earl's aunt had her way; but the vagaries of the law meant that any intruder attempting to enter the grounds, over the wall, could take a law suit out if they injured themselves in the process. Glass was a deliberate attempt to injure, so the Earl's aunt had settled for decorative but sharp jagged flint, just as sharp, if not sharper, but obviously purely for decoration.

"May I help you?" A voice sounded via the intercom.

"We are here to see the Earl. We telephoned earlier he's expecting us."

"Oh yes, that's me." A young male voice said, "I'll buzz you in."

Pancardi wondered why the Earl would answer the buzzer

when such a huge place was obviously maintained by servants, and at least a butler.

There was an electronic whirr and the heavy gates swung back and the green Ford Fiesta, belonging to the wife of Michael Stokes, crunched along the gravel drive and parked near the front entrance of the house.

A young teenage boy with long unkempt hair greeted the men and led them through the hall to the rear of the building and across a large expanse of lawn, and on toward a walled garden and an ornamental arch. In the distance stood a huge Chestnut tree which looked as if it had been ravaged by lightening or torn apart by the weight of old age. Around the base ran a circular bench which had seen better days and needed immediate repair. Pancardi thought he had read about it somewhere, seen a photograph, something was struggling in his memory, but the reference eluded him. It seemed a place where romantic trysts could be made; a place where lovers could make commitments and live. Try as he might, the reference in his mind would not be released.

"We thought you'd have butler?" Pancardi chirped as they walked. "Your name is Edward isn't it?"

"Well Inspector Pancardi, it is Pancardi isn't it?" the boy smiled broadly. "This is not the seventeenth century. Servants, sorry employees," he checked himself, correcting his own language, "have days off. The days of us owning vast sugar plantations run by slaves are over. It's more egalitarian now you know. And please call me Edward; it was the name my mother gave me just before she died."

Stokes studied the young man. He was well spoken and intelligent with a cruel hard edge to his mouth. His voice was slow and methodical almost coldly robotic at times.

Pancardi listened and noted his intelligence too, but there was something else there; he tried to evaluate as they walked.

"Yes your family made their money in sugar? Antigua wasn't it?" Stokes asked.

"That's correct Inspector Stokes? It is Stokes isn't it? You're from the Met? And you were in charge of the investigation into my father's murder I believe?"

"Correct, how did you know? Betty's Hope wasn't it?"

"So you've been to Antigua then?" the boy asked, casually avoiding the reference to the case of the 14th Earl.

"My wife and I went there some years ago," Stokes replied, "for a holiday."

"It's a lovely place," the young Earl retorted, "but Betty's Hope, was the Codrington family, not us. We were more to the south of the island, but our land holdings there have long since been sold."

"That is a pity," Pancardi interjected flippantly; "I am rather partial to good rum."

"I don't think I'd drink it," the young man laughed, "not having seen how it's made. But I believe they pickled Nelson's body in a barrel of it after Trafalgar."

"Yeah I heard that too," Stokes laughed; "foul stuff. And the men were supposed to have drunk the barrel dry once the body had been removed. I think there's a drink named Nelson's blood which has Antiguan Rum and something red in it. But I can't remember what it's called. It's a bit like that stuff in a Harvey Wall Banger."

"Galliano," The young Earl chirped.

"Bloody hell, I must be getting old. I'll remember the damn stuff in a minute. It'll come to me just when I'm least expecting it," Stokes laughed.

"Well whatever it is, I'm afraid I would not drink it," the young man jovially replied.

In the corner of the walled garden there was a woman in green Wellington boots and a floral cotton dress standing on a set of steps snipping roses from a bush and laying them in a trug. Her back was turned toward them but Pancardi noticed the neat black and obviously dyed bob of her highly styled hair.

"Aunt Geraldine?" the Earl said, "these two men wanted to see us. About Grandmother's unfortunate accident."

As the woman turned she dropped her trug. "You shouldn't creep up on someone like that," she scolded. "You could make me have…"

"An accident?" the young Earl scoffed.

Stokes thought he recognised the woman; there was something familiar about her. Her figure was good and she looked as if she exercised. He had seen her somewhere, of that he was certain, maybe on the cover of a magazine. The hair had been styled and the face aged by both surgery and some weight gain, but the eyes were the same. Eyes which spoke of raw sex and femininity. They were the eyes which belonged to a woman who knew the ways of men. A woman who could make a man fall into the abyss, if only with the promise of an hour of unspeakable sexual pleasure. Those eyes were the eyes upon which male fantasies were built and that, despite cosmetic surgery, could not be veiled, altered or removed.

Pancardi's eyes scanned the face of the woman. The shape had altered but the ears were the same. There was something familiar here and his mind was trawling the files of the Strathmorton case as weird and disjointed facts flew into a semblance of order in his brain.

Stokes recognised the eyes, the Marilyn eyes. They were the same eyes which had made the hairs on the back of his neck stand to attention in the quadrangle of the Scottish commune years before.

The voice of the woman oozed out like molasses, "I'm so sorry we don't seem to have been introduced," she said. "I'm Geraldine Singleton and that," she nodded, toward the unkempt youth, "is my nephew the 15th Earl of Strathmorton, though you wouldn't believe it by his manners. His hair needs a cut too; he looks like a hippy."

"Grandmamma didn't mind it," the boy spitefully replied. "She understood fashion."

"Yes and we all know what a wonderful style guru she was don't we?" the woman replied with vitriol. "Just how much sense can one get out of a stumbling alcoholic?"

"She wasn't an alcoholic," the boy snapped in reply

The word hippy sent the mind of Pancardi racing, and the penny suddenly plummeted.

"You should be a little more careful Miss Eyre," Pancardi remarked as he lifted the trug and offered it to the woman. "Fact is often stranger than fiction no?"

Briefly Geraldine Singleton's eyes met Pancardi's and at that moment Pancardi knew they only had the one unsolved case in their detective history.

"Malmsey," Stokes blurted, "Nelson's blood, Rum and Malmsey. You see if you wait long enough it all comes out in the end."

Pancardi's Pride

Out of the darkness and through the rat infested sewers of Florence; under the ancient treasure houses of the Palazzo Pitti and into one of the strongest bank vaults in the world; the best cracksmen in the business are on the take.

They have done the research, analysed the problems and now they are ready to make the biggest score of the century. But something history has forgotten, a myth, a legend; only this is no fairy tale, this is for real – a dream come true. All they have to do now is get away clean.

The score is every safe-crackers dream, the big "A" number one, the last job before retiring into luxurious obscurity – only this dream is about to become a full blown nightmare of insatiable greed.....

"More ups and downs than a scenic railway; more twists and turns than a high speed rollercoaster ride. A must read book!"

"for once with a book I couldn't guess the ending"

a measure of wheat for a penny

If you had something valuable and lost it – what would you risk to retrieve it? Would you lie for it? Kill for it? Even dice with death for it? Some things are worth a sacrifice – the skill is knowing that someday you might have to choose. The nerve – knowing that you might lose.

The hunt for mastermind and lethal beauty Alice Parsotti is on. Months of tracking, searching, watching and listening are about to pay off and Alex Blondell is now ready. Ready to follow her down any rabbit hole into which she may run.

But there are other forces at work too, forces that have their talons in family histories and roots in hidden political prophecies.

The recovery of the missing Romanov jewels is about to unfold in a tale of death and destruction, double dealing and dark demonic deception.

Alice is back and this time it's not Wonderland she's in.

"Ron Clooney takes us to places where only those with the stongest psyche dare to venture - another triumph"

"Dark and sexy and un-put-down-able: Ron Clooney's writing is breathtaking"

459

40th ANNIVERSARY OF
UNTIMELY DEATH

But is Mr. Mojo Risin really dead?

Ron Clooney examines the evidence and adds context in the form of what it was like to live through and grow up in, the late 1960's and early 1970's.

A life-long admirer of The Doors, Ron Clooney, like Danny Sugarman before him, explodes some of the myths surrounding this legendary front man; one of the most influential and revered to come out of the late 1960's.

During the heady days of flower power and free love, Jim Morrison stood apart; a leather clad harbinger of the Punk and Goth movements that were destined to follow him. Ahead of his time, Morrison was the dark flipside to the bell gingling, long-haired hippies that protested and preached, make love not war. Morrison, an intellectual in his own right, warned that not everything in the garden was rosy.

As the self proclaimed "Lizard King", Morrison assumed the role of Serpent in the garden - the serpent bearing the forbidden fruit of challenge - challenge to the established order. A reader of Nietzsche, Kerouac and the beat poets; a lover of the dark and chaotic art of Hieronymus Bosche; Morrison exploded onto the music scene, lucky to be in the right place at the right time.
As he himself claimed, "The history of Rock and Roll coinciding with my birth."

Marketed as a male sex symbol, the "God of rock and cock," an image he himself bitterly came to regret. He first embraced - he then railed against it. He gained weight, drank more heavily than ever, became even more unpredictable and even less conscious of his personal safety; all of this culminating in the infamous Miami incident and his self-imposed exile in Paris in 1971.

Ron Clooney, an accomplished crime novelist, embarks on a journey through misrepresentation, red herrings and illogical assumed truths and enters into a series of possibilities exploring Morrison's motives to disappear. The trapped long to escape and Morrison was both clever and charming enough to execute his – just how did he do it?

Mr. Mojo Risin ain't dead.

To Be Published – OCTOBER 2011

Reserve your copy now

www.ronclooney.com

Latest News

Mr. Mojo Risin ain't dead

The book, due for release in October 2011, coincides with the 40th anniversary of the legendary front man's mysterious death. Ron examines the truth behind the case of Mr. Mojo Risin and his sudden departure from decadence - with shocking results.

We are reliably informed that he is also starting to work on a third escapade for his Italian detective Giancarlo Pancardi. If the last two Pancardi books are anything to go by it will be an explosive, erotic and graphic page turner. Ron is saying possible completion 2012/13.

Based in Europe and the USA – this will be an eagerly awaited thriller.

For more information about the author and his work visit:
www.ronclooney.com